Like Carlos Fuentes's *The Old Gringo*, this absorbing novel . . . tracks Ambrose Bierce (1842–1914?) south of the border as the American journalist and short story writer journeys with Pancho Villa into the maelstrom of the Mexican Revolution. . . . Fans of Bierce's writing should enjoy this semibiographical tale with a suspenseful plot as wild as some of his more fantastical works.

—*Publishers Weekly*

In *The Assassination of Ambrose Bierce: A Love Story*, expect to be entertained—to laugh and sneer and shiver—expect to think—on life, on death, on love—and expect to feel—pain, anger, desire—but most importantly, expect to find out what happened to Ambrose Bierce when he left his home without looking back, and faded into the white dust of Mexico.

—Michael G. Kellermeyer, publisher, Oldstyle Tales Press

Ambrose Bierce is alive again in Don Swaim's new novel. A harrowing, often terrifying tale of love and adventure.

—Bill Diehl, entertainment correspondent, ABC News Radio

You might have thought Ambrose Bierce is dead. Wrong. Don Swaim has brought him back to life. And a colorful life it *is*. Exciting, in fact (and fancy). Fascinating, too.

—Mervin Block, founder of the
Television Newswriting Workshop in New York

Mystery solved. Written with spellbinding prose and subtle humor that befits the topic, and dare I say it, in a way that the bitter literary giant this speculative mystery embraces might actually have found satisfactory. A highly entertaining read.

—C. G. Bauer, author of *Scars on the Face of God: The Devil's Bible*

The Assassination of Ambrose Bierce:
A Love Story

BY DON SWAIM

The Assassination of Ambrose Bierce: A Love Story
Steampunk Electroblaster Romance
Bright Sun Extinguished: Ode to Norman Mailer
The H. L. Mencken Murder Case

THE ☆ ASSASSINATION ☆ OF AMBROSE ☆ BIERCE

A LOVE STORY

Don Swaim

Introduction by S. T. Joshi

Hippocampus Press

New York

Get your facts first, then you can distort them as much as you please.

—Mark Twain

The first duty in life is to assume a pose.

—Oscar Wilde

My Country 'tis of thee
Sweet land of felony

—Ambrose Bierce

BIOGRAPHY. The literary tribute that a little man pays to a big one.

—Ambrose Bierce

Tauri excrementum.

—Ambrose Bierce

Introduction

Few literary figures led a more interesting and event-filled life than Ambrose Bierce. Born in 1842 into a large family (all of whose siblings' names began with the letter A) in rural Ohio, Bierce enlisted in the Union army at the outset of the Civil War and served with distinction for nearly the entire conflict. He participated in some of the grisliest battles of that hideous war—Shiloh, Resaca, Kennesaw Mountain (where he suffered a serious injury when he was shot in the head)—and was also briefly captured by Confederates before escaping. After the war Bierce went out west with his former commander, Gen. William B. Hazen, on an inspection of western forts, then worked briefly for the San Francisco mint. Taking up writing, he wrote prolifically for a succession of San Francisco papers—the *San Francisco News Letter,* the *Argonaut,* the *Wasp,* and, most significantly, William Randolph Hearst's *San Francisco Examiner.* Along the way he worked briefly as a general agent for the Black Hills Placer Mining Company, spent months in Washington, D.C., lobbying against the railroad baron Collis P. Huntington, and became the focus of a thriving literary community in the Bay Area, with such luminaries as W. C. Morrow, George Sterling, Gertrude Atherton, and Jack London. He wrote some of the most chilling Civil War tales of anyone who had served in the war, and some of the most harrowing tales of supernatural and psychological horror. As a fitting capstone to his multifaceted life, in late 1913 he made a nostalgic tour of Civil War battlefields before disappearing in a cloud of smoke in Mexico.

It is remarkable that Bierce's life has not served as the basis for all manner of fictional treatments. Carlos Fuentes's *The Old Gringo* (1985) is a notable and poignant novel, but it is really more of a fanciful prose poem than an accurate recounting of Bierce's life and thought. Don Swaim, who operates the leading Ambrose Bierce website (donswaim.com)—is much better prepared to chronicle Bierce's life and accomplishments in fiction, and he has done so with deftness and panache in *The Assassination of Ambrose Bierce.*

But why has Swaim affixed the subtitle "A Love Story" to this novel? Bierce in his day developed a notorious reputation as a vicious satirist, lashing out against all manner of persons and causes he despised—politicians, feminists, poetasters, and perhaps the human race in general. It may be something of an exaggeration to call Bierce a misanthrope, even though some of the nicknames that were fastened upon him in his time ("Bitter Bierce," "The Wickedest Man in San Francisco") suggest it. It would be fairer to say that Bierce was *disappointed* in a human race that was constantly falling below the lofty standards it professed. A species that believed itself the product of a deity of love, mercy, strength, and benevolence was all too often addicted to the vices of fear, cowardice, hypocrisy, duplicity, and outright evil—and Bierce was not slow in pointing them out.

And yet, Bierce *was* a lover. He had a boyhood love affair in Indiana with a young woman named Fatima—an affair that ended abruptly after he went off to war. He married young, and even if that marriage (to Mollie Day, a wealthy socialite in San Francisco) was more than a little rocky, it led to the birth of three children, two sons and a daughter. (Bierce experienced the pain and horror of seeing both his sons predecease him.) And, as Swaim so eloquently portrays, he was constantly subject to the lure of the eternal feminine: Swaim's winsome heroine, Elizabeth Dumont, evokes in Bierce a memory of the feisty Gertrude Atherton, the prolific novelist who laughed in Bierce's face when he made a pass at her.

But Bierce was an extraordinarily complex man, and love—whether it be love of a woman, love of the greatest jewels of literature and culture, or love of the bravery and heroism of soldiers in battle—was only one element in his makeup. Death was another. The critic Edmund Wilson thought that death was the sole focus of Bierce's writing, but this is both an imprecise and a myopic view. What Bierce really emphasized in his writing was not death but *the fear of death*. In story after story, he relentlessly dissects the psychology of fear as it applies to death—whether it be the mere proximity of a corpse ("A Watcher by the Dead," "A Tough Tussle"), a foolhardy bravery in war that laughs at death ("Killed at Resaca"), or a fear that paralyzes one into inaction ("The Man and the Snake"). Bierce's most famous story, "An Occurrence at Owl Creek Bridge," testifies to the extent to which a disturbed psyche will go in repudiating the inevitability of death. Did Bierce himself feel such a fear? Don Swaim plausibly thinks so, and he underscores it with his depiction of the nebulous entity Bierce can only call "the Damned Thing."

The Assassination of Ambrose Bierce is a work as complex as Bierce himself. It is a love story; it is an elegantly constructed historical novel; it is a tale of terror. But most of all, it is a tale of a human life—a tale of a man who belonged to the "damned human race," however much he may have wished he didn't. Readers of this book may come away moved, amused, or terrified—but chiefly they will come away with a profound understanding of what it means to be human.

—S. T. JOSHI

The Assassination of Ambrose Bierce:
A Love Story

Chapter One

Under the mid-morning sun, the summer of 1915 nearing its coda, they assemble in the weedy cemetery near the Delaware & Hudson station. The tombstones are carved with the names of Putnam, Borch, Coo, Covell, Dostie, Kiff, Osgood, Van Woert—moldering dead, now mostly relegated to local lore and wilted flowers. An overworked graveyard, laid out at the beginning of the previous century by a nephew of some Revolutionary War hero. Most Saratogans now prefer to be buried in the more fashionable Greenridge Cemetery a few blocks south. The mourners include Mrs. Elizabeth Dumont of Buffalo; her young son Master Jonathan Dumont; Señor Doroteo Arango of Chihuahua, Mexico; his manservant Pedrito Gómez of El Paso, Texas, who first led the deceased across the Rio Grande and into the desert; and, last, the cordial undertaker and his assistant. There's no chaplain, just as the departed would have wanted, demanded. Mrs. Dumont had arranged for the mortician to obtain the death certificate, call for the corpse in an eight-cylinder Studebaker hearse, and prepare the body for burial. Señor Arango signed the papers as next of kin, the departed's Mexican cousin. No one wonders about this oddity. Or cares. Señor Arango pays in good American currency. Lots of it. Was the deceased's name spelled Grile or Grill or Grimes? Someone from too many places to pin down. Ohio, it's said, or is it Indiana? California, perhaps? District of Columbia? A white-haired septuagenarian who succumbed while on holiday here in upstate New York with no one outside of this forlorn little band standing at his grave. Mrs. Dumont thinks it strange that, despite his relatively long life, so few are present at the end. He managed to outlive the killer diseases: cholera, dysentery, typhoid, influenza, yellow fever, malaria, tuberculosis, even that uncharted fiend called cancer, only whispered about, not fully understood. By his own accounting he survived not only a war but a revolution. Wars and atrocities have claimed—*will* claim—the lives of untold millions, human gnats ground into oblivion. Why then did he survive as long as he did? And forget the rubbish about the good dying young.

Wait, she thinks, wait. Yes, by the saints, she's at this very moment figured it out. There's no design, no beastly god to plot our wretched little lives. Life's a damned crapshoot, and his death is irrefutable proof of that. He'd suggested the notion to her again and again, but she wasn't ready to accept it. Now, now she is. She laughs, but not aloud. No longer is there an iota of confusion in her calculating, feminine mind. Ah, peace, such peace. Before, she was a feisty young widow, but uncertain. Now, she's feisty and certain. In his lifetime he fired sallies at the powerful, the rich, the ignorant, the cruel, the wicked—and did so with lacerating humor. Was he as angry, bitter, as he sometimes made himself out to be? No, she thinks, no more than anyone who experiences the vicissitudes of life. Imperfect? Certainly. So what if he once insisted man would not, could not, fly, and believed the electric light was a parlor trick? He wasn't an aeronautical engineer or an expert on alternating current. So what if he was a troglodyte when it came to women's suffrage? So what that he despised dogs to the point of irrationality? So what if he believed the novel was, in his half-baked words, a short story padded? So what if he drank too much? Even geniuses have the right to go off half-cocked and destroy their livers and their brains. But how many, in addition to her, ever knew of his solicitousness, his courtesy, his consideration—or felt his passion as a lover? Not to mention his bravery, his fierce independence. And might a man, physically, be described as beautiful? He was, even in his late age. She must tell the world about him, the circumstances of his death, his final . . .

Hold on! Wait one goddamned minute. What would *he* have wanted? Had he not returned from Mexico pseudonymously in stealth and secret? Had he not renounced his former life? Had he not at the end refused to fully reveal himself—even to her? Perhaps, perhaps . . . Okay, dammit, okay. She'll keep his secret, for now at least, nor will she compromise the perspiring Mexican gentleman choked by the stiff Arrow collar he obviously despises. She knows now who this copper-skinned warrior really is, thinks she does, but his secret, too, is safe with her.

Johnny's bored. At first fascinated by the idea of a corpse, then disappointed at not being allowed to inspect the body, he's impatient and begins hopping up and down. He wants to look at someone dead. Particularly the old man. He hated him. The minute Johnny spilled Cracker Jacks on the old man he hated him.

"Mean old man," he says. "Dead, dead." Then, "Look at me, Mommy, I'm bouncing."

Johnny jumps, jumps. She grabs her son's arm to control him, which accomplishes nothing. She bears down on his arm so that her nails leave narrow puncture wounds in his flesh. "Stand still, you damned little shit," she hisses.

Johnny stops, startled more by the vehemence in his mother's voice than the pain in his arm, although he doesn't know the word shit and is only vaguely familiar with damned. In a few years, when he's blessedly far away, missing after his gunboat comes under warlord fire in the Yangtze River, China, she'll remember him jumping uncontrollably in front of the coffin. The ambivalence she feels toward her son has resulted in excruciating guilt, with which she'll never come to terms, not unlike what she feels about Oakleigh, the boy's late father. Damn you, Oakleigh. Why the hell did you have to pull the trigger? And in our bedroom of all places? My god, the mess you made on the counterpane.

The old man's casket rests on slats placed across the open grave. Soon the boards will be pulled away and the coffin lowered into the pit.

"We'll need a headstone, Mr. Arango," Mrs. Dumont says.

"Why, señora?"

"To mark his grave, of course."

"Thousands die in my country. We bury them. We burn them. We don't mark no graves. We die like *cucarachas*."

"Did he die like a *cucaracha?*"

"He would say he was assassinated, but he was kind of loco at the end. He wouldn't care about no tombstone. Trust me, *por favor.*"

"We should say some words."

"I ain't good with words, señora. Not gringo words, anyway. You are good, I think."

She should be. She's a writer. Hopes to be. No, *intends* to be—more than ever, thanks to her late literary guide and coital confidant. She tries to dredge up all the pious comments made by all the dim-witted clergymen she's ever known. She can only remember a few words. Dust to whatever. Ashes to who cares. The Lord is my goat herder, I shall not wait. Yea, though I ride through the valley . . . Shit, dammit, fuck. She looks helplessly at Señor Arango, who comes to her rescue.

"Señora, I was going to give this to you after the *entierro*—how you say?—burial. He wanted you to have it." He removes a piece of paper from his pocket. "Maybe it will help, although I think it's a joke. At night, after many drinks from the bottle, he would write down certain words and tell me what they mean. Like death. And wrath. And truth. Then he would destroy them because he said he had written too damned many words, and the world didn't need no more. Not from him. He told me once that he put all the words he knew into books. Señora, I can't read no English. Hell, I can't barely read no Spanish." He hands her the scrap of paper. "This maybe don't mean nothing. What do I know?"

She unfolds the note written on Grand Union Hotel stationery and reads it, the handwriting neat and precise, much like the man. She smiles, but no longer the coy smile of the ingénue she once affected. The words come flashing at her with all their bite and humor. Many would think them inappropriate under the circumstances, although that endearingly sardonic scalawag would have believed otherwise. He behaved as if he had no fear of death, not even his own, but she somehow doubted that. Fear or not, he certainly had no respect for what he called the Damned Thing.

Aloud, she reads, "Death is not the end. There remains the litigation over the estate."

No one knows how to react until she begins to chuckle, and they all join in, even Johnny who has no idea what's so funny.

"One more thing, señora," the Mexican says. "I almost forgot. He also wanted me to give you this. It's a silly trinket, I think, but *bonito*, kind of pretty. Ain't worth much, maybe."

She unravels the cheesecloth wrap to unveil a peach-tinted cameo pin on which is the delicately carved face of what might be a goddess.

"He told me that long ago it belonged to a very old woman who taught him to—what did he say?—think, breathe. He said he carried it throughout his war, the one between your blue and your gray. Even in Mexico he had it, along with his watch. Bet you could get five dollars for it."

"My god," she says, "this isn't the sort of thing a man carries, not through wars, not throughout his life."

"Unless, señora, it is something he was saving to give to a woman, a special woman. At the end, he didn't have much else to give you."

"Incorrect, Mr. Arango. This cameo epitomizes, only and just barely, what he gave me."

"Huh?"

The commander in chief of the *División del Norté* and his man are to take the steamer down the Hudson to New York City the next morning for their return to Mexico, while Mrs. Dumont and her son are poised to end their holiday in Saratoga Springs and depart for Buffalo on the Delaware & Hudson line to face the despotic Lake Erie winter. They fall silent as the earth carpets the remains of the man they've gathered to celebrate. Then she begins to hum. "Humoresque" by Dvořák. It was the old man's favorite melody although he could never remember the title.

Chapter Two

He leaves Washington, D.C., for the last time on a Thursday night. Carrie Christiansen's the only one to see him off. She writes in her diary, dated October 2, 1913. Describes how he pecks her cheek on the platform at Union Station as he boards the 10:10 for Chattanooga en route to . . . well, he *says* Mexico, but who in his right mind would go to a place like that in the middle of an insurrection? How he stands on the Pullman's steps until the locomotive's wheels begin to gnash. How she glimpses him through the coach window. He waves. She blows him a kiss. Secretary, confidante, lover, she's been with him a long time, but not long enough. Their friends joke that they're secretly married, even though she's three decades younger than he. He controls his lusts but not his passions, and she understands and accepts him for what he is. Her expectations being few, she's grateful for what she's had. They both understand he's never done right by her, and she knows she'll never see him again. Of his three children only one survives, Helen, but Carrie's the lone beneficiary in his will. After she returns to their rooms in the Olympia Apartments on Euclid Street, her bedroom across the hall from his, she runs her hand over his books. He's given away most of his library, but a few choice volumes remain. Works by Gertrude Atherton, Jack London, Edwin Markham, H. L. Mencken, and everything by George Sterling. All people he admires, even grudgingly the socialist London. What he sees in George Sterling she doesn't know. Over the next several weeks she receives letters from him, the content of which she neatly summarizes in her diary. Then the letters stop, never to resume. The last one's postmarked . . .

Chihuahua, Mexico, where under the moon they travel and during the day hide in the arroyos. Nine of them, *federales,* mangy and prickly with the heat. They wait in a steep dry arroyo, unseen by any on the dusty road above, knowing sooner or later another unsuspecting traveler, just right for the kill, will pass. They've bagged six this afternoon alone, the victims pulled down from the road, bodies now baking, bloodless among the mesquite. One of the dead was a twenty-four-year-old pregnant señora violated in ways she never imagined until just before the knife rose slowly upward through her flesh from her vagina to the carotid artery in her neck. For her, death wasn't quick enough. Along with her agony she felt her blood pumping in wide spurts from her body, mixing with the semen. Her fetus, at least, knew nothing and never would.

The soldiers plan to hightail it to a new hiding place after landing their next quarry because vultures are starting to circle to feast on the remains of the dead, and the sweeping wings will no doubt attract the curiosity of some alert *Villista.*

Not long ago they were cocky bastards, still in their teens, in clean, khaki uniforms and sidearms, used to getting their way with women, shopkeepers, and peons. Now, they're exhausted, hungry, hurt, filthy, frightened. Days before, happily swilling tequila in the brothels of Juárez, they celebrated Mercado's great victory over Villa in Chihuahua City, never suspecting Pancho would regroup, change direction, and swoop into Juárez without a casualty. The nine young men, all drinking pals from Galeana, escaped with just their rifles, pistols, and the clothes on their backs. There's safety in Chihuahua City, they think, but that means crossing Villa territory, and friends of the *bandido supremo* are everywhere.

They've taken to murder and thievery, plundering ranches and shacks and robbing isolated crossroads stores. They leave no witnesses. So far, they've captured two horses and one mule and need at least six more animals to make good their escape. They're unaware that Villa, after taking Juárez, has annihilated their comrades at Tierra Blanca, and that the hapless Mercado, with the remnants of his army, has fled Chihuahua City, crossing the desert to Ojinaga on the American border. His escape will become known in Mexico's history books as the Caravan of Death, but the boys won't live long enough to read the history books.

From the arroyo they observe a plume of dust spiraling from the north. They check their weapons and maneuver into position, preparing to stay hidden should it be a platoon of *Villistas,* but ready to leap at an unsuspecting traveler. They've learned not to open fire from too far a distance for fear of hitting the horses. Horses are infinitely more valuable than men. Two riders approach, one tall and straight and wearing a black coat, perhaps a gringo, the other short in a serape and sombrero, no doubt a Mexican. To capture a wealthy gringo would be *terrifico*.

The gravel road follows the curve of the arroyo and, as the horsemen pass, the *federales* leap from their hiding place swinging their rifles and shrieking to panic their victims. The mounted Mexican is struck in the head by a rifle butt. He catapults from his bucking horse and slams onto the barren ground, his wound gushing blood, and instinctively buries his head under his arms as the soldiers beat and stomp him. Others grab and calm his skittish horse, leading it down into the arroyo. Terrorized by the sudden bedlam, the older man's mare rears on her back legs, and then on her forelegs, the flaying of hooves preventing the *federales* from getting too close. He's an excellent rider, good at most of what he does, in fact, but he can't control the frightened horse, whose back legs crack one of the soldiers painfully in the midsection, crushing three ribs. The soldier falls, screaming in agony. The gringo digs his boots into the stirrups and pulls up on the bridle, and even though he tries to grab the horn, the mare throws him. His shoulder takes the fall, his forehead scraping against the tiny knife-like stones of the road. The pain is excruciating, made worse when his attackers pummel him with their boots. His horse bolts away, kicking up clouds. A couple of the soldiers dash after the mare in frantic but useless pursuit. The older man and the young Mexican lay groaning. Their attackers stand over them, rifles aimed at their heads. The American's Stetson has fallen onto the road, exposing his white hair. He's older than he first seemed.

"Say, this one *is* a gringo."

"A rich gringo, no doubt."

They drag their captives by the feet to the killing place in the gulch, where six other travelers found eternal peace.

"Damn," a breathless soldier says, sliding down the slope of the arroyo as he returns from pursuing the older man's horse. "We didn't get his nag or his saddlebags."

"We'll have fun with this gringo anyway. Look at them boots. Twenty bucks American easy."

They tear open the man's coat, revealing his Colt .45. One of the youths grabs the gun and spins the chamber.

"Loaded."

Another *federale* tugs roughly at the old man's boots, pulling them off.

"Feel this leather."

"I want them boots."

"Go to hell. I saw them first."

"Hand 'em over."

"Damned if I will."

"Shaddup, both of you. I got rank. Boots are mine."

The soldiers notice the pouch at the old man's waist and tear it away. They break it open and shake it. Hundreds of dollars in American bills pour out.

"*¡Caramba!*"

"Look at the dough."

"American dollars."

"On this we can retire."

They scoop up the bills and throw them over their heads and dance as the money floats lazily to the ground. Their captive's silver watch is ripped from his pocket, and one of the soldiers swings the timepiece wildly by its chain. They find his billfold. More dollars inside—and pesos. They shake the wallet. A photograph of a young woman flutters out. Mollie. No one would accuse their victim of being sentimental, but he's carried her picture for thirty years. The soldiers discover the *Villista* order authorizing the American's travel through the State of Chihuahua. They tear it and the photograph of the woman into pieces and stomp them into the dirt. Still on his person, however, is something that remains undetected. Sewn deep within the lining of his coat is a cameo pin he's carried since his youth. On the cameo is carved the face of the goddess who once saved his life. He moans from the pain in his shoulder and scalp. His forehead's bleeding, blood running into his eye. His mind wanders. Strange images appear. He sees lines, angles, curves. Wheels, countless circles, turning, twirling. The wheels of a wagon train or of . . . bicycles? He loves to ride bicycles. As he feels his body being violated, stripped of its clothes, he begins to analyze the essentials of the bicycle. It costs nothing when not in use, unlike a horse or an automobile. It feels no heat or cold. It has no aches or illnesses. A rudimentary knowledge of mechanics is all it takes to become master of a bike and thus of one's destiny. There are no intellectual requirements, only subconscious control. One can fold his arms, smoke, eat, drink, and converse while the feet interact with the pedals. His mind drifts to the rolling hills of northern Indiana with its lakes and groves of oak and maple. He sees on a bicycle a young man gripping the handlebars. Himself. Next to him, on her wheel, is his first love, a sixteen-year-old named Bernice Wright. They're riding along the Tippecanoe River. He calls her Fatima. Tima. She rides ahead of him. Fast. Too fast for him to catch up. Disappears. No, no. He couldn't have cycled with Tima. He never rode a bicycle as a youth. He's not sure they even made them back then, and if they did his father would never allow such an indulgence. What were they once called? Velocipedes, that's right. Wait, now he remembers. It's after the Civil War that he mounts a bike for the first time, in San Francisco shortly before he weds Mollie. The city's too hilly to ride accelerators, another silly antique word. So they cycle through the Presidio, the old fort long vacant, past the officers' quarters, under Fort Point, through the groves of pine, cypress, acacia, and eucalyptus. Suddenly, he sees it from above, a panorama. He's floating in the gondola of a hot-air balloon emblazoned with the boastful stars and stripes. Smells gunpowder. The rifle he's just fired is at his feet. Did he just try to shoot a man down on the ground? Yes, he did. Someone he wants to kill. Floating down, down. Down.

Bleeding, Pedrito Gómez is also stripped of his clothes. Like his companion, Pedrito is sure he's doomed. *Madre de Dios.* Why the hell had he been so greedy as to abandon his wife and children and the safety of El Paso to undertake this fatal mission back to the country of his birth? Now he's about to die. He'll leave a good woman and two little girls. He sees the past, not that long ago. His brother, Manuel, immigrates first, leaving Ascensión to stay with an uncle in El Paso. Good with his hands, Manuel lands a job with a blacksmith. Like his brother, Pedrito learns to speak a little American from the local priest, a hopeless alcoholic who sobers up enough on Saturday mornings to give English lessons. To be able to speak rudimentary English provides Pedrito with enough aplomb to wade with his wife and two babies in arms across the shallow water of the Rio Grande into Texas to join Manuel. Pedrito finds only occasional labor in the O'Hara and Kruger Slaughterhouse and ignores the blood and offal he carries off with him each workday. Mostly, he waits, smokes, drinks a lot when he can afford it. He's playing dominoes outside the slaughterhouse, hoping to be called for work, when he hears that some loco gringo, wanting to join Pancho Villa, is looking for a Mexican to guide him to Chihuahua City for a hundred dollars American. Villa? Who could ever get close to Villa? No one gets close to Villa. Pedrito seeks out the *gringo*, who is sipping Coca-Cola spiked with whiskey, at the Elite Confectionery at the corner of Mesa and Oregon, his ebony walking stick propped against the table. Madness, madness to cross into Mexico right now. They could be killed, would be killed. Money or adventure might lead some daredevil into the midst of this bloody revolution, but only a lunatic would go for any other reason. One of Pedrito's daughters has the yellow jaundice, the other the cough that doesn't stop. His wife is bleeding from her rear orifice, her cheekbones pressing against her eyes. They're sick and hungry and he can't afford a doctor and Manuel's money doesn't stretch far enough. Neither O'Hara nor Kruger is likely to give him any breaks. He's a beaner, after all. Pedrito humbly offers his services to the *gringo*, who says, "You appear to be a decent chap, Gómez. But let me warn you in advance that if you deceive me, I carry a fully loaded Peacemaker and I'm not afraid to use it." Maybe the Americano ain't no lunatic. Maybe. But he doubts it.

"Now we're going to play a game," one of the *federales* says, pulling the knife used to disembowel no fewer than five men and one woman that day. "What do you say we cut off the old gringo's cock while he's still alive and stuff it in his mouth?"

The others laugh.

"Do it, José."

"Cut his balls off too."

"*Sí,* now."

"Ram a cactus up his ass and see how he runs."

Soldiering has been forgotten. The brutality of a war that takes no prisoners has made them brutal. José puts his knife at the top of the American's drawers and slits the cloth, exposing his genitals. A murmur of approval.

"Ah, not bad. The old man's well built. For a gringo."

The youths laugh again.

José grabs the American's penis and holds it up.

"Say goodbye to your cock, old man." He sweeps his knife downward. The knife doesn't reach its target.

The gringo, through half-lidded eyes, hazily watches José's face take on a comedic expression, which changes into one of astonishment as his forehead erupts, drenching the American with blood and snippets of flesh. The knife drops from José's hand. Then the American sees. Above, on the roadway, are men firing into the arroyo. ¿*Villistas?* Pancho's boys? One of the *federales* tries to aim his Mauser at the attackers but is rewarded with a bullet through his eye. Another soldier, the one with the crushed ribs, receives two bullets in the gut. The other youths throw down their guns and bring up their hands, hoping for a miracle, or at least a temporary respite from death. The attackers slide down the arroyo's bank and use their rifles to prod the six survivors into a frightened little group. A man—tall for a Mexican—kneels beside the gringo. Like the American, he's dressed in black, his coat reaching his ankles, his chest draped with bandoleers. Wears a familiar black Stetson. Quite familiar. A smile is on his face, but there's no smile in his eyes.

The man in black shakes his head in what might otherwise be a gesture of sympathy. "Ah, señor, you are one miserable piece of dung." He speaks in Mexican-accented Spanish.

The American doesn't understand. Tries to raise himself but is too weak.

Pedrito, lying at his companion's side, translates haltingly. "He say you are a mess, señor."

The gringo begins to laugh his non-laugh. Tears come to his eyes. He uses his hand to wipe some of the blood and flesh from his face.

The man in black says, "I speak a little American lingo. Let me try it on you. Something tells me you're on—what are the words?—a *jornada del muerto.*"

"Journey of death," Pedrito interprets.

The man in black says, "The *federales* left a hat in the road like a marker. Your hat, maybe? *Estúpido.* Fools. The hat pointed the way. I am wearing it now. Fits me good." He spits. "They must have been trying to get to Chihuahua. Wouldn't have done them no good. Mercado's retreated to Ojinaga. Chihuahua's ours now. *Victoria!*"

The gringo says, "My horse . . ."

"The white mare? We got her. Galloped right up to us, saddlebags and all."

The American heaves with relief, but embarrassed that his genitals are still exposed. Painfully, he drapes his torn drawers over his crotch, intending to preserve what dignity he has left. His mind, after being muddled by spokes and wheels and balloons, is now clear.

"We saved you from misfortune, señor," says the Mexican though Pedrito's translation.

"Sir, misfortune is the only kind of fortune that *never* misses. Indeed, you spared me from imminent dismemberment and the loss of my appendage, for which I'm in your debt."

"Anything I want I can take, so you owe me *nada*. Personally, I'd enjoyed seeing your cock carved off and jammed into your *repugnante* gringo mouth. I might do it myself."

"You are a prince, sir. May I ask your identity?"

The Mexican stiffens in importance. "I'm General Rudolfo Fierro, attached to the *División del Norté*, third in rank to General Francisco Villa. I'm in charge of the *División's* railroad system. But before you think my only interest is in steam engines and coal cars and crossing signals and timetables, let me tell you they call me The Butcher. Why do you think they call me The Butcher?"

"I hesitate to speculate for fear I'd be right."

Fierro snorts. "I slice meat. I dig into flesh, human flesh. I sever arteries. I slash muscle and carve away fat. I hack at cartilage and saw through bones. Always I am asked to show mercy. Do you think I, The Butcher, should show you mercy, señor? Any more than these dogs I have captured?"

The American pushes himself into a sitting position, aggravating the pain in his shoulder, but somehow relishing it. "Mercy is an attribute welcomed by offenders who are found out, General Fierro. But regarding myself, the entire issue is in your hands."

Fierro holds up the man's watch. "Nice timepiece, señor. I took it from one of the lice we captured. Yours?"

A nod. The sun flashes from the watch's silver surface.

"Maybe I'll keep it for myself. A souvenir." Fierro puts the watch into his pocket. "I despise foreigners. Especially Americanos and Chinamen. I've been known to stand many a man of them against the wall. *¡Ejecular!*"

"I quite understand, General Fierro. A foreigner, such as I, always belongs to another and inferior country."

"Huh?"

"What I mean, sir, is that a foreigner is a villain tolerated only up to a point—depending on your own eternal standard of conceit."

Fierro shakes his head as he hand-rolls a cigarette. "I don't know what you say, gringo. I think maybe you're *delirante*—how do you say?—delirious." The general, eyes narrowing, ignites his cigarette with a match scraped on the sole of his boot. "No, I think you are a spy for your Colonel Pershing. Or maybe an agent of the Wall Street trusts here to steal more of our land. You may be on a secret mission for the loathsome Huerta, enemy of the people and assassin of the gentle Madero. I should shoot you right where you are. Yes, I *shall* shoot you." He fingers the barrel of the gun holstered at his side.

The American takes a deep breath.

"And yet, yet . . ." Fierro drags on his cigarette and expels the smoke. "With your white mustache and all, you remind me of my uncle. I loved my uncle. He carried me on his back when I was a boy. He played games with me. He pulled cactus thorns from my feet. He gave me *marzipan* and *aguas frescas*—how you say, candy and sweet drinks. He showed me how to ride and shoot." Fierro wipes a tear from his eye. "I shot him dead. *Sí,* between the eyes. Ah, but it was necessary, you see. He betrayed me. I'm a very compassionate man, gringo. Ask my soldiers. Ask my enemies. Tell you what." He throws the cigarette into the dirt and grinds it with his boot. "I'm going to take you to my *jefe* and let him decide what the hell to do with you."

"*Gracias,* General, *gracias,*" Pedrito says.

"I wasn't talking to you, you miserable little shit. *Mierda.* What's your name?"

"Gómez, sir, Pedrito Gómez. From Ascensión."

"And why the hell ain't you carrying a gun for Pancho? Are you some *Huertista?*"

"No, General, I swear it."

Fierro grins. "Then we're going to have the doc fix you up, Pedrito Gómez, and give you a rifle and ammunition and then you're going to ride with Pancho Villa."

"But—"

"You *do* want to ride with Pancho Villa?"

Pedrito sighs. "*Sí,* General."

Rudolfo Fierro turns to the Americano. "And you, gringo. Yes, you. I like to be amused, so I got plans for you. Tell me your fuckin' name."

Ambrose Gwinnett Bierce has outlived most of his friends and enemies. Hazen, Eaton, Twain, Harte, Mulford, Stoddard, Bowman, Pollard, Miller, Pixley, Huntington, Gladstone, Barnum. All dead. But not the despised Hearst, the very man who resurrected his reputation and livelihood. Bierce carries with him an unfinished manuscript that will, he thinks, expose the newspaper magnate for what he is, assuming Bierce gets around to finishing it. These days he has a tendency to put things off, just as it's gotten harder and harder to piss and to sleep at night.

His journey from Washington, D.C., has been an exhausting combination of train, auto, steamer, horse. He walks across the battlefields where he fought as a young soldier. Shiloh, Chickamauga, Stones River, Missionary Ridge, Nashville, Franklin, Kennesaw Mountain. He was wounded in the head at Kennesaw Mountain. At Chickamauga, he visits a monument erected in honor of his brother's regiment. From Nashville, he steams up river to Pittsburg Landing. At Shiloh, he sees the graves of twenty souls from his own regiment. All through his odyssey the food tastes like crap, the water foul, the sleeping accommodations mean and filthy, not unusual in the wretched South. Could darkest Africa be worse? At Corinth the weather turns chilly and his hand trembles as he signs the hotel register, his usual precise signature nearly illegible. He knows then he's seen enough. The soundless battlefields and unmarked graves are forlorn monuments to an old war, which make him question the reason he's returned. There was a day when conflict was exhilarating, when the nearness of death made him feel alive. Now he's seventy-one. He needs a fresh war to bring back the boyish feelings of anticipation, danger, and battle he once so loved, which is why his ultimate destination is—*¡Caramba!*—revolutionary Mexico. He's breathing hard because of his asthma and is anxious to reach New Orleans to rest. When he steps from the Crescent City Limited he's attired for assassination, garbed completely in black, only his cuffs, collar, mustache, and hair are white. Carrying an ebony walking stick, he strolls the narrow Creole streets of the Vieux Carré, gazing at the low-slung buildings crossed by ornamental grilles shaped like vines.

He still fancies New Orleans, a city he visited often enough just after the Civil War when he was a Treasury agent in Alabama. Then, he was charmed by the city's contradictory atmosphere, somnolent in the delta humidity but buoyant with songs and love of life. Enchanted by the big-toothed Negroes who sang and strutted and danced. He never cared much about music, but even his foot tapped to the infernal infection that came to be known as jazz, a woeful yet exuberant blend of cornet, trombone, drum, and banjo. He enjoyed watching the sharpies play billiards, listening to the clack of the balls. He stood for hours sipping the city's strange and exotic drinks, brews of red or green or yellow, and all sweet to the tongue. He adored the saloons. He loved standing at bars intricately carved and rounded, varnished to a high gloss, set off by reflections, and punctuated by flashes of color and Tiffany. But now it's different. Again his asthma flares. It's hard to breathe in the city's swamp-suffocating air. He starts to hate this low-lying, mosquito-ruled fen. The streets are dirty, lined with garbage, excrement, urine, and vomit. More filthy than he remembers. Everywhere are deformed beggars and diseased whores and ungodly men waiting for something—anything—in the shadows. He wants to push on to Texas and to the dry climate of the border and Mexico.

The weather turns oceanic, as does his breathing. It rains steadily for two days so he spends most of the time gasping in his cramped room at the St. Charles Hotel waiting for his asthma attack to subside, trying to ignore the city's damp and gloom. Then, feeling better, he saunters into the hotel's hushed lobby where he encounters a newspaper reporter for the *States*. The youthful journalist, who's been tipped by the cunning innkeeper with a flair for publicity, convinces his editor that interviewing the visitor will make news. Long harboring an ambition to write serious prose, the reporter is anxious to meet the famous author, who hasn't penned a major story or article in years. Bierce's *Collected Works,* however, is being published in twelve morocco-bound volumes with gilt edges, which the young journalist has his hungry eye on. But at $120 a set, it's way more than an apprentice on a Dixie newspaper can afford. Or most reasonable readers for that matter.

"So you're just passing through?" the reporter asks, jotting notes on a pad with the stub of a pencil. They sit on upholstered chairs by the lobby window.

"I'm en route to Mexico, young man." Unaided by spectacles, his eyes are as blue as they were at eighteen when he was on his way to battle.

"There's a war on in Mexico, Mr. Bierce. Some sort of revolution. They take no prisoners I understand."

He laughs a sort of non-laugh. "I like the game. I like the fighting. I want to see it. I don't think the American landowners there are as oppressed as they claim they are, my former employer William Randolph Hearst and his mother included. They own an enormous cattle ranch down there, the Babicora. One million acres. I want to get the facts. In any event, I plan to meet up with Pancho Villa himself."

"I hear it's dangerous to go there, sir, even for Americans."

Bierce crosses his legs and leans toward the reporter in a confidential way. "Unsafe or not, I intend to cross the border. More fun, the danger and all. Eventually, I hope to reach South America and climb the Andes."

"Are you serious, sir? The Andes?"

"Have I been known to lie? I'm aware that as a gringo in Mexico I might be stood against a stone wall and shot to tatters. But that's better than dying under the sheets, isn't it?" His non-laugh again. "Trumps old age, disease, or tripping down the winery stairs. An innocent bystander in a Mexican war. That, young man, is rare quietus."

"Your family . . ."

"I've no family to speak of. My wants are modest. My royalties give me enough to live on. I've retired from writing and I'm leaving the field to the younger authors. In any event, one who's as old as I has been discredited by the lapse of time and is offensive to the popular taste."

"Unlikely, Mr. Bierce." Although the reporter knows Bierce is right.

Reporter and author adjourn to the hotel's saloon where they stand, feet on the brass rail, drinking mint juleps. Bierce pulls the disgusting mint from his glass and carefully places the sprigs on the bar. Tentatively, the reporter, revealing his literary ambitions, asks Bierce for advice.

"The first duty of an author is to be interesting," the visitor says. "He who does not obey this first commandment of the literary megalogue will incur the inevitable punishment of not being read."

Suddenly, a rotund man, hair in disarray, bursts into the taproom and staggers against the bar.

"I heard you were here, Bierce. Word gets around. I've waited a long time for this."

"And just who are you, sir?" He blanches at the stranger's breath, the mixed odor of privy and malt.

"You won't remember me, Mister Famous Author, but you'll remember my father, the late Reverend Foster P. Taggert, pastor of the Second United Methodist Church on Clementina Street in San Francisco, California." The man bangs his fist on the bar, rattling the drinking glasses and little bowls of peanuts. "Bartender, pour me a glass of rye. A big one." The bartender complies. The stranger grabs it, drinks it in a single swallow, and slams the empty glass back on the counter. "Another."

Bierce says, "Sir, the name Taggert doesn't register."

"The Reverend Foster P. Taggert was my father and it were you that destroyed him."

"I?"

"In them columns you wrote for that weekly rag in San Francisco comparing him to a fornicating pig and a swilling swine."

Bierce sips his julep. "Ah, it's coming back. Taggert. Rather heavy-set man, as I recall. Once known as the Reverend Two-Ton Taggert."

"Bierce, it was you that drove my father out of the church and out of San Francisco. He had to flee to Nevada where no one heard of him."

"As I recall he was involved in some sort of love nest. Eleven and twelve-year-old girls, I believe. Daughters of some of the church's parishioners. Quite a titillating story for my column. Boosted the *Wasp*'s circulation by twenty-five percent, I'd say."

"They was all goddamned lies."

"*Tauri excrementum.* He pilfered the church's treasury, as I remember."

"Liar."

"And one drunken night the Reverend Two-Ton Taggert was caught consorting with three Oriental prostitutes in a single bed at a fleabag hotel room on Grant Street, his trousers and suspenders well below his knees."

"Bierce, because of you the deacons of the church brought my father up on charges."

"But, Mr. Taggert, you must recall I defended your father in print."

"Say again?"

"I wrote that, in the interest of morality, the deacons shouldn't fire the Reverend Two-Ton Taggert. I pointed out that no respectable harlot who cared for her reputation would ever consort with a man as unsavory as your unlamented parent."

The stranger staggers backward, then recovers his balance, his words slurring. "My father was sick and penniless when he died. He put the barrel of a gun into his mouth and killed himself."

Unmoved, Bierce drains his mint julep and returns the glass to the bar. "Certainly, Mr. Taggert, you don't think I'm responsible for your father's premature demise, worthy as it may have been?"

"Sure as hell I does." Taggert, tottering, raises his fist. "I don't care how old you are, you cur, I'm gonna beat hell's candy out of you."

Before the drunk can act, Bierce whips out his Colt .45 and rams the barrel into the thick flesh below Taggert's Adam's apple. With his other hand he clinches the lapel of Taggert's coat. Taggert's mouth opens in surprise, his head pushed far back, his bulging eyes seeing only the ceiling. The pressure of the gun on his windpipe closes off most of his air supply.

"Mr. Taggert, you know what an Adam's apple is, don't you?" Taggert makes a gagging sound. "Then I'll tell you. It's a protuberance in the throat of man thoughtfully provided by Nature to keep the rope in place. In your case, it's a node that makes a perfect target for a bullet." A rasping noise belches from Taggert's throat. "Let me explain to you, sir, this gun is fully loaded and a bullet is set to discharge into your Adam's apple, through your chin, into your brain, and out of the back of your head. You're a worthless drunkard, sir, and just as dirty and fat and swinish as your father. I'll give you to the count of three to leave these premises or, so help me, you'll be as dead as your late, ignominious parent." Bierce shoves the fat man backward. "One . . ." Taggert pitches into a table, knocking it over, glasses, plates, and silver crashing to the floor. "Two . . ." He recaptures his balance, then lurches from the taproom and runs howling into the Louisiana night. Bierce returns the Colt to his belt. "I loathe a man who can't hold his liquor," he tells the journalist. He pulls out a silver watch. "Why, I believe it's past my bedtime. I must absquatulate."

The reporter is astonished by the author's audaciousness and composure. "One more drink, Mr. Bierce, please. After all this rambunctiousness you deserve another. My treat."

Bierce sighs. He rarely turns down the opportunity of alcohol, treat or not. "At my age bedtime becomes earlier and earlier by necessity. It's a fact that old age is a state of usefulness consistent with general inefficiency. Signal the bartender, young man."

The reporter asks if he might mail some of his better literary efforts to the author for an opinion. Bierce agrees, although he's vague about when he'll return to the States. The reporter is giddy when he leaves the hotel, the drinks having gone to his head. But he's managed to obtain Bierce's autograph on a hotel postcard. On his way back to his Rue Iberville room he's nearly run down by a streetcar on Royal Street, and that sobers him up.

Bierce leaves by train the next day for San Antonio, where he is hosted to a dinner of prime rib, baked potatoes, steamed cauliflower, fried onions, and barbecued beans at the Officers Club at Fort Sam Houston. A few of the cavalry officers are those he occasionally drank with at the Army and Navy Club in Washington, including a much younger man named Lack, a major he once struck in the jaw during a dispute over the qualitative advantages of certain brands of malt beverages. Lack was drunk and abusive at the time and undeniably deserved the blow. Now, the major approaches Bierce as he is about to enter the bar.

"I've never forgotten that night in Washington when you clobbered me on the chin, Major Bierce."

"Nor have I, Major Lack. It was one of the finest evenings I've ever had. I'd almost relish repeating it."

"I could shoot you, Major Bierce."

"You'll be dead before that happens, Major Lack."

"In that case, let me buy you a drink, Major Bierce."

"An honor and a privilege, Major Lack."

Bierce buys two horses, both mares, and a used but firm saddle. One horse for himself, the other for his small trunk. Much of his week at Fort Sam Houston is spent exploring the prairie and collecting bluebonnets and four-leaf clovers. He rides through the sage until the sun falls. He plays tourist at the Alamo where, seventy-seven years before, the entire Texas garrison led by William B. Travis was slaughtered by the troops of Mexico's Antonio López de Santa Anna. The city with its tacky little shops has grown up meanly around the old mission. He stands in the silence of the San Fernando Cathedral on Main Plaza where some of the defenders of the Alamo are buried. William Sydney Porter once lived in this city. Bierce is convinced his favorite literary device, the twist ending, was plagiarized by the jailbird Porter, who called himself O. Henry, a larcenous purveyor of smoke and mirrors. He meanders along the muddy creek the locals call a river, the San Antonio, which curves through the downtown. He drinks half a bottle of tequila in the bar at the Hotel Menger.

He reaches Laredo, more than two hundred miles to the south, on November 7 and visits Fort McIntosh on the banks of the Rio Grande. He'd planned to cross there into Villa territory, but that proves to be impractical. Victoriano Huerta's troops still control Nuevo Laredo on the other side. He eats roast beef, fried okra, and stewed tomatoes, and fortifies himself with brandy in the Hamilton Hotel. He stashes his trunk in the hotel's storage room. The trunk contains a few favorite books and some of his own manuscripts, including the unfinished monograph on his old boss Hearst. He assures the manager he'll be back for the trunk in due time. A fabrication. He visits the oldest chapel in Laredo, San Augustine Church, but has no time to pray. Making his way along the Rio Grande, he looks for a crossing that will lead him to Villa. He stops at Eagle Pass, Del Rio, Presidio. But their counterparts remain in the hands of the Huerta government. He rides for two weeks, past yucca, agave, sotol, cactus, and desert willow. Six hundred miles west of Laredo he reaches El Paso, where he discovers that Villa has taken Ciudad Juárez across the river. Capturing a *Huertista* troop train at Terrazzas, Pancho forces the telegrapher to send a wire to the garrison in Juárez claiming Federal reinforcements are on the way. Then eight hundred rebels glide into the railroad yards and seize Juárez by surprise. El Paso's citizenry stand on their rooftops to enjoy the fray on the far side. After the battle, the firing squads work at a feverish pace while the *bandito supremo*'s main body of troops moves south to invade Chihuahua City.

Engaging a youthful Mexican, not much more than a peon, to lead him from the border south through the desert, Bierce purchases supplies and still has one thousand five hundred dollars in green American currency left over, rolled and stashed in a leather pouch strapped to his waist. Unchallenged, he and Pedrito Gómez cross the Rio Grande over

the Stanton Street Bridge into Juárez. Villa's victory is still being celebrated as the two ride down *Calle Diablo* past the cantinas, casinos,
dance halls, and bordellos. Slot machines clang. Roulette tables clack.
Pesos and dollars change hands. Signs in the gambling halls warn the
players not to stand on the tables or piss on the floor. Music pours
from the doorways, the year's hit songs directly from the U.S. of A.
pounded out on mechanical pianos. "Ballin' the Jack," "Danny Boy,"
"Snooky Ookums," "The Trail of the Lonesome Pine." Drunken soldiers are everywhere, as are the whores raising their red skirts to show
their freshly shaven legs. The hookers are the same, but a new army of
soldiers has replaced those now in their graves. The odor of pulque
and day-old beer and urine drifts into the street. Gamblers step over
dozing *Villistas* snoring on the wooden sidewalks. Occasionally, a gun-
shot cracks as an insult is repaid.

They tie their horses in front of the Customs House, now the
command post of the *Villistas,* who swagger and strut in their white
sombreros and bandoleers, most in sandals or bare feet, Springfields
and Mausers slung over their shoulders. Villa's soldiers aren't used to
saluting or even obeying their officers, who freely execute their men to
keep order, and in reprisal are often murdered in their sleep. The *Villistas* never march in step or ride in formation. Their bombs are tin cans
stuffed with powder and nails and chunks of metal and capped with
five-second fuses. Villa's strategy is secrecy, surprise, and speed. Bierce
reports to an unshaven major who sprawls in a chair, his feet on the
desk, chain-smoking from a pack of Sweet Caporal cigarettes. His
boots, recently removed from the feet of a dead federal officer, are
polished to a mirror shine.

"*Comó estás,* Major."

"Your name, meester?"

"Bierce, sir. A. G. Bierce."

"And who's the hombre with you?"

"My colleague, Señor Pedrito Gómez."

The major says, "So, Gómez, I suppose you're a Mexican. How
come you ain't fightin' for Francisco Pancho Villa? You some *federale*
swine?"

"Señor Major, I'm a *pacífico.*"

"On no one's side?" The major tosses his cigarette butt to the floor and peels a revolver from the holster at his waist. He opens the gun, peers into the barrel, and blows into it. "*Amigo,* there's just one side in this war. Pancho's side."

"*Si,* Major, I assure you I'm on Pancho's side. I hate the *Huertistas.* It's just that this North Americano—"

"Shut the fuck up." The major returns the revolver to his holster. He expectorates in the direction of a spittoon but misses. The major can afford to be arrogant. He and his men have won a great victory and will one day be in control of all Mexico and he'll have a high government position in his hometown of León, maybe in charge of the water works, and will sit behind the wheel of a Stutz-Bearcat, his boots flooring the accelerator, making chickens and peons jump out of the way. The major asks Bierce, "What is your business in the State of Chihuahua, meester?"

"I'm an observer, sir, intending to make my way south in the company of Señor Gómez. Chihuahua City's our destination. I plan to rendezvous with the illustrious leader of the Division of the North, your own General Francisco Villa. I wish to observe at first hand this conflict of yours. We Americans need to have a better understanding of what's happening here."

The major spits again. "You with a newspaper or something?"

"My journalistic record is impeccable, sir. For two decades I was employed by the San Francisco *Examiner* and the New York *Journal.* I might now be described as a consultant. Major, I need safe-conduct papers. And I'd like to make arrangements to take the train to Chihuahua along with my two horses."

The major snorts. He rolls his boots off the desk and shuffles some papers. "You're a crazy gringo, meester. Civilians can't ride no trains. The trains is commandeered by the *División del Norté* for military purposes."

"Then perhaps I might engage an automobile and driver."

"All the cars is commandeered. For the *Revolución.*"

"I trust horses haven't been commandeered. For the Revolution."

"If Pancho needs your horse then you'll walk."

"Walk or ride, Major, I respectfully request your authorization to go to Chihuahua."

The Mexican shrugs. "As long as you ain't no spy, meester. Because if you is a spy you will be stood before a wall and shot like a dog."

"My dream, sir, my dream."

"It ain't safe in the desert. A few lice-ridden *federales* escaped the firing squads and are hiding in the cactus just waiting for a rich gringo like you."

"Consider it mere folly on my part, Major."

"What is this—what you say—folly?"

"The divine gift whose creative and controlling energy inspires man's mind, guides his actions, and adorns his life."

"Huh, *comó?*" The officer shifts his boots from the desk, opens a drawer, and takes out a sheet of paper on which he laboriously writes permission for Bierce to travel through Villa's lines into the interior. "Loco gringo." He signs the paper, stamps it, and holds it out. As Bierce reaches for it, the major snatches it away. "Ah, meester, I forgot. A formality." He smiles. "There is a small fee for the credentials." The major shrugs in a helpless way. "Fifty dollars American is all."

"Quite reasonable, I'd say, Major."

The major raises his fist in a victory salute. "*¡Viva Francisco Villa! ¡Arriba la Revolución! ¡Viva Villa!*"

Bierce and Pedrito leave the garrison with their freshly initialed papers and ride through the pockmarked streets of Ciudad Juárez. They pass the now deserted federal barracks, outside walls splattered with dried blood and crossed with bullet holes. Burned-out autos angle into the streets. In doorways women squat, pounding tortillas into shape with their fists. Naked children with bloated bellies titter and tiptoe in the alleys. The two travelers pull their horses sideways to avoid the carcass of a dead dog, bloated, festering in the middle of the street, the corpse perhaps never to be moved.

"The major isn't an amiable man, Pedrito."

"He don't need to be amiable, señor. He is a revolutionary."

"My friend, the problem with revolutionaries is that their revolutions are always now, now, now. When they win, they don't know what to do next except to unleash the firing squads. Socialists, anarchists, revolutionaries. They all might as well be hanged."

"Señor Bierce, please don't say that so loud. If the *Villistas* hear you you'll be shot."

"A fitting conclusion to an overly long life."

It's nearly two hundred miles to Chihuahua City. On the outskirts of Juárez they see lines of refugees—women, children, old men—some on horseback, but most on foot, bearing their meager possessions, hoping to escape the bullets and the bombs. Bierce whips his riding crop against his horse's flank. Pedrito spurs his horse forward. Their mounts' hooves kick up spirals of dust as they set out toward what the refugees had left, and where the two men have a fateful encounter with nine desperate *federales* on the run.

Chapter Three

He's seen death before, so much that he's lost respect for it, much like a forensic examiner who, without qualms, impersonally dissects one corpse after another. The carnage of his own war left bodies on the battlefield as far as the eye could see, but, friend or enemy, he took little pleasure in it. Here, in Mexico, no prisoners are taken, and there's something almost gleeful in the way the adversaries put men to death. Take General Rudolfo Fierro, attached to the *División del Norté,* third in rank to General Francisco Villa. Fierro's a man who enjoys his work. In amusement, he turns his attention to the six surviving *federale* soldiers captured in the arroyo. He grinds his cigarette under the heel of his boot.

"Gringo," he says to Bierce, "pay attention for *un momento, por favor.* I learned this from Pancho after the battle of Casas Grandes when we almost ran out of bullets."

Fierro lines the prisoners into two rows of three men each. He hefts Bierce's Colt, admires the gun for an instant, and cocks it. Legs wide, he plants his boots before the first row of cowering men. "Stand up straight, you cowardly dogs."

He shows his teeth as he fires into the chest of the man standing in front. The bullet exits the back of the first victim, then into the hearts of the two behind. All go down, their blood commingling in the sand. Fierro moves to the men in the second column, who stand moaning, frozen in fear, and fires a single shot through their hearts. They, too, fall. A few questions will be raised about the disappearance of the young men from Galeana, but after a while no one will ask about them anymore. Soon it will be as though they had never existed.

"See, six men, two bullets." Fierro blows a wisp of smoke from the barrel of the .45.

The American says, "General, I once fought in a war. It too was a revolution. The republic survived it. While the mutineers failed to destroy the nation, their descendants live on in various guises, burning crosses, repudiating man-made rights, lynching those they itch to tyrannize. We may never civilize that squalid quarter of my nation. I was wounded in the discord. We captured prisoners in butternut gray, most of them pitiful and more like slaves than slaveholders, but we never executed them with quite your aplomb."

"The *federales* was cowards."

"I'm not certain that to fear for one's life while lacking any alternative is quite the same thing as being cowardly."

"You think I am bloodthirsty, señor?"

"Not at all. In your case, blood is probably an appropriate beverage."

"Ay, yi, yi, you make my mouth dry. *Caramba!* Also I'm so hungry I could eat a goddamn horse." Fierro pulls Bierce's watch from a pocket and dangles it by its chain. "I've decided to return your watch to you, señor. Just to prove I'm an honorable man. And because you remind me of the uncle I had to kill. But don't let my generosity go to your head."

Bierce, Pedrito, and their horses are taken to a rail junction, and when the next troop train comes through the two men are put into a hospital car, whitewashed and clean inside, supervised by a gringo doctor, Ira Bush, who shows no curiosity about his patients other than their wounds. Hundreds of Americans have joined the fight, and the old bird with the white mustache is just one of them. The old bird in question finds it prudent not to identify himself. Far better to remain incognito in this barbarous land, in some respects not unlike the American South he helped to subdue. The doctor patches the injuries: a scraped scalp, a dislocated shoulder, a cracked rib. Some iodine, a few bandages. He'll live, although the wounds will take weeks to heal. It's a hard ride on the Mexican rails. The coach shakes and lurches, halting repeatedly for no apparent reason before moving again. He sees himself years before on another train, riding a flat car, a bullet wound in his head. It's in Georgia after the Battle of Kennesaw Mountain.

He lies on the splintery surface of the car, blinded by the moon, a perfect ball. He squeezes his eyes shut, but the light has no pity. He hears the crunch of metal, then a screech. Feels a lurch. With the jolt, the pain shoots through his skull. It's as though the bullet has struck him again. A whistle wails through steam. He feels a jarring side-by-side motion and the sensation of wheels gathering speed. He breathes in the odor of wood smoke and is stung by the tiny cinders that fall on his face. From close by he hears a moan. Then another. Someone begins to cry, then to yowl. A groan. A curse. More moans. He tries to raise himself but he feels strong hands on his chest, holding him down.

"Don't move, soldier. You're in bad shape. Bullet in the head."

"The light."

"I'm puttin' a wet bandage over your eyes. That'll keep the moon out."

The cloth is warm, damp. There are bitter fumes in his lungs, a wrenching odor he has smelled on the clothing of the surgeons. Ether.

"Who are you?" Bierce asks.

"They call me Charley. I'm with the Sanitary Commission. We gotta nurse you fellas till you get to Chattanooga. It's a sin to Crockett how they treat you wounded."

"Chattanooga?" He reaches out his hand, groping. "You said Chattanooga?"

"Easy, soldier." Charley pushes Bierce's arm down to his side. "You're headed to the army hospital. You and the rest on this flatcar."

"I helped to break the rebel siege of Chattanooga."

"Do tell," Charley says. "I reckon you and about forty thousand other boys in blue. Thanks to the anti-fogmatics."

"I don't—"

"Weren't for the fact all your generals at Chattanooga was drunk they wouldn't have planted a sockdologer on them rebs. Had to get corned to get off their asses, they did."

It takes some doing and the ornery crackers are driven back, but it's too soon to write their epitaphs. Bierce supposes the insurrectionists deserve what they're getting, but he doesn't have a particular position on the politics of the war; slavery, however, seems a touch excessive and hard to validate. Not that he has any particular admiration for the Negro, nor does he know any up-close, and he's certainly not in favor of amalgamation. They're a breed apart, and it seems strange to be dying for them—although preserving the nation appears to be a righteous cause. What he likes is the fight, the strategy of it, a chess game with lethal consequences, which is why Ambrose Gwinnett Bierce became the second man in Elkhart, Indiana, to follow President Lincoln's call to arms. Age eighteen. Late of George Steeple's Brickyard and A. E. Faber's Saloon. He can recite *Evangeline* and *Hiawatha* and almost all of Poe. *I was a child and she was a child* . . . Proud member of Company C. The recruiting officer certifies Bierce as qualified to perform the duties of an able-bodied soldier, having blue eyes, dirty blond hair, fair complexion, six-feet-one-inch in height, one hundred fifty pounds. He marches in civilian clothes and drills with a tree branch. Weapons and uniforms are still to arrive.

He sees his brother's face. Grizzly's voice pleading.

"Don't do it, Brose. Don't join just yet. Uncle Lucius is raisin' a field artillery company in Ohio. We'll sign up with Uncle Lucius and be together."

"Hell, Grizz. That'll take weeks. I can't wait. War might be over by then." Bierce has the patience of a horsefly. "Grizz, I'm only joining for three months."

He tries to open his eyes. Realizes he can't see because the cloth Charley put over his face is still there. The tracks curve and he hears the shriek of steel against steel, feels drops of liquid on his face. Like spit. A miserable rain.

"Okay, you men. I'm going to cover ya'all." Charley. "Looks like the clouds are opening up a little bit on this here death train."

He feels a tarpaulin being draped over his body. The raindrops tap like fingers. He begins to sweat in his uniform under the tarp. The way he sweats on the fairground at Indianapolis where he drills for two weeks. They're days of drums and bugles and flags and cherry pies and pretty girls. And Tima's proud of him, tall, straight, handsome in his blue uniform. He intends to marry Tima, his nickname for her.

At last, the Ninth Indiana Infantry marches through the midnight streets to the railroad station. The troop train presses south to the Ohio River. Western Virginia's a ferryboat away and war's waiting. The first thing he notices are the uniforms as the troops gather at the railroad siding on the Virginia bank. Clean. Neat. Mostly blue, a few gray. Some of the militia regiments wear garish clothing like that of the French Zouaves: blue coats, baggy red breeches, scarlet sashes around the waist, fezzes on their heads. He's heard talk of a New York regiment called the Highlanders that marches in kilts. The regimental flags are silk and not yet blemished by the stains of body and earth.

From Parkersburg, the Baltimore and Ohio Railroad carries them far from the river. The Ninth's first skirmish is at a place called Philippi. The Federals intended to attack at dawn to the signal of a pistol

shot. But Mrs. Thomas Humphreys, who sympathizes with the seces-
sionists, observes the Union troops dragging two cannon to the crest
of a hill near her home, so she fires her pistol at the Yanks, and that
sets off the attack prematurely. As battles go it isn't much. But it's
Bierce's first. The boys shoot off a Confederate's leg, while a Union
colonel is wounded in the breast.

The Indianans are sent to the Cheat Mountains. He's never seen a
hill much higher than a steeple. Spruce. Pine. He inhales as though he's
never breathed such a scent. Laurel. Roots hard. He carves the roots
into finger rings. Gathers spruce gum and sends it home in his letters
to Tima so that even before she opens the envelopes she smells where
he's been. He stands on the mountain and looks across the valley, dark
and green. The rebs are dug in somewhere in that valley.

The Ninth sleeps in wedge tents. They upend their bayonets in the
earth to serve as candlesticks. Smoke their pipes. Pass the time with
cribbage and euchre. Violin serenades from a sensitive youth who
doesn't know he's about to die. Huddle in rubber ponchos when it
rains. Quinine for toothaches, headaches, coughs, fever, and ague.
Postage stamps as currency when they use up all their silver coins. Fill
their tins with boiled meat and potatoes from the mess kettle. Hoard
coffee and sugar. Eighty rounds of ammunition while on patrol. Chew
on hardtack when they run out of honest food. Rip open packages
from home containing smoked turkey, clean socks, and tins of Bor-
den's condensed milk. Their pay is twelve dollars a month.

On sentry duty one dusk, hidden among the laurel, he nearly dozes. There's harmony in the katydid buzzing and sparrow lullaby. Then
he feels a human presence and becomes alert. He raises his head from
his arm and closes his hand around the stock of his rifle. Not seventy-
five feet away on an outcropping of rock above him, outlined against
the sky, is a man dressed in gray astride a white horse. He sits straight,
soldierly. One hand holds a carbine, which lies across the pommel of
the saddle, the other hand grips the bridle. The rider has the serenity of
a Greek god carved in marble. Sharp, pronounced features. A neat
beard. Silhouetted against the sky, the horseman not only appears to be
heroic but *is* heroic and of colossal size. How did he reach that prom-
ontory so close to Union lines? What secret forested path did this
Confederate enemy find to bring him so near to his death?

Bierce slowly cocks his rifle and aims it at the horseman's heart. His finger tightens on the trigger. In a moment the ball will fire and the enemy will fall. In just a moment. Then the rider turns his head and looks into the direction of the young rifleman hidden in the laurel, impossible to see. Yet the rider seems to see directly into Bierce's eyes. Into his heart. As if to say, to kill me you kill courage, you kill bravery, you kill nobility, you kill the essence of what man seeks to be. Duty, Bierce, *duty*. You have an obligation to kill the enemy. Pull the damned trigger and be done with it. Duty, Bierce. His hands begin to shake. His finger drops from the trigger. He can't fire. Suddenly, the rider, as though hearing some inner warning, pulls at the bridle and turns his horse. In the next instant horse and rider vanish. There's only the sky, darkening, over the rock above. Bierce rises, holding his rifle at his side. He's shaken, perspiring. Unimaginable. No horse could have reached that outcropping. He must have imagined it. A hallucination. Or the horseman in the sky was a phantom come to haunt him, just as the apparitions of his childhood dreams torment him still. He thinks, I must write about that supernatural horseman in the sky. Some day, some day.

Memories of his war fade as Fierro's train rolls into Chihuahua City, sprawling low and plain over a brown desert with a backdrop of gray, jagged mountains. The streets are wide. Colonial churches are the principal landmarks. Commanding the main square is a pink, quarry-stone cathedral with twin bell towers. The illustrious leader of the *División del Norté*, General Francisco Pancho Villa, who rarely smokes, is puffing a victory cigar as the engine pulls into the railyards. Pancho's feet itch in his new boots, and the bandoleers crisscrossing his shoulders aggravate his flesh, and yet he's in good humor after leaving to his firing squads three local merchants who, despite their protestations, are known to have sold supplies to the enemy. At first, he's inclined either to send the gringo with the white mustache on his way or to have him shot. Doesn't much matter which. But the older man seems to amuse Fierro, who is like a son to the *bandito supremo*. Rudolfo works hard, kills hard. He's entitled to a little entertainment.

Pedrito, haltingly, translates.

Villa says to the Americano, "General Fierro tells me you were carrying much American money. You were planning to buy weapons for my enemies."

"Indeed not, sir. My traveling money."

"Which is now safely in the possession of the *División del Norté.* Just why are you here?"

"I came to see if you Mexicans could shoot straight."

"You is a fake and a liar."

"General, you mistake me for a preacher or a lawyer. I was given credentials by your very own headquarters in Ciudad Juárez."

"Let me see them."

"Unfortunately, the papers didn't survive our confrontation with the luckless federals back in the desert."

"Señor, I could end this conversation and any more speculation about who or what you are by puttin' you into a grave."

Bierce shrugs. "A grave's a place in which the dead wait for the coming of the medical student."

The general begins to laugh. Then he laughs some more. This gringo's a witty old gent on the verge of death. But an example must be set.

Fierro says, "My *jefe,* may I suggest that the *idiota* play The Game. Give him a gun and a single bullet. Have him put the gun against his head. Make him pull the trigger. If the gun fails to shoot, the gringo will go free. If the bullet accomplishes its task, well . . . Such fun. *Muy diveritido.*"

"*Sí,* The Game. Rudolfo, I got to hand it to you. You always got good ideas."

They thrust into the American's hand his own Colt .45 and a single bullet. Without hesitation he puts the bullet into the chamber, spins it, places the gun to his head, and pulls the trigger with an eagerness that surprises the general.

Snap

"*Bastardo,*" Villa says. "Again."

Snap

"Gringo luck. If you keep winning I'll have to honor my word and spare your life."

"What makes you think I'm winning, General?"

"You're awful casual about your own fate. Even in Mexico worthless, diseased, shit-covered dogs that forage through garbage and eat their own vomit try to protect their skins."

"Death is merely being done with the work of breathing, sir. I've had my share of breathing. Shall I continue to play The Game?"

"Do it."

Snap

Snap

But the expectation becomes too much, even for Pancho.

Snap

"*¡Dios mio!*" He snatches the gun from Bierce's hand. "You're a little too thirsty for death, you *larva de mosca peluda*. Maybe we'll resume The Game some other time."

"In that case, General, perhaps you might direct me to where I can obtain a schooner of beer. I'm a thirsty man. After which a warm bath would be most agreeable."

Villa laughs. "Ah, but it's Sunday. The bath yes, but I strictly enforce the liquor laws in Chihuahua, although in your case I might make an exception." His eyes narrow. "Gringo, what do you want to do with the little time that's left of your *duración*—how you say—life?"

The American smiles his non-smile. "I understand Mercado's troops have retreated hundreds of miles across the desert to Ojinaga. Trapped now at the American border. It'll be a tough tussle, General, but I want to be there. With you."

"You wish to observe our battle."

"No, to fight in it."

"*¿Librar batalla?*" Villa spits. "You're loco, gringo. An old man like yourself, all patched up with bandages and splints."

"I heal quickly, sir, and I'm no stranger to war. Once, I was even called a hero and written of in the newspaper. I hope to fight in at least one more battle before I climb the Andes."

"What you mean, Andes?"

"They're mountains, is that not true?"

"*Sí.*"

"What's the use of mountains, other than for climbing?"

Villa, amused, thinks for a moment. What the hell. "Gringo, I'm going to let you go with me. On one condition. That every night you play The Game. Because if you play The Game long enough you won't live to see Ojinaga."

Famished, the American ignores his aches and devours a dinner of red meat with chiles, yellow rice, tortillas, and frijoles. Swallows the schooner of beer to the last drop and asks for a supplement, *por favor*. The Division of the North picks up the tab using the gringo's own money. That night, drifting into sleep as he lies on a pallet in the *Villis-ta* camp at the edge of the city, recollections of his war rush back. In his early days of the crusade, even the waiting for battle is like a dream.

The mountains of western Virginia stretch away to places too distant to comprehend. He sees far in the distance thin lines of blue smoke: enemy campfires rising above the firs. Mist rises from the rivers. The valleys only pretend to be asleep. Imminent danger is unseen, but death waits. He revels in the suspense. It's like something in a book, but he also welcomes the chance to fight, which comes soon enough. He's now a sergeant. Bayonets flash at Buffalo Mountain. The boys march past the corpses, faces clay-yellow, eyes staring, teeth like fangs, blood congealed. Frost has turned the bodies white. The Ninth gets licked. In retreat, the soldiers happen upon the same bodies, the corpses different somehow, a bit askew with an added blankness to their expressions. Expressions? The bodies have no faces. A herd of swine is feasting on the dead. Bierce, furious, is the first to aim his rifle and open fire at the hogs. The rest of the company join in, slaughtering the beasts.

The regiment pauses at the Tennessee River. On the far side, big guns throb in cadence. The shells make the water churn. Smoke clings just above the water's surface. What's the name of this place?

"They call it Pittsburg Landing," the lieutenant says. "And when we get our asses across that ditch we'll be marching to a place called Shiloh Church."

Bierce hears a bugle. Other bugles take up the chorus. The regimental flag, which was limp, tries to flutter. The men board a steamer, low in the water, heavy with its human cargo. He sees in the distance two gunboats at the mouth of a wide bayou. They look like tortoises, he thinks. I'll have to write that down. Someday, I'll write about all this to let the world know what my war was like. The river trembles in its banks as the boats fire their guns at the enemy. Standing on the steamer's upper deck is a fiery young woman holding an ivory-handled pistol. She's plainly visible in the flash of the cannons.

"My God, madam!" Bierce tries to make himself heard over the thunder of the guns. "Get down!"

Her mouth opens in a shout, but Bierce can't hear the words. She raises her pistol into the air and fires at the battle clouds.

A shell spirals from the dark and smashes into the steamer. A portion of the upper deck gives way, wood and metal falling on the soldiers below. Screams and cries of agony come from nowhere and everywhere. He's knocked to his knees. The ferry lists to one side but keeps steaming toward shore. When he climbs to his feet he no longer sees the woman on the deck above. He pushes his way through the soldiers, stepping over the injured, and finds a ladder, swinging precariously, leading to the upper deck. Gun and haversack heavy on his back, he climbs to the top. Several bodies lie on the damaged deck. He sees her. She's on her hands and knees trying to raise herself, her head down. The pistol's still in her hand. He struggles to her, puts his hands on her shoulders. Her head jerks. She looks up at him in fury, dark hair in wild strings over her face, sweat bubbling through the pores. Blood oozes from a jagged wound stretching down the side of her head. Her eyes are fierce.

"Madam, let me help you."

"Who the hell are you?"

"Bierce. Sergeant. Indiana Volunteers. Ninth Regiment."

He tries to lift her into a sitting position.

"Get your hands off of me, sergeant. I said to get your stinking hands off me." She raises her pistol and aims it between Bierce's eyes. "If you don't think I won't pull this trigger then you're one dead soldier."

He does as he's told.

"I was trying to help you, madam."

"Save your help for those who need it, and there's going to be a lot of 'em. I'll live."

The woman pushes herself into a sitting position. She uses her forearm to dab at the blood flowing from her head.

Bierce says, "What are you doing up here? You're likely to get killed."

"I'm where I want to be."

"You should be home with your family, your husband."

"My husband was killed on the first day of battle, so if it comes to duty, sergeant, I'll do it like a man. Like *some* men. My husband died a hero. He might still be alive if it hadn't been for the cowards in his regiment who deserted him. Bastards, they are. That's why I'm here. To let them know what courage is."

"Madam . . ."

"Get the hell out of here, sergeant, or I'll kill you with no regret."

Courage. To confront danger, even death, without displaying fear. He isn't sure he would willingly die for a cause, no matter how right, but dying in the name of courage is something else. When the steamer bumps against the dock, throngs of howling deserters, fearful the rebs are just behind them, struggle to get on board, but are kept at bay by bayonets.

Bierce leads his platoon through the black fields. Soldiers are everywhere, but no campfires. They encounter men who belong to strange regiments and generals with unfamiliar names. Tents are hidden in the hollows. Moans come from inside, while outside are long rows of dead with covered faces. The tents steadily receive the wounded but are never filled, the dead ejected to make room for the new. In a single row, Bierce and his men walk in tiny steps through the dark, frequently bumped by the men behind. Often their feet strike the lifeless. Sometimes they trod on the living who responds with screams.

A corporal says to Bierce, "Sarge, help me lift this man off to the side so's nobody else walks on him."

The man shrieks in agony.

"Easy, soldier," Bierce says. "We're trying to help you."

The soldier says, "Water. Do you have water?"

"I've got water," the corporal says.

"No, corporal," Bierce says.

"What's that, Sarge?"

"Don't give him water. What little we have we're going to need. Besides, we have to keep moving."

"But—"

"That's an order, corporal."

"Whatever you say, sergeant."

As dawn breaks, they come to a battlefield after the enemy's retreat. Bierce sees knapsacks, canteens, haversacks, and blankets beaten into the soil. He sees rifles with bent barrels and splintered stocks and wrecked caissons. He sees waist belts and hats and sardine boxes. He sees dead horses and dead men. A Union soldier, barely alive, lies face upward, his breathing coming in convulsive snorts. Bierce halts his platoon. A red froth sputters from the mouth of the injured man. A bullet has carved a groove in his skull. From the opening the brain protrudes, a mass of strings. A farm boy, probably. From Washington Court House, Ohio, or Connersville, Indiana, or Johnstown, Pennsylvania. Planned to finish his tour and go back to help his daddy with the mules and the plow.

The corporal says, "Should I put my bayonet through him, Sarge? Put him out of his misery?"

Bierce considers the idea.

Then . . . "I don't think so, corporal. It's not what we usually do. Besides, too many people are looking."

They come upon some woodland where Bierce walks through a growth of saplings, every one detached by bullets and each burned and charred. Men have been roasted here, cornered by cannon and flame. Everywhere he sees bodies half buried in the ashes. Their clothing broiled away. Some are swollen to double their size, others shriveled to mannequins. The contraction of their muscles gives them claws for hands and on their faces are hideous grins.

"Sarge, they're coming! The damned rebs!"

"Steady, corporal."

"Thousands of them, Sarge."

"Fix bayonets. Damn you, men, I said to fix bayonets! We've got the advantage—and the artillery."

A great gray cloud surges toward the Union ranks from the forest, bayonets glittering, walking into certain death, but Sergeant Bierce and his platoon never earn the glory of meeting the enemy head-on. The Union artillery does the work for them. The mutilated gray line falls back as the cannonballs plunge into their midst, exploding, deafening, deadly. Tasting the scent of victory, the blue presses forward, laughing hysterically as they pursue the retreating enemy. The victors are as confident as boys in a schoolyard. It's like a game. For the moment, at least, the fear of war is gone.

"We got 'em licked, Sarge."

Now come the stretcher-bearers, the surgeons, and the chaplain.

Bierce enlists for a third tour, and on the eve of the Battle of Pickett's Mill he runs into an old enemy from Indiana, a Yahoo he once bested in a bar brawl, now a member of the Seventh Indiana Infantry.

"If it ain't the kid who cold-cocked me at Faber's Saloon. See you got stripes now, boy."

"It's *sergeant* to you, Private Purvis."

"So you gone military. Well, *sergeant,* you caused me no amount of grief. My nose is still out of shape and I needed a new upper bridge in my mouth on account of you."

"I'm warning you, Purvis . . ."

"Warning me, *sergeant?* Let me warn you. This here's a big army. There's a lot of bullets let loose on these battlefields, so watch your back."

"Is that a threat?"

"Sergeant, would I threaten a fellow soldier fightin' a common enemy?"

Bierce is transferred to General Hazen's staff to serve as topographical engineer, his one year at the Kentucky Military Institute at last put to use. At the start of the Battle of Kennesaw Mountain, he learns that the Eighteenth Ohio Field Artillery has been deployed not a mile away. His brother's unit.

The two brothers throw their arms around each other. Hug. Dance.

"There's a hundred thousand men, blue and gray, on this battlefield, Brose, but you found me anyway."

"I asked around for the Eighteenth Ohio Field Artillery, Grizz. When I saw an artillery company that just wouldn't stop shooting I figured it had to be yours."

Unremittingly, the battle seethes. Albert continues to direct the cannon fire.

"So it's First Lieutenant Ambrose Bierce," Grizz says.

"And it's Second Lieutenant Albert Bierce."

Bullets thud around them.

"Better get down, Brose. They're gettin' a tad too close."

Suddenly a Confederate sharpshooter's bullet strikes one of Albert's gunners in the brain. The man falls backward at the brothers' feet.

"Damn," Grizz says. "That's Corporal Crawford."

Blood gushes from the hole in the man's temple. Brose and Grizzly drag the soldier's body to a tree and prop him up.

"He's gone, Grizz."

"One of my best men too. Shit. Say, Brose, my captain gave me this cigar. Been savin' it for a special occasion. Let's split it."

"With pleasure, Grizz."

Bierce is barely twenty. He sometimes archly describes himself as a plain, common soldier, but he knows in his heart he's more than that. He has military pretensions. He's found his calling. If he has to die he wants to die a hero. He asks only one thing: when to expect the bullet. Such is the ardor of youth.

His company pushes through the shrubs. Rebel bullets whine past their ears. Off to his right he thinks he sees Harley Purvis, his rifle in firing position. Suddenly there's a cannon blast. The ground thumps. For a moment Bierce loses his balance. Then he feels the pain in his head. He drops his rifle. Puts his hand to his temple. It's wet. Is it raining? So much water pouring into his hand. That's when he falls. He awakes in a field hospital tent and sees Grizzly leaning over him.

"Brose, they stopped the bleeding and I washed the wound. They say when you wash a wound it gets better. They're going to take you on the train to the base hospital in Chattanooga. Brose, can you hear me? Listen to me. Open your eyes, Brose. They don't think it was a rebel sniper that shot you. They think it was one of our own men. Someone named Purvis."

After his convalescence, he seeks out the Seventh Indiana Infantry Regiment, looking for his assassin, but Purvis has disappeared, either an unknown casualty on the battlefield or a deserter. So long ago, yet still so vivid.

Pancho toys with the Americano, a diversion after a hard day of work. Almost as good as getting laid. Or whooping it up at a cockfight. They sit across a table from each other in the red railroad caboose Villa uses as an office in the field. At night, Pancho sleeps in a fifty-room mansion he's commandeered in the center of Chihuahua City at Calle

10 Norte and Mendez. He calls it Quinta Luz, named for the most recent of his wives. Pancho's put in a hard day, planning with his generals his assault on Ojinaga. Chintz curtains flap at the caboose windows, and on the walls hang theatrical posters of fleshy gringo ladies posing with umbrellas or less. Candles illuminate the railroad car. A bottle of tequila is balanced on the rickety table between them. The general's taste for alcohol is newly acquired. He dances and he eats and he screws but—until now—he rarely drinks. Because Bierce drinks Villa does. He refuses to be bettered by an old gringo who isn't afraid of him or of The Game, and who can hold his liquor. In the privacy of the caboose, Villa's bodyguards outside, the general and the Americano swallow tequila until it rings in their ears. Bierce has consumed two bottles that day, but his hand is as steady as steel as he spins the chamber and places the gun to his temple. He hears the snap of the hammer. There's a little circle embedded in his flesh from the pressure of the barrel. He can't see the mark, of course, but he feels it long after he lowers the gun from his head. He spins the cylinder again, hearing the click, click, click.

The gun.

God, how he loves the gun. More than people he loves the gun—certainly more than people. He once cynically described a revolver as an argument used by temporary maniacs. He doesn't completely believe that. The gun is his defense against blackguards, railroad tyrants, feudal barons, newspaper publishers, and Mexican bandits—not to mention his opponents in the art of war, which he defines as a by-product of peace. In the greatest sense, the gun is not only protection from his enemies, it allows him to determine his own destiny. While the gun can be used against others, it can also be turned on himself. He loves the gun. Its hammer, hammer spur, loading gate, rear sight, front sight, cylinder latch, butt, grip, bore, side plate, trigger guard, trigger. Especially the trigger. The firm, even pressure when the finger tightens on it. He also loves the bullet. The single bullet. The bullet's nose, case, rim, crimp, primer. The light-heavy feel of it in his hand before he inserts the cartridge into the chamber. He loves spinning the cylinder. Click, click, click. And putting the gun to his head. Again. Such a game. The stakes are the ultimate for the player, unlike dice, poker, blackjack, roulette, or dominos. He's carried a Colt since his war. It's known as the Peacemaker. It was at the hips of Indian fighters, prospectors, sheriffs, and cowboys. He holds a bird's head model, so called because when turned upside down the gun's grip resembles the head of an eagle. And one day an eagle will soar over his bones, which will roll about in the alkali winds of the desert. Or maybe not. One may not know exactly where, when, or how he will die, but he has a pretty good idea about his own fate.

He pulls the trigger.

Snap

Villa says, "Put the gun down, *amigo*. The Game is over for the night. And maybe forever. You're too fond of this sport."

Bierce complies. At first, Pedrito serves as their interpreter, but in mere days Bierce and Villa learn to speak a pidgin mixture of Spanish and English, enough to communicate, although each loses some of the nuances of the other's language. As the candles' flames flicker, the grooves and creases seem to expand and contract on the faces of the two men, one older, the other not yet in his prime.

"Shall I tell you something funny, señor, a *divertido?*"

"Certainly, General."

"I saw a flush toilet for the first time just three years ago. Until then I did not know there was such a thing. I did not know how to use it, so I went outside to shit as I always do."

"I grew up in Indiana, sir, also unaware of flush toilets."

"You were poor?"

"Not poor, although I was born to farmers in a two-room cabin in Meigs County, Ohio, not far from the banks of the Ohio River. I remember, barely out of infancy, how Virginia seemed to rise mysteriously on the far shore. Or maybe I imagined it. When I was four my father moved the family to a village in Indiana."

"You were close to your father?"

"He was a man who spent his life failing, although he had a substantial library. Longfellow, Poe, Emerson, Cooper. His favorite poet was Lord Byron. 'I had a dream, which was not all a dream.' He believed in God and the power of the hickory switch."

"And your mother?"

"My mother believed in my father. She kept the chickens in the yard, the pigs in their sty, and the children in their place. Like my father, she never went to a dance, played a game of cards, rolled a pair of dice, sipped a glass of beer, or slept with another person other than her mate. My mother's lord did not sanction the pastimes of the profane. My mother was not profane."

"I was born Doroteo Arango, and I'm a killer. My parents were sharecroppers on the *Rancho de la Coyotafa* in the state of Durango, although my father died when I was very young and I became head of my family. You mentioned your father's library. My parents were illiterate, as was I until a short time ago. I killed my first man when I was sixteen to avenge the rape of my sister. They captured me and sentenced me without a trial to hang." The past comes rushing back with fury. Villa grabs a half empty bottle of tequila and throws it against the wall where it disintegrates into stars. If laughter comes to him quickly, anger comes even faster. "My jailers made me work like a slave grinding corn, but one day I took a heavy stone roller and crushed the skull of one guard and then another's. With their guns I escaped to the hills. I renamed myself Francisco Villa. I joined the gang of the best *bandito* in all Mexico, Ignacio Parra. He was like a father to me. For fourteen years I roamed without fear across the state of Chihuahua. I robbed the rich. It was where the money was. I was not stupid. I was called the Robin Hood of Mexico. Despite everything I stole, I never owned more than three hundred silver pesos at one time. I was an honest thief, you see.

"Then a little man named Madero asked me to join him in a revolution to oust the dictator Diaz. Madero gave me a silver watch, the only watch I have ever owned. I fought for him at San Andrés, Santa Isabel, Bajio del Tecolote, Cerro Prieto, Santa Rosalía, Camargo. At the first battle of Juárez, I, Francisco Villa, with a six-shooter in each hand, personally led the charge into the Plaza de Toros." The general uncorks a fresh bottle of tequila and refills their glasses, the liquor splashing over the sides and onto the table. "Diaz fled. Madero was inaugurated as president. I was rewarded with the sum of ten thousand pesos by a grateful nation. I retired to Chihuahua City to fulfill my life's ambition, operating a butcher shop. Then a man named Orozco came with guns to overthrow Madero. Orozco carried a red flag with the words 'Reform-Liberty-Country.' Such shit. I closed my butcher shop to help General Victoriano Huerta to put down Orozco on behalf of

Madero. How did Huerta reward me? Had me arrested for stealing a horse. He put me in prison. Huerta is a liar, drunk, and dope addict."

One of the candles has melted to its core. Villa takes a fresh candle and plunges it into the melting wax. Then he scratches a match to start a new flame. "Because of the deceit and *conspiración*—how you say?—complicity of the American ambassador, Huerta murdered Madero and took over as president. Blood ran in the streets. A day after Christmas, I cut through my bars with a saw. Dressed in a Spanish cape and bowler hat like a lawyer, I walked unchallenged through the prison gate and into the street, where I hailed a cab." The *bandito* begins to laugh. "'Take me to Tacubaya,' I ordered the *taxista*. I shaved my mustache and rode the train to El Paso. Once again I became Doroteo Arango.

"I waited. Zapata in the south, Obregón in the west, and Carranza in the north all declared against Huerta, so with seven men I rode across the Rio Grande to join them. I had eight horses, eight Winchesters, nine pistols, thirty-six pesos, two pounds of sugar, a pound of coffee, a pound of salt, and three whores, although one of the whores got strangled on the way. An accident. Another whore, the ugly one, I had to leave behind after she got *embarazada*—how you say?—knocked up. Also I had my silver watch." A wind kicks up outside, shifting the sands. The gusts can be heard whistling through the wood cracks of the caboose, trying to break in. "We grew by twos and fours and eights and finally to thousands. Now, we follow the First Chief, Venustiano Carranza, and we ain't afraid to die for the revolution." He thumps the table. "Señor, you would have been much safer remaining in the United States. See the trouble you got yourself into."

"General, why should I remain in a country that's on the eve of women's suffrage? And Prohibition as well. To be henpecked while at the same time forced to remain sober would be worse than the *beso de la muerte*. I knew when I was licked. And see how I'm becoming familiar with your lingo?"

Villa laughs, displaying his large white teeth. "I spoke into a telephone for the first time two years ago. I was thirty-four years old and I ain't never held a telephone to my ear. I didn't know what to say into it."

"General, the telephone is the invention of Beelzebub, who, if you may not know, is a surrogate name for those who believe in Satan. I've received word on the horn on several occasions, and the news has inevitably been bad. In addition, the phone does away with the advantages of making a disagreeable person keep his distance."

"You amuse me, old man. I'm starting to like you Americans—even though once I thought you were no better than the Spanish, the Chinese, and the devils of the Catholic Church. I got many gringos on my payroll."

"Gunslingers, General, and those who'd like to be. Desperate men flocking across the border to find action and adventure."

"Ah, just like yourself. *Estúpido viejo.*"

Bierce, in the small notebook he always carries with him, jots the names of his potential rivals. Edward "Tex" O'Reilly of Dennison, Texas, is a major in Villa's army. Lou Carpentier, a French-American, is in charge of the rebels' cannons at the first battle of Juárez. Death Valley Slim, who killed a dozen men in gunfights in the States, now fights in Mexico for universal peace and brotherhood. A former stockbroker from New York, Oscar Creighton, specializes in blowing up bridges—while federal troop trains are crossing—and is known as "The Dynamite Devil." Dr. Ira Bush is chief surgeon in the revolutionary medical corps. Dick Brown serves as a registered nurse. Notre Dame graduate Eduardo Hay loses an eye at the battle of Casas Grandes but goes on to become a general. George "Buck" Connors once rode in Buffalo Bill's Wild West show. Louis Wolheim, a graduate of Cornell, leaves his post teaching physics to fight for the *insurrectos*. Rodeo performer Tom Mix, who has made a few short Western movies, is captured by the *federales* at Juárez and rescued by the *Villistas* just before he is to be shot. There are so many Americans, many of them cattle rustlers, killers, and thieves, involved in the Mexican revolution they're known as The Foreign Legion. But Bierce doesn't associate with them. He's protecting his identity.

Pancho strums his guitar. He takes lessons. He also sings, not always in key but with heart. He sings his battle song.

> *La cucaracha, la cucaracha*
> *Ya no puede caminar . . .*

"I tell my soldiers we're cockroaches, little cucarachas grabbing for our tiny bit, our crumbs. I tell them we're humble, ugly, and indestructible. Words, words, words. If damned words were as simple and direct as bullets we would all be wise men. I wish my brain could give me the power to use words instead of guns."

> *Porque no tiene, porque le falta*
> *Marijuana pa fumar . . .*

"If it's any comfort to you, General, it's my belief the brain's merely an apparatus with which we only think that we think."

The general, not quite comprehending, strums a chord on his guitar.

"My wireless operator has been picking up a strange song, apparently an Edison recording, on the gringo radio. It is played over and over. What is this song, 'Aba Daba Honeymoon'?"

"It must be a popular tune, General, one which I thankfully haven't heard. Most likely it's used to accompany dancing, which is the process of leaping around to the sound of tittering music, preferably with one's arms around his neighbor's wife."

Villa props his guitar against the wall of the caboose. He yawns, stretches his arms. "Get some rest, señor. In a few days you'll have a chance to test yourself at Ojinaga."

Test himself? In battle? He's done it before, the first time at Girard Hill in western Virginia. The Indianapolis *Journal* prints an account of one Private A. G. Bierce, Company D, who runs to the assistance of Corporal Dyson Boothroyd, Company A. Boothroyd's wounded in the neck by a rifle ball and paralyzed. In full view of the enemy, Private Bierce carries Boothroyd to safety. But Boothroyd's wound is fatal and he dies two days later, while Bierce is on his way to receiving his stripes.

Chapter Four

Villa finds the gringo *simpatico*—the old hombre has grit, little obvious fear, and above all is a hoot—but he's not sure he can trust him. However, Pancho trusts no one. At night, far in the field, he drapes a serape over his shoulder, sneaks from the caboose, and traipses alone into the desert to sleep on an opulent bed of rocks. He's had many traitors posing as friends, and some old *cabron* who imbibes with him in comradely mirth just might turn out to be his executioner. The general knows he'll die in a geyser of gore. In Mexico, nearly every insurgent dies savagely. He's a warrior, not some scaredy-cat who'll perish of smallpox, scarlet fever, mumps, measles, dysentery, tuberculosis, or even from some unnamed and unmentionable disease, of which he's had several. But he vows not to die until the Revolution is over. *¡Caray!* God is watching over him. He despises the contemptible Church and the curs responsible for it, but he does obey God—when he has time. Sometimes obeying God is inconvenient, especially in the middle of a war. But he'll never grovel on his knees, not even for the Creator. Villa is quick to learn that his new friend also detests the church, and not just the odious one with a capital "C," nor does the Americano have use for anything spelled with the letters G-O-D.

A kerosene lantern projects furtive shadows on the slats of the red caboose, where the formerly abstemious *bandito supremo* matches the gringo jigger to jigger.

"You ain't no Christian, are you, *amigo*. You make too much sense."

"General, camels and Christians accept their burdens kneeling. I never kneel. As I see it, a Christian is one who believes the New Testament is a divinely inspired book admirably suited to the spiritual needs of his neighbor."

"Before this war is over I will hang from the fruit trees the padres who keep my people in ignorance and superstition."

"But consider the opposite point of view, General. It is in the interest of those soul snatchers to keep your people in ignorance. Otherwise, there would be no Church."

Villa spews cigar smoke into the air, then stubs out the cigar on a porcelain plate decorated with a crude image of the Last Supper. "The Church has worked in league with the government and the rich. The padres preach about virgins and bleeding images and apparitions and ghosts. They make the poor spend what little money they have to buy candles to waste. They tell pilgrims to kneel before the Virgin of Guadeloupe. The ignorant beat themselves with whips and chains. They press crowns of cactus thorns into their heads. They hang iron weights on their legs. It's loco. This cannot be allowed. Priests are paupers of the mind and body. They are too weak mentally and physically to make a living for themselves, so they live like lice—on the body of others. Parasites. Once, I had to beat my wife Luz without mercy on account of she built an altar in our home. *Compadre,* I need no bullshit altars or priests to explain the nature of God to me."

"General, I am ill-equipped to advise you with regard to the clergy, but I can tell you my system for answering theological questions. I developed it after a lardish, doltish clergyman couldn't make up his mind about a certain question dealing with the Bible and threatened suicide as the result. This delightful entity was known as the Reverend Two Ton Taggert of the Second United Methodist Church in San Francisco, a formerly breathing creature of no loss to humanity, thanks to his swallowing the barrel of a gun. Whenever I come to a theological issue that is too tough for me, I simply take out a deck of cards and decide the question directly and forever by turning a jack. A red jack is always yes, a black one is no. I state one of two opposing interpretations, such as 'there is a heaven' or 'there is no heaven.' I then shuffle the cards and keep drawing off the top of the pack until I come to the answer. In that way I've proved there is no heaven, hell is cold, the wicked have no souls, the devil was baptized by immersion, Peter's real name was Hiram Johnson, Abraham's bosom was a mountain in Mesopotamia, the first hundred fifty of the Psalms of David were composed by someone else, and Calvinism is a nice thing for an early tea party. Mine is the most perfect system of theology the world has ever seen."

Villa's infectious laughter is heard from far outside the caboose.

Bierce's antipathy toward all things religious begins early enough. He is twelve when he's dragged to a camp meeting on the bank of the Tippecanoe, where the holy and those who want to be have gathered to confess their sins. The faithful travel for miles on horseback and wagon to reach the meeting ground. Hand-lettered signs nailed onto trees guide them the last mile. Even before they get to the clearing they hear the singing of the hymns, voices clinging to the air. They pitch tents and build fires, the excitement growing. The forest has been thinned out along the river bank and hundreds of horses are tethered among the trees. The dusty open space is lined with wagons, carts, and buckboards.

On a wooden platform, the Reverend Ebenezer Baldwin stretches his arms to the Lord on high to remind the congregation they all have been born of depravity. Sinners and dogs of hell, they were spawned in the grip of Satan. "But in Jesus' name you can be sanctified. Hallelujah, amen."

Ambrose and Albert, squatting at the rear the crowd, sneak off to where the horses are tethered.

"Sure this is going to work, Brose?"

"Never been wrong yet."

In the river they soak a ratty blanket and tie it dripping around a docile old mare. On the blanket they lash a huge load of straw, dry and crisp and combustible, and with one of their mother's kitchen matches touch fire to straw.

"Now, Grizz, give the nag the whip."

Panicked, the mare rears, then shoots forward into the congregation, which splits like the parting of the Red Sea. Little children, crying, bolt to their mothers. Men once considered brave roll to safety. Women burst into fearful prayer. To Preacher Ebenezer Baldwin, the mare, which is hurtling directly at him, resembles nothing less than Satan invading the assembly to transport him to hell, where he knows he belongs after rolling with the twelve-year-old daughter of one of the faithful back in Fostoria last week. Hell, he wasn't the first to diddle the little bitch. He couldn't understand why the girl's old man hauled out the shotgun. Buckshot about ruined his new straw hat, and, besides, the girl gave him the worst pubic rash he's ever had. Baldwin, feeling the heat from the flaming horse, dives for his life as the mare vaults onto the raised platform, hooves thundering over the wood, leaving behind a plume of smoke. On the far side of the stage the horse, trampling over tents and cots and cooking pots, splashes with a boom into the Tippecanoe River, where the soothing baptismal waters snuff out the sphere of flame. Preacher Baldwin swears he can smell brimstone. *A revelation!* shouts the crowd. *A sign, the wrath of the Lord!* The Reverend Baldwin sees his camp meeting collapsing all around him. What if word of this disaster gets out to Watseka, Kankakee, or Minooka? He'll have to return to his loathsome job blacksmithing.

The conspirators, chewing on straws, sit under a tree giggling and poking each other with their elbows. Then they see standing before them their righteous sister Almeda.

"Ambrose, Albert," she says, her lips thin like her mother's. "Pa wants to see you. *This instant.*"

Now, Bierce remembers the painful tanning the brothers received, but it was all right because it was done in the name of the Lord.

Pancho says, "*Amigo,* do not make the mistake of thinking I do not believe in God, because I do. But I serve, first, the *Revolución* and, second, God, who governs the stars above and who will protect me until I have eliminated my enemies. The Lord favors me."

"Interesting, General, that you think God has taken sides in your fight. I won't ask how you've reached this conclusion. But to the point. Thanks to your revolution, you've already launched a system of education in Chihuahua. Schools, real schools, not church schools. Please don't make the mistake of creating a new generation of martyrs. In the long run, firing squads and ropes never prevail over religious superstition. Only enlightenment. Ridicule the Church, don't try to obliterate it. You'll only fail."

"I am not so sure."

"General, a long time ago, eighteen-seventy I think, I did what I could to strip the church of its most precious symbol—the cross. It was New Year's Eve and I was well fortified with brandy, as were my accomplices, three literary pals: Prentice Mulford, Charles Warren Stoddard, and James Bowman. The cross was huge, erected for the purpose of intimidation, on the highest elevation of . . ."

Golden Gate Park. Far below, San Francisco sparkles from lights in the windows of the revelers. Occasionally a rocket lights the sky. Sporadic bursts of celebratory gunfire herald the imminent arrival of midnight. In the Bay, the boats are asleep at their anchors.

"Gentlemen," Bierce tells his comrades, "the cross above us was erected by missionaries. I maintain the sons of bitches constitute a perpetual menace to the tranquility of the human soul."

Amen!

"The reprobates never give up. My sister Almeda is somewhere in Africa trying to save the souls of cannibals. If mankind is lucky, she will be boiled in a pot and eaten before it's too late."

Amen!

"Let us go forward, men."

Instead of pulling down the crucifix, the young men, hopelessly inebriated, entangle themselves in their ropes. Before long they are lashed haphazardly to the cross and, exhausted, finally gave up the struggle. In the morning, awakened by the sun, Bierce, head heavy, realizes his predicament. "Get me the hell out of here," he screams. "I'll *not* be bound to a cross. Better a bullet in the brain, which would have the additional advantage of ending the pain in my skull."

The careers of the four young men take divergent paths. Bierce survives his friends and, improbably, finds himself in Mexico on a mission not even he fully understands.

Pancho assigns Bierce sleeping accommodations in one of the many bedrooms of Quinta Luz. The accommodations are spartan—a bed, desk, chest, and a light that swings from the ceiling like an electric onion, just enough illumination to read by at night. A few books in English, mostly second-rate novels, are stacked on a nightstand. He's not sure not how they got to his room, and he tires of most of them after the second page. By god, this Bulwer-Lytton fellow is rank. Tommyrot about ancient Romans covered by volcanic ash? Good riddance, I'd say. And Wilkie Collins, the sensation novelist. Clearly this codswallop about a purloined diamond is a book with its covers too far apart. And drivel by someone or something called Bram Stoker having to do with eternal bloodsucking . . . Hogwash. But one of the books is *The Sea-Wolf* by his old foe Jack London. He's read it before, but what the hell? There are flaws in the damned thing, of course. Too long and sprawling, and London can't write a hoot about love, with its absurd suppressions and impossible proprieties. Well, he, Bierce, can't write about love either, but at least he's astute enough not to try. He's as happy here, in Quinta Luz, within these four adobe walls, as he's ever been; at the least, he has privacy, something he never enjoyed growing up in Indiana as one of ten siblings. Christ, how did his mother do it? A veritable baby-making machine. Carries thirteen to term.

The three most recent members of the clan don't make it, so Bierce reverts to his position as the youngest of the surviving siblings. His father, a man overwhelmed with piety, isn't without a peculiar sense of humor. Marcus Aurelius Bierce gives each of his children a name starting with the first letter of the alphabet: Abigail, Amelia, Ann, Addison, Aurelius, Augustus, Almeda, Andrew, Albert, Ambrose. It's not until they're grown that they appreciate the old man's whimsy.

The quiet of his room at Quinta Luz doesn't spare Bierce from the nightmares visiting him since childhood, the most frequent being of a great white horse that speaks to him in an indecipherable language. Stop, I pray to you, speak to me no more—on account of I know, I think I know, what the hell you're trying to say, and I want none of it.

Bierce is ten when the Dammed Thing visits him for the first time. On the streets of Elkhart, Indiana, where the buildings crowd together as if defending one another from attack. Wood and brick and glass. Advertising signs and barber poles and cigar store Indians. Horses and wagons and buckboards and carriages. Newsboys and flagpoles. Chimney smoke floats in the air, an open sewer oozes in the street. Mysterious men in high hats and women in bonnets rush to appointments known only to themselves.

The family rarely leaves the safety of its farm in Walnut Creek, but there are times when errands are necessary and the trip to Gomorrah can't be put off. To Brose, Elkhart's a metropolis. In the cluttered stores is a child's universe. Peppermint sticks marked by red spirals down the side. Whips of licorice so black and tart their very promise stings the roof of the mouth. Thundering hobbyhorses. Newly tuned banjos waiting to ring. Startling patterns of calico and gingham. Hammers and saws and drills. Fistfuls of nails overflowing in the bins. It's also a zone of fear. Kids risk being crushed by rigs driven recklessly through the muddy streets. Men stagger out of saloons and collapse in the gutter. Painted, reeking women shout obscenities. Sinister men crouch in the shadows waiting for night. Constables patrol the streets in blue uniforms, guns strapped to their sides. It isn't talked about at home, nor would Brose dare bring the subject up, but he's heard on the school playground shocking rumors of certain Elkhart men who take into their mouths the penises of other men.

Brose runs beside the wagon with his brother Albert. Their father, in the driver's seat, slaps the reins to encourage the mule. Laura Sherwood Bierce sits next to her husband, her back straight, lips thin as thread.

"I tell you, husband, Elkhart is a place of whores and drunkards. Sinners infest the streets here. The blasphemous jeer at God. Leprous, tubercular fiends sow disease."

"Easy, wife. It will be over in due time."

"Beggars reaching out with gnarled fingers, husband. Murderers wiping blood from their hands. Madmen maiming their own bodies with razors. The theaters are homes of Devil worship. Not even church is safe for God-fearing Christians."

Once, a neighbor loans her a copy of *Godey's Lady's Book*. She leafs through it looking at the pictures of fancy women, all puffs and curls, dressed in ruffles and trimmings and bows and endless buttons. For a fleeting moment she is intrigued, then she becomes indignant, embarrassed at reading such presumption. She has contempt for women who wear profligate store-bought clothes, city folk mostly, like those in Elkhart, the kind of women who drink sherry, sing strange songs, and perform aberrant acts with men at night. It can't be true that men actually put their . . . their things into the anuses of women. Why, that's sodomy! She walks two miles in the dark to return the blasphemous *Godey's Lady's Book* to her neighbor.

Pots for sale! Pans for sale!

Approaching the Bierces is a wagon pulled by two defeated horses, kitchen vessels lashed to the conveyance's every surface. The driver wears a bushy black mustache and stovepipe hat. The wagon's sign identifies him as Mr. Mose, who announces his wares in the voice of a dead man. It isn't Old Man Mose or the pots and pans that attracts young Bierce, but the specter trailing behind in small but hurried steps, running in a stupor. A monkey of a man, stooped, dazed, mouth open, eyes mere slashes, flesh bloodless. On his head, dangling from a tight-fitting cap, is a long plaited tail of hair. His pantaloons billow as he runs in sandaled feet.

Pots for sale! Pans for sale!

Ambrose and Albert stop short.

"Grizzly, you see that?" Brose's voice is a hoarse whisper. "That's a Chinaman. Like we read about in school. I've seen pictures. They wear pigtails and eat dogs."

"That's bunk, Brose."

"Everyone knows Chinamen eat dogs. Cats too. Marco Polo found out when he crossed the mountains and discovered China. The Chinamen had firecrackers and a printing press and goldfish and they bred grubs to make silk."

"Why would some Chinaman come here to Indiana?"

"To see the center of the world. Like Marco Polo in his time. Think about it, Grizz. We're in the exact geographic center of the earth. The side of the earth to our left is just the same distance as to our right."

"Damn, you're right, Brose. How'd you ever think of that?"

Old Man Mose snaps the whip at his horses. A wheel of the wagon dips into a rut, making the kitchen receptacles clang together like chains. The Asian comes abreast of the boys. He slows. His head turns. Suddenly his eyes open. They look directly at Bierce. For that moment the Chinese man's eyes are alive and fierce and on fire, flaming balls commanding Ambrose to throw himself into them. The boy knows those eyes. He's seen them in the dreams that rupture his sleep and make him cry out at night. His body starts to shake with a chill that won't stop. His mouth opens, but he swallows his scream. Grizzly grabs his brother's arm until the convulsions stop. The ferocity of the eyes vanishes as fast as it comes and the eyes sink into nothing. The Asian stumbles on blankly, forever trapped in the wagon's wake. Ambrose won't forget those eyes. Nor will he forget in his dreams the pure white horse that attempts to tell him something, something horrifying.

"Brose, snap out of it." Grizzly shakes his brother's shoulder. "You got the shakes again."

"Grizz, did you see the eyes on that Chinaman?"

"A little squinty is all."

"Last night after dinner Pa read us a poem by Longfellow. Don't you remember that line about the Reaper? 'There is a Reaper whose name is Death.'"

"Forget about it, Brose, we gotta catch up with Pa."

"Don't you understand what we just saw, Grizz? We just saw the Reaper!"

"Tell me no."

"It's damned, Grizz. A thing that's . . ."

. . . damned. Bierce's childhood vision of the Damned Thing re-

visits him as he accompanies Villa to the bleak border town of Ojinaga, part of the journey by train, some by automobile, the rest on
horseback. Men will die here, perhaps himself, all victims of the Reaper. Ojinaga is a place of such treeless desolation it makes Presidio, its
dilapidated American cousin across the Rio Grande, seem prosperous.
The Mexican town's composed of square, adobe houses and white,
dusty streets. Few houses have roofs; most have walls fractured by
cannon blasts. Chickens, children, and dogs use the gaping holes in the
walls like doors. The warring sides have exchanged Ojinaga six times
during the revolution. Maybe seven. No one remembers anymore. For
the moment, it's in the hands of General Salvador Mercado, leader of a
deadly hundred fifty-mile retreat across the desert after his denoue-
ment by the *Villistas* at Tierra Blanca. Mercado begins his campaign
with an army of fifteen thousand men. By the time he reaches Ojinaga
there are just three thousand five hundred left, including eleven generals, twenty-one colonels, and forty-five majors. Under siege for the
past several days, Mercado has managed to withstand the *Villistas*—but
now the fiend himself, Villa, has arrived to take command.

"Chiefs and soldiers of liberty," Pancho roars to his men, "we're
about to charge into the belly of that yellow dog Mercado. Take courage, because any man who turns back in the face of battle will be shot
then and there. By me personally. And if you get away I will bring you
back and hang you from your feet from the nearest eucalyptus tree before shooting you."

The gringo with the white mustache and attired in black nods his
approval as he sits astride his horse next to Villa.

The general's strategy is simple and effective. First an artillery
pounding, then a head-on assault. *Un golpe terrible.* It succeeds every
time. Wearing two crisscrossed bandoleers and a sombrero, Villa is
mounted on his favorite horse, a stallion named Seven Leagues. He
has owned many horses, but he gives them all the same name. A white
silk scarf flows from the *bandito*'s neck. He wears buckskin trousers,
jodhpur boots, and big-rawled Mexican spurs. Just behind him is the
Americano on a white mare. The gringo's Colt .45 is holstered at his
side, a Winchester cradled in his arms. Villa is amused when he sees
that his boozing buddy's in discomfort, still hurting from his beating at

the hands of the *federales* in the desert, but Pancho grins knowing the tough old hombre will die before admitting it.

"Sure you're up to this, you old buzzard?" Villa says.

"I can still pull a trigger," Bierce replies.

"You're about to get your chance, señor. What I said to my men applies to you as well. No turning back."

"A coward thinks with his legs, General. As you can see, I'm astride a horse, so I only need to think with my crotch."

Villa bellows with laughter.

The sun flashes on the menacing sight of the *Huertista* field guns protecting Ojinaga, but the *guerrilleros* know the *federales* are low on shells and ammunition, that they're exhausted, depleted, starving, terrified, and after several days of siege are weary of fight. Their uniforms are in rags, and most wear no boots or shoes.

"*¡Viva la Revolución!*" Villa shouts to his cavalry. He waves his rifle over his head.

¡Viva Villa!

¡Viva Villa!

A crater from a cannon blast erupts not seventy feet from the gringo, scaring his horse, which rises on her hind legs, but Bierce is steady at the reins and urges her ahead. The *federales* are dug into trenches. They hide behind stacks of sandbags, overturned cars, and piles of debris; however, they have no will. The *guerrilleros,* ignoring the cannon blasts, swarm through the makeshift positions, slaughtering without mercy the wretched defenders. Those who survive the initial charge retreat in backward steps, then start to run. Villa gallops down the main street, firing indiscriminately. But as he nears a decrepit windowless church, three huge Spanish bells hanging on a rack outside, Seven Leagues stumbles on a discarded automobile tire and the general is thrown to the ground, his gun skittering. Two of the fleeing *federales,* on foot, see their chance to become heroes. They raise their Mausers and start to fire at the fallen general. Bierce's horse gallops past Villa. The Americano pulls on the reins sharply, turns the mare, raises his Winchester and fires two shots, each bullet reaching its target. The *federales* fall, the gringo's bullets lodged neatly in their brains, their blood contrasting red with the street's dull white earth. Villa gets up and brushes the dust from his clothes.

"Not bad shooting for a broken-down old gringo."

"I learned my skills in the Ninth Indiana Infantry, General."

Bullets whistle over their heads. Villa, in his pigeon-toed way, finds Seven Seas and grabs the bridle. The desperate *Huertistas*, firing over their shoulders, splash across the shallow water of the Rio Grande. On the far side they are greeted by unsympathetic American soldiers led by Colonel John J. Pershing and herded like goats into a great, unsanitary corral. Later, the captives will be moved to Fort Bliss and crowded into a stockade enclosed by barbed-wire until the Americans can figure out what the hell to do with them. In good conscience, the defeated *Mexicanos* can't be turned over to Villa, who takes no prisoners.

At dusk, Ojinaga becomes tranquil except for the odor of smoke and burned rubber and death. Exhausted soldiers sleep, buzzed by mosquitoes. Near a campfire a soldier strums a guitar and sings "The Morning Song to Francisco Villa." It will be a long time before the smell of the battle goes away. The odor is not unfamiliar to Bierce, save for the stench of burning rubber. He sleeps, not all that badly.

Over breakfast of tortillas, dried beef, and black beans, Pancho says to his friend, "You saved my life, *amigo*." He raises his morning tequila in a salute. They sit in the ruins of the old church with the three Spanish bells outside.

"My compliments, General."

"You faced cannon fire and bullets. A foolhardy man, you are."

"Who is understood to be a man unlucky in the execution of a courageous act. I the exception."

"You loco old coot. But just because you saved my life don't mean I'm going to let you die of natural causes. You still got to play The Game."

"I wouldn't have it otherwise, General, and I remain in your hands. You, sir, have power to abate in me the ravages of senility and to reduce the chances of my being drowned."

Villa takes out a cigar and puts it in his mouth. A dog barks. The animals have emerged from their hiding places to chew at the bodies of the dead. He checks his pocket watch.

"I got a busy day, gringo. Colonel Pershing has asked permission to cross the Rio Grande so he can confer with me, and I said okay. It'll do no harm. The photographers are impatient to take my picture. And

I promised an exclusive interview to a fellow gringo of yours, John Reed. A journalist from New York City. You know him?"

"No, General, but I know of the magazine he works for. The *Metropolitan* is a muckraking rag read by socialists, anarchists, and radicals of all stripes. Before it turned to politics it featured pictures of women in provocative poses, and I prefer to be provoked than pissed."

"Señor, I do not know these words, muckraking, socialists, anarchists, radicals. One day you will explain them to me. Sometimes I feel like, how do you say, an ignoramus."

"You're far from being an ignoramus, which is a person unacquainted with the unique knowledge familiar only to one's self."

"You make no sense, *amigo*. Maybe you should meet this Señor Reed. You are a journalist. You might teach him something."

"I demur, General. I must protect my anonymity. I am, after all, in hiding. I've had enough of a world in which I played such a minor role."

"Perhaps, then, you are some famous Americano that I ain't never heard of."

"Perhaps, General. However, one who is famous is conspicuously miserable, while I'm having the time of my life."

"It can be a nuisance to be always the center of attention like me. Did you know that they're about to make a movie here in Mexico about the life of Pancho Villa? A gringo director named Thayer has come from the Mutual Film Studio in your Los Angeles, and guess who is playing Pancho?"

"If I were to speculate, General, I'd say you were portraying yourself."

"*Si,* Pancho Villa, movie star. I signed what you call a contract. I am to get twenty percent of the—how do you say it?—net. But I had to agree to carry out my attacks during the day so the cameras have enough light to film, and if the battle scenes turn out to be no good I got to reenact them. No problem. They're bringing in an actor called Raoul Walsh to play me as a young man. *¡Fabuloso!*"

Villa swaggers off to meet his public, while Bierce remains alone in the rubble of the demolished church. He sips at his tequila. With each year of his life, his drinking day begins earlier and earlier. Like Villa, Bierce has been photographed often, and he recalls the time as a child he desperately wanted an Elkhart photographer to preserve an image, the first and only, of his family—and failed. The sign outside read . . .

Wm. Lassiter, Photographer, Elkhart

Arrayed in the window are sepia-toned portraits, tiny and large, framed in wood, leather, brass. Pachyderms, camels, marching bands, mustachioed men and bonneted women in stiff, formal postures, pouty children posing on ponies.

His mother snorts. "It's the Devil's work. A body's not meant to be put on exhibit like that." She folds her arms.

"Aw, Ma," Ambrose says.

Marcus Aurelius squeezes the fleshy part of his son's arm so there will be a colorful blue welt in the morning. The shop's door jangles and a man walks out in shirtsleeves and suspenders, his mustache jaunty, curled up.

"Folks, I see you're admiring the daguerreotypes in my window. I'm Mr. William Lassiter in the flesh. You too can be assured a place in posterity. Come and let me take your picture. I've got a box, a *magic* box. You're quite a brood, so you qualify for the family rate. A mere five dollars for the group. Let us proceed while the sun favors us."

"Pa, let's get our picture taken," Ambrose says.

Marcus Aurelius shushes his son. "Just what are these, these . . . what do you call 'em?" he asks the photographer.

"Daguerreotypes, my man. Some Frenchy invented the process, which has been refined to perfection. It's done with silver-coated copper metal plates and the fumes of iodine. A complex technical process far above the knowledge of the average person. But I, dear sir, have studied in Paris, New York, and Chicago to learn and to master the technique. You're looking at the brilliance of my work in the window. Imagine! Your images will be captured forever, preserved under glass in a handsome leather case, perfect on the mantel over your fireplace or on your bedside table."

"Pa, can we do it?" Ambrose says.

"God doesn't want us to have our character taken," his mother says.

His father nods in agreement. Marcus Aurelius is not an unread man. Has a decent library, follows politics, detests slavery, and, in some ways, is intrigued by the technological marvel of photography. And yet he finds it difficult to reconcile his fundamental faith with newfound gadgetry, of which there is no mention in the King James Bible.

"I tell you, husband, it's the Devil's hand." Laura shakes her head righteously. "You heard the man say it was a magic box."

"Merely an expression, madam," says Mr. William Lassiter.

Marcus Aurelius concludes on the side of the Lord. "We're God-fearing Christians, we are. We don't hold for magic."

"Science, sir, science."

Laura says, "Looks like magic to me, all those images in the window. We don't want your magic box sucking the souls out of our bodies."

Ambrose says, "Ma, that's crazy. You heard Mr. Lassiter. It's done with silver and copper and iodine, not magic."

"Silence," Marcus Aurelius says.

"Damn!"

Laura gasps in shock at her son's expletive.

"Your language is vile, son," his father says. He slaps Ambrose in the face. "You're disrespectful to your mother and father." He cuffs Ambrose again. "Mark my words, unless you change your ways you'll burn in hell." He hits the boy once more to dramatize the goodness of God. Ambrose staggers from the blow. Tears well in his eyes, but he'll be damned if he cries. "Burn in hell, you will, son."

The photographer says, "No need for a family dispute, folks." To Marcus Aurelius he says, "You shouldn't be so hard on the boy, sir. Everybody's getting their pictures taken these days. I'll wager you'll all change your minds some day."

"We never wager."

"Amen," says his wife.

"I truly understand that." As he retreats into his store, Mr. William Lassiter says to Ambrose, "Cheer up, lad. Someday you'll have your photograph taken. Maybe your picture will be in the pages of a book. Have faith."

"Faith?" Ambrose wipes the back of his hand against the tears in his eyes. "That's when you believe in something you can't see or hear or know or understand. You do it because you're expected to. My father explained it to me."

Mr. William Lassiter smiles. "Ah, but faith in yourself—that's different. You can surely learn to know and understand yourself."

Late that night, back at the farm in Walnut Hill, the boy's awakened by still another nightmare. Albert holds a candle close to his younger brother's face. Brose sits up in bed. He's drenched in sweat. He opens his eyes wide, trying to fathom where he is.

"You're burnin' up, Brose. Like you've been in a fire." Albert puts his hand on Bierce's arm. "I'm gonna wake up Ma. Think you got a temperature. Maybe you're down with the fever. Could be the pox."

"Grizz, I don't want none of Ma's cure."

His mother's remedy for everything from bad dreams to bad breath is castor oil.

"You was really dreaming this time, Brose. A real bad one."

"I was burning in hell, Grizz."

"Aw."

"Just like Pa said I would."

"Only a nightmare, Brose."

"It was real, Grizz. I was in hell."

"So what's hell like, Brose?"

"You wouldn't like it if I told you."

"Tell me anyway."

"Grizz, there are rivers and oceans of blood, and trees with branches of tattered flesh instead of leaves. Fields of picked human bones, all white and clean. Giant bears and man-eating pigs and venomous snakes and poisonous spiders. Dark castles with endless rooms."

Albert covers his ears. "I've had enough, Brose. Don't tell me no more."

"I got to tell you about the bears. Chasing me. Their mouths open and dripping, jagged killer teeth all chalky. They're right behind me. And then a vision appears, floating, in white. She's in flowing robes. Her hair's long and light. Her skin is so pale it might be made of African ivory. She's a goddess. She opens her arms as if to take me in. She tells me to follow her. I see a huge stone castle. It's got towers, parapets, turrets, ramparts. She leads me to the castle. The bears are so close I can hear them pant, smell their breath, feel the earth thud under their paws. I pull the chain on the castle's door as the goddess floats upward, breaking into a million particles like crystals. Nearer and nearer are the voices of the bears. Grizz, they're growling, salivating, anticipating their feast. The door opens, slowly, screeching. I squeeze through the narrow opening just as the first bear heaves its huge body against the door, slamming it shut. I release an enormous wooden plank, which crashes into place locking the door. On the other side, inches away, I hear the bears clawing at the wood. Grizz, the goddess saved my life."

"You got me scared, Brose. Now I'll never get back to sleep."

"You need to know about the wind and fire and noise. Plague. Pestilence. Pain. Corridors of fire. That's what it's like, Grizzly. I've *been* there."

"Brose, you have nightmares 'cause you climbed the mound at Mr. Kissell's farm."

"So what?"

"You disturbed the mound. The Injins built it, and they put a curse on it to make sure their sacred burial place wouldn't ever be bothered. You know what's inside, Brose? Skeletons, that's what. Spirits and ghosts and devils and banshees wailing for the dead."

"Grizz, has anyone dug up the mound to see what's really in there?"

"They can't do it on account of the curse. Anyone who disturbs the mound will surely die."

"I climbed all the way up it."

"Now you know why you have those dreams, Brose. And about that white horse that always comes to you."

"I've got the curse, Grizz."

"And you gotta die."

Ambrose doesn't believe it, and yet . . .

Ojinaga. Such a wretched place. It too is a place of fire and noise, pestilence and pain. Why would anyone fight over it? Then, he realizes, the battle wasn't about a place but about an objective. As he leaves the ruins of the church, he sees a crowd of reporters and photographers clustered around the celebrated Villa and his generals. He recognizes one of the reporters as young John Reed. The photographers are taking a group portrait while a newsreel cameraman from Pathé grinds away. Bierce pulls his hat down over his eyes, as if that will make him invisible.

Chapter Five

The *guerrillero* sits, smoking a cigar in the chapel of the pink sandstone cathedral in Zacatecas, the quaint silver-mining city carved among the slopes of the *Cerro de la Bufa*. He's turned the chapel into his office. He thinks it fitting to appropriate the local cathedral as his temporary headquarters, and so he puts his feet on the table and with a crucifix scrapes the mud from his boots. Pancho is serene. Twenty-three thousand of his *cucarachas* have just crushed fifteen thousand Federal *soldados*, including a brigade of Pascual Orozco's hated Redflaggers.

Since Ojinaga, his new American sidekick has followed Villa into battle at Santa Rosalía, Camargo, Conejos, Mapimí, Bermejillo, Torreón, San Pedro de las Colimas, and Saltillo. When Pancho triumphantly enters Zacatecas the morning after the battle, the residents emerging from their hiding places step over piles of corpses, already starting to rot in the heat. To demonstrate his solidarity with the people, Villa orders that the bodies be thrown into the shafts of abandoned mines and filled with dirt. He decrees that looters among his own soldiers are to be shot, so seventeen are publicly executed. In Mexico life's not only hard but dirt cheap.

"*Buenos noches,* General," Bierce says as Villa's bodyguards usher him into the chapel.

"*Amigo,* I have our usual bottle and two nearly clean glasses."

Villa rolls his feet off the table. He pulls two Havana cigars from his pocket and hands one to the older man. Each bites off the tip of his cigar. The general lights for both of them.

"I am an uneducated man, señor. I carry a pocket watch and I can barely read the time."

"Let others tell you the time, General. You're a superb military strategist."

"Any fool can fight."

"General, it was the fool who invented letters, printing, the railroad, the steamboat, the platitude, and the sciences. He created patriotism and, like you, taught the nations the art of war. He founded theology, philosophy, law, medicine, and the city of Denver. The fool established monarchical and republican governments. He is from ever-lasting to everlasting. In the morning of time he sang upon primitive hills. In the noonday of existence he headed the procession of being. General, after the rest of us retire into the night of eternal oblivion, the fool will sit up to write the history of human civilization."

"*Compadre,* the fool before you learned to read and write just two years ago. Let me tell you how. My superior, the vile General Victoriano Huerta, ordered me shot for stealing a horse, but the sentence was commuted to life imprisonment, which is how I became an inmate at the Military Prison of Santiago Tlaltelolco. Until I escaped to El Paso, Texas, I put my seven months behind bars to good use. Now I can read simple books of short verse and folk tales. I look for my name in the newspapers. Sometimes I read aloud, although not without effort, to my lieutenants. My handwriting is bird-like, but with one finger I can type words on an Underwood."

The *bandito* considers himself literarily deficient and unschooled, but he believes in the concept of formal education.

Bierce says, "General, consider your progressive efforts on behalf of schooling. You ordered your soldiers to help build fifty new schools in Chihuahua. You imposed a truancy law. You required that English be taught."

"Maybe I ain't so dumb."

"Have you ever studied the lives of some of the recent presidents of the United States? Men barely competent enough to defecate in a toilet, much less govern. You, sir, are the last person in the world I would consider dumb."

Unlike the *guerrillero* turned military genius, Bierce refuses to publicly acknowledge his own shortcomings, although he too is aware of his educational deficiencies, despite his one year at a military school in Kentucky. He does, however, owe a debt to one Mrs. Octavia Oona Rich, retired librarian, grand and regal in her later years, her husband dead prematurely as the result of a carriage accident. In Bierce's seventeenth year, while he is briefly employed as an Indiana printer's devil, he visits Mrs. Rich at her home twice weekly. They speak of words and wisdom.

She pours Ambrose a cup of tea. Below the collar of her dress is a peach-colored cameo pin on which is the carved face of a goddess. He can hardly take his eyes off the cameo.

"Ambrose, you must stop pooh-poohing Jonathan Swift." She holds up the book he's been reading. "Don't you find Swift's use of the term Yahoo amusing?"

"Swift is silly, Mrs. Rich. In Lilliput, Gulliver is merely a giant among small men."

"And is Brobdingnag unreal to you as well?"

"The Brobdingnagians are grotesquely large. All I see is that in their country, Gulliver himself becomes a Lilliputian. It's a child's tale."

Mrs. Rich smiles. "Do you observe no differences between the Lilliputians and the Brobdingnagians other than size? Think, Ambrose."

"Well, the Lilliputians are not only small but contemptibly small. They seem to personify meanness of mind and character."

"And the Brobdingnagians?"

"They appear to represent morality, reason, strength. Although they still have flaws, like greed and envy and lust."

They sit beside each other on the velveteen sofa in her parlor. Before them is a small table with a marble top. Several books are on the table as well as a silver teapot. She lifts the pot and refills their cups as the columnar Seth Thomas clock chimes on the mantel.

"Do you understand the meaning of the word allegory, Ambrose?"

"Of course, Mrs. Rich."

"Then I suggest you read Jonathan Swift in the allegorical and satirical way he intends. Swift was a Whig minister in Queen Anne's court, but he switched his allegiance to the Tories after being betrayed by his own party. If you consider *Gulliver's Travels* in the context of Swift's life you'll see the book is an assault on political dishonesty and treachery."

"The Yahoos in the book, Mrs. Rich . . . they're a filthy, soulless, jabbering species motivated only by their appetites. They're a symbol of man's animal nature."

Mrs. Rich applauds silently. "Now you understand, Ambrose, that our best literature takes on other, if not deeper meanings. Fiction often exposes truth in ways nonfiction cannot."

They sit quietly for a few moments. Mrs. Rich puts a finger, the nail filed flat, against her cameo.

"I'm pleased you've advanced beyond stories of the frontier, Ambrose. That dreadful Mayne Reid. Look what is before you. Alexander Pope, Samuel Johnson, Henry Fielding. Superior literature. The books on the table are yours to borrow."

"Thank you, Mrs. Rich."

"And return them to me in the condition in which I gave them to you."

"Indeed, Mrs. Rich."

"Ambrose."

"Yes, Mrs. Rich?"

"Come here, Ambrose."

As he moves closer to her she puts her hand on the belt at his waist, opens the buckle, undoes the buttons, lowers her head.

Later, as she sips her tea, she says, "Ambrose, I have something to give you."

"You've given me enough, Mrs. Rich."

She unpins the delicate cameo and puts it into his palm, her two hands enclosing his.

"I want you have this brooch as a symbol, Ambrose. Of intellect, of imagination, of love. I saw how intently you were looking at it."

"Mrs. Rich, I know the face of the woman on this pin. She is the goddess in my dreams. Once she rescued me from being devoured alive by man-eating bears in a land of pestilence and plague."

"You don't say."

"I was walking across a stream in my bare feet, and when I looked down I saw the steam was a river of blood. I ran in horror. Into a desolate, burned-out landscape. The trees were blackened, leaves long scorched into ashes, limbs in grotesque shapes reaching out for me. The bears were just behind me."

"You have a most active imagination, Ambrose."

"The goddess, the angel, on the cameo—she saved me."

"And one day you'll find the right person to give it to."

"Never, Mrs. Rich. There will never be the right person. I will always keep it."

"Life is empty without sharing, Ambrose, so I hope you're wrong."

At the time of his weekly teas with Mrs. Rich, he is laboring as a printer's devil for Reuben Williams, owner and publisher of the *Northern Indianian* in the town of Warsaw. The shop's on the first floor, the Williams family lives on the second, and Ambrose sleeps on a straw mattress under the attic eaves. He sweeps the floors, stokes the fires, carries the water, pours the ink, and bundles the papers for three gold dollars a week and the promise of two new suits of clothes a year. He watches as the newsprint rolls through the steam press. The odor of the ink is more intoxicating than the hard cider he and Albert as kids would filch from their neighbor's back step. The churning of the press is like the music of a chorale. Inside are crank handles, gear boxes, rollers, camshafts, locknuts, pressure bars, springs, screws. When the myriad parts of the press work in unison they achieve the single and dazzling purpose of conveying words to paper. Words. Carriers of meaning and mystery. The young man learns to set type. He pulls the letters one by one from wooden cases, each letter molded in metal, and tediously deposits them into a composing stick. As the letters go in, so do the spaces. The letters begin to take shape first as words, then as sentences, then as paragraphs. When the stick is full of meaning, he passes it to Williams. The publisher sets the stick into a galley, the paragraphs lined into columns demanding to be inked and stamped onto paper, then to be read. The ink blackens Bierce's hands, the grease of the press softens his fingernails. He snatches the first page as it emerges from the press. His eyes fall on a headline about one John Brown, who is facing the gallows for attempting to instigate a slave rebellion in Virginia.

Williams says, "Bierce, I'm about to write an editorial on behalf of John Brown for the next edition. If you were me what would you say in the headline?"

"How about 'John Brown Should Be Spared'?"

"For Christ's sake, Bierce. Too damned namby-pamby. In the interest of abolition, John Brown should *not* be spared."

"But, sir, would he then not become a martyr?"

"Precisely. The headline shouldn't sentimentalize Brown. Or appeal for mercy. It's got to scream. Scream, dammit."

Williams writes furiously in block letters on a sheet of paper, then holds up what he wrote. BROWN'S FATE IN HANDS OF MALIGNANT BUTCHERS AND KILLERS.

"Bierce, be as reticent as you wish in private, but in print assert yourself."

A lesson learned.

Bierce would luxuriate as an apprentice at the *Northern Indianian* were it not for one Harley Purvis, the publisher's errand boy, yard man, and dung cleaner. Purvis and the young printer's devil take an instant dislike to each other. He is carrying a gallon of ink when Purvis's boot suddenly shoots forward and Bierce trips. The jar falls to the floor, the glass shattering, ink splattering, black and oozing.

"Gee-whillikins, boy, you is as clumsy as shit," Purvis says. "An accident. Real sorry about that."

"Sorry?" Bierce climbs to his feet. "I don't believe you."

"Who gives a fuck what you believe?" Purvis hooks his thumbs into his bib overalls. "Boy, you and that cunny-catcher Williams is two of a kind. A real goosey gander, you is."

"The mess on the floor, Purvis. What's Mr. Williams going to say?"

"Clean it up, asswipe. You know what I gotta do for that sap-head? Break my bum carrying his damned Republican newspapers from one end of the county to the other. Far as I'm concerned the Africans oughta stay slaves. They ain't real humans. Gotta clean the shit from Williams's stable every day. Wipe down his horse every night. 'Do this, Purvis,' he says, 'do that, Purvis.' And the bloodsucker pays me five stinkin' dollars a week. But I'm buildin' a nest egg, I am, and not just on what the old bastard pays me. I'm about to mosey off to Elkhart. Job's openin' up at a brickyard. Owner says I'll be foreman in no time. Besides, I been courtin' this little Elkhart bitch. She gives me a real good time. We might even get hitched before long. Then I'll get it any time I want without havin' to pay for it. Say, boy, to show I don't have no hard feelings for you trippin' on your bum, how about a little fun tonight? The ass-fucking, cunt-fucking kind. I know you been jerkin' your gherkin up in your room all alone. There's this coon gal I know whose bubbies are big enough to keep the British navy afloat." Harley pushes his hands under his shirt as though balancing a huge set of breasts. "She lives in this shack by the cemetery. Boy, I'm gettin' us a bottle of tiger sweat and I'm takin' you to old Stinky's. She charges a quarter, but she gives discounts for regular customers, and I'm a regular. My treat."

"Purvis, I have to clean up this mess you caused. Not only that, I could puke at the thought of sharing a bottle of tiger sweat with you, or a colored whore for that matter. Someone said once ignorance isn't innocence but a sin."

"You sayin' I'm ignorant?"

"I'm saying you're a Yahoo."

"Huh? What's a Yahoo? I don't know what it means, boy, but it don't sound good, and I'm gonna make you eat that word. Wait and see."

Bierce ignores Purvis's threat, and the following Sunday, his day off, skates on Goose Lake with Bernice Wright. He calls her Tima, short for Fatima, favorite daughter of the Islamic prophet Muhammad. When they're ten Bernie Wright gets even with Brose for sticking his tongue out at her in church. She teases him mercilessly. "Ambrose, your shoes are too big. I'll bet you're wearing Albert's hand-me-downs." She sits in the second row of the one-room school where they are students. He sits behind her. "Ambrose, how come you never volunteer in class when the teacher asks us to recite? Too shy, Ambrose?" One day as school is letting out he accidentally drops his books in the dust. "Ambrose, you read too much. Why don't you ever play games with the rest of the boys?" In the schoolyard her eyes are sapphire. "Ambrose, I bet you've never even kissed a girl because you've always got your nose stuck in some book." He's a tall boy and his muscles are hard from the hated work behind the mule. Bernie Wright can tease him. His other classmates can't. "Ambrose, would you like to kiss me? Oh, I forgot! You're too busy reading." He blushes, too reticent to reply, and digs his heels into the dirt. They were a lot younger then.

Now, they skim across the ice, their skates leaving straight, thin grooves. The sound of blade against ice is almost like a mother's sigh. The wind blows across the solid lake raising gusts of snow that twist upward like spirits. As they warm themselves by the bonfire at lake's edge, he recites a sappy love poem he's written in her honor—*Fatima, should an angel come from heaven / Bright with celestial ardor from above*—but she dismisses it, suggesting he's too intense, that they're both just seventeen, and that they might be better off if they each see other people.

She asks him, "Ambrose, have you ever been . . . intimate." She blushes. "With a girl?"

"Well . . ."

"Tell me the truth, Ambrose."

"I've never consummated a relationship with a woman, Tima. In the regular way, I mean."

"In what other way is there, Ambrose?"

"Uh . . ."

"Oh, look! Who's that skating out there? Why, it's Gabe."

"Gabe?"

"The new boy from Saginaw, Michigan. He's working in Mr. Fair-weather's dry goods store. He came by to call on me last week and my parents were very impressed. Gabe has such a handsome smile. And he's earning good money, eight dollars a week."

"Gabe? You call him Gabe?"

"Let's skate out to meet him."

"I think not, Tima."

"Then I'll go by myself."

She wobbles in her skates down the embankment to the ice, and then skates into the arms of Gabriel Vaughn.

Ambrose hands her his heart as a valentine and she brushes it away as casually as a snowflake on the sleeve. Mrs. Rich tells him that in love there's always one who kisses and one who offers the lips. Red-faced, he removes his skates and puts on his boots, intending to return to Mr. Williams's home, but somehow makes a wrong turn in the woods. It's nearly dusk and the snow has begun to fall heavily, fine and powdered, whipped by the wind. It feels as though tiny glass particles are being flung against his cheeks. He's wearing his oldest boots, the pair with an ever-widening hole in the right sole. Should he stop walking his foot will freeze. Might have to be amputated. What if he stumbles and falls in the snow, unable to get up? His snow-covered corpse might repose for months under nature's blanket until a thaw. He stops short. A few yards ahead of him he sees a dark, sibylline shape. It moves. The chimeras of his childhood have returned. He starts to back away. The eyes of the beast open, glowing and furious. He hears a growl like that of a huge cat. Then the beast springs, not at him, but sideways, and disappears with an angry roar.

"A cougar," he says aloud. "Damned bastard cougar."

He breaks off a heavy tree branch. If the cat comes back, begins to track him, he'll use the limb to beat the animal off. He stumbles on. Who was it who said death never takes the wise man by surprise? He isn't a wise man. Not yet. There are so many things he has to learn. What is the world like outside of Kosciusko County, Indiana? He has amends to make. The day he leaves the farm to work in town, he and

Grizzly have words, a trivial thing, something to do with a borrowed shirt. Grizz refuses to come out to say goodbye. Brose also needs to make peace with his father. No, he'll never make peace with his father.

He's lost in the woods. Such an ignominious way to die. To be later found hunched into a ball, rigid, corpse unyielding. So embarrassing. A bullet in the brain, blown apart on a battlefield—that's a hero's death. That would make dying worthwhile. But this ... this ... Wait! What does he see? Human footprints in the snow. Whoever it is just ahead of him. Can't be far. He's not done for after all. He begins running, following the tracks. He discards the tree limb. He gasps for air. Since early childhood he's had a breathing problem and doesn't know why.

"Help me, for Christ's sake. I'm lost. Lost!"

He falls. Picks himself up. Runs. Comes to a clearing. Standing in the center is a man in black clothing, back turned. Bierce falls again, crawls, climbs to his feet

"Thank god I've found you."

The man turns. He's holding a rifle. Aims it at Brose's temple.

"Wrong, boy. I found you."

"Harley?"

Purvis pulls the trigger. The rifle explodes. Bierce feels his head disintegrate. Pieces of bone and brain and flesh scatter into the air. He screams, the sound of one who knows his life has been taken, swiftly, violently, and by surprise. He lies still, head throbbing. Opens his eyes. Puts his hand to his forehead. It's wet with blood. As he sits up a heavy branch from a tree rolls from his shoulder and sinks into the snow. A swath of blood on the limb. His blood. The branch must have collapsed under the weight of the snow, striking him on the head. The crack he heard was the branch splitting from the tree. He laughs with relief. How long was he been out? He rises to his feet. The image of Purvis seemed so real. The cold, the wind, the fear must have conspired to play tricks on his mind. He staggers off, unsure of the direction, until he sees in the distance, through the trees, a flickering light, then another, and another. The town. He's nearly home. Jesus, he'll live. He opens the front door and finds Reuben Williams sitting at his roll-top, shadows from the oil lamp playing on his face. He's smoking his favorite meerschaum pipe.

"Egad, Bierce. You look like tarnation. What's that on your head?

Blood?"

"I fell in the woods, sir. Nothing serious."

"Good, because I have some bad news for you, boy."

It's then the publisher accuses Bierce of thievery and gives him ten minutes to collect his things.

"They were skillfully designed andirons of bronze and iron and glass that had been in my wife's family for years. Stolen. How did you think you could escape from being discovered, Bierce? I want those andirons returned."

Ambrose stands erect. "I did not steal your andirons, sir. Have you ever known me to steal?"

"The temptation was simply too much for you."

"I repeat, sir. I did not steal from you, and you cannot prove I did. I suspect it was—"

"I do not care to listen to your suspicions, Bierce. What I should do is contact the constabulary, so you're fortunate I'm letting you off so easily."

Protests ignored, tears welling, he walks the three miles in the dark through the slush and snow home to Walnut Creek. Over his shoulder is a bag stuffed with his dress suit, long johns, razor, skates, his Poe and his Longfellow. He has failed as a printer, as a lover, as a scholar. After he walks into the house he brushes off his parents, Grizzly. Damn them too. In the glow of the oil lamp he takes out pen, ink, and paper and writes to his Uncle Lucius Verus Bierce—Ohio University degreed, thriving lawyer, dynamic mayor of Akron—about the false accusation of theft and the loss of his job. Uncle Lucius is a man of action. He once staged an ill-conceived invasion of Canada, was declared a fugitive with a price on his head. Armed John Brown with the sword the insurrectionist used to annihilate five slavers in a place called Pottawatomie Creek, Kansas. Uncle Lucius writes back to say military school will change his nephew's outlook, build his character, mold him into a man, and that Ambrose Gwinnett Bierce has herewith been enrolled for one year at the Kentucky Military Institute, where he is to report posthaste. In a separate mailing, Uncle Lucius sends a silver watch to remind the young man of his responsibilities as an adventurer in a world to conquer. "If you keep it well it will tick forever," Uncle Lucius says.

In the coach to Kentucky, Ambrose reaches into his bag and removes the cameo brooch with the face of the goddess once belonging to Mrs. Octavia Oona Rich. It's a woman's thing, but she wanted him to have it for whatever use he might have. It had been a part of her. It's now a part of him. No one needs to know he has it. And maybe if the right person comes along . . .

"I feel as though I'm blind, Mrs. Rich," he tells her upon their parting. "I can't see my way ahead."

"Ambrose, you don't need a candle to see the sun."

Pancho thumps the table with the half-empty bottle of tequila "You seem lost in thought, *amigo*."

"The reveries of an old man, General."

"I too have, how you say, reveries."

Few would guess a man like Villa could be sentimental. He reaches under the table and produces a dented tin box. He opens it and shows Bierce the odd little treasures inside, small objects understood only to Pancho. A piece of a candle, a few coins, some torn and faded photographs, several newspaper clippings in which his name appears, the stub of a pencil, and a piece of paper, neatly folded. There are writings in Spanish on the paper, the letters laboriously, even painfully, printed in a cobwebbish, childish hand. It reads, "When man was born, he was not born to be alone."

"What's the significance of the phrase, General?"

"None, *amigo*. They are the first words I ever wrote."

Bierce is impressed by the effort if not the sentiment. He looks at his watch and then at the general. Villa nods. Bierce places his .45 on the table, but hesitates.

"Perhaps you're not in the mood for The Game tonight, *compadre*?"

"Perhaps not, General. Thoughts of my youth keep flashing through my mind."

"Tell me about them."

Bierce puts the glass of tequila to his lips. "I had a brief sojourn at military school before I returned to Indiana. I survived the hazing, learned to walk like a military man, became intimate with firearms, and studied what I loved best of all, topographical engineering. I savored the drill, liked the march, relished the discipline, accepted the order, admired the precision of men falling into line. But after the year ended, I had no choice but to return home and take whatever job I could find, which was in a brickyard in Elkhart. The foreman turned out to be a Yahoo I'd encountered before, a Harley Purvis, who rode me mercilessly, until I quit to work as a waiter in a saloon. But, worse, my mentor, Mrs. Octavia . . .."

. . . Oona Rich has suffered apoplexy and can no longer speak. He learns that she sits for hours staring into space as the clock on her mantel chimes each quarter hour, that she's incontinent, and that her eldest daughter must feed her by hand, that the food oozes out of her mouth and runs down her chin. He can't visit her, too embarrassed by the thought of their carnality and what she is now. But he treasures the cameo-faced goddess she gave him. Her secret, his. He keeps it with him, a kind of phylactery, if he understands the term.

A. E. Faber's saloon overflows with carpenters, blacksmiths, foundry hands, and rail workers guzzling their hard-earned but easily spent dollars. The piano player, derby cocked on his head, knocks out tunes like "My Old Aunt Sally" and "Old Dan Tucker." Clifton Gump, a genial giant, works the bar, his more than two-hundred-pound frame moving with unexpected grace. Old Faber busies himself countin' the money in the cash drawer under the counter. Hell, Faber thinks, with all the lucre pourin' in he'll soon be able to sell this here joint in Elkhart, move out of the sticks, and open up a palace on Michigan Avenue in Chicago. In his imagination the bar's already built: mahogany with intricately carved gargoyles; marble top as smooth and cold as ice; brilliant gold rail on which to rest one's best boots; leaded glass windows of greens and reds and yellows behind which are stored luxury lines of spirits; and a grand mirror filled with reflective swirls that runs full-length behind the bar. No sawdust on that floor. Expectoratin' is to be aimed strictly into brass spittoons imported from Bridgeport, Connecticut. The floor is constructed of oak, so burnished you can see your face in it, and polished enough to use as a shavin' mirror if you have the notion to kneel and wield the razor. The waiters are to be dressed in dickies and string ties. And one day someone will invent a new-fangled cash register machine that clangs when you open the drawer to make change. Faber's name will come to be celebrated in Chicago. They'll trek all the way from Milwaukee and Detroit to drink at his saloon, eat his famous oysters. Freshest, best-prepared steaks and chops in the Midwest. He'll run for alderman. No, mayor. Or better, governor. The governor don't have to actually *live* in Springfield.

At night—after the dishes are washed, the pickles back in their jars, the mops hung on the wall, and the customers home in bed— Brose and Gump sit on Faber's back steps and talk about the ghosts they've met. Bierce is chilled by their mutual tales of spirits and the supernatural. If he were a writer, he'd put the stories down so people would read them and remember them and be terrified by them. But he isn't a writer. He's a mere waiter. But isn't that what a writer is? A writer *waits* for inspiration, *waits* for the truth, *waits* for the strength to put words to paper, a person who . . . waits.

Among the saloon's regulars is the ubiquitous Harley Purvis, whose weekend binges are legendary. After cramming Faber's oysters and roast beef sandwiches down his throat, hardly bothering to chew, Harley always springs for the hops. "On me, gents." Purvis's generosity makes him popular with his buddies, even among those who would ordinarily cross to the other side of the street when they see him coming, but his mood gradually changes from generous to sentimental to cocky to angry to abusive. Eventually he'll stagger home, broken windows and broken noses in his wake, to knock his habitually pregnant wife around the bedroom before attempting, usually unsuccessfully, to penetrate her.

Purvis yells to Bierce from across the room, "Boy, I said to hurry up! I got a damned thirst that won't quit till next Friday. Hear me, boy? Or am I gonna have to whip your ass, like I used to? Back at that two-bit printer's and when you worked for me at the brickyard."

Bierce's cheeks flush.

Gump says, "Don't pay no attention, Brose. You know how Harley gets when he drinks. Besides, he's one hell of a fireman. Saved a lady and her baby from a burning building a few weeks ago. He's a hero. Got written up in the Elkhart *Review*. He just goes a little crazy on weekends."

Bierce serves the beers to Purvis and his pals.

"That's six beers, sixty cents," Bierce says.

"My treat, boys," Purvis tells his pals, producing the coins and throwing them onto Bierce's tray.

As Bierce starts to walk away Purvis snatches a small book from the young man's back pocket.

"Give me my book, Harley."

"Hang on, boy. I ain't going to steal this book. I ain't never stole no book in my life."

Purvis thumbs though the book as he would a deck of cards. "Who's this, this Edgar . . ."

"Edgar Allan Poe. A poet."

Purvis thrusts the book back into Ambrose's hand. "Read us a little poletry, boy. Read us a pome. Just one pome."

"I've got other tables to wait on."

"Sissy boy, if you don't want me to kick your ass across the room you open that damned book and read us a little poletry."

Bierce sighs, weighs his options, decides on civility. He doesn't have to read from the book. He knows Poe by heart.

"'It was many and many a year ago . . .'"

"Are you countin' leap years?" Purvis says.

The drinkers burst into laughter.

"'In a kingdom by the sea . . .'"

"You talkin' about Lake Erie or Lake Michigan?"

Laughter.

"'That a maiden there lived whom you may know by the name of . . .'"

"Lu Lu Schultz. Fuckin' broad gives it to everyone. For only a quarter too. And on bad nights for a dime."

Laughter.

"' . . . Annabel Lee.'"

"*Animal* Lee, you mean."

More laughter.

"'I was a child and she was a child . . .'"

"Oh, so you got your ashes hauled with a butter-cup." Purvis succumbs to laughter. Tears come to his eyes at the moment Bierce's fist connects with Harley's nose. He pitches backward in his chair, crashes into the sawdust. Blood sprays the air. Eyes disappear into their sockets. The piano stops. A couple of screams. A few people stand up. Somebody laughs. Then everyone laughs. Laughing at Purvis is easy now that he's head-down on the floor.

Bierce rarely smiles, but he almost does now. He guesses that Purvis won't know anything until the morning when the doc will come by and try to rebuild his nose. He still owes the doc after his wife's last two miscarriages. Most likely he'll have to pay the doctor's bill by selling off another piece of loot, possibly a prized set of andirons handcrafted of bronze, iron, and glass.

A. E. Faber ducks under the bar and runs to where the blood from Purvis' nose mixes with the sawdust.

"Bierce, you hit a customer." A. E. sees piles of legal papers, circuit court, lawyers' bills. His dream of Chicago and Michigan Avenue all going to hell. "You're fired, Bierce. Hang up your apron and leave the premises."

Bierce carefully drapes his apron over Farber's shoulder. Gump catches up with Bierce under the gas lamp outside the apothecary's on Main Street. Moths are skittering into each other under the light.

"Brose, you was lucky you got Harley with that first punch. He don't fight the way you do. He'd have stabbed you in the gut with that knife he hides in his boot and called it self-defense."

"Go back to work, Gump, or Faber will fire you too."

"No, he won't, Brose. I just quit. I hear there's going to be a war, with Lincoln in and all. They tell me them Southern swine is already shootin' at some fort in South Carolina. I ain't cut out for city life. I'm joinin' the army."

Uncle Lucius Verus has already written Bierce to alert him of the clarion call of the bugle, and to warn him that war spares the coward, not the brave.

"Maybe you can read *me* a little poletry sometime, Brose. I'd like to know more about this Animal Lee."

Bierce's narrative of his youth is interrupted by the sound of Pancho Villa's snoring. Perhaps Bierce isn't the storyteller he'd like to be. He stands and starts to blow out the candle when Villa jolts himself awakes.

"You're calling it quits for the night so soon, *amigo?*"

"It's late, General, and I'm afraid I put you to sleep with my wistful tales of youth."

"Have you heard the expression, sleeping with one eye open? I heard every word you said. Why don't you recite for *me* that poem about Animal Lee, if you still remember it?"

"Well . . ."

"That's an order."

"General, there are certain things one never forgets."

When Bierce finishes with, "In her sepulcher there by the sea / In her tomb by the side of the sea," there are tears in the eyes of Pancho Villa.

Chapter Six

General Rudolfo Fierro, injured in the leg by a piece of shrapnel at the battle of Zacatecas, is slightly annoyed. Twice he slaps the face of the gringo doctor who washes and treats the wound. The pain pulsates and keeps him from sleeping. He has chills but is hungry at the same time. He swallows eggs and tortillas and black coffee in the officers' mess. Finally, he feels better. Is restless. The battle's over and he has nothing to do. He decides to visit the stockade where Villa has imprisoned several hundred *federale* soldiers. Fierro spits. In the old days there'd be no prisoners. Now, Villa is giving the enemy a choice. Join the revolution or face the firing squad. It's the gringo's fault, putting ideas into Pancho's head. Then Fierro observes Bierce leaving a side door of the cathedral, where Villa has set up his temporary headquarters. The gringo's been taking up too much of Pancho's time lately and Fierro doesn't like it. Fierro and Urbina and Villa used to sit into the night talking strategy and discussing dreams. Now, Pancho spends hours practicing his English with the gringo and talking about things that make no sense.

"Gringo," Fierro calls to Bierce. "I want you to come with me. That's an order. *¡Ahora!*"

"Certainly, General Fierro."

Bierce follows the limping Fierro to the stockade. The pens were made for cattle but are now encircled by barbed-wire. The prisoners are penned in so tightly most have to stand. They've already been stripped of their boots, watches, rings, and coins. The sick and the wounded lie in the dirt, often trampled by the men standing above them. Bierce, too, had been a prisoner of war in Alabama, but briefly and under considerably less stressful conditions, so the sight of these wretched men is pitiful. At one end of the stockade cluster a special group of prisoners, the surviving Redflaggers of Orozco. Fierro summons the officer in charge of the prisoners.

"How many colorados would you say there are, Captain?"

"More than three hundred, sir."

"Good. Bring me a blanket and two revolvers. And five hundred rounds of ammunition. And Captain, tell your men to fix bayonets."

"Sir."

Bierce says, "General Fierro, may I ask what you have in mind?"

"An amusement, gringo, and you're going to help me."

When the blanket comes, Fierro settles down on it and makes himself comfortable. He hands Bierce both handguns. "I want you to keep these guns loaded until I tell you not to. *¿Comprende?*"

"Indeed, General." Bierce loads the weapons.

The Redflaggers are prodded by bayonet out of the stockade and forced to stand in a long line. The first man, his face white with fear, stands trembling before Fierro. About a hundred yards from them is a low adobe wall.

"You see that wall over there?" Fierro tells the prisoner. "When I say go, you're going to run to the wall. If you reach the wall and jump over it without getting shot, you're a free man. I'm a pretty bad shot, señor. So I think maybe you'll make it."

Bierce speaks into Fierro's ear. "General, the man's a prisoner. Captured fairly during war. You can't just—"

"Don't tell me what I can or can't do, you fucking gringo cur. I'm Rudolfo Fierro, third in command of the *División del Norte*. I can do anything I want. I can even have *you* shot. Hand me a gun." Bierce complies. "Go!" Fierro yells to the prisoner. Petrified with fear, the man doesn't budge. "I said, go!" Again the man hesitates. Fierro shoots him where he stands. "Next one forward." The second prisoner wastes no time. Despite a foot wound he runs, limping, with all his strength toward the wall. Fierro sights. Then he lowers the gun and shakes it as if it's jammed, which it isn't. He looks into the barrel. He shakes the gun again, sights again. The captive almost reaches the wall when Fierro's shot plugs him between the shoulder blades. "Next," Fierro says. The third man runs and is easily cut down. Fierro decides to fire the guns in two hands so he orders two prisoners to run at the same time. He kills them simultaneously. "Anyone who moves out there after I've shot him is to be bayoneted." By one, by twos, the prisoners run for the wall, only to fall with bullets in their backs. Some of the prisoners, seeing the slaughter, try various strategies to avoid Fierro's bullets. They run in circles. They duck. They dodge. They weave.

They crawl. By the time they reach the wall they fall. When the gun in Fierro's right hand becomes empty, he thrusts it at Bierce for reloading while continuing to fire with his left. The gun is hot, smoking. Finally, Bierce refuses to take it. He's sickened.

"Load the fucking gun, gringo."

"I shall not."

"You disobey me?"

"I do."

"Then instead of merely loading ammunition *you* will fire the gun at the prisoners."

"I refuse."

"In that case . . ." Fierro aims his gun at Bierce's forehead and begins to squeeze the trigger. Then he stops. He'll suffer Villa's wrath if he kills the Americano. Bierce is Villa's plaything, his gimcrack. Fierro spits. The gringo ain't worth it. "Get out of my sight, you filthy piece of pig shit. *Pinche pendeja.* You make me want to vomit."

"Fierro, I have but one thing to say to you. Those who believe there's a God obviously never heard of you."

"*Besa mi culo,* gringo."

Fierro keeps shooting. He fires until noon when it's time to eat. But he doesn't stop. He has his lunch brought to him. Tacos of goat meat, frijoles, pieces of chicken, fried bananas, and pickled cactus. He eats with one hand and fires with the other. When the guns become too hot to hold he has them dipped into cold water to cool them off. As he fires his hands begin to swell. The guns become heavy. His eyes are tired. The wound in his leg throbs. But Rudolfo Fierro is no shirker. The bodies pile up. The remaining prisoners find it harder and harder to get to the wall because of the proliferation of corpses. It's dusk when it's over. Three hundred forty-two men lie dead in bloody, chaotic piles, waiting for burial in a common pit. Poor Fierro's exhausted.

"Captain, it's getting chilly. Bring me another blanket." Fierro covers himself and takes a nap before dinner.

Bierce complains bitterly to Villa about Fierro's atrocity. Pancho is amused.

"Rudolfo did *what?* That *muchacho!* I don't know what I'm going to do with him. Did I tell you once Rudolfo shot dead a total stranger on the street in Chihuahua just to prove a dying man falls forward, not backward. I was mighty annoyed at the time, I tell you. Once I had to remove him as my railroad superintendent because he shot an engineer for bringing in a train thirty-five minutes late. I had to discipline him on account of the railway men were complaining. But later I restored him to his post. It was only fair."

"To whom, General?"

"To Rudolfo, of course."

"General, if it's fairness you want, you must court-martial him. The man is evil incarnate."

"*A la chingo con eso.* He is like a son to me, and the bravest of all my generals."

"He committed a war crime."

"Ah, but the men he killed, they were colorados. They were going to be executed anyway. Do you not understand they fought under the flag of my bitter enemy, Orozco, a man who betrayed the Revolution to fight for Huerta? So Rudolfo had a little fun. What's the harm in that?"

"General, they were prisoners of war."

"They got what they deserved."

"I beg you to do something about Fierro."

"*¡Mantenerse en silencio!* Señor, sometimes you talk too much. I need no instruction from you, not in matters military. Leave me now before I become angry and make you apologize to Rudolfo. Or even better, allow him to have his way with you."

Bierce is furious, but dares not show it. He can push Villa only so far. He himself narrowly escaped confinement in the notorious Andersonville prison, where nearly 13,000 Union soldiers perished. He remembers it well, and how his capture all started as a lark, he and another lieutenant named Cobb, both assigned to General Hazen's staff, crossing the Coosa River into territory still controlled by the enemy. Atlanta has fallen, Hood's army is in retreat, and Sherman is about to invade. The South has little time left. For Bierce and Cobb it's an opportunity to enjoy a little fun at the expense of a dispirited enemy. The river is sluggish and wide. Dogwood and magnolia grow along the bank. On the far shore are cornfields but there's little other evidence of human life. Concealing their horses in a canebrake, the two young officers come upon an empty boat along the shore. They steal it, row across. It's an act of arrogance. Between them they have two Springfield rifles and two Colt revolvers. Hiding the boat in the weeds, they march through the corn rows until they come to a white plantation house where several children play in the yard and black men and women work the field. Bierce and Cobb are about to knock on the door to ask for a drink of water when several horsemen appear on the crest of a slight rise. Then a dozen more riders moving toward them at a trot. The rebs don't look quite as dispirited as they've been rumored to be.

Cobb says it first. "Let's get the fuck out of here!"

Bullets whine around them. Bierce hears what he believes is the ugliest sound a mortal can make, the rebel yell. The two soldiers separate in near panic, Cobb running toward a grove of trees, Bierce through the cornfield into a swamp. Both drop their rifles, not a soldier-ly thing to do, but the guns are too damned heavy to run with. Bierce splashes through shallow water. Around him grow sinister ferns and vines with dank leaves. An odor of decay fills the air. At last he comes to solid ground and flings himself, panting, into a patch of briars. Instantly comes the buzz of mosquitoes. He hears shouts and fast riding and an occasional rifle shot. Gradually, the sounds of the pursuers disappear. Swamp chatter takes over. He waits sleeplessly through the night, ward-ing off the insects, and when dawn comes he tries to find his way back to the boat. The dinghy isn't there. Perhaps Cobb has escaped across the river in it. He'll have to swim across. The river, cold as spring water, swirls around his legs. As the water reaches his waist, a surprise current sweeps him off his feet and drives him to the bottom. His mouth fills with water and he feels himself about to drown. So here's where it ends, Bierce. You survive the bullets and bayonets and cannons, and now the Coosa River claims your sorry ass. The current slams him into a tree, a sapling with roots growing in the water. He grabs a limb and pulls him-self to the surface, spitting out some of the river he's swallowed and drawing in huge gulps of Southern air. Exhausted, he crawls onto the bank, where he pulls off his wet boots and pours the water out. His watch, my god, the watch his uncle gave him, is it dead?—no, it's wa-terproof, still ticking. And the cameo, Mrs. Rich's cameo—nothing can destroy it. He feels weak. It would be good to sleep, but as he starts to nod off he hears a voice and stares into the barrel of a carbine.

"You're my prisoner, Yank."

The gunman has a foggy Alabama drawl. Unshaven with a long, narrow chin. His body is clothed in the remnants of a Confederate uniform and on his feet are tattered boots from which his bare toes protruded. He nods at Bierce's boots drying on the grass.

"Mighty fine shoe leather you got there, Yank."

"Best I could afford, reb. But they're wet."

"Seems to me it would be a shame to waste them boots on a Yankee. I don't mind if they're a little damp."

As the reb bends down to pick up the boots, Bierce springs from his exhaustion and rolls his body into the man's legs. At the same time he reaches for the Colt revolver holstered at his side. The reb stumbles but doesn't fall. By the time Bierce frees his revolver the man reverses his grip on the rifle and swings it like a club. A rifle butt, after all, can splatter brains, crush bone, reduce muscle to pulp. The stock of the carbine hits the revolver, sending it dancing. With the art of a juggler, the Confederate switches the rifle to a firing position and points it at Bierce's heart.

"You try that again and you'll be one dead Yank. Now get up. We got a bit of marching to do. I said get up! You behave and I'll turn you over to the regulars. If not, I'll sic Gatewood on you."

"Gatewood?"

"The meanest, scurviest guerrilla chief in these parts, Yank. Rides with the worst cutthroats and murderers in Alabama. Half of 'em are deserters from the Confederate Army, the other half deserters from the Union Army. If Gatewood's gang catches up with you you'll be swinging from the nearest crabapple tree before you get off the first line of 'The Battle Hymn of the Republic.'"

They plod along the dusty roadway, the Confederate, limping, wearing Bierce's boots, Bierce wearing the reb's.

"Name's Pemberton, Yank. Former Sergeant Jubal P. Pemberton. Late of the Confederate Army of the Mississippi under General Braxton Bragg."

"Bierce. Ninth Indiana Infantry. Lieutenant under General Hazen."

"They retired me on account of the bullet I got in the leg at Chickamauga. Doc says I'll probably have this limp the rest of my life."

"I also fought at Chickamauga."

"Maybe you was the one who shot me, Yank."

"I was wounded in the head at Kennesaw Mountain."

"I also fought at Kennesaw Mountain. Could be I was the one who popped you."

"I know who did it, sergeant, and it wasn't you. One of our own men, I think."

"So it's that way in your army too."

They pass unpainted farmhouses and unkempt fields. Curious families come to their doors and windows, farmers look up from their plows.

"Hey, Jubal, what you got there?"

"Got me a Yankee."

"Damned if you don't, Jubal."

They come to Pemberton's place, a rough cabin made of logs. It's set in a little grove of magnolias at the edge of a vegetable garden and a cotton field. Smoke spirals from the cabin's chimney.

"Ma, I'm home!" Pemberton calls. "And I brung us a Yank for dinner."

"Ah shucks, Pa. Dinner's on the stove. Besides, I hear Yanks is too tough to eat."

From the house pour a horde of delighted humanity, accompanied by mongrels, chickens, pigs, and goats. Women, men, grandpas, grandmas, aunts, uncles, cousins, nephews, nieces. Their ages run the spectrum. Jubal P. Pemberton is a lucky man.

"Before I send you off to Andersonville, lieutenant, I aims to feed you."

They sit at a long, crowded table in the front room to eat. Colossal golden biscuits. Slabs of ham. Squash and okra and sweet potatoes and white radishes hot enough to singe the tongue.

"We thought you Southern folks were starving," Bierce says.

"This here food is all home-grown."

Bierce suspiciously pushes his spoon into a strange whitish food with a gruelish texture.

"You ain't never seen grits before, Yank?" Jubal says. "You been missin' one of God's great pleasures. Good for breakfast, lunch, or dinner. Grits is made from white corn kernels. Try some of that red-eye gravy with 'em and mix in some country ham."

Neighbors drift in. Word has spread. A Yankee officer in full uniform, minus only his boots, is a sight worth seeing.

"That there the Yank, Jubal?"

"That's the Yank."

"He don't look like much."

Bierce ponders the curious faces around him. "It appears your neighbors are disappointed by the absence of horn, hoof, and tail on my body, Sergeant Pemberton."

"That's 'cause they ain't never seen a Yank up close. Alive, that is."

Night falls, the lanterns are lit, and Pemberton gets out the jug.

"Best corn liquor in the county, Yank. Make it myself."

Jubal fills a corncob pipe with tobacco and lights it. "Y'all hush down now. Lieutenant Bierce, I got a story to tell that'll make your hair stand on end. Want to hear it?"

"Indeed, Sergeant Pemberton."

"Took place at Chickamauga, it did. Seems our boys was in retreat. I have this here bullet in my leg to prove it. Christ, it's bleeding. And I'm limping, tryin' to run but barely able to walk. But I ain't the worst of the injured. Some is slithering on their hands and knees. Some just use their hands, dragging their useless legs. The walking, creeping wounded, arms dangling at their sides. Inching our way through the blood of the men ahead of us. I see out of the corner of my eye a boy. Must have been five or six. Happy little kid. Playing, laughing, running through the wounded. Then I see him run up to a man crawling next to me. The boy hops on the man's back as if to play pony. The man sinks to the ground but recovers and flings the boy off. The kid don't know that the lower part of the man's face is missing, just hanging shreds of flesh and splinters of bone. When the kid sees the face, he gets scared and runs off. Then we come to what had been a farm. The house is in flames. The fields too. There's the boy again. He's running in circles, helpless, in a panic. Appears it's his family's farm. There's a body of a woman. Her face is turned upward, hair all blood. Her brains sticking out through the hole in her head. The work of a shell, ours or yours. The boy waves his hands, makes these strange gestures. I hear him utter some cries. I can't describe them, maybe like the gobbling of a turkey. An unholy sound. I realize the dead woman's his mother. And the boy? Hell, he's deaf and dumb."

Silence in the cabin. Then the horror of the boy's predicament begins to sink in. The jug comes around to Bierce, who takes full advantage of it.

"Sergeant Pemberton, if I get out of the war alive, I'm going to put your story on paper. People who've never been in battle need to know what it's like."

They hear horses approaching from outside. Jubal's oldest son Tom peeks out the window.

"Pap, I think it's a couple of Gatewood's boys riding up."

Pemberton says, "Yank, you go into that back room and stay there until they're gone."

But before Bierce can disappear, the cabin's front door bursts open and two men with rifles over their shoulders barge in. Scruffy, arrogant, wearing Confederate butternut gray. Unshaven and dirty. One is heavy, the other thin. The thin one is . . . is . . . It can't be, Bierce thinks. Harley Purvis? Bierce turns his back as if that can keep Purvis from recognizing him.

Jubal says, "You Gatewood boys think you can just walk in and—"

Purvis says, "What do we got here, Pemberton? Looks like some Yankee to me. We heard you had one in tow. Word gets around fast in these parts. There was two of 'em, but one got away across the Coosa."

"This Yank's my prisoner, Purvis, and I'm turnin' him over to the regulars."

"We're takin' charge, Pemberton. We're runnin' things around here now. Yank, turn around so's I can get a look at your puss." Bierce complies. "Holy shit! It's sissy boy. I thought you was taken care of back at Kennesaw Mountain."

Jubal says, "Hell, you two know each other."

Bierce says, "Purvis here joined the Union army, but I see he's now wearing gray. So you're a deserter, Purvis."

"There was more opportunities on this side of the war, Bierce. Pemberton, this here sissy boy and I go way back to Indiana. He once smacked me in the nose. He's queer, he is. Reads poletry. Why don't you recite us a pome right now, sissy boy?"

"Go to hell, Purvis."

Purvis points his rifle at Bierce's middle.

"You know what we do to Yankee spies?"

"I'm no spy, Purvis. I'm wearing my uniform."

"That's right, Purvis," Jubal says. "I caught him fair. I aim to turn him over to General Hood. This man's goin' to Georgia."

Purvis says, "Sissy boy here won't live long enough to see Andersonville."

Then things happen fast. Jubal uses his good leg to ram his foot into Harley's groin. Purvis screams and drops his rifle in order to clutch his testicles. Pemberton's son Tom brings the whiskey jug down on the head of the other man, whose body slams to the floor. Luckily, the jug doesn't break and only a little corn liquor is spilled.

Purvis thrashes in agony, cupping his hands around his balls. "I'll make you pay for this, Pemberton. You can't—"

"War's about over, Purvis, and we've had enough of deserters and thieves and rapists like you. Tom, you take this man's rifle and stand guard over him and the other gent. I got somethin' to do."

Jubal walks Bierce out of the cabin's front door and into the starry night.

"Lieutenant Bierce, you're still a prisoner of war. Now you're to march due east until you come to Hood's army and tell 'em I caught you and you're ready to spend the rest of the war in Andersonville. You understand them orders, Yank? Of course, it's easy to get lost at night. If you make a mistake and follow the north star it'll lead you the wrong way back to the Coosa. And if you happen to come to a white church with a tall steeple you'll be right at that old river's shallowest stretch. There's a big sandbar in the middle. A man can wade across without hardly gettin' his knees wet. You could be back behind Union lines before the rooster crows. That is, if you get your directions all confused and you forget to report to Hood and go to Andersonville like I told you. Oh, and you better take your boots. They're a little tight on me anyway."

Bierce shakes Jubal's hand. "What about Purvis and the other man?"

"We'll leave 'em tied up in the slops out back till morning. We might run 'em behind the mule for a spell just to give the mule some exercise. Then we'll shoot 'em. Then maybe if I think they learned their lesson we'll let 'em go. Naw, the cornfield needs a little fertilizin'."

Bierce escapes the Confederate clutches by walking the wrong way in the dark, but no such luck for the poor devils gunned down by The Butcher in Zacatecas.

Throughout northern Mexico, Pancho is being hailed as the people's hero, and so in Chihuahua City thousands of men in wide straw hats and women with head scarves gather at the Governor's Palace in the *Plaza de Armas* to pay tribute to the celebrated leader of the *División del Norte*. Four military bands march as hundreds of flower girls throw rose petals. Although the civilians are dressed in clean white shirts and the soldiers in pressed uniforms, Pancho wears an old khaki uniform with half the buttons missing. His hair is tousled and it's obvious he hadn't shaved. He sits, yawning, through the speeches saluting his bravery, and when they present him his award, a gold medal, Villa sniffs. "This is a hell of a little thing to give a man for all that hero stuff you've been talkin' about." The crowd cheers their leader's humility. Pancho says, "*Amigos,* let's go to the bullfights. And when the bulls is dead we'll go to the cockfights. And when the cocks is dead it's off to the whorehouse."

As the crowd disperses, a young American news correspondent wearing a yellow corduroy suit corners Bierce, tells him he looks familiar, and asks if he's from New York. Bierce says no and starts to leave until the reporter offers him a drink from a pint of bourbon. Even though Bierce has assiduously avoided the newspaper men for fear of being found out, he never refuses a drink. The reporter, who writes for several papers, including the *Masses,* explains he's been following Villa since the battle of Ojinaga. The reporter isn't sure what the revolution's all about although he supports it. In fact, he supports just about any revolution anywhere at anytime. He plans to write a book about his experiences in Mexico. The reporter asks the older man's name.

"Grile," Bierce says, voice surly.

"Glad to meet you, Grile. Name's John Reed. Have another drink. General Villa has a nickname for me. *Chatito.* Means pug nose. I'd like to stay longer to report on our Latin American Napoleon, but war's broken out in Europe, so I'm leaving Mexico tomorrow to cover the conflict. By the way, Grile, are you familiar with the writings of Karl Marx? No? How about Lenin? Trotsky?"

"Confound it, Reed, you ask too many damned questions. Ask one more and I'll shoot you. But not before I have that drink you're offering."

His threat to shoot is mere bluster, of course. But shoot he does— back in his war, and, like Pancho, earns his share of honors. Shortly before being mustered from the army he's elevated to brevet major.

He wants to make the military his career, but at war's end there are too many officers and not enough men to command. However, through the efforts of his former commander, General Hazen, he's taken on as a Treasury agent in Selma, Alabama, at a salary of one hundred five dollars a month. The first thing he notices about the place is the stink—the smell of smoke and death. As Bierce, astride his horse, rides slowly down the muddy, shell-pitted main street, the residents watch him with eyes of hate. Hardly a building still stands. What had been a large hotel is a burned-out shell. The blacksmith's shop is a ruin of blackened timbers. The apothecary dispenses his medicines from a tattered tent. The windows of the dry goods store are shattered and empty. But, as he notes gratefully, no fewer than three saloons stand unscathed.

He knows the man he is to replace, Sherburne Eaton, formerly of the 124th Ohio Infantry.

"Bierce, I bet you're wondering about the terrible odor in this hellhole. In the last days of the war our soldiers, many of them drunk, set the town on fire. They looted it, and when that was over they rounded up all the mules and horses they could find, drove them into the middle of town, and slaughtered them, leaving the carcasses to rot in the streets. It took days before the corpses could be burned. By that time the smell had invaded every crevice. They hate us here, and for good reason. Yesterday, I saw the bodies of two U.S. marshals lying by the road. Their throats slit. That's what we're up against, and now that you're here, I plan to spend more time at the district office in New Orleans. It's a hell of a lot safer."

Bierce's duties are to locate and confiscate, in the name of the United States, cotton formerly owned by the Confederate government.

Eaton says, "No doubt you'll be approached by certain citizens and offered genuine U.S. currency in exchange for overlooking this contraband cotton. That means you must make a moral decision. You may accept the money and chance a Federal indictment. Or risk getting your head blown off. I can't give you advice, other to say that my head has yet to be blown off."

As Bierce hunkers in at the Widow Morgan's guest house, he senses the anarchy around him. The occupation troops are undisciplined, drunken louts. Guerrillas hide in the bushes. A growing movement of madmen in white robes burn crosses and swing nooses in the air.

There are no churches, no newspapers, virtually no constabulary. The judges are daft. Then there are the McLaws brothers, Charles and Frank, who have a business proposition to offer—but not before plying Bierce with food and intoxicant.

Frank says, "We fought with Hood at Franklin in Tennessee."

"I fought at Franklin as well," Bierce says. "On the opposite side, with Hazen."

"That's funny," says Charles, stroking his chin. "I don't remember you there."

The brothers burst into laughter.

"'Twas at Chickamauga I get riled, Mr. Bierce," Frank says. "Everywhere I see corpses, and ruins, and torn-up land. I didn't think much about it until one day I'm standin' in front of a tree, shavin' and lookin' into this little mirror I got propped up on a branch. All of a sudden I hear this rushing sound and a Yankee shell explodes not fifty damned feet away. When I pick my ass up I see I cut my chin with my own razor, and my mirror's smashed all to hell. I got mud on my nice, clean uniform. So I gets riled, Mr. Bierce, because now they're shootin' at *me!*"

More laughter.

Charles says, "Old General Hood calls our Captain Maddox up to headquarters, and he says, 'Maddox, the Confederate Army has been supportin' you and your lazy fellows for years, only you just eat and shit and drink your heads off, and you don't do no fightin'.' And our captain, he says, 'Ain't true, General. The drummer knocked the bugler silly only yesterday, the first sergeant has a black eye most of the time when he ain't drunk, and I punch the first lieutenant's head myself quite frequent.'"

Howls of laughter.

The McLaws' business proposition is a simple one. They know the whereabouts of seven hundred bales of cotton and offer Bierce one-fourth of the value if he'll declare it a shipment of private property rather than contraband. Bierce makes a counter-proposal. The McLaws will receive one-fourth the value if they surrender the cotton. A stand-off.

On the way home, in the dark Selma street, the three men realize they're being followed by a shadowy figure.

Frank says, "I figure it's someone out to get you, Mr. Bierce. Gimme your gun."

Before Bierce can protest, Frank reaches under Bierce's coat and removes the revolver. As Frank turns on the stalker, words are exchanged, a single shot is fired, and, with a yowl, the stranger falls to the dirt. Windows are thrown open, lamps are lit, folks run from their doors, and a meddlesome crowd gathers around the body of the man writhing in the street.

Frank says to his brother, "Just felt right to shoot the bastard. It's that Dixon fella. Been runnin' contraband down the Tennessee and Tombigbee Rivers."

Charles says to Frank, "Perhaps, Brother, you'd best mount up and skedaddle."

"Good advice, Brother. Here's your gun back, Mr. Bierce."

The wounded man is lugged to the Portland Hotel, where he's chucked, groaning, onto a sofa in the lobby.

"Damned knee's shattered," Dixon moans. "Get me the doc. And bring Judge Henry. I got a complaint to put in about Frank McLaws, the man what shot me. And for no reason other than I wanted to make a business arrangement with this here Yank Treasury cuss."

The doc, hair wild and woolly, rushes in carrying his black bag. His trousers are held up by suspenders over flannel underwear. He takes a look at Dixon's bleeding leg and shakes his head.

"It's got to go, son. Someone get me a wood saw."

Then comes the judge, a wizened old man with two days of white stubble on his jaw.

"This here court will come to order. The Honorable Judge Henry presidin'." He goes behind the hotel counter and perches on a high stool. "Who's the plaintiff in this here case?"

"I am," bellyaches Dixon from the sofa. "Shot in the leg by that ornery Frank McLaws."

"You provoke him?"

"No, sir, Judge. I was standing in the street minding my own business when Frank McLaws runs up and pops me."

"Where's that *saw*?" the doc roars. "It's gettin' late and I have to get myself back to bed."

"Order in this here court." Judge Henry bangs the counter bell. "Any witnesses to the shootin'? You there, Charles McLaws. I never seed you without your brother. What happened? Remember, you're under oath."

"Well, Judge, this here Dixon was trailin' us, and we could see he was up to no good. My brother went to Dixon to remonstrate. Dixon must have went for his gun. And that's when my brother fired."

"And while you're gettin' that wood saw, get me some grog," the doc yells.

The judge says, "That right, Dixon? You go for your gun?"

"Judge, I never had no chance to."

"But you do got a gun, don't you?"

"Well . . ."

Doc reaches into Dixon's breast pocket and withdraws a tiny silver derringer.

"Aha!" says the judge. "So you *was* armed."

"But as you can see, Judge, I never got off a shot. Bullet's still in there."

"I call the Yankee to the stand," the judge says.

"Me?" Bierce says.

"Now listen close, Yank, you're under oath. What's your version of this here crime?"

"It's correct, Your Honor, that it appeared we were being followed by the wounded man here, and perhaps menaced."

"Where's the grog?" the doc yells. "Where's the saw?"

"Just why was you followin' these fellows, Dixon?" the judge says.

Dixon moans again. "You see, Judge, I was merely tryin' to get close to the Yankee here. Purely business. Little matter of cotton. But these McLaws brothers, why, they was always in the way. All I wanted was a chance to talk to the Yank by hisself. Personally, I think the McLaws was tryin' to make their own deal."

A man runs into the lobby and throws a rusty old saw at the doc's feet. Dixon grimaces as the saw rattles on the floor.

Doc says, "About time, dammit. But I'm still waitin' for the grog. Can't start sawing till I get some grog in me."

"Order," the judge says. "Now this here shootin' business is mighty serious. Man's about to lose his leg on account of it. I got to make an example out of this case. Charles McLaws, where did your brother hightail it to?"

"He was feeling mighty poorly, Judge. His stomach's been actin' up all week. He had the runs. So he—"

"Order, order. I don't give a damned hoot about his runs. This here court finds Frank McLaws guilty of disorderly conduct. The sentence is a five-dollar fine plus one dollar in costs. This court is dismissed. Let it be a lesson to you all." The judge trots into the night.

The doc picks up the saw and ripples it back and forth. It makes a whining sound.

"Don't worry, young man," the doc tells the terrified Dixon. "It's only going to hurt while I'm doing the actual sawin'."

On leave in New Orleans, Bierce takes a steamer to Panama, where he writes in a notebook what he sees and hears, the words of the mulatto girls as they sells lemons in the streets, the impudence of the native black boys competing to carry his luggage, the color of the cocoa palms, the sight of buzzards perching on every roof and tree, how the people hang beef in long strips from racks in the sun to dry, the look of the ring-tail monkeys, the parrots whose feathers are bathed in color, the smoky train ride on a track through the malarial swamps. For the first time he entertains the idea that he might actually become a writer. But there's so much to learn. Perhaps too much.

The McLaws' cotton is finally turned over to Bierce, who loads the contraband on a steamboat plying the Tombigbee River to Mobile. At a curve in the river the boat comes under fire from the shore. Bierce ducks behind a cotton bale. The river bank is lined with armed men who are almost close enough to the boat to jump on board. Pirates? Bandits? Guerrillas? The boat seems to be drifting helplessly, washing ever closer to the shore. Bierce sees that the pilothouse appears to be empty.

Dodging the bullets, Bierce makes his way to the pilothouse, where the captain, burly, with a flowing black beard, cowers on the floor.

"Captain, the boat's drifting into shore. Get up and take the damned wheel."

"Mister, look at the pilothouse windows. They're shattered. Must be a hundred bullet holes in the wood. And the bullets are still coming in. If I stand up I might be plugged."

Bierce puts his revolver to the captain's head. "And if you don't stand up, Captain, you *will* be plugged."

As the steamboat returns to the Tombigbee's main channel, the firing begins to subside. The boat's whistle shrieks. Black clouds start to form above. Then rain patters on the deck. Bierce finds shelter below deck, where he takes out his notebook and begins to write. "The din of the firing, the rattle and crash of the missiles splintering the woodwork and the jingle of broken glass made a very rude arousing from the tranquil indolence of a warm afternoon on the sluggish Tombigbee."

The South of Bierce's post-military career was in a virtual state of anarchy, but here in northern Mexico, Pancho Villa rules with an iron fist. As governor of Chihuahua, he enacts laws the most direct way, simply drawing them up and signing them. He sets prices for beef, milk, corn, and avocado. When he needs currency he prints Villa money on the press in the basement of the Governor's Palace. He lowers railroad fares and gives the poor free passes. He raises taxes on merchants, bankers, cattlemen, and the churches—especially the churches. He confiscates the haciendas and gives every male citizen of Chihuahua sixty-two and a half acres of land.

Over their nightly tequila, Bierce warily asks Villa if he knows the definition of socialism.

The general says no. "Perhaps you will explain it to me, *amigo*. That reporter who was here, Señor Reed, tried to tell me, but it was too complicated for a man with no education, except for riding and shooting."

"Socialism's a political theory advocating state ownership of industry, General, as well as being an economic system based on state ownership of capital."

"What does all that mean?"

"General, I hesitate to explain, since I don't wish to put certain ideas into your head."

Pancho laughs. "Tell me or I'll turn you over to Rudolfo."

"In that case . . . Socialism aims to eliminate the inequities between rich and poor."

"Ah. That is good."

"No, General. It doesn't work. Socialism would repeal the economic laws of nature, which isn't feasible. There's simply no redress for the poor and feeble who suffer at the hands of the rich and powerful—only escape from it. The victims themselves must emancipate themselves by acquiring their *own* wealth and power. That's known as capitalism."

"Emancipate?"

"Free themselves."

"But what if they are too poor and feeble to—what is your word?—emancipate themselves and adopt capitalism?"

"I'm afraid that's the contradiction that mitigates my own argument."

"*Amigo,* I've given Chihuahua's own rich and powerful, the Spaniards and the Chinese, orders to leave the state or be put against the wall. The Spanish steal our gold, the Chinese our jobs. Good riddance."

"General, in many quarters of the United States the wall is a symbol of sin. I refer, of course to Wall Street."

From outside, they hear the sandy wind blow against the caboose. Then Villa remembers.

"Say, you ain't enjoyed The Game for weeks, ever since I decided not to make you play it. But at first you wanted to. Are you tired of it?"

"For the moment, General. Let's say I'm enjoying myself too much. The Revolution is far from over, and there's much more left to fight."

Chapter Seven

Death has always been a preoccupation, but at the moment it's not Bierce's worst fear. It's of being revealed. He has a dream that the odious Jack London materializes in Chihuahua like a ghost. London? Here? Impossible.

"*Amigo,*" Pancho says, "pack your grip. Saddle your horse. We're leaving in the morning by train to Tacuba. From there we will ride in style into Xochimilco."

"And the occasion, General?"

"The Centaur of the North is forming an *alianza*—how you say, alliance—with the Attila of the South, Emiliano Zapata. *¡Caramba!* Zapata and I have new enemies to fight."

The players in the revolution keep shifting, onerous for an outsider like Bierce to fully keep track of.

"It's simple, my American friend, but *prestar atención.* Alvaro Obregón, my former ally, beats me to the—what's the word?—punch and captures Mexico City. *El Presidente* Huerta, *El Chacal,* flees to Cuba with two million pesos. First Chief of the Revolution Venustiano Carranza declares himself premier *jefe,* which I did not mind so much, except he makes Obregón his supreme *generalissimo.* This I cannot abide. No longer do I have faith in Carranza. Also, we have little in common. He is, in his heart, a *hacendado* while I am a peon. And Obregón? I will fight this *bastardo* to the death."

Bierce bids Pancho *buenas tardes,* and as he walks through one of the courtyards at Quinta Luz he sees a man standing outside the door to his room. He puts his hand on the gun at his belt just in case.

"That you, Bierce?" calls the man. *"Hola,* as they say in Mexican."

The voice. He knows that voice. By god, it's— Damned if his nightmare hasn't come true.

"Thought I'd find you here, Bierce, if that don't beat the Dutch."

A cigarette dangles from London's lips.

"Hell's fire, if this revolution doesn't attract you socialists like flies to dung," Bierce says. "I've already had to fend off some fool named

John Reed. You two pirates are peas in a pod."

They face each other outside the door to Bierce's room. He's been happy. Until now. And Jack London's come to ruin it all.

"How the hell did you find me, London? No one else in Mexico knows who or where I am—as far as I know."

"There was some talk among the correspondents in Veracruz about an older man with a white mustache who appears to have Villa's confidence. Perhaps his personal servant or secretary. Most believed he's a light-skinned beaner, but a few others thought he just might be an American. So I decided to find out for myself. Quite a hubbub back in the States about your disappearance, Bierce. I drove here all the way from Veracruz. Ever ride in an open Dodge on dirt roads for three hundred miles? Pardner, if that don't give you hemorrhoids nothing will. Once I got past Villa's bodyguards, tracking you down was easy. To them I'm just another reporter, and I've got the credentials to prove it."

"You came all this distance just to sniff me out? You're like a hound with its nose in another mutt's rectum."

"Actually, *Collier's* is paying me eleven hundred dollars a week to cover this asinine revolution, or whatever you want to call it. So it's not just you. I got to Mexico on a steamer from Galveston along with my wife Charmian and Nakata."

"What in Sam Hill is a Nakata?"

"My valet, of course. I never travel without Nakata. The Americans captured Veracruz, you know. We're spooning the spics a little of their own medicine for the hard time they gave to one of our Navy boys who happened to be in town buying supplies. These taco jockeys need to have a little respect for Old Glory."

"London, a flag's just a colored rag borne above troops and hoisted on forts and ships."

"Anyway, there's no action on the Gulf coast. Christ, every night I sit in the bar of the Diligencias Hotel and roll dice with Ford Madox Ford, John T. McCutcheon, Vincent Starrett, and Richard Harding Davis."

"Dice, London? Little polka-dotted ivory cubes constructed like a lawyer to lie on any side."

London snorts. "Same old cynical Bierce. Anyway, they're not letting correspondents out of Veracruz into the interior, but when Davis got through to Mexico City, I thought if that son of a bitch can scram out of Veracruz I can too. So I hired some greasers with Mausers to take me to Chihuahua, and I just up and went. Frankly, I believe the Americans oughta march across Mexico like Sherman in Georgia and straighten things out once and for all. Like old Rudyard says, it's the white man's burden."

"What ever happened to Jack London, defender of the socialist revolution?"

"Ah, the spics here aren't fighting in the true revolutionary spirit. They're a nasty bunch of half-breeds with no idea of what socialism's all about. It's all a fraud. The white man's up against big obstacles, Bierce. I covered that war between the Japs and the Russians, you know. Hired a fishing junk to cross the Yellow Sea and got myself arrested, so I know something about the yellow peril."

Yellow peril.

A high-pitched voice repeats London's words. A green and red parrot flutters in a cage hanging from a courtyard beam.

Yellow peril.

London laughs and lights another cigarette. The two Americans find a bench by a eucalyptus and sit. A hairy spider crawls along the side of the tree, which sprouts thumb-sized green bananas.

"Bastards in the War Department tried to hold up my credentials as a correspondent on account of my politics, but I got it fixed. I consider myself a peaceful man."

"Who carries an automatic pistol."

"Exactly what I said. A peaceful man who carries an automatic pistol."

"London, I've read some of your articles. You've called soldiers murder machines, and the army and navy killing institutions. Tommyrot. You're a walking contradiction."

"I admit I'm a lousy socialist, Bierce. I think I'm gonna quit the party. At heart I'm only a humble writer."

"I'm not convinced you're even a writer, much less humble."

"I've written dozens of books with more to come, pardner, so obviously you're not aware of my output."

"Unfortunately, I am." Bierce stands, then paces. "London, you've come to the wrong place to watch the war. The last big battle was in

Saltillo. Chihuahua's quiet and Villa's in firm control."

"The way I see it, bub, you're the big story. You caused a sensation back home by vanishing into Mexico. Everyone wonders what happened to you. Been all sorts of rumors. You were put to death before a Mexican firing squad. You're a member of Carranza's staff. You went to Europe to join Lord Kitchener. You're a military adviser to the Kaiser. You're confined in an insane asylum in Napa, California. Wilson named Franklin K. Lane to head a committee to investigate your disappearance. Pretty ironic when you recall that the Interior Secretary once called you a hideous monster so much like a mixture of dragon, lizard, bat, and snake as to be unnamable. General Funston was ordered to search for you along the border. The San Francisco *Bulletin* sent private investigators. The Pinkertons were called in. And here you are. Under their very noses. Who would have thought Ambrose Bierce would actually be living in Pancho Villa's mansion? Looks like I'm gonna have a hell of a scoop for *Collier's*." London flicks a shred of tobacco from his lower lip. "But I have an idea that'll make this an even better story. Bierce, you're one of Villa's pals, right, a *gran amigo?* That greaser needs to be retired and retired soon, and you're just the man to catch the weasel asleep. Get him drunk one night. Make sure his lamp is out. Then put a piece of lead into the back of his head. That'll end this revolution, so called. The scheme's brilliant. Came to me as a revelation."

"London, a revelation is when you discover late in life that you're a fool."

"If you knock off Villa they'll make *you* the military governor here."

"Jack, Jack, Jack. I recall you and I once spent a memorable day and night in California drinking together."

"It's been a coon's age. Two white men sharing a bottle."

"We became friends then."

"'Twas quite a frolic, old man."

It happens at the Bohemian Club's summer high jinks in a redwood grove along the Russian River in Sonoma County, just as Bierce is beginning to toy with the idea of personally invading Mexico. Coincidentally, his brother Grizzly owns a plot of land for a summer camp just across the river. George Sterling, the sycophantic poet and now London's best pal, dares the contrarian Bierce to publicly confront the socialist London over a bottle of cognac. Bierce loathes London's political notions. Set up socialism and you create a race of sloths and slugs, he thinks. So Bierce takes the challenge, promising to treat the son of a bitch like a Dutch uncle.

Bierce makes no concession to the California woods, damp and lush from the rain, just ended to clear the way for a pure and unambiguous sky. He wears his usual black suit, tie, and derby, and the soles of his shoes are already damp. The Bohemian Club's primary drinking establishment is a rustic affair, open on four sides, with a roof of redwood. Bierce stands at the bar to sip his favorite cognac, Martell. Nearby, London, wearing a wide-brim hat, plays poker under a tent and chain-smokes. He throws his cards down when he's told Bierce has arrived and is spoiling for a fight. It's a bad hand anyway, it's always a bad hand. London wears Levi's and a red vest over his workman's shirt, and when he leaves the tent the others follow his wake like Coxey's Army. Indeed, London trailed Coxey back in '94. The year he'd been a tramp, the year he played dodge with the brakemen on the Cannonball Express, the year he was clubbed on the head by a cop in New York City just for being there, the year he served thirty days in the lockup for the crime of having no money. As London marches the crowd behind him grows larger. London is thirty-eight, a man of average height with a short neck and the physique of a middleweight. His mouth is quick to smile despite the loss of his two front teeth, the result of a friendly barroom brawl. He collects people. White people. He hates Japs, chinks, darkies, and half-breeds of all categories. He believes in racial purity—unlike Bierce, who believes nothing is pure except Martell VSOP. Bierce, leaning against the bar, sees the crowd approach with Jack in the lead. Either a revolution or a mob of drunks, which are one and the same, he thinks.

"Comrade Bierce."

"Mister London."

"Bierce, I'd recognize your mug anywhere from those Swinnerton cartoons in the Hearst papers."

"And I you from the police blotter."

London grabs the bottle of cognac on the bar. He pours it into Bierce's nearly empty glass.

"It's on me, Bierce, if you don't mind accepting a drink poured by the wildcat of literature."

"To your health, London. Never thought I'd be drinking with someone who thinks civilization is a slum."

"Civilization's a slum only when it's cluttered with literary critics like you."

London puts a cigarette in his mouth and blows smoke into Bierce's face.

"You do that again, London, and I'll shoot you between the eyes."

"Just wanted to see if you were still alive, Bierce. Old men like you lose touch with the latest scientific knowledge and become defensive."

"If you're making the claim that socialism is the latest scientific knowledge, then I must remind you socialism isn't a science. It's a philosophical notion that embodies certain economic presumptions. In other words, an opinion. Like Christianity and every other damnfool religion."

"Bierce, I suspect that one day you may surprise even yourself and might join our little revolution."

"London, revolution is merely an abrupt change in the form of misgovernment. Have you no idea what revolution means? It's the bursting of the boilers that takes place when the safety valve of public discussion is closed. You're in a pitiful minority."

"I admit we socialists don't have a fighting number. Yet. It's a philosophic war we're waging in which our goal is the confiscation of the wealth of the world and the complete overthrow of your society. It's a matter of equality. Every Fourth of July we celebrate our independence—but independence from what? Poverty, discrimination, injustice? Bierce, we're going to take your governments, your palaces, and all your purpled ease away from you. Someday, when we get a few more hands and crowbars, we'll topple your society, along with all its rotting life and unburied dead. Then we'll clean the cellar and build a new habitat for mankind in which all the rooms will be bright and airy, and where the atmosphere will be clean, noble, and alive. When that day comes, the capitalist will work for his bread just as the toiler in the field works for his. It's equality we seek."

"Tauri excrementum."

"And horse manure to you. Have another drink."

"I notice you have a long, lovely neck, London. Someday I hope to be the one who'll put a rope around it."

London's laugh booms. "What a delightful thought. A hangman's rope against my neck. And Ambrose Bierce the man who puts it there. You're terrified of our revolution, old man. Admit it."

"London, even if your damned revolution comes I'm not sticking around for it. There's now a revolution in Mexico, and I'm going down there to watch the show."

"They're just a bunch of half-breed bandits in Mexico. Who the hell even knows what they're fighting over? Besides, you're too old to go. You'd die on the trail."

"London, one is never too old to die on the trail."

"I *knew* I was going to like you."

"I thought I might dislike you too."

A Bohemian with a Kodak Brownie snaps a photograph of the two writers. The picture will never come out. It's too dim under the roof of redwood. Then comes a shout. "The games are about to begin!" The congregation, disappointed that the only exchange of blows has been verbal, retires to the playing field for some real sport. On the field, the Bohemians abandon what few adult sensibilities they've managed to pack with them to indulge in sack races, greased pig wrestling, one-legged racing, blindfold boxing, egg-throwing, and tug-of-war. The sides are evenly matched for the tug-of-war, twenty men at each end of the rope, eighty sweaty hands, with a pit of mud in between.

"You're not playing tug-of-war, Bierce?"

"I've no wish to be pulled into the mud, London, even if it takes twenty men to do it. Have another drink."

The sun rolls above in a lazy fashion as the tug-of-war ends as expected. Forty men manage to drag each other into the mud. Their clothes and faces caked, they mill around in circles like survivors of a Zulu slaughter. The revelers move on to the cooking fires where a pig, apple in mouth, is turning over a spit. They chew on sliced ham, chow-chow, cole slaw, baked potatoes, ears of corn roasted in the husk, and sourdough biscuits. As dusk arrives, Bierce and London take turns at the crank of the ice cream maker, a job usually relegated to children with the enthusiasm to turn and keep turning, but there are no children at the encampment, at least not in terms of age. The ice cream churn—its container filled with a mixture of cream, sugar, and vanilla—is packed solid with crushed ice and coarse rock salt. Bierce is the first to turn the crank, a comforting and highly domestic sensation that leads him to ponder so much he has abandoned in his life. Christ, he thinks, do not become a sentimental old fool over the repetitious task of concocting ice cream. Bierce samples it. The ice cream's texture is soft and smooth, the taste redolent of vanilla. It's so cold it sends a lightning bolt through his head. He passes the spoon to London, who puts his tongue to the ice cream and nods his approval. The campers line up with their cups and spoons to eat fresh ice cream on a warm evening after a rain.

Bierce and London talk for hours, sitting on a blanket, their backs against a redwood, a bottle of cognac between them. They watch the fireflies signaling. They slap at mosquitoes and drink and talk and drink, then send Sterling for more booze. London tells Bierce about his lousy childhood and the poverty of his youth. How he was five years old when he first got drunk, guzzling beer from a pail intended for his father, an itinerant astrologer. How he worked as a sailor, a longshoreman, a roustabout. How he mowed lawns, cleaned carpets, and washed windows. How he learned the great truth, that it was better to sell brain than muscle. How he wrote thirty books in twelve years because life is expensive, as are former and present wives, experimental farms that always fail, and prize animals that win no prizes. He tells about building the world's most expensive ketch, the *Snark*. How he never turns anyone from his door or refuses a loan. How everyone he's ever trusted has cheated and deceived him. How he always loses at cards.

"That's why I write one thousand words a day, sick or not, hangover or not. What would you do in my place, Bierce?"

"Personally, I'd commit suicide."

"Which is what you'll do if you go to Mexico. Bierce, the literary critics are already calling my *Call of the Wild* and *Sea-Wolf* classics."

"London, I hate to admit it, but you have come out with some rattling good stories. When you created that ruthless sea captain, Wolf Larsen, you made a permanent addition to American literature."

"Never thought I'd receive a compliment from the great Ambrose Bierce!"

"Never thought I'd give one."

The two warriors get very drunk—even for them. London theorizes about the two types of drinkers, the first whose brain is filled with maggots, blue mice, and pink elephants; the other whose brain is infused with wit, imagination, and cheer. The men agree on two things: they oppose both the temperance movement and the women's vote.

"London, demon rum is a fiery liquor that produces madness—in abstainers."

"Bierce, the first thing the ladies will do if they get the vote will be to close down the saloons. The bitches would have us drink water. M'god, water!"

"I drink water only to cure the disease known as thirst."

Bierce notes that he drinks in precise numerical order. The second drink immediately after the first, the third immediately after the second, and so on. They drink. And drink. And become silly. Tears of laughter flow down London's cheeks. Even Bierce smiles out of turn.

"Bierce, I love you. Pass the bottle. And may I call you comrade?"

"Not without a thrashing."

"Then may I call you Ambrose?"

"If I may call you Jack."

London raises the bottle in a salute. "To my dearest friend, Ambrose."

"I didn't mean what I said to you, Jack,"

"About what, Ambrose?"

"About wanting to put a rope around your neck."

They fall asleep, their backs still against the tree. Bierce pulls his derby over his eyes. He's tired, so tired. An old man who talks too much, who thinks too much, who drinks too much, who hates and loves too much. He awakens when he feels cold steel against his cheek. A massive man, cigar in his mouth, stands before him with a gun in his hand.

Bierce pushes his hat back from his eyes. "Who the hell are you? What do you want?"

"Name's Larsen. And it's you I want."

"*Wolf* Larsen?"

"Wolf's my brother. He's the gentle one. I'm *Death* Larsen. I need deckhands, seal hunters, and a cabin boy. You're going to be my cabin boy, Bierce. You're coming on the *Macedonia* with me, so get the hell up."

Bierce screams.

Grizzly hollers, "Dammit, Brose, you're yellin' in your sleep again. You're having those bad dreams. Quiet down, Brose. You'll wake Ma and Pa. Ma'll give you the castor oil, I tell you."

"Grizz, don't you see him?"

"See who, Brose?"

"He's standing right here, Grizz. With a gun. Death Larsen."

"Go back to sleep, Brose. We'll be goin' to the camp meeting tomorrow. You better brush up on your prayin' and your hymns."

Bierce is yanked to his feet. As he rises he grabs Death Larsen's hand, the one with the gun. But Larsen's fist seems to be made of iron and Bierce can't twist the gun away. Sweat rolls down his face as he pulls at Larsen's hand, but the hand remains firm. Bierce runs. He trips over the sleeping body of Jack London. The Prince of Drunkards barely stirs. Bierce staggers to his feet and runs some more. He feels Death Larsen behind him like a panting bear. Bierce's legs are weak. It's agony to lift them. Lead balls might have been chained to his legs. Death is catching up to him. He trips on a root and pitches head first into the ground. Larsen stands over him, Death's legs spread on either side of Bierce's body. He feels the gun barrel against the back of his head.

Grizzly. "Brose, you hush up now or I'm coming out to wallop you like I did when we were kids on the farm."

Bierce lies on the deck of the *Macedonia*. He hears the rumble of the steam engines below. Smells the smoke pouring from the stacks. Feels the sea breeze. Tastes the salt. Hears the screech of the gulls. He isn't a seaman. He's a landlubber. He's been shanghaied. He remembers the Sioux. They drag him, beaten and tied, to Red Cloud. "You've been hallucinating, Bierce," General Hazen says. "Not another word about Indians." There are gangs. New York gangs. He fights them. The Plug Uglies, the Gophers, the Hudson Dusters, the Gas Housers, the Shirt Tails, the Five Pointers, the Dead Rabbits. He hears his brother's voice on the battlefield. "Brose, I think Harley done it, shot you in the head." A bell. A foghorn.

"You're a dead man, Bierce," Larsen says. "You ain't good enough to carry shit and slop. You ain't worth twenty dollars a month in sailor's pay. You're supper for the sharks, that's what you are."

Larsen starts to squeeze the trigger.

Another voice. "Don't do it, Larsen!"

Jack London's voice. It's commanding. He holds a scarlet banner on a staff with one hand and a bottle of Martell in the other.

"Drop the gun, Larsen, or I'll brain you with this bottle. Ours is a peaceful revolution. But if you want violence—"

"Of *course* I want violence!"

"Larsen, there are a million revolutionaries in our ranks. We demand the reins of power and the destiny of mankind. Nothing less. So if it's death you prefer it's death you'll get."

"Oh, I want death, London. *Your* death."

Larsen pulls the trigger. Bierce sees the flash. Hears the explosion. Smells the smoke. London shrieks as the bullet enters his brain. The banner falls against the wind. The bottle of Martell flies into the air and hits the deck, smashing into pieces.

"Now it's your turn, Bierce."

A blazing horse wreathed in fire booms across the deck, which shudders as though hit by an earthquake. Bierce's sister, Almeda, impervious to the flames, stands on the horse's back holding the reins.

"Pa warned you, Ambrose. You've done it now. It's too late for you, Ambrose, just like Pa said. You're goin' to hell. You *all* are goin' to hell."

The horse, hooves of steel and stone, bears down on Bierce and Death Larsen. Cigar clinched in his teeth, Larsen fires at the horse, but the bullets pass through the beast as though through air. The horse tramples Death Larsen first, turning Larsen's flesh into juice and meat. Then the Apocalyptic monster thunders over Bierce, unable to escape the crushing avalanche of hooves.

Bierce screams again.

"I'm tellin' you, Brose, you're gonna get whupped if you keeping yellin' in your sleep like that. You know Pa thinks it's the Devil's work."

In the morning when George Sterling wakes up, head throbbing, he sees Bierce, his derby pulled over his eyes, sleeping fitfully against a tree, his hands shaking like the palsy. London lies on his back on the ground. Both men are wet with dew and sweat, both snoring desperately. A smashed bottle of Martell is between them, glass glistening in the weeds.

Now, here in Mexico, Bierce remembers his hallucination. And he knows what he has to do about Jack London.

"Jack, we had a marvelous drunk that summer at the Bohemian Club, did we not?'

"One of the best drunks in my life, Ambrose."

"Let's do it again."

"Are you kiddin' me? You mean now?"

"Let's mosey down to the finest cantina in the state of Chihuahua."

The two men drink tequila as a mariachi band mercilessly performs the popular ditties. Girls swirl in their fiery dresses. A young woman photographer armed with a Kodak tries to take a picture of the two gringos. They shoo her away. Later, London is sorry they did. He would have liked to have had a picture of himself with Bierce in Mexico. To prove it really happened. The two writers talk about their years, about their books. They talk about California. They talk about their friends Joaquin Miller and George Sterling and John Barleycorn. They talk about men and women and friendship. They talk about right and wrong, truth and justice. They talk about values. Outside, when they're through talking, Bierce pulls his gun and puts it to London's head. They're both drunk. But London is more drunk than Bierce.

"Jack, drinking with you is enough to make me want to vomit. I think I'm going to kill you now."

"I actually think you would shoot me, Ambrose."

"I'd prefer to hang you, but in Mexico bullets are cheaper than rope."

"I thought we were friends. Why do you want to kill me?"

"Because you're not the man I had a tug-of-war with at the Bohemian Club."

"We didn't have a tug-of-war, Ambrose. You wouldn't play because of the mud."

"We had a tug-of-war, all right, but mud had nothing to do with it. It was an intellectual tug-of-war. Remember you told me what you felt about the rights of man. How the Fourth of July meant nothing without equality. Now I hear your garbage about breeds and yellow peril and white man's burdens. I thought you had ideals. I didn't like a lot of 'em. But at least I believed you stood for something. It was all a scam. Like your books. All you do is write for money. Your books are lies,

London, and you're a lie. I'm at the end of my life. I care nothing about the past. Nothing about the things I've written, about the remnants of my family, about my lost friends. I'm with Villa now. We're planning my death. If it doesn't come in battle it'll come as the result of something we call The Game. I don't want my death violated by you. You're not to reveal to anyone that you found me here. Do you hear me, Jack?" Bierce pushes the barrel of the gun deeper into London's temple. "If you were ever a man of integrity I want you to show that integrity again. Show it, Jack, in the name of the god that doesn't exist. Show it or I'll kill you. If you agree I'll let you live. And if you don't honor your word I'll track you down to Glen Ellen and kill you there. Yes, I'll shoot you dead in the Valley of the Moon."

"I'll honor my word, Ambrose."

"You won't give me away?"

"I won't give you away."

Jack London flees from Chihuahua the way he arrived and returns to Veracruz. He's drunk tequila until the flow reverses. He's eaten raw chopped meat, underdone chicken, uncooked seafood, unwashed vegetables. Brushes his teeth with the local water. Now he's sick. Really sick. Diarrhea. Dysentery. Pleurisy. Vomiting. Shitting. London can hardly distinguish one end of his body from the other. Barely tolerates his own odor. He is carried from the Dodge into his room at the Diligencias Hotel. The U.S. Army sends an American doctor to his bedside, but when he fails to improve, his wife Charmian hires a Mexican physician who seems to know what he's doing—until he starts applying leeches. Jack lies under a soaked white sheet and shivers. He shakes so violently, rattling the bed, the guests at the hotel complain, banging on the walls. Charmian boils his water and cooks his food on an electric plate in their room. He vomits before he eats and after he eats. Before his illness, before he made the mistake of driving to Chihuahua City, he'd written seven articles about the Mexican conflict, mailing them off to *Collier's*. He's now so ill that writing is impossible. He rallies enough to be moved to a cabin in a cattle boat, the *Ossabaw*, bound for Galveston. He's delirious on the train back to California. He has nightmares about Ambrose Bierce. Bierce slipping behind him with a noose. Bierce slitting his throat. Bierce firing a bullet into his brain. Bierce strangling him with his bare hands. London screams in his delirium. Charmian holds his hand. He loses eighteen pounds. When he finally emerges from his fever he's sure Chihuahua never happened, that he had never seen Ambrose Bierce. It was only a dream—no, a nightmare, the result of Montezuma's Revenge, the old Aztec Two-Step. Charmian asks him how far he had gotten on the road to Chihuahua. "Less than halfway before they turned me back," he lies to her. Jack London's a man of integrity. Dammit, he's a man of principle, a white man . . . and a socialist. He'll keep his word. Besides, he doesn't need a madman like Ambrose Bierce tracking him down at Glen Ellen.

Chapter Eight

Pancho is a man of the desert. "I was born with a saguaro spine up my ass," he tells his American friend. Here, in Xochimilco, Villa has never seen so much water. "Ay, yi, yi, *compadre,* if I had all this water in Chihuahua I would flood the desert and turn it into a heaven on earth."

"Indeed, heaven," says Bierce, "where the wicked never bother you with their complaints, but the good always listen to yours."

Villa and his entourage are in Xochimilco to seek a union with the rebel chieftain from Morelos, until now an ally in name alone. Pancho is anxious to know this farmer turned soldier, whose slogan is *Tierra y Libertad,* although Villa realizes the two men have little in common other than the same enemy. The *bandito supremo* has nothing against those whose preferred weapon is a hoe, but he can never be like them. The closest he ever came to domesticity was during a short stint as a butcher in Chihuahua between revolutionary flare-ups.

Villa and Bierce ride together side-by-side.

Bierce says, "Unlike you, General, I was born in a mythological land of gently rolling hills and lakes."

"Where is this place?"

"The poets call it Indiana. It's in America's heartland. However, I'm not a stranger to the desert. I was once on an odyssey through an unfriendly territory to visit a chain of American forts. A barren waste, marked by sagebrush and cactus, forbidding and inhospitable, with little more than prairie dogs, owls, and jackass rabbits. This desolate land was granted by treaty to the Indian, under the assumption it was worthless, and taken away from them when the assumption proved mistaken."

"I know of what you speak, *amigo.* Both Emiliano and me is Indians, so we know the curse put on us by white men."

"A curse, General? I sometimes believe the Indians of North America put a curse on me. Did you ever hear of a chief called Red Cloud?"

"Your stories are as tasty as tequila, you old *cabron.* But tell me later when I'm drunk. I got business to do here."

The cobbled streets of Xochimilco are narrow, dusty, and un-promising, but it all changes when Villa's party arrives at the floating gardens, bordered by leafy, overhanging willows. Everywhere, canals cross through islands of foliage. Flowers explode in rainbow colors. Marigolds, tiger's paws, lilies, poinsettias, dahlias, sunflowers. Bees dart from petal to petal. Songbirds cock their heads. The channels are crowded with bright flat-bottom boats navigated by gondoliers push-ing long poles into the muddy bottom. Mariachis stand on rose-blanketed barges to spill carnival music into the air. Pungent food smells float in the breeze. Narrow columns of smoke rise from the cooking fires on boats where women fold pieces of meat into tortillas and hold them out for sale. Vendors pole their way from boat to boat selling worthless trinkets of tin, tiny stuffed dolls, papier-mâché orna-ments, cheap shawls, candles, beads, jumping beans.

Villa says to Bierce, "Now I know why the name of this town means place where flowers grow. They tell me that in the old days the Aztecs grew their crops here on rafts filled with sod. Over time, the rafts became rooted to the bottom, forming miles of canals. *¡Maravil-loso!* Have you ever seen so many blossoms, so much water?"

Surrounded by children clutching posies, Villa's party is guided to an open canvas tent, where Emiliano Zapata reclines in the shade. The *bandito* dismounts and the two generals throw their arms around each other in a bear hug. As Bierce tries to reach Villa's side, his way is barred by Zapata's gunmen, wearing huge sombreros, white peasant shirts, and sandals. They wield carbines and are obviously not shy about using them. In turn, Villa's vaqueros, dressed in American-style khaki uniforms, raise their rifles.

"The gringo is with me," Villa says. "Let him through."

Zapata waves his men off. "*Sí,* let the gringo pass." The Zapatistas back away. Zapata's eyes, always suspicious—darting here and there looking for enemies—fix on Bierce. "Who is he?"

"This man not only saved my life, but he is my secretary. I hope you don't mind if he takes notes because he has also agreed to help me write my memoirs, if I ever get around to them."

Zapata says, "Your soldiers are dressed as if to fight a war, *compadre.*"

"And yours as if to dance at a fiesta."

Both men laugh and give each other another *abrazo.* Tears come to

Pancho's eyes. It's like a reunion with an old friend, even though he's never met Zapata before. The two can't be more dissimilar. Villa is heavy-set. He wears a white pith helmet, thick brown wool sweater with buttons down the front, khaki trousers, army leggings, and black riding boots. Emiliano is thin, face narrow, cheekbones high. An enormous sombrero casts shadows across his dark face. Under a black coat he wears a blue shirt. A silk handkerchief is tied around his neck. Silver buttons run the length of his tight trousers. Two gold rings glisten on his fingers.

Beyond the two generals are the floating gardens.

"Chinga tu madre," Villa says. "The flowers are beautiful. Let's go for a boat ride."

Zapata shakes his head. "General, I've arranged for us to talk at the municipal school building."

"¡Chingao! To hell with some musty school building. We'll talk on the water among the flowers and the birds and the music. I come from the desert, *compadre.* The only birds I know are vultures. The only flowers are on the tips of cactus. And we both know there's no water."

Although Mexico's conquerors, the Spanish, lacked any qualms about procreating with the autochthonous population, Villa and Zapata, of Indian stock, possess few classic Mediterranean characteristics. They are what Jack London, despite his claptrap about eternal brotherhood, calls half-breeds. Mexico's native population at last overthrew their invaders, something the Indians in what became the United States failed to do.

Nothing could have gotten worse for North America's native people, as Bierce learns at first hand. Sick of his job as a Treasury agent in Alabama, young Bierce leaps at the chance to join an expedition into Indian territory led by his former commander, General Hazen, who promises Bierce an army commission as captain once the party completes its odyssey from Omaha to San Francisco. For the duration, Bierce, as topographical officer, is assigned his old rank of lieutenant. Their mission is to inspect a line of Union forts.

Hazen says, "Bierce, we're getting a paid vacation through some of the most spectacular country in the world. But the mission's not without its dangers. It's Indian territory, after all. My enemies in Washington would no doubt relish the thought of a tomahawk in my brain.

Grant, Sherman, Sheridan. I piss on 'em all. By rights we should have lost the war. We suffered twice as many casualties as the rebels. All we did was overrun 'em."

"That's probably how the Indians feel, General. Overrun."

Their guide's a man named Jim Beckwourth, Jim the Breed, born in Virginia to a mother who was a slave and an English father. The pass Jim discovers over the Sierra Nevada in '51 is named for him.

Hazen says to Bierce, "Jim may be a mulatto but he knows the trail better than any white man. His mind is like a steel trap. He was apprenticed to a blacksmith as a boy, but he got the wanderlust. Became the best damned trapper in the Rockies. He's also an honorary chief in the Crow Nation. And there's something else: he took the first white child across the mountains into California, a girl named Josephine Donna Smith."

The horses of Hazen's column kick up the summer dust. It's a land only hinted about in the novels of Mayne Reid. Everything flat, then from nowhere a sudden mass of earth springing upward. Faraway clouds twisting into human-like shapes. Sun-bleached bones are bright along the trail.

Bierce says, "Jim, those bones . . . Buffalo?"

"They ain't all buffalo bones, son. See that skull over there? I knowed that fella once. Good pal of mine, he was."

That night Bierce stays close to the campfire. At intervals he hears the howl of a wolf. Or might it be . . . ?

"Jim, if Indians attack us what should we do first?"

"Hell, son, first thing I'd do is to spit out that fire. You make a mighty nice target for an arrow in the ass."

In the morning Bierce fingers himself to confirm there are no arrows in his ass, grabs the camp kettle, and sets out to find water. He sees some willows about three hundred yards away, but the farther he walks the more distant the willows get. The sun rises hot and its rays sting his head, making him dizzy. When he stops, the willows also stop. Leaving the kettle behind he dashes toward the willows, which disappear over the crest of a hill. As he climbs to the top he sees under an intense sky a barren waste of sand stretching infinitely, and then to his horror what appears to be a long line of monsters rolling across the prairie. They take the shapes of animals, buildings, machines, ships.

Within them are the bodies and fragments of men. Anatomical beasts. Mechanical nightmares. All intertwined and superimposed. Hell's fire, the demons of his childish dreams are about to devour him. Then the spectral monstrosity recedes, gradually replaced by a mile-long train of mules and wagons, far on the horizon.

"Bierce!"

Hazen. Standing slightly behind the general is Jim the Breed.

"We wondered where the hell you were. I knew you wouldn't absquatulate, so we thought the Indians got you. Bierce, I'm talking to you. *Attention.*"

"Sir!"

"What's wrong with you, lieutenant? You look peaked."

"Sir, I saw, saw . . . things."

"What sort of things?"

"Willows. And then, then . . . I can't tell you, sir."

"What do you mean?"

"Sir, I don't think you'd understand. What I mean to say is sometimes I imagine things that may not be real. Often in my dreams I—"

"I don't care a hoot in hell about your dreams, Bierce. As for your seeing things—"

"'Scuse me, General." Jim the Breed bites off a chaw of tobacco. "I reckon he saw a mirage. Out here, the land plays sport on you. Bamboozles your eyes and your mind."

Bierce begins to gasp.

"What's the matter now, Bierce?" Hazen says. "Are you having a conniption fit?"

"Doctors say it's something called asthma. Has to do with the lungs. Gotten worse since the war, sir. Sometimes it becomes difficult to breathe."

"Then the clean, fresh air of the Powder River country is just what you need."

"You mean, sir, I should keep my powder dry?"

"Haven't lost your sense of humor, have you, Bierce? And lieutenant . . . Keep your damned dreams to yourself. It's time to pull-foot."

They call on Forts Laramie and Reno along the Bozeman Trail, and at last near Fort Phil Kearny. As the expedition reaches the top of a rise they get their first glimpse of the garrison. The fort is nestled below the rolling, treeless hills that surround it, a quarter-mile from a shallow river that no doubt serves as its water supply. A wall of logs encloses a scattering of buildings. Fluttering bravely on the parade ground is an American flag, while a man behind a mowing machine cuts the grass.

Jim the Breed spits. "Damned fools, they are. They put that fort in the low ground. If we can look down at 'em so can the Sioux. There's no cover between the fort and the stream. How's they going to haul water in if they're attacked? And there's no trees. When they need timber they got to ride miles for it."

The members of the Hazen party are greeted as honored guests, plied with food, wine, a dress parade, and a concert by Colonel Carrington's forty-piece brass band. Bierce sits with the other officers in rocking chairs, smoking, as they listen to "The Girl I Left Behind Me" and "Hail Columbia."

"You seem to be comfortable here at Phil Kearny, Henry," Hazen says to Carrington.

"Bill, I intend to show the Indians we aren't afraid. That's why my officers and I brought our wives and children here—and why I made a point of letting the Indians know we had."

"We heard you were under siege."

"I admit it was difficult for a time. It used to be impossible for the weekly mail to get through. I had to send platoons to escort the woodcutters. It took two squads of men to fetch water, one squad to protect the other. No one was allowed to leave the post. Not a day went by a man wasn't scalped or wounded and robbed of their uniforms. But now the Indians seem to have disappeared."

"How can that be, Henry? They must be out there somewhere—waiting for an opportunity."

"I'm convinced they've learned their lesson."

"Really? And you're sure this fort is safe?"

"With our walls it's impregnable, Bill. It's a model fort. No attacking force can penetrate it."

The concert ends with a prayer and the playing of "Garryowen." Bierce retires to the officer's club for drinks with a Captain William J. Fetterman. Joining them is artist-correspondent Ridgeway Glover of *Frank Leslie's Illustrated Newspaper*. The place smells of freshly cut wood and whitewash. Through the window Bierce hears the call of insects in the grass. And from far away the sigh of a harmonica against the lips of a soldier.

Fetterman says, "I tell you, Bierce, a company of U.S. regulars can whip a thousand Indians. I'm not trying to undermine Colonel Carrington, you understand, but I feel he's sometimes more, shall I say, cautious than he needs to be. A single regiment is all we need to annihilate the entire array of hostiles. Give me eighty men and I'll destroy the Sioux nation."

Bierce says, "I hear that fellow Red Cloud is trying to unite all the various tribes, Fetterman."

"I don't care how many tribes that savage pulls together. I'd sorely love to meet the bugger head on. He's a bad egg. More port, Lieutenant?"

Ridgeway Glover's a short man whose mouth curls in a perpetual smile. "The public's fed up with this Indian business, Bierce. We've found veins of copper, gold, and silver near Virginia City. It would be the California gold rush all over again if it weren't for the damned hostiles. Our economy depends on those gold fields."

Bierce says, "It appears the Indians are taking a mighty unreasonable attitude about our economy, Glover. Perhaps the savages should be instructed about how much gold is prized for its convenience in the robbery known as trade."

The newspaperman leans back, elbows against the bar. "It's the Indians' destiny to lose and ours to win."

"I understand destiny to be a tyrant's authority for crime and a fool's excuse for failure."

"You're mighty glib, Lieutenant Bierce, and perhaps a trifle more inflated for your own good."

"Would you care to repeat that to me outside, Glover?"

Fetterman interrupts. "Gentlemen, enough. Bierce, when your General Hazen leaves the region he'll have a better understanding of our frustration. We're being forced to deal with the savages on their terms, not ours. It's a sin to Moses. They're not a trained enemy. Not a West Pointer among them. Spear-carriers is what they are. Lazy, idle vagabonds who never labor, who have no profession except that of arms."

"Bravo," cheers Glover.

Fetterman says, "The Indian's highest honor is to own a scalp taken by himself."

"Obviously, we've taught them well," Bierce says.

Fetterman says, "The belligerents must be driven to reservations and compelled to remain there."

"Where, no doubt, they'll be taught the value of Christian virtues," Bierce says.

Fetterman's eyes take on a faraway look. "Just give me eighty men . . ."

Glover catches up with Bierce outside the officer's club. Dusk is falling fast.

"No hard feelings, Lieutenant Bierce. May I stroll with you?"

"Suit yourself, Glover."

Bierce has a low opinion of newspapermen. Lickspittles, most of them. Unlike soldiers, newspapermen are a drunken, undisciplined lot. Besides, he views non-combatants like Glover as little more than dead Quakers.

"What do you say we stroll down to the Little Piney, Lieutenant?"

"Is it safe to leave the fort?"

"Pshaw, there've been no Indians for days. Besides, I'm carryin' a rabbit's foot for luck."

"It may bring luck to you, Glover, but it brought none to the rabbit."

The two men walk unchallenged through the gate. The sandy ground is covered by low bushes and knee-high weeds. They hear the gurgle of running water as it washes over the stones of the river bed. Two uniformed figures walk toward them along the side of the stream.

"I see we're not the only ones enjoying an evening constitutional, Lieutenant Bierce. Yonder comes a couple of our boys in blue."

Glover picks up a flat rock and hurls it over the stream. The stone skips across the water kicking up little white splashes. The two approaching soldiers are now just yards away.

"Howdy, boys," Glover says. "Nice evening for a stroll."

"Howdy, boys," one of the soldiers says.

"Top of the morning," the other says.

Morning? Bierce thinks. But it *isn't* morning.

The next moments are a blur. One of the uniformed men brings a tomahawk down in the center of Glover's head. Blood sprays. Glover's face contorts in an expression of shock and surprise. Bierce fumbles for his revolver but is unable to get off a shot. One of the Indians swings a carbine, the stock first glancing from Bierce's head, then hitting his shoulder. Bierce staggers back, dropping his gun. He falls, stunned. Through half-lidded eyes he watches the Indians strip the murdered correspondent of his clothes. They discover Glover's lucky rabbit's foot, snort, and throw it away. Then an Indian puts a knife at the top of the dead man's forehead. He runs the blade under the scalp and lifts off the hair almost as if it had been a rug. The Indian waves the scalp as still more blood oozes to the surface of the late Mr. Glover's wound. Desperate, Bierce springs to his feet and runs. The attackers are blocking his retreat to the fort, so he splashes in the opposite direction across the Little Piney, the Indians in pursuit. His breathing becomes heavier as he reaches the far shore and scrambles up the bank. The pain in his head and shoulder throbs. He runs through weeds and tall grass, drunkenly now, the air in his lungs nearly depleted. He stumbles, falls, picks himself up, runs some more. Then he collapses, his breathing coming in great gulps. The Indians stand over him. It's curtains now, he thinks.

"Get to your feet, American."

He becomes disoriented as night falls. If he stumbles he's prodded by a rifle barrel. His hands are tied behind him. The Indians can see in the dark what he can't see. They're joined by more Indians in battle dress, riding ponies. As the sun begins to rise, they come to a camp, and Bierce sees teepees and campfires. He's taken before a commanding Indian sitting cross-legged. A single feather rises from a band circling the crown of his head. His nose is flat, lips thick, eyes penetrating. On his cheeks are painted lines of white, green, and yellow. Bierce is pushed to his knees.

"You're the chief?" Bierce says.

The Indian doesn't answer. Instead . . . "You are wondering why my warriors didn't kill you. Why I had you brought here. Because I want to tell you a story, and for you to return to your Colonel Carrington and repeat it to him so he will tell it to the Great White Father in Washington. Do you agree to listen?"

"I do."

"Soon, the People will fight as one, for we gathered in a great meeting to forge a new, stronger nation. The Oglalas, Hunkpapas, Brulés, Miniconjous, Cheyenne, Gros Ventres, Arapahos. It was decided there will be no peace until the white man leaves or the Indian dies in the land where his fathers died."

The campfire pops and sizzles. The sun sets off the creases and lines in the chief's face. Bierce hears a baby crying in the distance. The whinny of a horse.

"Ours is a buffalo nation. I am the son and the father of the buffalo. But the buffalo is being killed as the Indian is being killed. The white man's words are not sweet like sugar but bitter like gourds. They want to put us on reservations and into cabins. I was born on the prairie where there is nothing to break the light of the sun. I do not want to die within walls. They have told us to give up the buffalo for the sheep.

"At first, the People thought the white man could create great magic to punish them. One evening a Sioux warrior left his teepee and looked up. He let out a great shout. 'The stars are falling! The whole sky is falling!' The People came running out of their teepees. They looked up too and saw the stars shooting downward. They shouted, 'Is the world coming to an end?' They thought the white man had brought disaster onto the camp because seven days before a war party stopped a wagon train, killed the teamsters, and stole from the wagons. The People believed the Americans were punishing them for the raid by making the stars fall. The stars kept falling, and it didn't seem there could be any stars left in the sky at all. The People were terrified. All of a sudden the stars stopped falling and the People were still alive.

"Later, a war party attacked the homes of some white settlers and killed them and burned their buildings. The next day at noon, the sky began to get dark. Darker and darker. Like midnight. And the People were frightened again. 'The sun is dying!' they yelled. 'The white man has released a snake from under the world and it is swallowing the sun!' But before long, the People saw a rim of light, like the edge of a fingernail, against the sun. The light grew and grew and the whole sun reappeared and the world was alive again. The birds flew from their nests and began to sing once more. The young men and women laughed. The mothers went back to cooking their dinners.

"The People learned that no matter what power the white man has, the stars will stay in the sky and the sun will always return. Now, the people know the only magic the white man has is his bullets. The People are not afraid of bullets."

Bierce knows the white men have more magic than mere bullets. They also have sheer numbers and they carry with them a multitude of diseases, known and unknown, that will decimate the unprepared.

The Indian says, "Let me tell you what the buffalo means to the People. We eat it. We use its gall as dressing. We make sausages by stuffing the buffalo's dried meat into its small intestine and smoking it over a willow fire. Its brains, tongue, and nose are its greatest delicacies. We make soup by boiling its hoofs. We thicken its blood into a pudding. We mix its fat with the dried sap of a box elder tree and eat it like candy. We use the hide for making teepees, moccasin soles, and shields. Its bladder we use as a bucket. Braid its hair into rope. Split its tendons for thread. Children slide on sleds made from its ribs. Its paunch is used as a stewpot. We boil the thick hide of the neck to make glue. We fry its scrotum and load it with pebbles for a baby's rattle. We steam its horns and bend them into spoons and ladles. We burn its dung for fuel when there is no wood. Blend its dung into our tobacco to produce a rich flavor. Its bones are cracked and boiled for grease. Its hide is stretched over the hoop of a drum. Its beard and tail decorate our lances and the heels of our moccasins. And a buffalo robe keeps us warm and dry. When the buffalo disappears the heart of the Indian will stop. The white men are killing the buffalo to the last calf. This is another reason we must fight. And why we will never give up. Explain this to your Colonel Carrington. And tell him the story of the stars and the sun and of our buffalo resolve."

"I shall," Bierce says, but he knows it'll be hopeless. "May I ask your name?"

"I am Red Cloud."

Bierce walks for hours, blindfolded, led by a rope. He staggers against rocks, falls against shrubs, trips on vines. His head pounds. The old bullet wound and the new ache from the rifle butt. His breathing comes in gasps. At last he's released, his captors disappearing into the prairie haze. A scouting party from Fort Kearny finds him and takes him to Hazen.

"We thought you were a gone coon, Bierce, that the Indians really got you this time. Especially after we found that fool newspaper correspondent without his scalp. You've got grit, son."

"Sir, the Indians did capture me. But they freed me after I promised to deliver a message to Colonel Carrington."

"By the horn spoons, what are you saying?"

Bierce tells Hazen the story of the stars falling from the sky and the sun that disappeared. About the buffalo nation. When he's through Hazen stands up, shakes his head.

"No, Bierce, you're not telling that story to Carrington or anyone else. It's bunkum."

"I promised Red Cloud, sir."

"I don't care beans if you promised the Queen of England. Don't try to hornswoggle me. It's a goddamned fairy tale. What does some cock-and-bull story about stars and suns and buffalo have to do with putting the savages in their place? As far as I'm concerned you're delirious. You've been hallucinating. Another one of your so-called mirages. I'll tolerate no more talk of Red Cloud."

"But, sir, it all seemed so real."

"Our military mission will not be compromised by mirages and hallucinations and Indian myths. Not a word about it. That's an order."

Relations are strained between Bierce and Hazen as they leave Fort Kearny. In his journal, Bierce makes a drawing of a bison's head. He pencils maps, noting the Big Horn Mountains, Crazy Woman's Flat, Clear Fork, Tongue River, the Little Big Horn, and the Judith Mountains. He makes copies of the Indian inscriptions he sees, pictographs carved into the stumps of trees in the Yellowstone Valley and on rocks along the Powder River. It's near Fort Smith they encounter their first buffalo herd. Enormous. As far as Bierce can see are bulls, cows, calves—miles of them. He wonders how the world could ever run out of buffalo. How could Red Cloud—if Bierce had actually met Red Cloud—possibly be right?

Jim the Breed confesses he once shot and killed one hundred buffalo in the space of two hours. "Then, I says to myself, 'Jim, that's all the killing you'll need to do for the rest of your life.'"

Hazen's men still have their scalps when they reach Fort Benton. In the evening, they're treated to Corporal R. Kohler playing "The Last Rose of Summer" on the cornet; a trio of privates performing "Wait for the Wagon"; and Miss Hortense Beveridge, daughter of Captain

Beveridge, singing a medley consisting of "Gentle Annie," "Kattie Avourneen," and "Killarney." The entertainment is interrupted by a commotion. A young lieutenant by the name of Clinchfield, breathless, bursts into the room.

"It's Captain Fetterman! He's dead. And so are eighty of his men. The Indians massacred them outside of Fort Kearny."

Cries of disbelief.

"Are you sure his men numbered eighty?" Bierce says. "Fetterman told me he could lick the entire Sioux nation with eighty men."

"A feckless boast, I'm afraid," Clinchfield says. "After a wood train was attacked by the Indians, Colonel Carrington ordered a relief party and put Captain Fetterman in charge. Fetterman was warned only to protect the train, not to pursue the hostiles, but I guess he couldn't resist. He and his men went in pursuit. The Indians were concealed in the rocks and brush, and Fetterman fell into a trap. He and all the others were killed and scalped. To the last man. One of the soldiers' dogs, a little mutt, was found with an arrow through her heart."

Someone shoves a mug of beer into Clinchfield's hand. He drinks it in a single gulp. "The fort's numbers were badly depleted by the massacre. We were so vulnerable Carrington ordered fuses set in the powder magazine. If the Indians attacked, the wives and children were to be put into the magazine and destroyed. He vowed not to allow them to be captured alive. But inexplicably Red Cloud failed to attack. The Indians lost their opportunity, and finally our reinforcements arrived from Fort Laramie."

"If that doesn't cap the climax," Hazen says. "A tragic setback for the U.S. Army, and the end to Carrington's military career. I tried to tell him but he wouldn't listen. It's a calamity."

Bierce says, "There are two kinds of calamities, sir: misfortune to ourselves, and good fortune to others."

"No more sarcasm out of you, Bierce. This is neither the time nor the place." The general doesn't care much for dreamers, men tormented by nightmares, and ungrateful underlings who fail to recognize their station in life. Nor is he sure that Bierce has earned his commission as captain. "By God, the United States will never hang up its fiddle because of a bunch of ornery, no-account savages."

Hazen proves to be right. Bierce becomes a virtual witness to

America's own brand of genocide and knows his country's moral standing will forever be suspect. But, here in Xochimilco, he puts those doleful thoughts out of his mind as streamers flutter from the gaily painted barge. Pancho reclines luxuriously while the boat rocks gently in the sluggish current.

"Ah, this is the life, boys," Villa says. From an *anciana* he buys a set of jumping beans in a tiny cardboard box. He spills the beans into the palm of his hand and watches them hop, almost like the gamboling of headless rabbits. "*Compañero,* we call them *frijoles Mexicanos,*" he says to Bierce. "A little worm has made a home inside each bean, and when the worm moves so does the bean. Here, you take them. For good luck."

"General, worms are the finished product of which we are the raw material, so I gratefully accept your gift."

Then Villa and Zapata talk. They agree to stand up to their former revolutionary allies, Carranza and Obregón, in the name of agrarian reform. Villa boasts he has forty thousand men, seventy-seven cannon, sixteen-million cartridges, dozens of troop trains, a score of aeroplanes, countless horses, wagons, cars, and trucks. The rebel chieftains make a list of Carranza's supporters who will face the firing squads. Emiliano vows to launch an offensive against Puebla in the south while in the north Pancho is to attack Veracruz, recently abandoned by the Americanos. "Remember," Zapata tells his new best friend, *"la lucha sigue."* To celebrate their partnership, Zapata opens a bottle of cognac. Villa declines, saying he will just have some mineral water. He saves his drinking for his nights with Bierce. Zapata insists. The cognac is poured into two huge tumblers. Villa drinks his in one great gulp. His throat and chest seem to catch on fire. His face turns red. His eyes bulge and tears run down his cheeks. He nearly chokes. Bierce slaps him on the back.

"General," Bierce says. "Cognac is for sipping. As I know well, having sipped many, many gallons of it."

Villa throws the empty tumbler into the canal. The glass floats among the other debris for a moment before it fills with water and sinks. Villa's voice is hoarse. He can barely speak, but he manages to say to Zapata, "I'd like that glass of water now if you don't mind." A mariachi band floats by, playing the old songs.

Chapter Nine

Girls shower the heroes with flowers, and the brim of Zapata's sombrero bends with the weight of the petals. When Villa's military hat falls off, Zapata, without losing his horse's stride, scoops it up and returns it to his new ally. A Hearst newsreel camera team films the two generals as they ride side by side behind a military band through the streets of Mexico City. Bierce, dressed in his customary black, follows on horseback. The parade lasts seven hours; fifty-five thousand soldiers marching to the Zócalo before dispersing. Inside the National Palace, Villa and Zapata pose for the newspaper photographers along with a nervous old man named Gutiérrez they hand-picked to serve as Mexico's acting president. The correspondents keep pestering Villa to sit in the gilded presidential chair. Villa finally agrees just to feel what it's like as a gringo photographer named Robert Runyon—with a flash of light and a puff of smoke—takes his picture. "One more shot, General," Runyon says, "just to be safe." Villa complies, then gets up, only a little sheepish. Zapata tries the chair, equally self-conscious. Zapata doesn't see himself as more than a farmer from Morelos, and never wants to be what Villa's become, strutting and posing.

Pancho celebrates with Bierce under the lights of the city, where the *bandito supremo* takes up temporary quarters in a wealthy merchant's house in Colonia Juárez on Liverpool Street. The home is furnished with antique furniture and Persian rugs, and a library filled with rare books.

"How can I resist staying in this fine house, *amigo?* After all, it was offered to me in friendship, so I could not refuse."

"General, I've always viewed friendship as a ship big enough to carry two in fair weather, but only one in foul."

Pancho roars with laughter.

"Besides, General, did I not see the owner of this house led away by your men at gunpoint?"

"For his own safety, *compadre,* for his own safety."

At night they dine in the best restaurants, dance the flamenco in the nightclubs, fornicate in the sporting houses, and in the mornings, despite enormous hangovers, eat whopping breakfasts at the Hotel Palacio. Over coffee, Villa plans strategy against Carranza and Obregón, who control a wide swath of the nation from Puebla to Veracruz, as well as the Isthmus, Yucatán, Jalisco, Tepic, and Sinaloa.

Villa says, "*Amigo,* there's something about this Zapata I don't like. He don't have no ambitions. He don't think big. And I think he's easily influenced."

"But he's a good revolutionary, General, and he's revered by his soldiers."

"*Si,* and a brave man as well. But his men don't wear uniforms. They dress in white pajamas. Also I think maybe Emiliano has surrounded himself with the wrong sorts."

"Such as . . ."

"David Berlanga and Paulino Martínez."

"They were early supporters of the Revolution."

"They no longer speak good of me. I learned they've cursed my name and are plotting against me. They're trying to make Emiliano my enemy. I think maybe they will have to go."

"Into exile?"

"I do not believe in exile, *compadre.*"

"General, if you execute those men you will incur Zapata's wrath."

"There is always wrath in war."

"In which case the Villa-Zapata alliance will be stillborn at a time when Carranza's forces are growing."

"Carranza is a gnat on the executioner's wall." Villa's eyes widen as he plunks his coffee cup on the table. "Ay, *caramba!* Do you see what I see? *Fantastico!* Behind the cash register. The girl with the blond hair. *Hermosa!* How did I not notice her when we first arrived?"

"She's quite attractive, General. French, I believe."

"I've been struck by Cupid's arrow."

"Indeed, Cupid. The notion of symbolizing sexual love by a sexless baby, and comparing the pains of passion to the wounds of an arrow."

"Shut up, *amigo.* Let me feast on my vision of loveliness. This morning I will pay the breakfast bill personally."

Villa swaggers to the cashier's counter and leans against it as he hands the young woman a wad of pesos for the bill.

"Señorita, let me introduce myself. I am General Francisco Villa, leader of the esteemed *División del Norte.* I am better known as Pancho."

"Everyone in Mexico knows of you, *monsieur.*" The young woman's accent is decidedly French.

"And your name, señorita?"

"*Madame.* Madame Yvette."

"I wish to marry you, Madame, and take you away with me."

"No doubt, General Villa, that my husband would object."

"Not a problem. I will have him shot in the street like a dog."

"I'm certain President Gutiérrez would have something to say about that."

"Madame, perhaps you did not know, but President Gutiérrez does my bidding. He is the president of Mexico because I made him so."

"Then I shall complain to the French Embassy."

"And I will have the French Embassy sacked and burned."

"Here is your change, *monsieur.*"

"Keep the change. Buy yourself a jeweled comb and put it into your beautiful hair."

"Please, *monsieur,* I do not want your change or anything else."

"Madame, you spurn my attention when all I want you to do is to *chupame mi pinga* and *besa mis huevos.* That is not asking very much, and I guarantee you will like it. I have never had a complaint. Why, just last night—"

The young woman turns white, her hands shaking. "*Monsieur,* I beg you."

Bierce taps Villa on the shoulder. "General, I apologize for interrupting. But you're already late for an important meeting at the National Palace with President Gutiérrez and the cabinet members."

Villa says, "Yes, of course. I'm very late. Madame, I shall return for breakfast tomorrow. Perhaps you will be more receptive to my overtures. In fact, I'm going to insist on it."

Villa, of course, isn't late for his meeting. His plans are to visit the military prison at Santiago Tlatelolco, where he'd spent part of his seven months as prisoner of the vile dictator Huerta, killer of Pancho's idol Madero and predecessor of Carranza. No doubt a number of Villa's jailers and wardens remain on the job and he wants a few words with them.

Outside the hotel, Bierce says, "General, it's none of my business, but I suspect you were frightening that young woman."

"You are right, *compadre*. It is none of your business. I want that woman and I shall have her."

"She's a French national. It could cause—"

"You are my friend, but sometimes I lose patience with you. *¡Vete a jalar el pescuezo al pollo!*"

Bierce's Spanish isn't good enough to fully translate Villa's malediction, but he knows it has something to do with pulling on a chicken's neck.

"*Hasta la vista*, the *bandito supremo* says."

Villa climbs into a Packard 238 open touring car with his bodyguards and roars off, leaving Bierce alone on the sidewalk. Rather than return to his room on Liverpool Street, he decides to walk to the *Museo Nacional de Antropologia*, which is housed in the *Casa de Moneda*, the national mint. Bierce himself once worked in a national mint in San Francisco. As he turns a corner he encounters a ruckus outside a Chinese laundry. Some of Villa's boys have dragged an Asian man from the shop and are tormenting him on the street, yanking his queue and prodding him with their rifle barrels. They have Pancho's tacit approval. He once ordered all the Chinese in Chihuahua to leave within forty-eight hours or face the firing squads. It wasn't so much different in San Francisco back in '67 following Bierce's odyssey with Hazen through Indian country.

Ah, yes. San Francisco, where he spends his free evenings at Bob Dunphy's Saloon on Powell Street. Failing to win his promised commission as captain, his rank now merely that of mister, Bierce's gainful employment is that of a watchman at the United States Mint at Mission and Fifth, where he earns the lordly sum of one hundred twenty-five dollars a month.

Bob Dunphy's is where the reporters at the *Morning Call* and the *Chronicle* stand at the bar to sip and spit, denigrate their editors, and ridicule the most sacred of San Francisco's institutions, especially the most sacred. O'Leary of the *Call*: "So I goes into the gents and I see Chief of Police Thomas on his hands and knees in one of the stalls, and I says, 'Are you all right, Chief Thomas?' And Thomas—everybody calls him On-the-Take Thomas—he gets all red and embarrassed and says he's lost a collar stud and has to get down on the floor to look for it. So I goes into the adjoining stall and what do I see rolled up and hidden almost out of sight behind the toilet but a thick wad of greenbacks. When I finish my business, Thomas is still down on the floor poking around, so I says to him, 'Chief Thomas, you're looking in the wrong place. They put your stud in the stall I just left.'"

"Bob, Bob." It's a little man with several days growth on his ferret-like face who slithers through the swinging doors. "Some heathen Chinee is drinkin' out of your horse-trough again."

"Son of a bitch," Dunphy says. He stashes the bottle he's been tippling from all day, wipes his hands on his apron, grabs the ceremonial shillelagh from the wall, and ducks under the bar. "Ah Wee!" he screams. "Where's that chink when I want him? Ferret, go find Ah Wee. Tell him to get his yellow ass out front quick."

Dunphy storms from the saloon's front door. An emaciated Chinese man is on his knees leaning into the horse-trough, lapping up the water like a dog.

"Yellow bastard," Dunphy yells. "That there water's reserved for horses and mules." Dunphy pounds the shillelagh against the trough. The Chinese bolts, pigtail floating behind him. "I don't waste none of my water on Godless, heathen, yellow asses."

Ferret's waiting back at the bar. He clutches at Dunphy's sleeve. "I looked for Ah Wee, Bob. Couldn't find him, Bob. Honest."

"I've about had it with that chink," the barkeep says. He swallows a slug from his personal bottle, which he keeps below the bar at all times.

Dunphy out-tipples his customers. Bierce has heard it said Dunphy is often overcome by the DTs and that he frequently claims to be surrounded by fiendish shapes and grotesque beasts. Several times Bierce, haunted by his own nightmares, has tried to question Dunphy about his violent mental images, but Dunphy always insists it's a passel of damned lies.

"Bob? Bob?" Ferret leans over the bar and again grabs at Dunphy's sleeve.

"All right, Ferret, I'll give you a whiskey on the house. But you ain't worth more than one."

Ah Wee, holding a broom, appears at the door to the back room. He bows. Five feet tall perhaps. Delicate, almost feminine face, black hair covered by a tight fitting cap, a queue dangling from the back.

"Where the hell have you been?" Dunphy yells.

"In stable, sir. Sweeping, sir." Ah Wee's voice is musical, pitched high.

"Lying son of a bitch. Listen, Ah Wee, your fellow heathens have been drinkin' out of my horse-trough again. What do I have to do to make 'em stop? Piss in it?"

"Yes, piss. Very good. Piss."

"Get your yellow ass back to the stable, Ah Wee. Make sure all the horseshit's cleaned up or I'll have your ass."

"Shit. Ass. Piss. Yes, sir." Ah Wee runs out of the room in little steps.

Bierce downs his bourbon and signals for another. "A little hard on the Chinamen tonight, aren't you, Mr. Dunphy? Hardly the Christian spirit."

"Mr. Bierce, I ain't read nothing about Chinamen in the New Testament, so I can treat 'em as hard as I damn well please. Ah Wee don't know nothing and he don't give himself airs. And when I kick him in the ass he thanks me." Dunphy moves down the bar and sets up a bottle for a new group of drinkers, sailors in starched whites. He returns to Bierce and leans close. "You Easterners who don't know a Chileño from a Kanaka can afford to spout some liberal ideas about the Chinese. But an Irish fellow like me that's got to fight for his bone with a lot of mongrel coolies hasn't no time for such foolishness. They've started talking about running me for the state legislature. Now if I'm going to take a seat in Sacramento I'm obliged to tell the truth about how the chinks shit in our streets, take our jobs, depress our economy, stab us in our backs, kidnap our children, and sell our women into slavery." He sees the skeptical expression on Bierce's face and shrugs. "What can I say, Mr. Bierce? It's a popular issue. You don't have to back it up with facts. Hell, if I was the president of the U.S. of A. I bet I could lie my way into some war with a country that can't fight back just 'cause I wanted to and everyone would think I was grand."

Dunphy removes from a shelf below the bar a lacquered Oriental box, red and gold, with intricate carvings of dragons and eagles and bears. He's so unsteady he almost drops it. Bierce is dazzled by the glow of the container, which seems to have a life of its own. Dunphy clumsily opens the box and removes a wad of tobacco that he crams into the side of his mouth, causing his cheek to puff out like a tumor.

"That box . . ." Bierce says.

"My magic box," Dunphy says, his voice slurred.

"I've never seen anything like it."

"Courtesy of Ah Wee. Gave it to me, he did. Brings me luck." Dunphy returns the box to its place under the bar.

Suddenly Dunphy freezes. His eyes grow wide in horror. Then his arms begin to flail at no one. "What's that? Bloody Jesus, what's that?"

Bierce sees nothing but the drinkers, Ferret squatting in the sawdust on the floor, the pickle jar, the bowls of sardines and sliced onions on the counter.

"What, Mr. Dunphy? I don't see . . ."

"The eye, dammit, the eye," Dunphy screams. He points at a knothole in the wall.

"An imperfection in the wood, Mr. Dunphy. That's what you see."

"I'm telling you it's an eye. A human eye. The yellow heathens are staring at me again. Ah Wee!"

"Mr. Dunphy, you've tippled too much."

Dunphy staggers against the bar. "An eye, for the love of God!"

Bierce has his own visions, but they usually come in his sleep, including a recurring nightmare in which a decaying body on a bed inevitably turned out to have his own face. Then there's the milk-white horse that speaks to him in a human but unintelligible voice. When he first started at the Mint he shared a room with a fellow worker, but Bierce made so much noise at night, crying out in his sleep, he moved to a single room at the Russ House.

He reports for work at midnight, making his rounds with a lantern, walking through the counting offices and the cubicles of the clerks. The odor of the long-cooled machinery used by the melters and refiners hangs in the air. He checks the locks on the front and back entrances, inspects the barred windows, like those of a prison. He puts his ear against the cold metal of the great vault to hear its strange ticking, residual noise from the locking bolts, the cylinders, the various pieces of assembly waiting to be sprung. Inside the vault are untold tons of gold molded into bars and ingots. Bags of gold dust and towers of greenbacks. Pennies, half-dollars, quarters. Odd denominations made of bronze or copper or nickel. Double eagles, single eagles, half eagles, quarter eagles. Gold and silver dollars. Between his rounds, he writes, trying to break into a new magazine edited by someone called

Bret Harte, the *Californian*. Harte, a man with literary aspirations, also works at the Mint, but during the day in an office job, so Bierce has never met him. Bierce's writing efforts are clumsy, superficial, and met by repeated rejection. But at the age of twenty-five he's a fast learner, and he hopes to write his way out of his lonely job.

From outside the Mint he hears screams and shouts. Through the barred basement window he sees a tangle of running feet and shapes in the shadows.

The chink's around here someplace.

Where are you, heathen scum?

The Irish boys in action. Having a little fun with some unfortunate yellow gentleman who must have turned into the wrong street. Such is America, where an Irishman can stone a heathen in the morning and obtain the blessed sacrament in the afternoon.

We'll hang you by your pigtail.

Coolie son of a bitch.

Bierce cares little about coolies or Irish thugs.

We'll find you, yellow-belly.

Mongolian scum, we know you're around here.

But perhaps things have gone too far. The object of the Irish wrath is no doubt cowering in the garbage of the alley.

Come out, coolie, wherever you are.

Bierce walks up the stair that leads to the back door, which he opens with a brass key at his belt. Drunken Irishmen brandishing bottles and torches run through the street. Damned papists, he thinks, groveling at the altar one day, running berserk the next. He sees the shape of a human under a pile of discarded rags and forgotten newspapers, obviously the terrified coolie.

"It's all right, my man. I'm taking you inside until the hubbub is over. Get up, I say. It's not safe out here for heathens or even Presbyterians. Oh, do I have to pick you up? If you insist . . ."

Bierce, with his six-foot frame, kicks away the makeshift blanket and scoops up the small body in his arm. It's surprisingly light, like a child's. As he turns to re-enter the Mint he hears a shout.

"There he is, the chink!"

The mob run toward Bierce. One of them is a young man with a three-inch scar on his forehead his slouch hat doesn't quite cover.

"You caught the Chinee for us. Thanks, mister." The man is carrying a slab of walnut he'd grabbed from a construction site. "We'll take the Mongol off your hands now."

"Of just what crime is the Chinaman guilty?"

"Chinks ain't allowed in our part of town."

"I've not heard of that statute."

"Turn over the chink, mister."

"Under no circumstances."

"As sure as my name is Denis Kearney I ain't never heard of a white man in San Francisco protectin' some Chinee."

Kearney raises the walnut club. Bierce responds by withdrawing his Colt, which he jams against Kearney's forehead.

"Drop your stick, Kearney, or you'll feel a hole through what's left of your pickled excuse for a brain."

Kearney freezes. Reluctant sobriety begins to slap him in the face. His club clatters to the cobblestones. Kearney's pals inch forward.

"Don't do nothing, boys," Kearney tells his pals. He says to Bierce, "There's too many of us, mister. You can't shoot us all."

"I don't intend to. I need only to shoot *you*. I suggest you take your drunken friends home to sleep it off. Otherwise, your sainted mother will be grieving over your trifling corpse."

"You got a point, mister." Old whiskey oozes through Kearney's pores like sweat.

The boys begin to retreat. It's time to nurse their hangovers, empty their bowels, devour their cabbage and boiled potatoes, and recite their Hail Marys.

"But you ain't heard the last of Denis Kearney," he says, backing away.

"And I have two words for you, Kearney. Tauri excrementum."

Bierce locks the door to the Mint and carries the hapless Chinese to a basement cot. It's there Bierce gets a look at the man he's saved. And recognizes him.

"Ah Wee?"

"You save my life, sir. Thank you, sir."

"What were you doing so far from Dunphy's?"

"Sir, Mr. Dunphy gives me a package to deliver to a man on Mission Street. On my way back I become lost. A group of men coming out of a saloon begin to chase me. Last week, a Chinese crab fisherman was attacked. Red pepper was thrown into his eyes. He was beaten with hickory clubs and branded with hot irons. And then his ears and his tongue were slit. I run and hide and you saved me." Ah Wee's eyes glisten in the lantern light.

"There's a little stove upstairs, Ah Wee. I'll make some tea."

When he returns, he sees Ah Wee squatting over the chamber pot in the corner and hears the stream of urine against the porcelain.

Ah Wee pulls up his pants and runs back to the cot in little steps.

Bierce clears his throat. "Ah Wee, men don't usually . . ."

"Sir?"

"Squat. Unless . . ."

"Sir?"

"Ah Wee, you're not a man."

She covers her face with her hands. Bierce grabs her shoulders.

"Ah Wee, tell me why you're disguised as man, how you got here." He shakes her. "Tell me, Ah Wee."

She takes a deep breath. "Sir, I came to America on a big boat when my husband was sixteen and I was twelve. He came to America to work on the railroad, but they do not allow women, so I cut my hair like a boy. I dress like a boy. When we get to San Francisco my stomach is very round. My husband must go and work on the railroad and he leaves me in a stable and covers me with straw and says he hopes I will be better. I know I will never see him again. He gives me the only precious thing he has. It is a Chinese box that looks as if it was made from gold. I am in pain and I know I am about to have a child. I can still hear myself screaming because of the hurt. That is all I remember until I open my eyes and see Mr. Dunphy's face. I am in his stable. He gives me water and puts bread in my mouth and he buries the baby. He takes my magic box and lets me live with him. He teaches me to speak your language and I help him when he shakes and is sick. Mr. Dunphy does not tell anyone I am a girl because he needs me so much, and because Chinese women are not allowed in this country unless they were here before the law was passed. I do not like Mr. Dunphy very much, but I have no choice. He saved my life."

Bierce lets Ah Wee sleep until dawn. When he returns to wake her he looks at her childlike face, her fine features. She's beautiful. Her eyes open and stare into his. She pulls his face down to hers. Her mouth reaches his.

Ah Wee. What will happen to her in the merciful state of California will be far worse even than the depredations against the Chinese in Mexico, another blot on the rectitude of the land of Bierce's birth. Thinking about it delivers him into a downward emotional spiral. Pancho, however, is in fine spirits after his visit to the military prison at Santiago Tlatelolco. Feeling generous, he executed just two of the wardens who served at the prison before his escape, while a third jailer got off easy, merely suffering crushed knuckles of both hands. In the morning, famished and no longer at odds with his American friend, Villa and his entourage return to the Hotel Palacio expecting to find the young French woman with whom he's enamored. Instead, an older, darker, plainer woman is at the cash register.

Villa says, "Where is Madame Yvette? And who are you, señora?"

"Madame Yvette is not working today, and I am the proprietress of this hotel."

"You are also French?"

"*Oui, monsieur.*"

"I think you have hidden Madame Yvette, and I believe you have done so to ridicule me. It is insulting to a man celebrated as the Centaur of the North."

"Señor General, I would never insult a guest in my own hotel."

Villa is red-faced, but he stalks to a table and collapses heavily into a seat. He begins to mutter under his breath.

Bierce says, "What do you feel like ordering for breakfast, General?"

More muttering.

"How about an omelet? I also see on the menu they're serving jalapeño corn cakes and *machaca con huevos.*"

Pancho says, "They're whispering, laughing at me."

"Who, General?"

"All of them. The customers, the waiters, the busboys, the woman who runs this place. They've made me a laughingstock."

"General, I think you may be—"

"I'll show them." He rises so abruptly his chair slams to the floor. "Come on, boys," he tells his officers.

They march to the cashier's counter, where Villa says to the proprietress, "Señora, since I cannot have Madame Yvette then I'll take you. Grab her, boys."

They carry the screaming struggling woman outside to Villa's Packard and drive her to the house on Liverpool Street, where she's locked into a room. In less than an hour the news is out. The abduction makes all the newspapers, except for *Viva Nueva,* Pancho's own publication, which publishes pretty much only what he wants.

That evening, Bierce and Villa sit in the library drinking tequila.

Pancho says, "Look at all those books I will never read."

"Reading's overrated, General. In my country it usually consists of Indiana novels, short stories in dialect, and humor in slang."

Villa becomes pensive and stares into space.

"You seem subdued, my friend. I think I know why."

"What could I have done? They say I kidnapped that woman to satisfy my desires, but I did not. It was only because she laughed at me. A man I would have shot. She wasn't the one I wanted anyway, but Madame Yvette. The Minister of France came to see me. So did the Minister of Brazil, representing your President Wilson. They demanded I release her. They accused me of bringing her to this house to dishonor her. It's now an international incident. I've been slandered. *Compadre,* do you think I dishonored this woman merely by detaining her in one of my bedrooms? What can I say in my own defense?"

"You're a man experienced in the art of war, so you're in the habit of command. If you don't know what to do, what could I say that would help you resolve this dilemma?"

Pancho thinks for a moment. "Ah, but you have. You have told me, in effect, I cannot free myself from the slander. Therefore, I cannot allow her to remain in Mexico as living evidence that I, Francisco Villa, did violence to a woman I had no desire for. *Amigo,* I want you to go to the woman and tell her to vacate Mexico immediately on my orders. Tell her it is her punishment for ridiculing me."

"If you insist, General, but what about the hotel she owns?"

"I'll buy her damned hotel. You'll receive two hundred thousand pesos to make the transaction, and I want you to do it tomorrow. When men fall into the hands of a woman, they must either silence her or appease her with money. Anyway, the proprietress was not so good in bed. I still want Madame Yvette."

Chapter Ten

War is waiting and Pancho is tired of waiting. But before leaving Mexico City to whack Obregón he decides to indulge his Americano pal one final day. The gringo has somehow gotten it into his loco brain to climb the Pyramid of the Sun in Teotihuacán. They motor to the ancient ruins in Villa's Packard, Pancho behind the wheel, a retinue of bodyguards and officers following behind. The road is lined with clusters of impossibly poor shacks made of tarpaper and corrugated tin in which live Mexico's most impoverished, those who fled the farms, ranchos, haciendas, and revolution to find work in the big city—only to learn there was no work. Villa, tired of hitting the auto's horn when he encounters flocks of chickens pecking in the roadway, drives the Packard directly into them, raising squawks and feathers.

Pancho loves it. "*¡Caramba!* So much easier to kill chickens than men. I should always have it this soft."

Bierce, who long ago made sketches of aboriginal markings on caves and rocks as he traveled across Indian territory in the American West with Hazen, is fascinated by the pre-Columbian culture of the Americas. While Pancho is up to no good playing politics with his revolutionary chums, Bierce spends hours in the *Museo Nacional de Antropología* studying the artifacts left behind by the Aztecs, Olmecs, Tulas, and Toltecs. Although he revels at the thirty-ton Aztec calendar stone, he is particularly fascinated by the small items: kitchen pots and utensils, knives with sinister faces and stone inlays, incense burners with bizarre carvings. They tell you the most, he thinks, about people and the way we were then and are now.

Over the roar of the Packard's motor, Bierce says, "General, the name Teotihuacán. What does it mean in English?"

"City of the Gods, *compadre*. But don't ask me no more, on account of I ain't never been there before." Indeed, Villa has never even seen the vast oceans that frame Mexico to the east and west. The only place he's ever visited outside of Mexico is El Paso, Texas.

Bierce opens his Baedeker. "General, two centuries before the birth of Christ, Teotihuacán is the biggest city in the Western Hemisphere, perhaps one of the largest cities in the world, with a population estimated at one hundred twenty-five thousand. Then, mysteriously, it all collapses. Despite the excavations, surveys, and studies, the mystery of the vanishing city remains unsolved, although it's thought to have been built by the elusive Toltecs."

The place, an abandoned ruin and an archeologist's dream, bakes under the Mexican sun as Pancho's caravan enters the Avenue of the Dead. Among the ruins are two great pyramids, the largest the Pyramid of the Sun, which looks to have sheer sides, but as they approach, it's apparent rows of steps lead to the top. It's as high as a twelve-story building.

Villa brakes the car.

"You really want to climb that thing in all this heat?"

"Climb with me, General. The story of Mexico is hidden on the steps leading to the summit."

"You're one nutty old gringo. *Sí,* I drove you all this way to indulge your whims, but I got a war I got to get back to. Me, I'll stay in the car with a gallon of iced tea. By the way, you ain't dressed so well for climbing, in that suit and tie, and your shoes ... You'll die of a heart attack before you reach the top, you old *pedo.*"

"I'll be all right, General. Everyone in Mexico climbs the Pyramid of the Sun at least once."

"Sometimes you talk like a *baboso*—how you say?—idiot."

"I may, indeed, be a idiot. When I was a young man, I wrote a column of opinion in a lowly San Francisco weekly. Called myself the Town Crier. In it, I summed up the intelligence of my nation and divided it by the number of inhabitants. The quotient represented the intelligence of the average man. I discovered it was greater than that of a soft-shelled crab, but considerably less than that of a hippopotamus."

"And what is this, hippo ... hippo ... Never mind. I don't want to know. It's funny anyway."

Quetzalcóatl. Feathered serpent, god of air and water and of the ripples caused by the wind on the surface of a lake. It was to Quetzalcóatl that this edifice was dedicated. So goes the legend. If Bierce were Quetzalcóatl he'd soar and glide from the tallest peak. But he doesn't believe in gods or God or much else. The steps at the base of the pyramid are high and broad, and hard to climb. Then they narrow and the ascent becomes easier. He looks back and counts the steps he's climbed. He'll count each one from now on until he gets to the top.

Twelve, thirteen, fourteen.

Occasionally, when he takes a step, his shoe slips. Solid American leather, but not climbing shoes. The perspiration soaking his shirt starts to saturate his dark wool suit. Sweat trickles into his eyes. Stupid, he thinks, to have worn a suit in this heat. Several young Mexican men dart quickly down from the top, laughing and shouting in Spanish, sometimes taking the steps in twos. They seem to have limitless energy and boundless courage. Bierce is already beginning to breathe heavily.

Sixty, sixty-one, sixty-two.

His legs feel like anchors.

Seventy, seventy-one, seventy-two.

Higher and higher. He turns and sees below him Villa sitting in the Packard and waves. He begins to feel giddy. Perhaps he should keep facing the pyramid and not look out. What if he becomes too dizzy to stand and falls backward, tumbling down the side? There are no hand-rails to cling to.

One hundred twenty-five, one hundred twenty-six, one hundred twenty-seven.

He passes a smiling, toothless old woman who is slowly making the trek downward. Then a young boy in a sombrero passes him, whistling. It's a high-pitched, single note whistle, not a melody. As he nears the summit the steps again become tall and thick and he has to climb them almost like a ladder. The final step is the two hundred and forty-eighth. He pulls himself over it and squats at the top, panting like a dog, the sun pounding down. At the least he should have worn his hat. His suit is drenched by perspiration. He isn't particularly good at figures, but he estimates the flat stone crest of the pyramid to be forty, perhaps fifty, square feet in diameter. There are just two other people at the top, a young Indian woman in a dress patterned with red and green flowers and the baby she holds in her arms.

The sky is a deep blue, backdrop for a series of serrated, waxen clouds. A steady breeze is hot and fails to cool him. The Pyramid of the Moon lies to the east, its peak not quite as high as the edifice on which he stands. To the southwest he observes the low buildings of

Mexico City, faint in the haze. The stark, treeless landscape below stretches for miles before vanishing. Toltecs built the giant monument to honor their gods and to dispatch their sacrifices. How many thousands of victims were given to the gods at this very spot? He sees the Temple of Quetzalcóatl below him. When Quetzalcóatl returned to his home across the sea, as legend has it, the Toltec civilization fell.

Head aches. In the sun too long. Dehydrated. Needs water. He stands at the edge and gazes down. It appears to be a linear plunge and the first step looms large. He's sure he'll not be able to climb down by facing forward, so he'll have to descend backward like a painter on a ladder. But what if he slips in his hard-heeled shoes and plummets two hundred and forty-eight steps? He sees himself lying at the base, covered with blood. His stomach ripples at the thought, the way it does in his sleep when he has nightmares of a snow-white horse talking to him in a hideous language unknown. He, a man unafraid to charge directly into a Confederate battery, is now fearful of taking that first step down because the Damned Thing might grasp him. He's trapped under the sun. All of a sudden he feels isolated, alone in the world. Once he loved and was loved, and had more to wish for than a disconsolate death in Mexico. Once he had loved Mollie, and in print he let all San Francisco know. Oh, yes, those early days. So merry, so impassioned, so heady. Harte, Coolbrith, Twain, Miller. He knew them all.

He breaks into Bret Harte's *Californian* with a poem called "Basilica." Eighteen-sixty-seven. In succession he publishes stories and verse in the *Golden Era*, the *News-Letter,* and the *Overland.* Becomes a fixture in the close San Francisco literary community. Harte, at one of their Sunday breakfasts, notices that Bierce seems to have a breathing problem and asks if it might be a touch of consumption caused by sleeping in a graveyard.

Bierce denies it. "It's true, however, I do sleep in marble orchards, especially on bleak, damp nights, after many glasses of stout. While it's not wise to mix one's biers, there's nothing more coldly satisfying than reclining on the slab of a sepulcher and sleeping the sleep of the dead."

Harte says, "And with an empty skull as an ashtray."

Bret's a man whose sartorial impulses are more profound than his writing, as if a good suit compensates for a bad sentence. Typically, he wears a green outfit with wide lapels, a yellow velvet vest punctuated at the bottom by a chain linked to gold watch, a high white collar, and a blood red tie. His leather gloves are usually folded and tucked into a back pocket. His bank account is ordinarily empty, but his wardrobe is inevitably full. Bret's closest confidante is a poet named Ina Coolbrith, a pretty, no-nonsense brunette, who advances the notion that a versifier's name must have a romantic ring.

Bierce asks, "And my name, Ina, do you consider it romantic?"

"Ambrose Bierce," she says. "Hmmm. The name is somewhat romantic but dark. With you I feel as though I'm alone in a maze where all is black and I must grope to find the light."

Ina is a librarian in Oakland. Once she was Josephine Donna Smith, the first white kid to be led across the Sierras into California. Her guide was a tobacco-chawin' half-breed named Jim Beckwourth.

Bierce writes a column of cheerful invective called "The Town Crier" in the *News-Letter*, and is in the office when a visitor arrives asking for the publisher. Mr. Marriott is away, attempting to lure suckers into investing in the Aerial Steam Navigation Company, formed to create an aeroplane powered by steam. He calls it the Flying Aviator. Bierce knows it will never get off the ground because it's not possible to fly in a machine that's heavier than air. And that's a damned fact.

"You are Mark Twain?"

The visitor's lean with red hair and a mustache that curls on either side of his mouth.

"My god," Bierce says.

"Not quite, young man, although I have aspirations. I'm here to repay your Mr. Marriott the twenty-five dollars he lent me the other night at the Lick House. I always pay my debts, of which I have considerable."

"You may leave the money with me, Mr. Twain, and let me offer you . . ."

Bierce hauls out a bottle and two glasses.

"You may, young man. For my toothache."

"You're in pain, sir?"

"I consume whiskey as a preventative to toothache. I've never had a toothache and I never intend to have one.

"I admire your stories. The one about the jumping hog . . ."

"Frog. I too admire a good story, which is why I have to write 'em myself. I once had but two ambitions. First to be a riverboat pilot, second a preacher of the gospel. As I failed at both I had no other choice but to become a writer."

They hear from outside the cranking of a hurdy-gurdy, the creaking of wagon wheels on cobblestone, the clopping of hooves, the shouts of vendors, the cries of the children, and from the Bay the whistle of a steamer. Bierce, eager, refills Twain's glass. Twain is all but a celebrity in these here parts.

"Are you in San Francisco to stay, Mr. Twain?"

"Returning to New York tomorrow. This visit has been a grind. Bret Harte helped me polish a book about my travels. *The Innocents Abroad*. He told me exactly what passages, paragraphs, and chapters to leave out. I follow orders strictly. Harte is a year younger than I, but he seems twenty years older. And he's certainly better dressed. By the way, has he ever borrowed money from you?"

"Well . . ."

"Don't expect to see it again. Sometimes I think the only function of Harte's heart is merely that of a pump." Twain polishes off his whiskey, stands, counts off a number of bills, and hands them to Bierce. "Young man, kindly pass on this wad to your employer. And remember, when all the fools in the world die, god knows how lonely you and I will be."

Noting that to forgive is to err, to be human is divine, the Town Crier spares no sensibility in his column, male or female, Republican or Democrat, Christian or heathen. He is "fond of dunces of all grades and descriptions, villains of every size, shape and hue, thieves and imposters, and all unpleasant people generally. He trusts this statement will be accepted as a refutation of the rumor he might leave San Francisco. He likes society here, and thinks he'll damned well stay." TC does not hope to understand the sublime mysteries of the feminine soul. "He knows the female of his species is comely and vivacious, innocent, pure, holy—and that she will lie like Satan to get her ends. But she is very nice to kiss when you have nothing else to do." *He writes of a girl named Mollie. So cutesy a name.* TC notes that a court has ruled that the word "blackguard" is not libelous if applied to an editor. "It has been so often applied to the Town Crier that he esteems it a term of endearment, and does not see how he could get along without it." For the study of the good and bad in woman, two women are a needless expense, he claims. *Mollie, do not think of me as too harsh, for I only tell the truth.* He examines the preachers of San Francisco with an entomologist's eye. "Rally round the cross, O leather-lunged elect, for the recognition of Christianity, and its relentless enforcement by law! Let us jam our holy religion down the protesting throats of the heathen and the infidel, so that they shall be brought to know God, and to love him as we do; yea, that they may hanker after him, even as a baby craveth rhubarb, or a cat lusteth after soft soap." *He begs Mollie to save him from the masked ball because he can't hide behind a face that's not his own.* "On the walls of San Quentin State Prison, the one at Folsom and the lunatic asylums at Stockton and Napa, the following lines are set in letters of gold: Here lies the body of the Republican party / Corrupt and, generally speaking, hearty." When a thief tries to break into the safe in the office of the city treasurer, TC says, "This is rushing matters; the impatient scoundrel ought to try his hand at being a Supervisor first because the transition is natural and easy." He begins a lifelong crusade against the politician, all of 'em. "I hold that under our political system it is very rarely a man of brains, honor and good manners who gets into public life. In most instances a man who holds public office is a rogue, a vulgarian or an ignoramus; commonly he's all three." *Mollie, ride with me on the ferry to Sausalito so the west winds might blow salt into our hair.* The cruelty of the Christian to the Chinese knows no boundaries, he asserts, after a local newspaper asks when such lawless outrages will end. "I shall tell you. Whenever a perspiring pig shall decline to encase himself in mud; whenever a mad dog shall submit to the presence of a succulent rabbit; whenever a skunk shall become an agreeable footstool; whenever 'civilization' shall imply decency; whenever the Christian religion may be professed by a gentleman without a broad blush." He alerts San Francisco to the pending arrival of some visiting poet from Oregon, Joaquin Miller, and that, as a courtesy, TC will be there to greet him. "There are three hundred and sixty-five days in the year and the Sultan of Tangier has three hundred and sixty-four wives. On the odd day he goes fishing." *Mollie, dearest, walk down the aisle with me.*

The sanguine Oregonian steps off the steamer onto on the Broadway Wharf. Poetic hair falls to his shoulders under a red sombrero, a mustache flows around his lips. He wears a white linen duster over tight blue denim pants. Beaded moccasins are on his feet. "Joaquin Miller has arrived!" he announces. Toting a carpetbag in one hand and a bedroll in the other, the Byron of the Rockies, Poet of the Sierras, mounts the dock, as a yellow bear dances to "The Blue Danube" fluted by a bearded gypsy. The bear is enormous, sullen. Tongue protruding, the brute performs an ungainly somersault, which prompts an outburst of applause from the rabble on the wharf: sailors in pressed uniforms, Irish punks up to no good, Mexican women selling *frijoles* wrapped in tortillas, scruffy teamsters wearing red suspenders, Chinese men darting like birds through the crowd, black men with no place to go, beggars on crutches, fancy women with parasols, and perverts hoping to meet the eyes of others like themselves. The bear squats on his haunches to rest while he devours an apple the old gypsy thrust into the beast's mouth, which proves to be toothless. The gypsy oscillates among the crowd, hand and hat outstretched, soliciting coins. Endowments exhausted, the gypsy flips the cap to his head and starts to lead the bear from the dock. The beast balks, goes down on all fours, and takes a prodigious dump, an accomplishment even more impressive than his somersault. The enormous pile of fresh, shimmering waste on a pier crowded with people has the effect of clearing a circle fifty feet in circumference.

"By Jupiter," Miller says, circumventing the bear's turds, and shaking hands with Bierce, "a poet such as myself will find inspiration even in a dung-dancing bear. To wit. 'Oh! For the skies of rolling blue, / The balmy hours when lovers woo, / The dreamy call of the cockatoo . . .'"

"Did I hear you correctly, Miller, that you actually claim to be a poet?"

"Indeed, and there's more where that came from. Inspiration's derived from many sources, sir, among them fermented libations, so kindly lead the way to the nearest doggery."

Finally, the Town Crier confesses he's ill, that he needs careful nursing and medicine, that he requires someone to sit up with him, that his nights are feverish, that he craves crushed rhubarb with a woman on the other end of the spoon. He reveals that he's twenty-eight years old, robustly constructed, decent in appearance, and a bachelor, a man whom women are still sampling. He writes that he knows just the applicant for his needs and her name is Mollie. *Be of good faith, Mollie, for the cherry blossoms are beautiful in San Raphael and the seashells sing only to you.* At last, he discloses that San Francisco's most eligible bachelor is about to lose his eligibility.

Mary Ellen Day—Mollie—is the daughter of Holland Hines Day, a mining engineer who struck it rich, and who affects the title of captain after leading a skirmish against a pathetic band of redskins. On his wedding day, Bierce stands in the parlor of the Days' home on Vallejo Street, anxiously waiting for the guests to arrive.

"My boy," Captain Day says, "I've been reading your new column, the one with all those, those, what do you call them?"

"Dots and dashes, sir. I've named the column 'Telegraphic Dottings.'"

"Ingenious."

"Not unlike Morse code. That way I'm able to compile my view of the week's events in a succinct manner."

"But don't you think some of your dottings are a little, well, harsh? The one about President Grant, for example."

"About Grant's putting the wrong end of a cigar in his mouth and not being able to speak for a week?"

"Exactly." Captain Day slaps Bierce on the back. "My boy, you've got fortitude." He speaks into Bierce's ear. "I was going to tell you after the ceremony, but I can't wait. As a wedding gift from Mrs. Day and myself we're sending you and Mollie to London."

"I'm overwhelmed, sir."

"It means interrupting your career at the *News-Letter*."

"Writing is a craft that can be accomplished anywhere. And what better locale than London?"

"When you get there, don't be too hard on 'em."

"That, sir, I cannot guarantee."

Captain Day laughs. "My boy, the wedding guests are about to arrive. Perhaps you might go upstairs and hurry along my wife and your bride."

He's about to knock on Mollie's door when he notices it's ajar, and peeking through the opening he sees his future mother-in-law and his wife-to-be talking inside.

"It's not too late, my dear," Mrs. Day laments to her daughter even as the music of "Oh Promise Me" drifts upstairs from the piano in the parlor.

"Don't be ridiculous, Mother."

Mollie sits before the mirror at her dressing table. With a cameo brush her mother smooths her daughter's dark blond hair in long, even strokes.

"What do we really know about this young man?"

"Mother, we know he's handsome, he's witty, he's brave."

"He's just a writer on some awful newsletter."

"He's the editor."

"Mr. Bierce has upset all San Francisco."

"He's intrigued all San Francisco, Mother, and he intrigues me."

"Being intrigued by a man is hardly grounds for marriage."

"I also love him."

"You're barely twenty. You've just met him."

"I've known Ambrose for two years."

"He drinks."

"Everyone drinks, Mother, including Father with his whiskey and you with your sherry."

"He's an atheist."

"He's fair, moral, and honest."

"And no church wedding."

"He's asked the Reverend Stebbins to perform the ceremony."

"The Reverend Stebbins is a Unitarian. Besides, it's common knowledge Mr. Bierce sleeps on tombstones."

"Nonsense, Mother. He only did it once when the hour was late and he lost his way."

"And he collects human skulls."

"Really . . . Where do these rumors begin?"

"He carries a gun."

"Newspaper work is sometimes dangerous, Mother."

"Your young man attacks in print the best people in San Francisco."

"If they were the best Ambrose wouldn't attack them."

"The company he keeps. Bohemians."

"Writers, Mother. Poets. People of artistic temperament."

"And the thought of the two of you planning to live in that dreadful little cottage he rents in San Rafael."

"It's beautiful there, Mother. How the roses climb through the picket fence."

"Staying in a resort cottage in the winter."

"The climate is better for Ambrose's asthma."

"That's another thing, his health."

"It's the fog and dampness in San Francisco, Mother. When you get right down to it, this is not a pleasant place in which to live."

The wedding party, by design, is small. A few of the Days' friends and several of Bierce's. Brother Grizzly is best man. Albert, now settled in Oakland, is working at the Mint. The Reverend Stebbins stands before the marble fireplace in which crackles a blaze. Above the mantel, a mirror, overwhelmed by gilt, looks back at the guests who sit in chairs arranged in neat rows, separated by an aisle in the center. Ambrose, tall and erect and garbed in black, stands next to the clergyman. The pianist pounds out the wedding march from Wagner. From the rear of the room Captain Holland Hines Day advances up the aisle, daughter on his arm.

"Dearly beloved . . ."

Suddenly there's a brouhaha at the front hall, an exchange of words, the thumping of boots, and into the parlor storms a man wearing a sombrero with tassels around the rim, black leather knee boots on which spurs are attached, and a flowing white coat.

"Got here as fast as I could," says the intruder.

Mrs. Day rises at her seat. "Who is this, this man?"

Bierce says, "Captain Day, Mrs. Day, may I introduce a friend of mine. Joaquin Miller, the poet, formerly known as Cincinnatus Hiner Miller."

The Poet of the Sierras and the Byron of the Rockies embraces Ambrose and Mollie. "My children."

Bierce says, "I thought you were in London, Miller."

"My steamer docked not thirty minutes ago. I learned immediately that Almighty God Bierce was about to get hitched, so I high-tailed it right here without even stopping for a call of nature." Joaquin addresses the wedding guests. "My friends, in Scotland and England I met the poor and the meek, the rich and the famous. Before Burns's grave I paused for a silent devotion. I recited an ode as I stood before Scott's tomb. Byron heard my words as I knelt by his resting place in Nottingham." Joaquin recites a poem about the fire and the blood of youth. "I walked from Glasgow to London. In Westminster Abbey I prayed for the immortal bards who are buried there. Now I pray for this happy couple." Miller's prayer turns into a verse, something about the earth being an oyster and love being a pearl. Before he can be stopped he recites another poem, this one about sorrow, pain, virtue, and triumph.

"Joaquin, you seem to have a verse for every occasion," Bierce says.

"Every occasion calls for a verse," Miller says. "As I walk this mighty land my message is the love of beauty. The flight of a bird gracefully whirling through the air; the tint of a single autumn leaf; the voice of the wind in the forest; a rolling river between its leaning bank of trees; the curled moon in the heavens; the still, far stars; excrement at the side the road. Oh, if you don't love these things, I pity you. Yes, the greatest happiness is to be found in the love of the beautiful."

Mrs. Day says, "This is too much. Today's my daughter's wedding day and this, this man is standing here screaming about tombs and dead poets and birds and moons and excrement."

Miller recites a poem about love and kisses. Tears come to his eyes. "On with the ceremony, my children, and then lead the way to the bar. I'm in sore need of a tankard of hooch."

Mrs. Day elbows her husband. "Didn't I tell you about those Bohemians? And why is that man wearing spurs in my home?"

Bierce and his bride honeymoon in San Raphael. He loves her, as well as he can love anyone. In his final column, he claims his only aptitude is a knack at hating hypocrisy, cant, and sham. He advises his readers to be as decent as they can, not to believe without evidence, to treat things divine with marked respect but not to have anything to do with them, not to trust humanity without collateral security, to cultivate a taste for distasteful truths, and above all to try to see things as they are, not as they ought to be. That done, he pronounces that the Town Crier has not cried in vain. Then he and Mollie are off to London.

So long ago it was, so young he was. And so far away from Mexico.

At the Pyramid of the Sun, Bierce hears the sobbing of the young Indian woman who shares the summit with him. Shaking, she holds her baby tightly to her breast. He understands. She too is in horror at the thought of climbing down the steep face of the pyramid with a child in her arms. It seemed so much easier going up. Fearful she and her child will fall to their deaths, she, like Bierce, are prisoners on this thirsty crown. Without thinking, he reaches out his arms to the young woman.

"Down," he says. "I'll take the baby down. *Abajo.*" His Spanish is poor. *"Muchacha."* Maybe the child is a girl. He can't tell.

The woman thrusts her child at him.

"Gracias," she says.

The infant, probably not more than six months old, is wrapped in a cotton blanket. With one arm Bierce holds the child to his chest. With his other hand he grips the top step and lowers himself down. The young woman, still frightened, but no longer encumbered by her baby, follows tentatively. Stupid, stupid, he thinks. He's old, old for the time. No longer as spry. If he slips and falls then the baby falls as well. The brown-faced infant is asleep, its eyes peacefully shut. Backward down the steps they go. Don't look out, don't look sideways, just look up, he thinks. Perhaps Quetzalcóatl is surrounding them, protecting the air and the water and himself and the young woman and her baby.

Two hundred twenty-four, two hundred twenty-three, two hundred twenty-two.

Down.

Directly above him he sees the young woman's sandaled bare feet with their surprisingly clean nails. If she slips she might roll into him and the baby and they'll all plunge.

One hundred seventy, one hundred sixty-nine, one hundred sixty-eight.

The baby begins to weigh in his arm. Don't think about it. Think about something else. At Chapultepec Castle, the uniformed figure of a guard stood so still and stiff he might have been a statue. Probably was a statue. Bierce wanted to reach out and with a single finger touch the man to make sure, but he was afraid to do so.

One hundred-forty, one hundred-thirty-nine, one hundred-thirty-eight.

He and Pancho floating on a flat-bottomed boat at Xochimilco, surrounded by blazing flowers and mariachi music. He almost let his hand drop into the water of the canal but pulled it back sharply when he saw the headless corpse of a man floating just under the surface.

One hundred-twenty-four, one hundred-twenty-three, one hundred-twenty-two.

At the halfway mark he knows they're going to make it. Sweat trickles from every pore, salt burns his eyes. It's self-induced torture—unlike the bulls he saw tortured at the Sunday bullfights at the Plaza de Toros. Pancho loved the spectacle and the gore, and shouted *"¡Ole!"* along with the crowd each time the bull made a pass at the matador. Bierce has no objection to an equal contest, but the bull's slaughter, preceded by its torment and mutilation, was arranged long before the hapless animal entered the ring.

Twenty-two, twenty-one, twenty.

When they reach the base of the pyramid and stand on the firm, dusty ground, Bierce returns the baby to its mother.

"Gracias, señor. ¡Muchas Gracias!"

She clutches her infant tightly, a woman with a round face, her black hair dangling below a red bandanna. Can she read or write? Does she have a husband? A church? A god? It's Mexico, for Christ's sake. She must have a god. Quetzalcoatl perhaps? Bierce's legs, which felt so heavy on the way up, now feel strangely light. Perhaps his knees might float. My god, he thinks, the trust the woman put into him, a stranger and a gringo.

Pancho tells him, "You're exhausted, you old fart. Come sit in the car. Have some tea. *Pinche pendeja.* I told you not to climb to the top. You might have killed yourself. If you want to commit suicide, you should wait and let me do it for you."

Chapter Eleven

Pancho Villa respects the significance of books although he doesn't read them. It's Bierce's responsibility to peruse and summarize most of what Villa wants read, and that includes a little book given to the Centaur of the North by General Hugh Scott, commander of the American forces along the southern border with Mexico. Scott, Villa, and their subalterns meet at the center of the international bridge connecting El Paso and Ciudad Juárez. The two generals exchange gifts in the cold. The Mexican presents Scott with a red, green, and yellow blanket hand-woven in Durango. The American gives the book to Villa, who hardly glances at it before passing it to Bierce, who, as usual, is mistaken for Villa's valet. Despite himself, Scott likes the Mexican chieftain, especially his laugh. It bothers Scott little that Pancho is crude, loud. It's what one would expect of an uneducated Indian who has battled authority all his life. Scott, who for over forty years has warred on Indians, Spaniards, Cubans, and Filipinos, also has his rough edges. Both men admire weapons, war, women, and winning. Revolutionary bloodshed in Mexico keeps spilling across the border. Fifty-three Americans have been killed recently by Mexican bullets and mortars in the Arizona town of Naco, and the United States wants Villa to bring the warring factions under control. Scott also raps Villa's knuckles about the wanton killing of prisoners of war. Despite Scott's rebuke, Pancho is flattered to be courted by the American. But the Mexican has more consequential thoughts. His mortal enemy, Alvaro Obregón, is preparing for him in the city of Celaya.

After the meeting on the bridge, Villa questions Bierce about Scott's gift, which Bierce had been instructed to read. The two are sitting in Villa's little red caboose, warmed by a pot-bellied stove.

"It's called *The Rules of War,* General, adopted at the Second International Peace Conference at The Hague in nineteen-seven."

"What is this Hague?"

"The capital of the Netherlands."

"You have been there?

"Unfortunately not, although I did enjoy a period of exile that took me to England for some years and, briefly, to France."

"And what is this book about, *compadre?* There are no rules in war."

"Ah, forty-four nations, including your own, signed the agreement."

"Mexico did *what?* It must have been the work of that damned *ordinario*—how you call it, whore—Porfirio Diaz! May he die in agonizing pain from cancer in whatever rat hole he has exiled himself to!"

"I understand he's living comfortably in Paris. It was Diaz who said of Mexico, 'So far from God, so close to the United States.' Something I might have uttered. General, Russia convened the conference, and all the signatories agreed on how to treat prisoners and noncombatants."

Villa's eyes narrow to slits. "I do not think I am going to like what you are about to tell me." He clomps his boots on the table before him and begins cleaning his fingernails with a hunting knife.

"Article Four states that it is forbidden to kill or wound an enemy who has surrendered or no longer has any means of defense."

"*¡Chingalo!* Fuck it!"

"It also says prisoners of war must be treated humanely, and that all their personal belongings, except arms, horses, and military papers, remain their property."

"*¡Chingalo!*"

"Article Five states that prisoners of war may be used in labor, but they must be paid at the same rate as the soldiers who captured them."

"*¡Chingalo! Pay* a prisoner of war? Dammit, this book was written as some sort of amusement, was it not?"

"I'm afraid not, General. Article Five goes on to say that prisoners may receive letters, money orders, and parcels by mail, and may enjoy complete liberty in the exercise of their religion."

"*¡Estoy hasta la madre!* Enough."

"There's more, General, but I fear you'll like it no better than what you've already heard."

"Give me that damned book!" Pancho snatches it from Bierce's hand, opens the gate to the pot-bellied stove, and throws the book into the wood fire. "There. I feel better now. What do you think about all that *caca* nonsense anyway?"

"The intentions are admirable, General, but it's non-enforceable. Look at the depredations my own nation committed in the Philippines during which the United States Army routinely massacred and tortured insurgents who liked us no better than they liked the Spanish. We liberally applied a fiendish little device known as waterboarding. There may come a day when our own White House takes advantage of a major crisis to violate both national and international law in the name of, say, national security or whatever the moron-in-charge decides to call it."

"You Americans are no better than us. If you had your way you'd erect a fifty-foot wall from Tijuana to Matamoros to keep us out."

"That will never happen, General. America has a checkered past, and no doubt the future will be just as checkered. However, the rules of war adopted at The Hague deal with warring nations, so I'm uncertain how applicable the rules are to internal revolutions, such as your own."

"Aha! I knew the rules didn't apply to Mexico, no matter what that bastard Diaz did."

"Nevertheless, I suspect you'd win much favor among the populace if you treated your prisoners humanely. Would it not be wiser, say, to give your prisoners a choice between execution and joining your army?"

"I've tried that—over Fierro's objections. A decent army is not made from reluctant men. Are you familiar with our term *ley fuga?*"

"I think not."

"A handy practice. It is when we shoot a prisoner in the back and then assert he was killed while trying to escape. It resolves every sort of legal issue." Villa slams shut the door to the stove in which *The Rules of War* is going up in smoke. "And now I am in need of some female companionship. You will join me at Madam Blanca's bordello? I understand she has a fresh shipment of women from Havana. Barely used, and many not even thirteen."

"Not tonight, General."

"Your cock must be shrinking in your old age. How are you spending the evening? Tequila as usual?"

"That and thoughts of the past. It's what old men do."

"And just what portion of your past do you favor?"

"Hmmm. London, perhaps. The London of eighteen seventy-two when I became an expatriate. It was an intoxicating time, despite the fogs that aggravated my asthma. There were days I could barely breathe."

He and Mollie move first into rooms at 19 Downshire Hill, Hampstead, where he pores over maps and street guides. He sees that the cities of London and Westminster fuse with the boroughs of Finsbury, Marylebone, Tower Hamlets, Hackney, Chelsea, Southwark, and Lambeth to form the greatest metropolis in the world. London is a maze of Walls, Ways, Pavements, Courts, Streets, Alleys, Lanes, Acres, Ovals, Crescents, and Circuses. Ignoring his pregnant bride, he plays tourist. Guide in hand, he visits Madame Tussaud's, the Royal Alhambra Theater in Leicester, the Grand Barbaric Ballet, the Moore and Burgess Minstrels at St. James Hall, the matches at Lord's Cricket Ground, the Royal Academy.

Tom Hood, son of the celebrated writer and poet, publishes Bierce's sketches in *Fun.* An American named James Mortimer publishes Bierce's new column, "The Passing Show," in *Figaro.* Bierce starts grinding out stuff in no fewer than five publications. He adopts a nom-de-plume. Dod Grile. Hood's pals drink at the bar in the Ludgate Hill Railway Station. Bierce joins the tippling circle, which includes George Augustus Sala of the *Daily Telegraph,* the lyricist W. S. Gilbert (sans Sullivan), William Black the novelist, and soldier-of-fortune Mayne Reid. Bierce, overcome with childhood memories, speaks of how he and his brother quarreled over Reid's books when they were boys. In turn, Reid tells Bierce of his friendship with Edgar Allan Poe. "Eddie had the saddest eyes I've ever seen," Reid says.

The mists and vapors of London invade Bierce's chest, tighten his breathing, constrict his muscles, and sting his eyes. He and Mollie flee to Bristol, where Mollie gives birth to a son, Day. They move to Bath, where the medicinal hot springs fail to perform their ancient miracles, and finally to a cottage in Leamington, Warwickshire. Their second boy, Leigh, is born in Leamington.

Mollie says, "Ambrose, why are you always rushing off to London? You know it's not good for your health. And the children . . . You never spend time with them."

"There's plenty of time for the children, my dear. They're so young now they don't recognize me for who or what I am. Day does nothing but babble and Leigh does little but cry. And, of course, there's my career to think about."

"And what about me?"

The younger Hood's home is in the London suburb of Penge, where after dinner he and Bierce drink and smoke and talk of ghosts and wait for the dawn. The log in the hearth turns white as it cracks and spits. Hood maintains the greatest threat to man are machines with the ability to think. Bierce advances the theory that man's greatest enemies are life and the fear of death.

"A machine is only wires and gears and cogs, Hood, controlled by man."

"Bierce, let me tell you what would happen if the situation reversed and the machine took control. I once visited a man named Moxon who lived in South Lambeth. When we heard a pounding sound in the adjoining room Moxon ran inside. There were loud noises, such as a struggle, and when Moxon returned his face was bleeding. He told me, laughing, he had a machine that had lost its temper. When he left to make tea, I looked into the room. What I saw was horrifying. At first I thought it was a man, his back to me, sitting before a chessboard. It was no more than five feet in height, with a growth of black hair topped with a crimson fez. It reached for a chess piece in a slow, uniform, mechanical movement, and I saw it wasn't human at all, but a machine, an automaton chess player wearing a wig. It had no face, but it did have eyes, four of them in two rows, lanterns that glowed red and yellow with anger and hate. I slammed the door and leaned against it. I tell you, Bierce, I was in mortal fear. The next morning I picked up the *Times* and read to my horror that Moxon had been murdered, his body hideously disfigured. The police claimed the killer was an escaped convict from the Horsemonger Lane Gaol who's still at large. But I know different. When they found Moxon's body, it was next to an overturned chess set, his throat in the clutches of the iron hands of the machine. The machine murdered him!"

Bierce chuckles. "The machine certainly took its chess seriously, Hood."

"You laugh, but some day, you'll turn on a single machine and it'll make calculations, pay bills, organize paragraphs, spell words, create drawings, play music, telegraph communication to others, act as a secretary, be a chess partner. Even talk."

"Hood, that's as much nonsense as believing man will one day fly in a contraption heavier than air or flip a switch and turn on a light.

But you've told an entertaining tale. Perhaps I'll turn it into a story some day."

"Moxon wasn't just murdered by a machine. Oh, that was part of it, but his death was engineered by the Damned Thing. I swear, Bierce, the Damned Thing, in whatever form, will follow us until the end."

"To hell with the Damned Thing. I'll go when I'm ready."

Later, Hood's warning forgotten, Bierce publishes his first book, *A Fiend's Delight,* which contains an explanatory note claiming the author was assisted by his scholarly friend Mr. Satan. Bierce holds the book in his hands and flips the pages. He turns it upside down and downside up. He rotates it in his fingers. He puts it against his nose and inhales, savoring the smell of paper and glue and thread. He places his lips to it as he might to a woman. He stands the book on a table and surveys it from across the room. He hefts it on his palm to feel its weight. It's a small book, thin, brittle, unlikely to outlast time. But it's his book, his first. Two other collections of tales follow, *Nuggets and Dust* and *Cobwebs from an Empty Skull.*

Tom Hood dies unexpectedly, the very day Mollie, again pregnant, announces she's returning with their children to San Francisco on the White Star Line from Liverpool. Alone now, Bierce stands on Blackfriars Bridge. He'd enjoyed a meal at the Pall Mall on Regent Street, Waterloo Place, where he consumed more brandies than he could count, and where he easily put thoughts of both Mollie and Hood out of his mind. Staring into the inky water of the Thames, he sees—my God—Tom Hood looking up at him. "The Damned Thing, Bierce," Hood says, his voice echoing. "The Damned Thing got me and now it's coming for *you.*" Hood's image recedes into the murk, while Bierce in horror staggers to a place to vomit.

After Mark Twain invades London—where his book *Roughing It* is a smash and everyone's talking about his soon-to-be-published *The Gilded Age*—Bierce wangles an invitation to a banquet for the celebrated author at the Midland Grand Hotel. At the receiving line Bierce reintroduces himself as the San Franciscan who once conveyed Twain's twenty-five-dollar debt to Bierce's boss at the weekly *News-Letter.* "Ah yes, Mr. Bierce, I recall you as the young man who offered me a glass of whiskey as a preventative for toothache." Twain, not yet forty and in super health, consumes a quart and a half of rye a day with no outward ill effects, although he's discovered a new drink called an old fashioned.

"It's concocted of Scotch, lemon, crushed sugar, and Angostura bitters," Twain tells Bierce. "Old fashioneds taste so little like an alcoholic beverage I've taken to consuming them before breakfast, before dinner, and before bedtime."

They speak of such mutual friends as Joaquin Miller, Bret Harte, Prentice Mulford, and Charles Warren Stoddard, and Twain describes his newest project, a novel based on his boyhood in Missouri.

"The hero of my book is a young chap named Dick Sawyer, but I'm not quite satisfied with his first name."

Bierce says, "Mike, perhaps, or Bob."

"Hell, I'll think of something."

Twain inveigles Bierce to invest in "Mark Twain's Self-Pasting Scrapbook," patent pending. Bierce declines on the ground that he's broke, which is true.

The banquet's hosted by the Lord Mayor of London. Twain sits between Prime Minister William Ewart Gladstone and Poet Laureate Alfred, Lord Tennyson. A string quartet plays Liszt. The dinner begins with mock-turtle soup, fish in aspic cockaigne, roast leg of venison with sauce piquant, glazed endive with Beurre Manié, a hazelnut soufflé, and three types of wine. It ends with a verse by Tennyson—*Like glimpses of forgotten dreams*—and a rip-snortin' talk by Twain, who denies the English don't like to laugh. "They're just slower is all, and always catch up the next day or two."

After the speeches, Bierce is introduced to Gladstone, who picked up a copy of *A Fiend's Delight* at Kings Cross Station while on an odious journey to Balmoral Castle to call on the Queen. With the morbid excess of youth, Bierce writes of a decapitation by a mowing machine, of a child devoured by a dog, and of various murders and killings committed by mallets, pick handles, bootjacks, and shotguns.

"I trust the violence in my book isn't too intrusive for you, Mr. Prime Minister."

"Mr. Bierce, I find your various episodes of bloodshed *so* American."

Gladstone invites Bierce to 10 Downing Street. "I'd like you to meet my wife and to tell you about a curious mission we're on."

Gladstone's critics, led by Disraeli, portray him as stodgy, dull, and a pompous authoritarian. Bierce discovers otherwise. The prime minister waltzes and sings with the best of 'em. On a festive evening, Bierce sits in Gladstone's parlor and watches in amusement as the prime minister, his arm over Catherine Gladstone's shoulder, stands by the piano, man and wife swaying from side to side as they sing.

The prime minister has a preoccupation with prostitutes. So does his wife.

"We wish to save their souls," Gladstone says. "The police estimate there are ten thousand streetwalkers in London. I believe the figure to be much higher, perhaps one hundred thousand. It's not unusual for me—even after exhausting debate in the House of Commons—to slip away to the other side, the streets bounded by the Thames Embankment, Soho, and Piccadilly. I want nothing more than for them to accept my offer of money, food, shelter, and to hear me out. I tell them it's never too late to accept the Almighty and to find glory in the triumph of celestial redemption. You're a journalist and writer, Mr. Bierce. I propose that you join my mission to rescue fallen women as an observer. You'll see for yourself the sordid lives that must be changed. How promiscuity has condemned the souls to hell of so many poor women. And there's one particular young woman I *must* find."

So it is that Bierce and Gladstone venture into the darkness to stand near the Thames Embankment and wait. They hear on the cobblestones the occasional tap of heels. The slap of waves in the river. A foghorn. Someone laughs. A bottle breaks against a wall. The night twists around them. They smell piss in the corners and shit in the street.

"The police regularly patrol here, Mr. Bierce, should you be anxious."

"Which doesn't entirely encourage me, Mr. Gladstone."

"You must have Christian faith."

"For me, sir, that's impossible."

A woman approaches. "Hello, dearie," she mouths to Gladstone. "You want to have a little sport?" She might have appeared young if seen from a distance. Up close one could add thirty years. She notices Bierce, dressed in black and hardly visible. "Oh, two of you."

"Madam," Gladstone says, "I would much like to talk to you about your predicament."

"Predicament? Coo! I don't want to hear no sermon from some gong-farmer."

"In that case, madam, let me say I'm simply waiting here for a young woman."

"Just any kicksy-wicksy or someone in particular?"

"In particular, madam. Her name is Jenny."

"There's lots of Jennys walkin' this street."

"Perhaps you've seen her, madam. I—*we*—wish merely to talk to her."

"I'll bet you do, you gobslotch."

"I tell you sincerely I must find Jenny. Her last name is Domecy. Jennifer Domecy."

"I know what you and the other bloke is up to, Mr. Bum-balls. Two men. One woman. You'd like it at both ends. Some men just want a bloody spree."

"Madam, believe me. If you see Jenny, tell her an old friend wishes to see her."

"Bugger off, you old fart."

"A moment. Please accept this." He puts something into the woman's hand.

"You givin' me some French prints or somethin'?" He's a gentlemen all right, but there is lots of bleedin' perverts runnin' around and gentlemen could be perverts.

"A little money, madam. Enough to get you off the street tonight, give you a decent meal and a bath."

"And I don't have to do nothin'?"

"Nothing at all."

"Listen, mister." Her voice becomes a whisper. "If you'll just stand apart from that other gent, all you have to do is unbutton your front and take it out. Since I lost my front teeth my mouth is even better than my—"

"No, my dear . . ."

"I does it standin' up too."

"Please."

"You sure you ain't lookin' for a gap?"

"Madam . . ."

"You mean you ain't no sportsman? You're just givin' me the money? No strings?"

Gladstone clears his throat. "One small thing."

"Coo. I thought so."

"Your name. I'd like to write it down for my records. And if you have an address . . ."

"I ain't giving no bloke my name for no records."

"Perhaps I can help you some day."

"Bloody hell you can, Mr. Strut-fart. Nobody can help a woman who can't read and write, who can't find no job, who's got no place to live, and has no man to take care of her. I got this cough and I'm bleeding between my legs most of the time."

"There are . . . asylums that can assist women in your situation. And faith in a higher being will be your salvation. So if I knew your name . . ."

"I ain't givin' no names, you bloody rattlehead. Why don't you take your bald-headed hermit and screw it up your bum, you old tickle-pitcher. An arsehole is what you is."

She thrusts the bills into the private place between her breasts. Her head held high, she gathers her petticoats above her ankles and struts off. Out of sight, she breaks into a near run. She stops in the shadows, looks in either direction to make sure there are no spies, and counts the money. Bloody two pounds it is. No more work tonight. She knows of a safe place where she can drink a few pints and sleep warm and full next to the stove and not have to use her gash to pay for it. Then a ripple of guilt runs through her. Good old bloke, he is, quim-sticker or not. Gives me all that money and don't ask for nothin'. Shit, if the old cunny-hunter wants to find Jenny, what the hell. What's the whore-bitch to me? A rich, spoiled tart, that's what she is. Puttin' on airs. Thinkin' herself better than the rest because she's in a kip shop instead of streetwalkin'. You might think Jenny ain't no snatch-peddler at all. I'll go back to the old gent. Might be a few more quid in it. The woman retraces her steps.

"Say there, Mr. Dooflicker, you want to know where Jenny is at, do you? Cost you another two quid, it will."

Gladstone opens his wallet and counts off two more bills. The woman pushes the money into the slit in her bodice.

"Do you know of Maskelyne's?"

"I've heard of it, madam. The brothel on Milk Walk."

"That's where you'll find her, you old gully-raker."

The woman glides off again. Four bloody quid. That'll keep me in my cups for two nights or more.

Bierce says, "Mr. Prime Minister, about that woman. While I don't endorse her occupation, I must say she has a vocabulary that's vastly superior to my own."

Maskelyne's is a narrow brick building of three stories, identical to its neighbors on either side. Gladstone rings the bell. The door is opened by a woman wearing black. Her hair is parted in the middle and drawn back tightly. Her features are made even more severe by a nose that could serve as a hook.

"Gentlemen, may I help you?" She rubs her hands together.

Gladstone says. "Madam, we're here to see a certain young lady."

"A certain young lady, indeed, sir. We've several. Won't you please come in? I'm Mrs. Simmons. May I take your hats and walking sticks, gentlemen?"

They're led to a small parlor separated from the hall by a beaded curtain. A log burns feebly in the fireplace and the gas lamps on the wall are turned low.

"Would you gentlemens care for a spot of brandy?"

"That won't be necessary," Gladstone says. "If you could tell Jenny she has a caller . . ."

"Two callers, you mean. Jenny's one of our more popular girls. Excuse me while I inquire if she's available." Mrs. Simmons twirls her skirts and disappears through the curtain.

Bierce says, "Mr. Prime Minister, perhaps now you'll tell me why this Jenny is of such special interest to you."

"It's sad, Mr. Bierce, a particularly horrible case. Jenny is the daughter of one of my oldest friends, Lord Roscoe Domecy. I've known her since she was a child. She played at my knee. She always called me Uncle. She fell in with a bad crowd—gamblers and musicians and journalists and entertainers of the lowest sort. She ran away from home several times. Lord Domecy always took her back. She became, well, pregnant, if I may use the term. But she went off somewhere and took care of that. Lord Domecy placed her in a convent. She disappeared again. There were rumors. She was seen in public with certain loathsome men. In desperation, Lord Domecy turned to me to find and rehabilitate her."

Mrs. Simmons returns. "Gentlemen, may I present . . . Jenny."

The girl's tall, dressed in pale red, her skirts falling to her high-heeled boots. Her blond hair is swept high. Her features are childlike.

"Uncle William! What are you doing here? How did you find me?"

He takes her hand. "It's been a long, tiring search for you, Jenny."

She pulls her hand away. "And who is *that* man?" Jenny points at Bierce. "The police?"

"That's Mr. Bierce, my dear. An American. He helped me search for you."

"I wasn't lost, Uncle William. My life has changed."

"It's never too late to find salvation, my dear. I'm going to help you. I'm taking you away from here."

Mrs. Simmons moves between Gladstone and Jenny. "Say, what is this? You ain't got no business—"

"Stay out of it, madam. This is between Jenny and myself."

"Mister, this here's a private residence. You can't come in here and bother my girls."

"Jenny, collect your things. You're coming with me."

"No, Uncle William. I'm never returning to my father and mother."

"I'm taking you to Downing Street. Catherine is going to look after you while we—"

"I'm not going with you. Don't you understand, Uncle William? I have someone who's good to me, who treats me like a lady, like a woman."

"If you're talking about Mrs. Simmons . . ."

"I'm talking about a man named Muggsy."

"Nevertheless, Jenny, in good conscience I can't permit you to—"

Mrs. Simmons begins gesturing. "Permit? Who are you, my fine gentleman, to *permit* nothin'?"

"Come, Jenny." Gladstone takes her arm. She tries to pull away.

Mrs. Simmons runs to the doorway of the parlor and yanks on a bell. Then she shouts. "Muggsy, Earl! Get your arses downstairs!"

"Let's go, Mr. Bierce. We're taking the girl with us."

Gladstone pulls Jenny, screaming, into the hall with one hand while grabbing his hat and cane with the other. The girl is still shrieking when they reach the foyer.

"Let go of 'er!" Mrs. Simmons shouts as she follows the struggling pair. She clutches at Gladstone's arm.

"Stand back, madam," Bierce says, coming between the woman and the prime minister. He prods Mrs. Simmons in her midsection with his walking stick. Crying hysterically, Jenny is half pulled, half dragged into Milk Walk. But before they can reach the corner two men bound from the front door of Maskelyne's and run into the alley.

"Stop, you buggers," one of the men shouts.

"Keep going, Mr. Bierce," Gladstone says, hardly able to control the struggling girl.

Suddenly there's a shot, then another. Two flashes in the fog.

"They have a gun," Bierce says.

"Ignore them, Mr. Bierce. We've got right on our side."

"We can be right and we can be dead, Mr. Prime Minister."

Another flash. The bullet cracks against the cobblestones. Bierce opens his coat and removes the revolver from his waist. He points it between the shapes of the approaching men and pulls the trigger. The pair stop in their tracks. The man with the gun fires again. Bierce senses the bullet as it soars by his head. Bierce fires a second shot. There's a scream and the man with the gun goes down on one knee.

"Earl," the man moans, "the bloody bastard's got me in the leg."

Bierce fires again, aiming high. No further pursuit. He returns the Colt to his belt. He hears a window open, then another. "What the 'ell's goin' on down there?" a woman shouts. At the end of Milk Walk, Gladstone looks up and down the main street for a cab. Jenny ends her struggle and stands quiet, her shoulder against Gladstone's, strands of her blond hair falling over her face.

"That's better, Jenny. You'll see that—"

Suddenly she rakes her nails down both sides of Gladstone's face, severing the flesh in even rows. He screams in shock and pain.

"Muggsy, you shot my Muggsy," Jenny wails. "I heard him cry. Bastards you are. Both of you."

Gladstone puts his hands to his face, trying to staunch the flow of blood which oozes through his fingers. Jenny darts away but collides into Bierce, who grabs her arms.

She spits in his face. "Let me go you cunt-faced, bum-fucking, piece of shit!"

Startled by her vehemence and language as much by her spit, Bierce releases her. She runs back into the alley shouting Muggsy's name. Bierce removes his handkerchief and wipes away the spittle.

"My God," Gladstone moans. He sinks to his knees. Blood runs into his eyes.

"Mr. Prime Minister . . ."

"What have I done?"

"Let me get you to a doctor. Your face."

"Bierce, how did I fail?"

"You can't change the girl. It's hopeless."

"I must seek her out again."

Bierce clutches the prime minister's arm. "Sir, there's been shooting. The constables will come soon."

"I don't care."

"You have to think of your career."

"Hang my career."

"Then think of England."

Gladstone staggers to his feet. With the back of his hand he wipes the blood from his eyes. He stands erect. "No one must know about this, Mr. Bierce. No one. I'll be ruined. And England . . ." He takes Bierce by the arm. "Hurry, Mr. Bierce."

A cab stops for them. The barrel of Bierce's gun is still warm as Gladstone's body begins to shake. Tears stream from his eyes. He puts his fingers to his lacerated face. "I failed Jenny and I failed myself. This is an incident I'll regret all my life, Mr. Bierce."

"Mr. Prime Minister, regret is the sediment in the cup of life."

Bierce never mentions the incident to anyone, not even to his sometime friend Joaquin Miller, often described as America's greatest poet, who takes London by storm as the personification of the American West. Once in England, Miller consorts with the actress Lillie Langtry, whom he met at a lawn party at Lord Houghton's, a poet also known as Richard Monckton Milnes, said to have the greatest library of pornography in Europe. Bierce, barely trying to hide it, is envious of Miller's celebrity. One evening, after reading his verse to an audience of proper Victorians, Joaquin becomes so carried away that he rolls on the floor and snaps at the ankles of the ladies, insisting it's proper because he's nipping by the appropriate degree of rank. As a writer, Miller has his rough spots, notably spelling, punctuation, grammar, structure, dialogue, and narrative. Bierce, Miller, Stoddard, Mulford, and Twain meet for a riotous farewell dinner at the Whitefriars Club in Mitres Court, Fleet Street. Miller's about to depart for Italy. Bierce, planning to rejoin Mollie and the children, has already booked passage to New York on the *Adriatic*. At the dinner, Miller wears a huge bearskin rug over his shoulders with two Bowie knives stuck in his belt and spurs on his boots. Joaquin plunges his hand into an aquarium filled with goldfish. "Gentlemen, let me demonstrate how we eat fish in America." He grabs a goldfish by its tail and swallows it whole. It is, however, a small fish. Joaquin pulls out two cigars, puts both into his mouth like fangs, lights them with a kitchen match, and begins moving around, puffing like a locomotive.

Bierce smashes his fist on the table. "Dammit, Miller, you give all Americans a bad name with your buffoonery."

"You're bitter, Bierce," Joaquin says. "That's my name for you. Bitter Bierce."

"Miller, if this weren't a public place I'd thrash you here and now."

"The Almighty God Bierce has spoken," Miller says. "I shall take my leave. But before I go I have but one question to ask. Why did God make Ambrose Bierce?"

Even Bierce has no answer. Nor does he now in Mexico, about to accompany Pancho in what might prove to be a decisive battle. Celaya is a nondescript town known only for making candied fruits, delicacies so sickeningly sweet they turn the stomach after a few bites and leave an aftertaste that remains for hours. Most of Celaya's twenty-five thousand citizens have fled to stay with cousins who live anywhere but there. No one's quite sure which side is right or which side is winning. Skirmishes have already shown Pancho how Obregón has fortified the city's defenses, and Villa, furious, doesn't like what he's up against.

He paces in his railroad car, which has become untidy and in need of whitewash. A lurid poster of a dancer holding a fan provocatively over her derriere dangles from the wall. The picture's stained. Semen? Littering the table Villa uses as a desk are half-eaten pineapple, avocado, beef jerky, red beans, tortillas, and other former food too decomposed to identify. Candles have melted to lumps of lava. Dirty clothes are scattered on the floor. Bierce smells urine and notices one corner of the caboose is damp, below which is a puddle on the floor. Pancho's using it as a toilet. He stumbles over an empty tequila bottle, which then gyrates like a top.

"Are you all right, General?"

"Of course I am." He spits on the floor. Things have not been going well.

"You seem . . . tired."

"Damned right I'm tired."

"You need—"

"Let me tell you what I need. Obregón's head, that's what I need. And when I get it I'll hang it from the bell tower in Celaya. Then, I'll move west and take Jalisco." Villa puts his fingers to his chin and feels the stubble. He hasn't shaved for days. "I must send you on a mission."

"Certainly, General."

"I need to know exactly what fortifications Obregón has placed around Celaya. My army has been rebuffed and my scouts can't get near enough."

"What can I—"

"I want you to fly."

"As in an aeroplane?"

"I have brought my air force to the front. There's a gringo in charge. Señor Lester Barlow. You will report to Señor Barlow and follow his instructions. Then fly over Obregón's positions and get back to me."

Bierce pauses.

"What's the matter, *compadre?* You ain't going to fail me now?"

"It's just that, outside of floating in a balloon, I've never flown before."

"Now you will have your chance."

"You don't understand, General. For years, I maintained man could never fly, that the bird was the only entity heavier than air able to soar into space. I staked my reputation on it. And now . . ."

"And now, señor, you will—how do you put it?—eat your words."

Chapter Twelve

Their frames are made of spruce and ash, and covered with un-bleached linen stayed by piano wire. Despite their one hundred horse-power engines, the planes are so flimsy they must be staked to the ground to keep the wind from blowing them over. Pancho Villa's Tactical War Aeroplane Unit. Three Curtiss Jennies, two Wrights, and a Christofferson. The planes were trundled to Celaya by a locomotive protected by a Mexican artillery crew manning a cannon mounted on an armored flatcar. Bombs and ammo are stashed in a magazine car next to another coach serving as a machine shop. The pilots' headquarters are in a Pullman.

Bierce hears a distant thrum as soon as he dismounts from his horse. A young man squinting into the horizon squats along the rail spur.

Bierce says, "I'm looking for a Mr. Lester Barlow."

"You found him, mister."

Bierce's surprise is evident. Barlow can't be older than his mid-twenties.

"You were expectin' someone else?" Barlow says.

"You seem a bit young to be heading General Villa's air corps."

"Flying, like war, is a young man's calling, mister. Who might you be?"

"The name is, ah, Grile. General Villa sent me here to act as observer."

"Yeah, we were expecting you, Grile."

"I'm supposed to—"

"Quiet!"

Bierce hears a series of far-off pops. Rifle shots. Then he sees a biplane, a speck in the sky. As it comes closer the engine wheezes like an asthmatic.

"I think Fish is in trouble," Barlow says. "Damned cactus-assed greasers on the ground shoot at anything. Could have been Villa's men as easily as Obregón's."

"Fish?"

"Farnum Fish is one of my best pilots. Sent him up in a Wright on a test flight. We're experimenting with dropping bombs. Never been done from the air. Could be a whole new way of fighting—if we can figure out how to do it without blowin' ourselves up."

Two gringos, also hearing the plane's dilemma, dash from the Pullman to where Bierce and Barlow are standing.

"My other pilots," Barlow says. "Dean Lamb, Howard Rinehart."

The plane's motor continues to belch but then abruptly freezes, and the aircraft drops into a dive.

"Lost his engine," Barlow says.

Fish's Wright glides silently a few dozen feet from the ground until its wheels hit the dirt, lifting clouds of dust, then pirouettes to a precipitous halt. Barlow's men run to the plane and secure it from the wind. Fish lies in his seat moaning. Blood pouring from wounds in his shoulder and thigh, he is lifted from the cockpit.

Fish moans, "It was fucking Phil Rader that done it."

"Son of a bitch," Barlow says.

"Yeah, Rader. Still flying that Christofferson. Seemed to come from nowhere. Got me in the shoulder with a handgun. On the way back, ground fire hit the fuel line, and then I got it in the leg. Dammit to hell."

"Hell of landing though," Barlow says.

Fish says, "I'd go back up and get that bastard, but I'm finished with Mexico. Soon as I get healed, if I get healed, I'm going back to Los Angeles. Nobody ever gets shot in Los Angeles. If you guys know what's good for you, you'll leave too. Hey, I'm still losin' blood."

Lamb says, "Hell, I ain't gonna to leave. Not with Rader up there. I'm gonna knock that bastard out of the sky."

"Who is this Rader?" Bierce says.

Lamb says, "A damned mercenary fighting for the *federales*. First met him while we was barnstorming in Texas. Didn't like him then either. About a year ago I run into him over Naco. He's flying for Huerta, I'm flying for Carranza. I'm up about two thousand feet when he comes out of a cloud blasting at my plane with a handgun. I see his face—and his damned mustache—so I know in a second who it is. I return the fire and shoot until I run out of bullets. He keeps firing at me until he clips my fuel tank, so I hightails it back to camp. Now the bastard's got poor Fish here. So I got to get Rader."

"Hey, you bastards, I'm lyin' here shot and runnin' out of blood." Fish loses consciousness.

Bierce loves it. Airborne enemy against airborne enemy. Duels to the death. Certainly a more dramatic finale than chess, bridge, or euchre. While he always denied the practicality of motorized flight, he was no stranger to the hot air balloon. His first aerial ascent occurred not long after his return to San Francisco from London and his awkward reunion with Mollie and the boys.

Pregnant with their third child, Mollie greets her husband at the terminal. She holds Leigh, slightly more than a year old, in her arms. Day, three, clutches at his mother's skirts. Leigh sucks his thumb, Day's nose is running. The first change Bierce notices is a diminutive red cable car jangling up California Street. He's not sure the cable car deserves its accolades.

"I wonder how many of our worthy supervisors lined their pockets by issuing the franchise for that jarring, clattering birdcage," he tells Mollie.

"I read in the *Chronicle* it was invented by a man named Andrew Hallidie, Ambrose."

"My dear, an inventor is one who concocts an ingenious arrangement of wheels, levers, and springs and calls it civilization."

She laughs. Her husband's a wonderful storyteller who especially comes alive after absorbing a conspicuous amount of alcohol. At the center of a group, he never fails to release the mocking, lacerating remark that perfectly dissects the situation—or person. But alone with her he seems to run out of things to say and lapses into periods of moody silence. He isn't a demonstrative man. He's painfully reticent in matters of sex, embarrassed to reveal his lust, which he sees as the low side of a person's character. No woman, outside of his mother, has ever seen him completely naked. He and Mollie make love in the dark as fully clothed as possible. Since he utters no sound in the final moment of passion, Mollie is never quite sure he has actually climaxed. Once Mollie pads nude from the bed to the closet. Ambrose, lying in bed, says, "My dear, cover yourself this instant." "But no one can see me," Mollie says. "*I* can see you." Bierce feels contempt for men or women who unmask their bestial dispositions. He tries to hide his own nature.

He masturbates. In the woods. In the cellar. In the privy. Listening intently for the footstep of the intruder who might come upon him and give him away. He masturbates in secrecy and shame. He has to fulfill the urge in him, but he takes little pleasure in it. He isn't sure he can love, really love, despite the flowery Victorian language he uses when he writes to the women in his life. While he suppresses his need for sex, he also suppresses his need for love. In one of his columns he cynically describes love as the folly of thinking more of another before one knows anything of oneself.

In the cab on the way to Mollie's parents' house on Vallejo Street, Bierce proudly announces that he has brought presents for his sons.

"Can we have them now?" Day asks.

"*May* we have them now," Bierce says.

Day hasn't seen his father for more than six months, although he vaguely recalls him as distant, aloof, and seldom there. To Leigh, his father is an unknown, mysterious, and even threatening figure. Bierce produces two slim packages. Day is crestfallen, Leigh bewildered.

"Books?" Day says.

"Not just books, my boy. Shakespeare."

"Mollie says, "Dear, don't you think they're a little young?"

"No one is too young for Shakespeare." Leigh's book is *A Midsummer Night's Dream.* Bierce quotes Puck. "If we shadows have offended / Think but this, and all is mended / That you have but slumbered here / While these visions did appear." Leigh turns his book upside down in bewilderment. Tears well in Day's eyes. "No sniveling," Bierce orders Day. "Someday you'll appreciate *As You Like It,* from which comes the line, 'Always the dullness of the fool is the whetstone of the wits.'" Day buries his face in his mother's skirts. Bierce says, "So this is how you thank a father who has come all the way from London to introduce you to Shakespeare?"

"Dear, the boys don't know their ABCs yet. They're babies."

Bierce retreats. "Perhaps I overestimated the demands of Shakespeare on the young, my dear. I have mixed feelings about His Majesty anyway. He has no sense of proportion, no care for the strength of restraint, no art of saying just enough."

Mollie thinks, *Not unlike my own husband.* But . . . "I'm proud of you, Ambrose, so able to instruct Mr. Shakespeare in how to write."

The Bierces lodge with Mollie's parents while Ambrose looks for work. Unable to land a writing job, he returns to the Mint as a clerk in the assay office. The family moves into rented quarters on Harrison Street, where Helen is born, later into rooms on Guerrero Street. He renews his ties with the Bohemian Club and is elected club secretary. Ardent Republican Frank Pixley starts a new weekly, the *Argonaut,* and corrals Bierce as editor, which enables him once again unleash his venom in a column he calls "Prattle." His first target is Denis Kearney, the populist Sandlot Orator, whose slogan is "The Chinese Must Go." Kearney is threatening to burn the mansions of Nob Hill, hang Stanford and Crocker from the nearest lamppost, and dispatch the Chinese with buckshot. Bierce recalls with satisfaction that several years earlier, while protecting Ah Wee, he humiliated the Irish punk in the alley behind the Mint.

Ah Wee is now a widow and sole proprietor of Dunphy's Saloon. The day finally comes in which she and Dunphy abandon any pretense about her sex and her hiding as a man. No one is surprised when Dunphy announces to the regulars that he is taking Aw Wee as his de facto bride and partner—despite the goddamned California miscegenation laws, which don't mean a mound of maggots to them. There's a round of cheers and kicking of sawdust, and Ferret actually buys a drink with his own coins. A week later, Dunphy dashes onto Powell Street screaming that his brain is ablaze. He plunges his head into the horse-trough but can't put out the fire and begins rolling across the cobblestones, where he is crushed into blood and batter by the foaming horses of a fire truck. Ah Wee runs the saloon exactly as her husband had, right down to the right payoffs to the right people. She even leaves untouched the knothole over the bar from which rushed the demons that burned her husband's brain.

After his asthma flares, Bierce moves the family across the Bay to Marin County, where they rent a cottage in San Rafael. While walking alone through the woods he is felled by an attack. He falls to his knees, then lies on his back, coughing, wheezing. It is late afternoon and as he looks up through the umbrella-webbed foliage he sees the edge of the sun moving in a direction he can't delineate. Bierce hoped for a temporary escape from the distractions of his family. He has been trying to write stories based on his Civil War experiences and tales of his nightmares and fantasies. But the children have been difficult and Mollie spends most of the day whining, now her custom. Helen, the newest member of the family, bawls incessantly. Leigh dislodges the carefully arranged pages on Bierce's desk, sending them to the floor. Day asks interminable questions about the stars, sun, moon, planets, and grass-hoppers. Bierce's family is killing him, and so is his asthma. All are stealing the air from his lungs, sucking his life and art away. He has been to the doctors, read about the disease at the Mercantile Library. His asthma attacks come suddenly and without warning. They will last minutes or days, some are mild, others terrifying. He doesn't know why. An allergy, perhaps. Ragweed, a furry cat, feathers, dust, mold, Mollie's cheap perfume, newsprint, ink, smoke, fog, changes in the air, wheat, milk, red meat, exertion, pressure, anger, noise, the demands of children, wives, mothers-in-law. The doctors tell him asthma is a chronic condition that can't be cured. All a sufferer can do is to live in a warm, dry climate, curtail exercise, watch the diet, avoid stress and allergies. What the hell do the doctors know? Bierce thinks. They're men who thrive on disease and die of health. Medicine is useless. Like a stone flung down Park Avenue to kill a dog on Broadway.

He is more afraid of his fears than of death, but he jeers at both. An afterlife? A laughable contention among pitiful, hapless fools, the wishful thinking of the ignorant and superstitious. Yet paradoxically he is intrigued by the notion of ghosts and spirits and inner demons. He is fascinated by the idea of mystery and of puzzles with no solutions.

He hears someone call his name and struggles to sit up. Gradually his breathing becomes stronger.

"What are you doing down in the clover, Major Bierce?"

Staring down at him is the face of James Tunstead, local sheriff and hangman.

"I had an attack. How did you find me?"

"When you didn't come home your missus sent for me. Hope you get to breathin' real quick, 'cause I got a pint of prime drinking whis-key in my coat and a fresh deck of cards in my back pocket."

Back at the *Argonaut,* Bierce's duties require him to be office-bound a good portion of the week, and it's on such a day that the door bursts open and a man named Harry Widmer rushes in screaming and overturning chairs and tables. The object of Widmer's wrath is Bierce, author of an unfavorable review of Widmer's actress-wife, Katie. Widmer slaps Bierce in the face. The force sends him crashing into a bookcase, shattering the glass. Bierce pulls his .45 and aims it. Publisher Pixley grabs Bierce's arm just as the gun goes off. The bullet lodges in the ceiling, causing plaster to powder the room. Widmer, seeing the gun and hearing the blast, first thinks he's been shot and screams in terror. Pixley snatches the gun away from Bierce, manages to hustle Widmer out of the office.

"Good God, Bierce," the publisher says when he returns. "You might have killed that man."

"That was the idea, Mr. Pixley."

"Kill him if you want, but not in my office." Pixley returns the gun. "I have a feeling you're going to need this."

Bierce has no love for Pixley—his politics, his ambitions, his fawning over the likes of Stanford, Crocker, and Huntington—but the Prattler owes the publisher a debt for saving Bierce from a homicide charge.

Bierce's review of a book called *The Dance of Death* by a Mr. William Herman sets off an inflamed debate. The tome fiercely attacks the waltz as the open and shameless gratification of sexual desire. In his column, Bierce condemns the book as pornographic, a criminal assault upon public modesty, an indecent exposure of the author's mind, a sustained orgasm of a fevered imagination. Bierce demands that Mr. William Herman come forward so he can be shot. *The Dance of Death* sells eighteen thousand copies and Bierce finds the money mighty handy.

On a July day, after putting the finishing touches on his column, Bierce gets an unexpected visitor at the *Argonaut*. Sheriff Tunstead, red-faced and out of breath.

"Sheriff? Why aren't you back in Marin County stretching a few necks?"

"There's plenty of necks to stretch right here, Major Bierce. It's Kearney and his gang. I get word on the telegraph they's marchin' on the Chinee, so I hops the ferry and comes right over to warn you. Kearney's makin' the *Argonaut* his first stop. He wants you as much as he wants the chinks on account of all the bad things you been writin' about him. His gang could be here any minute."

Bierce pulls his .45 revolver from his belt and spins the cylinder to make sure the chamber's loaded.

"You don't hold much for anarchists like Kearney, do you, Major Bierce?"

"Sheriff, for anarchists I favor mutilation followed by death. If I cut out an anarchist's tongue would he have the law on me? Absolutely not. Anarchists don't believe in law."

Bierce goes to an armoire and removes a rifle with a battered stock. "This Enfield's old but reliable, and I know just the son of a bitch to use it on." He opens the loading gate and fills it with shells.

"We don't got enough firepower to fight off a mob, Major. Best we just skedaddle."

"A mob's unpredictable, Sheriff. It's capable of inflicting fire, flaying, torture, the murder of innocents—but sometimes a single bullet in the right place . . ."

They hear a menacing, unnatural sound, almost a rumble.

Tunstead says, "They's a-comin'. And I smell smoke."

"The end of civilization approaches, Sheriff. First rioting and fire, mutiny by the police and the troops, collapse of the government, a policy of decapitation, a parliament of the people, pandemonium, the man on horseback, and finally gusts of grape."

The noise outside swells. Men shouting, chanting, soles against the pavement, smashing glass, screams of the terrified. Bierce and Tunstead barricade the front and back doors with desks and chairs. A rock flies through the front window, showering the room with glass.

"Bierce!" screams a voice from outside. "Come outside and take your medicine. I owe it to you."

Kearney.

"Tauri excrementum!" Bierce yells back. He begins firing his Colt indiscriminately through the window. Tunstead lets loose with a shotgun blast.

A torch is hurtled through the window, then another. The curtains burst into flames. Tunstead rips down the curtains and tries to stomp out the fire. Two more firebombs are flung inside, igniting papers and books. Smoke fills the room.

"Major, if the flames don't kill us the smoke will."

"To the back, Sheriff."

They pull the furniture from the rear door, throw off the bolt, and open it. As they do, a back draft sucks at the flames and turns the *Argonaut* into an inferno. Tunstead's hair ignites. Bierce pulls his friend out of the building with one hand while clutching the Enfield with the other. In the alley, he beats the flames from the sheriff's hair. As the two men sink to the cobblestones, the mob moves on to fresh, less lethal, targets. From far off floats the sound of a fire bell. The *Argonaut* is lost to flame, along with Bierce's printed words and their sarcasm, cynicism, and invective. But only temporarily. A timber falls, adding sparkling decimal points to the destruction.

"Sheriff, we've just had a taste of anarchy. If the government had any sense it would come down hard on the masses. They're our natural enemy. We ought to have censorship of the press, a firm hand on the churches, supervision of public meetings, control of the railroads and the telegraph."

"And just who'd run the government, Major Bierce? You?"

"Why not? By god, government may have a thousand defects but at least it's government. And where the hell are the police?"

"Outnumbered, I suppose. Probably part of the mob."

Bierce and Tunstead venture into the street. Everything Chinese is in flames. Laundries, bathhouses, barbershops, vegetable stands, chop suey joints. Kearney and his rioters bay through the arteries savaging every yellow cast they find. Chinese hookers are dragged from their cribs and left bleeding on the stones.

All of a sudden Bierce feels a sense of dread. "Sheriff, Ah Wee. They're going after Ah Wee."

The mob is scattering as Bierce and the sheriff approach the blazing saloon on Powell Street. They see Aw Wee, engulfed in flames, staggering from the building. She carries Dunphy's old shillelagh in one hand and a blackened box in the other. As she collapses, Bierce rips off his coat and beats out the fire from her tiny body. The flames have eaten through her clothes, blackened her skin. Somehow she turns her head. Tries to speak. Her charred lips form the name Bierce. Her eyes stare into his and then through him into nothing. He recognizes the box she dropped. It's hot and smoking from the fire and untouchable. Once it had been beautiful. Lacquered in red and gold and graced with the carvings of eagles and bears and dragons. Once it had been Ah Wee's magic box.

Tears come to his eyes, which normally do not tear. "Sheriff, in no damned nation on earth is life so insecure as ours. In no place else is murder held in so little disrepute. Ten thousand homicides a year in this country. And Aw Wee is only one of them. If that's good government, then there's no such thing as a bad one."

The firemen come, horses straining to pull the pumpers. Dunphy's Saloon has already disintegrated and the firemen don't bother to unpack their hoses.

Teeth clinched, Bierce jumps to his feet.

"Hang on, Major Bierce. I know what you're up to, but you can't fight that mob by yourself."

"It's Kearney. He's all I need. And I know just how to get him."

Balloon Man is unhappy to be rousted from the safety of his basement home and dragged to the launch site. "It's dangerous, Mr. Bierce. All them Pope-lovers runnin' loose and settin' fires and things. Besides, there's too much wind today."

Bierce has been up in the balloon before, he and Mollie on their wedding anniversary, complete with champagne and cake. It's exhilarating in its way, all the houses below looking like building blocks. Telegraph Hill, Nob Hill, Russian Hill, and the white stretch of North Beach. Bierce picks out the streets he walks. Market, Sacramento, Dupont, Montgomery, Kearney, Clay, Washington, Pacific, Davis, Stockton. Wharves jut into the Bay along East Street. He sees Portsmouth Square; the dives of Devil's Acre; the saloons, dance halls, and melodeons of the Barbary Coast; the miserable little passageways of Murder Point, Moketown, and Dead Man's Alley; the gambling rooms, opium dens, cribs, and parlor houses of Chinatown. Ah Wee's place is down there, the saloon on Powell Street. Only last week she threw her towel on the bar and led him into the back room, locking the door behind them. She is no longer childlike, no longer boyish. She sits facing him on his lap, his trousers bunched around his ankles. "No one must ever know about this, Ah Wee," he says. "No one ever will, Bierce." She raises her torso, then slowly lowers herself onto him.

"Did you hear me, Mr. Bierce?" Balloon Man says. "Don't know if I can control it. Conditions ain't right."

"Take it up anyway, Balloon Man. We're following the masses." Conscious of Bierce's fury, as well as his revolver and rifle, Balloon

Man argues no more. He fuels the fire and fills the balloon. As it inflates, the nation's colors begin to expand in great stripes. Red. White. Blue. The gondola leaves the ground. From the air, Bierce sees the pall of smoke that blankets the city. Half of Chinatown is in flames. The Pacific Mail steamship docks are an inferno. The balloon drifts silently, then dips. Balloon Man adjusts the ballast. Through the smoke, Bierce spies the horde surging up California Street, nearing Nob Hill, smashing windows, looting shops, and torching buildings. It numbers several hundred and at its head, in his distinctive red cap, is Denis Kearney. Bierce kneels in the gondola and balances the Enfield on the swaying rim. He takes aim at Kearney and fires. He sees the brick pavement splinter near Kearney's boots. Missed, dammit. The basket keeps lurching, making it hard to get off an accurate shot. Bierce fires again. Again the bullet misses. Then the mob becomes aware of the airship above them. Before he can get off another shot a heavy gust arises and the balloon is swept upward and to the west toward the Presidio.

"Hold her steady, dammit," Bierce shouts to Balloon Man. "We're going too high, moving too fast."

"It ain't exactly science, Mr. Bierce. We goes up and we goes down. But sideways we can't always predict."

Balloon Man pulls at a cable that releases a valve at the crown of the balloon. Bladder-like, it sinks a little, then is pitched upward again by the turbulence. Bierce hears a muffled crack, then a thud, and finally a hissing noise. "They're shootin' at us," Balloon Man says. "We got hit." Another thud and another. The balloon begins to drop as its skin withers like an old woman before death. The cranberry buildings of the Presidio sweep into sight. Balloon Man slashes at the ballast, trying to slow the descent, but the balloon plummets into a grove of eucalyptus. All Bierce can see during the plunge is a confusion of color and the rush of air. The two men spill from the gondola onto the mossy ground. Balloon Man is bleeding from his mouth. Bierce is shaken and bruised, but manages to stand and dust off his clothes. Even in calamity he strives to be neat. The balloon has become a formless mass of fiber dangling in the trees. They hear running feet and the sound of men tearing through the brush. Men in the blue uniforms of the Sixth Army, rifles ready.

"Major A. G. Bierce reporting." He salutes. He is, at heart, a military man.

Denis Kearney's riot rages for two days before volunteers armed with hickory pick handles help the police and National Guard to wear the mob down. Kearney is led off in chains. Bierce stands before Ah Wee's grave in the Chinese Cemetery. He is a man who doesn't mourn easily, doesn't love easily, and is rarely sentimental. When his mother died, Bierce—as he had after his father's death—remained in San Francisco and allowed his brother to do the grieving for both of them. A low, spiked fence separates the cemetery from the street. On the far side of the fence someone sings, "I'll Take You Home Again, Kathleen." He begins to speak softly, as much to himself as to Ah Wee.

"The shadow on the dial of civilization is moving backward. Revelers with wine-dipped wreaths on their heads don't care about the hour. But there are signs and portents. Whispers and cries in the air, the stealthy tread of invisible feet on the ground, the sudden clamor of startled fowls at dead of night, crimson dewdrops on the roadside grass of morning. But pray, Ah Wee, let's not allow them to disturb themselves, for tomorrow comes . . . anarchy."

He puts his hand on Ah Wee's gravestone, for which he had paid. Into the stone is etched, AH WEE DUNPHY 1846–1877.

Bierce has had enough of San Francisco, its damp, blustery stench, the poverty of literary journalism, and the parsimony of his employer. Yes, he craves adventure, but even more he wants affluence, enough to protect him from the financial calamities that often afflict those with no trade other than writing. Through the military grapevine he learns that his old army buddy Sherburne B. Eaton is now a partner in a gold mine in the Black Hills and is looking for a new general agent. Bierce writes to Eaton that gold is a word once spelled "God," the letter "L" later inserted to distinguish it from the name of an inferior deity. He all but demands the job, maintaining he's eminently qualified, his father-in-law having earned a mining fortune, and that Bierce himself has twice been employed at the United States Mint. In his letter to New York he writes, "Sherb, send me a contract and I shall pack my grip, load my revolver, and be away to Rockerville, Dakota, to begin my new duties."

Not far from the battleground of Celaya, after Farnum Fish is carried to the hospital car, the injured pilot goes out of control. After losing so many fluids he becomes addled and starts seeing anomalies. He screams something about clouds and blood. "The clouds are turning red!" Fish yells. "They're stained. Clouds are supposed to be white, so it's blood, I tell you. My blood!" He has to be strapped to his cot. Fish sleeps for the next eighteen hours and when he wakes he asks for scrambled eggs and demands to be flown to El Paso.

Outside the hospital car Barlow says to Bierce, "When I got orders from Pancho Villa to take you up as an observer I wasn't expecting a geezer."

"I'm a geezer with a gun, Barlow."

"You're about to become a flying geezer with a gun, Mr. Grile."

"Barlow, when I hear the word fly, I think not of an aeroplane, but of the common housefly, a monster of the air owing allegiance to Beelzebub. The fly clouds the world. The sun never sets on him. In point of time, he is from beginning to end. Alexander fought him unsuccessfully in Persia. He routed Caesar in Gaul, worried Magellan in Patagonia. He spoiled Longfellow's meals in Boston. He's everywhere and always the same. He roots palatially upon the summit of Olympus, the sombrero of a Mexican revolutionary, and the goggles of an American aviator."

A fly buzzes from nowhere and lands on Barlow's cheek. The young aviator slaps at the insect and misses.

"See what I mean, Barlow? When the earth grows old it renews its youth. Seas flood the continents. Polar ice envelopes the tropics. Empires, civilizations, and races are extinguished. Where big cities stood jackals slink across the naked sands. Religions and philosophies perish with the tongues that created them. Cliffs crumble to dust. The goat's appetite fails him. The last office-holder is indicted for graft. But always the housefly remains like a run of salmon. By the fly's illustrious line we are connected with the past and the future. He walked in the eyebrows of our fathers. He will skate upon the bald pates of our sons. Barlow, the fly is the King, the Chief, the Boss. I salute him."

Barlow throws Bierce an aviator's cap and goggles. "Salute these, old man, because you're going to fly, all right. With Lamb first thing in the morning."

Chapter Thirteen

The April morning awakes clear and clean. Five men on one side, five on the other—the crew—push against the wing to ratchet the Jennie into position. Bierce, confronting his first aeroplane excursion, isn't unafraid to chart unfamiliar territory. He's done it before, notably back in the Badlands of Dakota, where he faced all odds in a gambit to launch a gold mining operation. It was insane, of course. What did a luckless writer such as he know about gold mining? Really. Mining for gold was never like excavating for, say, copper—or coal. He didn't know anything about those either. Greed it was, and he got caught up in it. In the long run, however, it was useful for a writer. Grist, as they say, like heartbreak, like disaster. Grist. Although he didn't quite see it that way then.

Bierce eyes Dean Lamb skeptically. "You've only been flying for three years?"

"Hell, I was a merchant seaman 'cause I enjoy going to strange places, like China, the Philippines, Nicaragua. Realizes I can't swim and hates the water. So I takes up flying lessons in Hammondsport, New York. Figure I can go just as far without getting wet. I'm in Texas working as a barnstormer when I hear Pancho Villa's starting an air corps. I crosses the border and goes to Villa and tells him I want to fly for him. Pancho laughs at me. Says I'm so skinny the wind would blow me away. Gives me a shove, sends me into the dust. Hell, I won't take that from no man. So I gets up and belts Pancho in the mouth. I hear rifles click all around me. I figure I'm a gonner. But Pancho, blood running from his mouth, waves off his men. He says, 'Boys, we've not only got a flier here but a fighter too.' So he gives me the job."

Bierce doubts Lamb would still be alive had he actually belted Villa, but it makes a good story, and Bierce is a sucker for a good story. He climbs into the cockpit's front seat. Lamb sits behind. What's disquieting is the biplane's fragility. All sticks, string, and cloth. Bierce feels the fabric surrounding the fuselage. If he pushes hard enough his fist will go through it. He puts his hand against his .45 to reassure himself, as if that can protect him.

"Noisy in the air, Mr. Grile. You want to talk to me, yell through this tube. When I'm trying to talk to you, put the tube to your ear. Otherwise I do the flying. You do the watching. And strap yourself the hell in."

Bierce does but can't understand how belting himself into this flimsy airborne tent can make much difference. Lamb gives the signal. The ground crew yanks the propeller. On the third turn it grumbles into life. The sound of the motor nearly deafens Bierce. Lamb raises his thumb. The crew kicks away the blocks holding the wheels and the plane, fuselage shaking, moves forward slowly. As it picks up speed the air rushes past Bierce, almost taking his breath away. The makeshift runway is rough. The wheels bump. Bierce is jarred in his seat. But there comes an eerie smoothness, and he realizes that not only is he still alive, he's actually in the air. He feels a whirling sensation in his stomach and a feeling of vulnerability. Lamb banks the plane, and Bierce at first feels as if he's falling. The Jennie makes a graceful circle over the rails where Villa's troop trains stretch for miles. Tens of thousands of soldiers are massed for the coming battle. The tents of their camps, smoke from the fires, surround in clusters the railroad cars. Villa's armies form so chaotically that horses, trucks, and cannon are spread out in a seemingly incomprehensible pattern. The land below is rolling, but brown and drab. It reminds Bierce of Dakota, where he so long ago tried his hand at prospecting for gold. Yes, gold. Dust. Flakes. Nuggets. The ancients mined it thousands of years before the birth of Christ. Egyptians hammered it into amulets. Celts wore gold ornaments. Incas prayed to it. Spaniards died for it. Everyone killed for it. He's amused by the thought that gold can't be consumed, won't quench one's thirst, and will never save a toe from frostbite. Still, he's captivated by gold's mystique.

If he is going to run a gold mine he needs a bodyguard, so he hires one Boone May, who greets Bierce at the Deadwood stage. May is famous in Dakota Territory for eradicating a notorious bandit named Frank Towle and burying him by the side of the road.

"True, Mr. Bierce. When I heard a two-thousand-dollar ree-ward was posted for Mr. Towle—dead or alive—I goes back to the scene of the killing, slices off the head, and brings it in a gunny sack to the sheriff to claim my money. That's all I got to say on this particular subject. Now let's skedaddle on to Rockerville."

Boone May is a man after Bierce's own heart.

Bierce is promised a salary of five thousand dollars a year plus a share in the mine's profits. By the end of the year he might be able to send for Mollie and the kids. Unfortunately, no one has told the previous general agent, Captain Ichabod M. West, that he has been replaced. Bierce confronts West in the Black Hills Placer Mining Company office. West tilts back in his chair, boots on the desk. His shotgun messenger, Leander Prong, leans against the wall, eyeing Boone May.

"Read about you in the *Rapid City Journal,* Bierce," West says. "Article said you're both a literary man and hydraulic expert sent here to replace me. Far as I'm concerned I still run the mine, since I've never been formally told I was removed."

"Then I'll make it formal." Bierce takes out a neatly folded document from his coat pocket. "A resolution dated June eighteenth, eighteen-eighty, approved by the board in New York appointing me general agent. Signed by the chairman and the company's vice-president, secretary, and treasurer. Therefore, I intend to take my rightful place as head of this mining operation. Should you have any doubts about its authenticity, I suggest you telegraph Major Eaton in New York. In the meantime, I expect you to vacate this office immediately."

"Christ-all-bleeding-mighty. Bierce, maybe you didn't know I got a separate contract puttin' me in charge of actually buildin' the dam and the flume—whether I'm general agent or not. How are you going to get around that?" West removes his boots from the desk and spits on the floor. "Besides, what the hell do you know about gold mining? I'll wager you've never been in Dakota before. Says in the paper you're a literary man. That hardly qualifies you—"

"I traveled through this part of the country on a military expedition in which I served as topographer. In matters of gold, I've worked in the Assay Office of the United States Branch Mint in San Francisco. And I've drawn upon the wisdom of my eminent father-in-law, Captain H. H. Day, a veteran of the California Gold Rush and the Comstock Lode of Nevada."

West looks at Leander Prong who looks at Boone May who looks at Bierce. West isn't going to win this one. Not here, not now. But neither is Bierce.

"Aw, no hard feelings, Bierce. Let's depart to Rockerville's finest watering hole, the Sanctified Bullet Cafe, and partake in a little Dutch cheer and some son-of-a-bitch stew. Little juniper juice would taste pretty good right now."

"Son-of-a-bitch stew sounds like a culinary delight, West, but I've just arrived and have work to do."

West gets to his feet, kicking the chair over. "This here's dangerous country. Would be a shame to see you martyred on behalf of a few investors back East."

"A martyr is one who moves along the line of least reluctance to a desired death. I have no intention of being a martyr."

West and Prong stride out, leaving the door open. The breeze catches the grit in the street and a whirlwind of prairie dust sweeps into the room.

Bierce turns to Boone May. "What is this son-of-a-bitch stew West was talking about?"

"Veal, Mr. Bierce. Thickened with brains and flour and spiced with chilies. Mighty tasty. Bet you can't never get somethin' like that back in Frisco."

Into the open door, tentatively, slinks a dog.

"Mr. May, please expel that animal and close the door." Bierce doesn't much fancy canines.

"Mutt's called Benjamin, Mr. Bierce. We all kind of adopted him on account of he don't have no home. Always chasin' after his own tail. Never catches it, though. You see, one afternoon Benjamin lays hisself down and curls up to sleep. What does he see when he awakes? His own damned tail, which he grabs with his choppers and bites down. Ouch! It hurts so much the cur lets go. Ole Ben's philosophical about it, however. He knows there's more joy in pursuit than in possession. Give him a few scraps and he'll be your pal for life. We all need a pal, even you."

Bierce gives in. Benjamin has a kind of needy charm. Besides, Bierce knows many humans he likes a lot less.

"Tell me about this place, Mr. May. I need to get the lay of the land."

"Used to be called Captain Jack's Dry Diggins for a man who found traces of gold down in the gulch."

"A rather forlorn place. Just a few jack pine, cottonwood, and pasqueflowers. Why was the name changed to Rockerville?"

"On account of nearly every shack round here has a rockin' chair on the porch. Now, we got more than three hundred souls. Also seven saloons, three hotels, four bakeries, a billiard parlor, ten general stores, an undertaker, a jewelry store, and B. Heuniche's Brewery. And spreadin' up the hills on either side of the gulch is lean-tos, tents, shacks, sheds, shanties, and shit-houses. We's gettin' up in the world."

"Still seems rather rough and rowdy."

"You don't know the half of it. Just last spring Ike Yarrow gets drunk on a bad batch of Heuniche's lager out at the mining camp and shoots Mick Mullins in the head. Undertaker fixes Mullins up pretty good. Fact is, Mick looks better than in real life. Sheriff comes and takes Ike up to the jail in Deadwood for hangin'. We all go up for the show, but get there an hour too late. Mighty disappointed, we is. Loved to have seen Ike's neck actually stretched."

A week later, Bierce walks from his hotel to the office. He notices the aftereffects of a prodigious rain from the night before. The mud is already turning to dust, but small, capriciously shaped lakes linger. He stoops by one of the puddles and stares into the water. Tadpoles are swimming in dark circles. Where the hell have they come from, the tadpoles? They spring from nowhere, it seems, then vanish, not living long enough to become frogs. They come and go like the inhabitants of Rockerville, miners, dreamers, drunks, whores, thieves, murderers.

Bierce notices West's shotgun messenger, Leander Prong, leaning against the hitching post outside the Sanctified Bullet Cafe. Prong removes a pouch of Bull Durham from his breast pocket, rolls the tobacco into a cigarette. Bierce sees something else. At first he thinks it's a heap of rags thrown in the street until he becomes aware of the unruly ring of red around it. A dog, lying on its side, legs askew. Benjamin. Hound's head is half blown off. Damned dog was bushwhacked. Bierce kneels and touches the corpse with a finger. Animal is still warm.

Bierce hears Prong spit.

"You kill this dog, Prong?"

"Mutt came around beggin' once too often so I got rid of it. You got a problem with that?"

Bierce does, but now doesn't seem to be the right time to deal with it. He's in limbo. Because West hasn't been sacked to his own satisfaction, he continues to supervise the building of the dam and the remaining distance of flume while Bierce is left to pay the bills. Infusions of cash from New York are slow in coming, so he's the target of anger from laborers and creditors alike.

When a shipment of cash finally arrives from headquarters, Bierce and Boone May set out in a buckboard to pay the men along the line. They come to the camp up the gulch where an oversized tent houses a makeshift saloon. A fiddler and a banjo picker are playing "Oh! Dem Golden Slippers" as Bierce walks in lugging the money-box, followed by Boone, Winchester slung over his shoulder. The bar is fashioned of boards laid over sawhorses, seats long plank benches. Sawdust absorbs some of the mud. No women. Only men, some hopeful, some desperate, some with pasts, some without. One or two are poets. Most just live and drink. The music stops. Seeing Bierce and his assistant, the men fall into surly silence. The tent is stifling. Unwashed bodies, unclean air, stench of old beer and fresh piss, and only the faintest scent of gold.

"Gentlemen, name is Bierce, new general agent of the Black Hills Placer Mining Company. It's payday so form a line. New York has sent a partial payroll and I've come directly from Deadwood to give you your money."

None of the miners carry the names on their birth certificates. They're known only by their presumed origins or by their deformities.

Minnesota Murphy. "About fuckin' time."

Canadian Jack. "Waitin' for our money for six weeks, we been."

Louisiana Len. "Say, what the hell you mean partial payment?"

One-eyed Otis. "We want our money. All of it."

Two-Fingered Tom. "How'd you like to work six weeks without nary a dime to show for it?"

The chorus of catcalls and curses grows. Bierce climbs onto a table so he can see above their heads. "Gentlemen, you have my word everyone will be paid—eventually." He says it but he isn't sure he believes it. All the promises and guarantees are in New York with Eaton, and Bierce pictures Sherb, that very night, at Delmonico's swallowing oysters and washing 'em down with champagne.

One-eyed Otis. "We been holding your IOUs for weeks."

"Gentlemen, don't make me responsible for Captain West's obligations."

Canadian Jack. "We don't give a hoot whose obligations they is."

"What'll you do if I knock your ass off that table, mister?" Minnesota Murphy.

Bierce removes his revolver and holds it to his side. "You'll go down permanently before I hit the floor, sir. And Mr. May in the back of the tent will make sure a few others will bite the sawdust as well."

The men back off.

Louisiana Len. "Some of the boys is talkin' about throwin' down their shovels for good. The dam and flume can go to hell."

"By gawd, that flume's only made of wood. This here's dry country. Lots of things could happen." The voice of Two-Fingered Tom.

"Boys, let's not be precipitous," Bierce says.

Huh? Huh? One voice after another. *Huh?*

"Don't be hasty, I mean. As general agent of the Black Hills Placer Mining Company, I—"

"When Captain West was in charge at least we knew who was cheatin' us." One-eyed Otis.

"I'm doing all I can to reimburse you. Let me remind you if the flume is damaged, or if you stop work, nobody gets paid."

The men grumble but line up sullenly to collect their wages. The cash is instantly converted to the thing of greatest value in these parts: hooch.

Back in the relative safety of Rockerville, Bierce drinks with Boone May at the Sanctified Bullet, a cafe named for sheer, unbridled truth. What more sacred purpose could one have for a bullet than to use it to purify and to make holy.

"Mr. Bierce, the first shootin' in the Sanctified Bullet occurred on its grand openin'. Pineapple Phil draws on an abusive drinkin' buddy and manages to shoot hisself in the foot. Ruins a damned good boot. Deputy comes down from Deadwood and decides God punished Pineapple Phil enough, since he's going to be left with a permanent limp. Doc removes the bullet, and Pineapple Phil consecrates it with a splash of good bourbon and wears the holy symbol on a string from his neck until the afternoon the timbers give way at the flume, crushin' him, and—one might say—makin' him even more pure and holy. Pineapple Phil used to boast he'd never seen a pineapple in his life, couldn't image what it tasted like, and wouldn't eat it in any event. That's how he got his name."

Bierce hears rumors his job is being shopped around, that New York has lost confidence in him, that it's he who is responsible for failing to turn around the fortunes of the Black Hills Placer Mining Company—as the bills pile up and not a speck of gold has been mined. Nevertheless, another infusion of cash arrives. Bierce and Boone May rattle to Deadwood in the buckboard to collect the money. On the way back to Rockerville the weather turns wet and sour. Bierce holds the reins. May sits next to him, hunched, rubber poncho over his shoulders, Winchester between his knees. From time to time May rubs his lips with Vaseline from a small jar he keeps in his pocket. Then he rubs the petroleum jelly over the bolt and trigger of the carbine to keep the gun waterproof and ready to shoot.

"Ever hear of the road agent's spin, Mr. Bierce? Sheriff gets the drop on an outlaw, see. Orders the bandit to hand over his gun. Outlaw reverses the weapon in his hand, but keeps his finger in the trigger guard. Then spins the gun and shoots. So long, lawman. If you hold it off to the side it'll work with a carbine too. Yessir, road agent's spin. Can come in mighty handy."

A horizontal rain follows a fierce gust of wind. Slash of lightning. Boone May sits up.

"What's the matter, Mr. May?"

"Thought I saw somethin' up ahead when the lightnin' flashed. All that cash we're carryin' would fix a lot of fellows for life. Includin' me."

"No one knows we're taking this route. Everyone in Rockerville thinks we're returning from Deadwood by way of Rapid City. I suspected the telegraph operator in Deadwood is on West's payroll, so I tried to throw them off."

May seems a trifle tense, so Bierce tells him about a story he wrote for the *Argonaut* called "The Famous Gilson Bequest."

"Won't scare me too much, will it, Mr. Bierce?"

"Hope so, Mr. May. About a mining camp pariah named Gilson."

"Pariah-what?"

"An outcast. Gilson's a petty gold dust thief, wrongly hanged for horse stealing. But he leaves a will, which bequeaths a considerable fortune to the man who set him up for death, the sheriff. However, there are so many claims against Gilson's estate that by the time the lawyers get through with it, the sheriff ends up with nothing. One night a flood washes out the coffins in the graveyard where Gilson is buried. Who should emerge but the ghost of Gilson himself, sprinkling dust into the open caskets. And in the morning there lies in the cemetery, none other but the sheriff, dead among the dead."

Boone May shudders. "Don't like your story much. Words has a way of scarin' people. I can face a man on account of I can see him, put a bullet in him. A man's real, but ghosts and phantoms and things, why, they're in your head. That's worse than anything you can see and touch. They get you at night when you're asleep."

"For me it's a white horse that stalks me in my dreams, trying to tell me something I don't want to hear in a language I don't understand. Something about the Damned Thing, I suspect."

"Damned Thing?"

"It comes for those who aren't ready to go, Mr. May."

They hear the clink of a horse's shoes against rock and a guttural shout. "Throw up your hands." Boone May sits upright, raises the Winchester. Bierce reins the buckboard to a halt, grabs his revolver. A shot. Feels the bullet pass close to his head. Another shot. "You're surrounded. Throw up your hands, I say."

"Do like they says, Mr. Bierce." May speaks from the side of his mouth. "Put your gun on the seat. But be ready to snatch it. I'm keepin' my Winchester right where I can grab it when the time comes."

Someone lights a torch. Then another. Shapes of men. Bierce sees at least three. In the light of the flame appears Leander Prong, West's gunman. Bierce isn't surprised.

"Thought I'd thrown everyone off our trail with a phony telegraph message, Prong."

"Shittletidee, son." Prong snickers. "We didn't pay no attention to no telegraph. We followed you all the way up to Deadwood and all the way down. Been circling you since you left. We was behind you or in front of you all the time. Now climb off the wagon and hand over your guns." He points at May. "You first, hombre. Pass me that Winchester."

Boone May complies. Or seems to. As he stands he lifts the Winchester, appears to hand it over, but then twirls it and squeezes the trigger. Road agent's spin. Prong's the first to go. Bullet in the brain. Blood spews like a banner in the wind. After him, fall the hapless men whose names no one knows. Death comes before they know it's death. The Damned Thing. Their torches fizzle in the mud. Bierce snatches his Colt .45 but never has a chance to get off a shot. Boone May is that fast. May takes out his Vaseline and rubs some on his lips.

"Think I got 'em all, Mr. Bierce." He smears petroleum jelly on the iron of his rifle, still warm from firing. "Know what else Vaseline's good for? Women. I mean, sometimes they don't all get as wet down there, if you know what I mean."

"What'll we do, Mr. May? Can't just leave these bodies here."

"Didn't you tell me you telegraphed to say we was comin' back through Rapid City? Then leave well enough alone. We ain't never been this way and we ain't never seen no bodies."

Back in Rockerville, things become more complicated. The First National Bank of Deadwood confiscates the remaining funds of the Black Hills Placer Mining Company. Creditors hound Bierce for their money. West walks off the job for a new mining operation, taking half the men with him. Work comes to a stop, the flume still unfinished. Bierce has no choice but to submit his resignation, but vows to go to New York and confront Eaton. Bierce wants vindication.

Mexico.

Bierce is flying. After less than twenty minutes in the air, it almost seems like a normal thing to do. As he looks to the west, he sees against the Mexican skyline what he thinks is the curve of the earth, but he appreciates it less as a glorious spectacle than as a confirmation of his own pessimism. All his life he's heard the claim the planet's ideally made for habitation. Spiritual guides, philosophers, and friends of the pulpit insist man has been blessed with an extraordinary place to live, thanks to the goodness of God. Tauri excrementum. Man's sweet little world's nothing more than a globe of liquid fire straining within a shell that, in relative terms, is no thicker than that of an egg, a shell constantly cracking and in imminent danger of falling to pieces. Three-fourths of the planet's covered with an element in which man can't breathe. Of the other fourth, half of that is uninhabitable by reason of climate. On the remaining eighth, man's faced daily with death, terror, lamentation, and laughter more terrible than tears, the fury and despair of a race hanging on by its fingertips. And, he argues, what's the prize? Something so worthless, so unsatisfying, so inadequate, so false, and at its best so brief, that for consolation and compensation man has set up fantastic faiths of an afterlife in a better world from which no confirming whisper ever reaches across the void.

"Heaven." He utters the word aloud.

"What?" yells Lamb. "Use the fuckin' tube."

Bierce puts his lips to the tube and shouts into it. "Heaven, Lamb. It's a prophecy uttered by the lips of despair."

"What the hell are you talkin' about? Are you daft, old man?"

He is now accustomed to the vibration and noise of the Jennie's engine. Can't imagine being away from the sounds of the valves, fly-wheels, rods, wires, hoses, pulleys, belts, pistons, cylinders, and shafts all screaming in unison. Were they to stop, his world will stop.

Lamb shouts something. Bierce looks back and sees the pilot pointing.

"Celaya."

Into view comes a collection of low buildings, white, red and orange roofs, the municipal landscape interrupted only by a town square and an occasional church spire. Celaya is built on a slight rise frowning down on orchards and scraggly fields. It is crisscrossed with narrow canals and drainage ditches turned into trenches fortified by sandbags and protected by layers of barbed-wire. Behind the trenches are Obregón's big guns, which catch the morning sun, metal reflecting the light like bursts of fire. Cannon, Bierce thinks, are instruments employed in the rectification of natural boundaries. The *federales* are there to stay, that's certain. He sees soldiers digging in the perimeter. It looks as if they're planting corn—no, land mines. As the plane flies five hundred feet above the ground, soldiers below gaze up, unsure. A few wave. He is tempted to wave back. Suddenly, a piece of the fabric wrapping the wing disappears leaving in its place a small hole, perfectly round. A bullet has gone through the wing. Someone down there has decided the plane belongs to the wrong side. Another hole. And another. Lamb pulls on the stick and the Jennie rises and arcs at the same time.

"We're gettin' out of here."

More bullets tear through the wing. The Jennie climbs to two thousand feet before it's comfortably out of rifle range. Lamb shouts. Bierce puts the tube to his ear.

"Too bad we're just on reconnaissance. Might've dropped a few incendiaries on them beaners before they even knew what hit 'em."

South of Celaya, Bierce sees more federal troops converging on the city, reinforcements. Obregón's leaving little to chance. Not only do the *federales* enjoy a strong defensive position, it looks as though they substantially outnumber Villa. Bierce becomes aware of the clouds rolling and shifting, turning into bizarre shapes, finally forming into the sudden and sinister contour of an approaching biplane. It flies directly at the Jennie. Bierce screams at Lamb to warn him. Then he remembers he has to yell through the tube. He grabs at the tube but in his haste drops it. Almost at the point of impact the other plane pulls up. He has a good view of the pilot, black mustache below his goggles, firing a revolver repeatedly. At least one of the bullets tears through the wires holding the fuselage together, but the Jennie hardly feels the damage. Lamb doesn't see the enemy plane until the last second as it swoops past.

"Fuckin' Phil Rader." The hearing tube into Bierce's ear throbs with Lamb's voice.

For a moment Rader has the upper hand. His Christofferson circles and comes in behind the Jennie, but Lamb pulls sharply on the stick to put his plane into a steep ascent. To hold it level and remain in Rader's line of fire would seal the Jennie's fortune. As the Jennie climbs, Bierce has a clear shot at Rader's plane. Bierce fires twice, aiming at the Christofferson's propeller. The shots tear holes through the wing. Rader, piloting alone, must realize that with two armed men in the Jennie the advantage is theirs, even if he manages to stay on their tail. As the Jennie goes into an upward spiral, Bierce finds himself upside down, his stomach seeming to fall into his chest. Now he knows why he was ordered to belt himself in. The Jennie levels out and goes after the Christofferson from behind. Rader leans out of the cockpit and fires back at the Jennie but apparently runs out of bullets. Both Bierce and Lamb fire their guns. At least one bullet hits the Christofferson's fuel tank, creating a trail of white smoke. Bierce continues to fire until his bullets are gone. As he reloads, Lamb pulls away from Rader, taking the Jennie into a gradual turn. Bierce snatches the speaking tube.

"What the hell are you doing, Lamb? We hit Rader's Christofferson. Let's go after the bastard and finish him off."

Lamb shakes his head. "We're almost out of fuel. We got holes all over us. It's hostile territory down there. If we go down in these parts, say goodbye, gringo. They'll shoot us dead. Important thing is, we winged Rader, and maybe put his plane out of commission."

And just when Bierce is starting to like this new-fangled aerial combat. Rader's Christofferson vanishes into the distance. Only its smoke lingers behind, forming into bleached clouds.

Chapter Fourteen

As sunrise nears, Pancho is alone in his caboose—and drunk or nearly there. Once he was a teetotaler, and as governor of Chihuahua he rigidly enforced the local drinking statutes. Now, what the hell? It's the gringo's fault. Bierce has turned him into a drinker. For that alone he should be made to play The Game. A Colt .45 and a single bullet. *Ay, yi, yi,* but why should he take out his fury on the white-haired Americano? *Chingalo.* It's Obregón he wants, and Obregón he will have, no matter how many lives it takes, and in Mexico lives are its most expendable commodity.

When Bierce, sheepishly, returns to deliver his reconnaissance report, he nods at the bottle from which Pancho is swigging.

"May I join you in toasting the gods, General?"

"Suit yourself, you old fool. Who would deny you a glass of tequila?"

"For one, the greatest charlatan on earth, an old fraud who was also my nation's leading temperance fiend. Man named Barnum. Tried to dupe me into giving up the habit, but I outsmarted him. It was in New York back in eighteen-eighty. Or was it eighty-one? No, I think it was eighty. Right after I left Dakota Territory. I'd been in charge of a gold mine, you see, and—"

"You're rambling again, *cabron.* It's what old farts do. Be quiet. Where the hell have you been? You were supposed to report back to me last night, and now it's morning and nearly time for the battle. I've had men shot for just grinning at me."

"I confess, General, I was intimately involved with one of your camp followers for much of the night, a particularly attractive señorita who—"

"*Mentiroso.* Tell me the fuckin' truth, dammit."

Bierce sighs. Yes, for the entire night, alone, he nurses a bottle of tequila in his tent, sleeping only fitfully. Even in half-sleep the dreams come. Images of P. T. Barnum and Tom Thumb; a huge brutal cop, the one who borrows his watch in the Tenderloin, Clubber Williams; a conniving barkeep called McGuirk; that incredible asshole Comstock;

and the Dead Rabbits. Wait, does he really fight the Dead Rabbits? Does he really help to lead the charge on the Vanderbilt Mansion? He is suckered, almost humiliated like a circus freak, by that old mountebank Barnum—but then, who isn't? But he's pissed, dammit. Still. After all these years he'd like to horsewhip Barnum, cold as his corpse may be. After all those dreams he hears a bugle call, sits up with a start, looks at his watch. M'god, he's late, too damned late. Should have reported to Pancho hours ago. He's derelict. Even in his war he'd face a court-martial, and deservedly so. Villa could have him shot, probably will. Pancho doesn't keep jailhouses.

"General, I have no defense, except to say it's human nature, including my own, not to want to confront the unpleasant. I admit I was hesitant to tell you what I observed of Celaya from the air for fear you would dismiss it. I can only throw myself on your—"

"Shut up, Mister Señor Aviator Asshole. I don't want to hear no more whining. Tell me what you got to say and make it pronto. I got no more time to waste on you."

Bierce describes the enemy's fortifications, cannon, reinforcements.

Villa paces the plank floor. "You say Obregón's built trenches, he's got barbed-wire and land mines, his big guns are in position."

"What does that tell you, General?"

"That Obregón's afraid to fight. Scared to send his soldiers to battle my brave *cucarachas*. He's a cowardly pig."

"It appears General Obregón is studying the techniques employed in Europe's most current war. They fight in trenches now. I understand the lines shift back and forth, often by mere yards a day, and weeks later the lines are as they were at the start."

"Pancho Villa don't fight in no trenches. I'll beat Obregón the way I always do. With *un golpe terrible*."

"In my opinion, Obregón's position appears to be close to impregnable. To throw your men directly against that sort of fortification—"

"*Besa mi culo*. I'm going to hit them with everything I got. I'll tame them with my artillery. My advance units will absorb the mines. My Dorados will cut through Obregón's barbed-wire like it's a cornfield. My riflemen will follow, shooting with no mercy. The enemy's trenches will serve as their graves. It has always worked. Pancho's men will again prove their valor."

"I fear valor is a soldierly compound of vanity, duty, and the gambler's hope."

The Centaur of the North is ready. He yells for Pedrito, who has served as Villa's man since he and Bierce were marched to the *bandito* by Fierro. "Bring me my gear." Pedrito complies, but when he hands the general his gold-handled sword, Pancho slaps it away. "No, dammit. Celaya's going to be a battle, not a parade. No sword, I want my best rifle." Villa snatches his bolt-action Mauser out of Pedrito's hands.

Bierce makes one last effort. "Your troops aren't fully in position, General, and you don't have sufficient cannon. Urbina and his brigade seem to have disappeared, and General Angeles won't arrive with the rest of the artillery for another three days. You have only Fierro's—"

"*Mantenerse en silencio*. You have ridden at my side for a year and a half. You and I talked like brothers, better than I am able to talk to my own *estúpido*, worthless brother. I have said things to you I could never say to Urbina. Or to Fierro. Or Angeles. You were my counselor on affairs of the mind and heart. I revealed my soul to you. We dined and drank and danced together. *Hacer el capullo.* You have disappointed me. I was expecting your report last night. And when it comes to military tactics . . ." Villa kicks the dust on the floor, raising a cloud that floats over the American's boots. "This will be a *batalla campal.*"

"Then let me ride at your side, General. I came to Mexico to fight."

"Not into this battle."

"At Ojinaga I—"

"You were too old to fight at Ojinaga."

"I saved your life."

"You barely breathed because of the asthma. You were stiff from the beating by the *federales*. It took two men to help you climb onto your horse. I thought any moment you were going to slide from your saddle. You aimed your rifle well, but I saw it was almost too heavy for you to lift. I took you with me to Ojinaga because I thought you were going to die there. The idea was a *diversión*. That some old gringo would come so far to die. It still amuses me." The general paces, Mauser in his hand. "This is what you will do. The damned newspaper correspondents are demanding information. You will go to their press tent and you will talk to them. You will be my—how do you say?—press attaché. You'll talk a lot and you'll tell them nothing."

"A flimflam. Like P. T. Barnum."

"I don't know what you say. What is this Barnum? Never mind. You will tell the reporters only what they know already, but you will make it sound new. And one more thing: find out where the hell Urbina is. So I can kill him."

Bierce knows Villa's frontal assault is bound to be suicidal, which is precisely why Bierce wants to go. He doesn't need to be analytical, but isn't death the reason he rode to Mexico in the first place? A way to stay ahead of the Damned Thing. Pancho is an impulsive man, but more often stubborn and unyielding. So is Bierce, which might explain his affinity for the *guerrillero*. He recalls his own impetuous invasion of New York to confront the head of the Black Hills Placer Mining Company. Would Villa have done less? Hell, no. Pancho would have shot Sherburne Eaton between the eyes.

He remembers now. His dreams have brought it all back. The cab from the Twenty-third Street ferry terminal to Eaton's Wall Street office. No time wasted. Noting his agitation, Eaton ushers his former Army chum to the relative tranquility of Trinity Church's graveyard. Robins and starlings flit, pigeons peck in the dirt. In the distance are the rattle of carriages and wagons, the shouts of newsboys, the calls of the fruit vendors, the candy butchers' cries, and the occasional shriek of a policeman's whistle. Eaton points to the graves of Robert Fulton, William Bradford, Francis Lewis, and Alexander Hamilton. Bierce likes graveyards, the way some people like railroad stations, but he doesn't give a farthing about this one or who's in it. Not at this moment.

"Dammit, Sherb, you hired me to oversee a mining operation doomed from the start, and you knew it."

"Ambrose . . ."

"My predecessor was a confidence man who ran the company into the ground, and yet I couldn't fire him because *you* signed him to a contract. I was underfinanced, undercut, and underpaid."

"Ambrose, face reality."

"Reality is the dream of a mad philosopher. I demand to speak to the full board of directors. I insist on compensation and an apology, and I want it now."

"The company has been dissolved. There is no more board."

"What?"

"We're out of business. Ambrose, gold mining is highly speculative, and we failed. It's an episode that's over and done with. I know you're distressed—"

"Distress is a disease incurred by the prosperity of a friend."

Eaton places his hand on Bierce's shoulder. "Put Dakota out of your mind and play the tourist now that you're in New York. We've a brand new opera house. There's a wonderful farce at the Standard Theater."

"A farce is nothing more than a brief drama commonly played after a tragedy for the purpose of deepening the dejection of the critical. Sherb, I was put through a goddamned farce."

Bierce knows he's licked, but he's made himself heard, which is the important thing.

"Ambrose, I'm about to be named president of the Edison Electric Light Company, which is going to launch the world's first central electric power station in Manhattan. Tom believes electricity will some day power the streetcars, light our homes, and run the factories. I might be able to find a position at Edison for you."

"I decline. I know nothing of the economic application of electric power, but no doubt it will propel a street car better than a gas jet and give more light than a horse. No parlor tricks for me."

Bierce, once the Wickedest Man in San Francisco, author of four books, and head of a gold mining operation, is now a nobody with no job and no prospects, but he'll be damned, after what he's been through, that he'll gamble on something as speculative as electric lights. Nothing Eaton says will placate Bierce's anger, other than dinner at Delmonico's.

"Some special friends will be joining us, Ambrose. Delmonico's is so exclusive it's a virtual club."

"I always thought of a club as an association of men for the purposes of drunkenness, gluttony, unholy hilarity, murder, sacrilege, and the slander of mothers, wives, and sisters."

"Oh, you've been there before?"

The restaurant, at Fifth Avenue and Twenty-sixth Street, is so discreet that when a midget in a high hat accompanied by a tall bald man walk into the oak-paneled dining room to sit at Eaton's table no one appears to notice.

Eaton says, "May I introduce Major Tom Thumb and his associate, Mr. P. T. Barnum."

Charles Delmonico himself stacks Tom's chair with books, so when the midget sits he is almost at eye level with the others. Bierce is introduced, not as a hydraulic and mining expert, but as a published author.

Barnum says, "I too am an author, having written an autobiography that has sold in the millions. I encourage readership by giving a free circus ticket to anyone who buys a copy." When the waiter takes their orders Barnum announces loudly that he's a teetotaler and asks for mineral water.

Bierce, who orders absinth, says, "A teetotaler is one who abstains from strong drink, sometimes totally, sometimes tolerably totally."

Barnum chuckles and rubs his hand over his bald pate. "All my circus employees must sign an agreement abstaining from the use of either malt or spirituous liquors. I bill my circus as 'Barnum's Great Moral Show,' which contains nothing professed Christians wouldn't approve of, and no entertainment a Christian mother couldn't patronize with her innocent daughters."

"Thank God, Mr. Barnum, that I'm not a Christian, a mother, nor a daughter."

"My initials P. T. stand for Piety and Temperance. What do *you* stand for, Mr. Bierce?"

"I stand for common sense, common courtesy, and common decency."

The showman shakes his head in pity. "I'm seventy years old. All my museums have been destroyed in flames, as was Iranistan, my home. I served in the Connecticut legislature. I was mayor of Bridgeport. My traveling circus is the most famous on earth. But I still have inexhaustible energy and I use it to save souls. Mr. Bierce, have you been baptized?"

"I was, unfortunately, as a defenseless infant into the Congregationalist Church. I'm aware that baptism is a sacred rite of such efficacy that he who finds himself in heaven without having undergone it will be unhappy forever."

Barnum's eyebrows raise. "Since you're a skeptic, I wish to demonstrate to you the power of righteousness and the influence of religion. Periodically I join members of the cloth in making the rounds of the Tenderloin. The purpose is to enter saloons and convince the poor souls therein of the folly of their ways. While I'm not usually a wagering man, Mr. Bierce, I'd like to bet that within the course of a single night I'll be able to redeem at least one soul. I have the power to change a sinner into a God-fearing man, and shall do so in your presence. If I fail, then I'll give you—*give* you—my share of the Barnum and Bailey Circus."

"And if you succeed, what's my penance?"

"You will publicly repent and renounce your alcoholic and heathen ways."

"As you've said yourself, there's a sucker born—"

"Never did I say that, sir. Long have I been misquoted. But to the point. Do you accept my offer?"

"I accept. You have a circus to lose, while all I have to lose are my sins and a measure of pride."

The next night, Bierce meets the pious outside of his hotel, the Navarre. Accompanying Barnum are New York's noisiest clergymen. Dr. Henry Ward Beecher of the Plymouth Church in Brooklyn Heights; Dr. T. De Witt Talmage of the Brooklyn Tabernacle; the Reverend Asa D. Blackburn, pastor of the Church of the Strangers; Dr. Charles H. Parkhurst of the Madison Square Presbyterian Church; and Bishop Simpson of the Methodist Episcopal Church. Anthony Comstock, Secretary of the New York Society for the Suppression of Vice, is present as an observer. For protection, the group is escorted by Police Inspector Alexander S. Williams. Also joining the band is a young reporter, Arthur Brisbane from Charles Dana's New York *Sun*. Bierce considers most of the clergymen of his acquaintance as little more than dunderheads who fancy ghosts and devils and pregnant virgins over reason. To describe a clergyman as an intellectual is, to Bierce, oxymoronic. Intellectuals work for the arts sections of newspapers, reside in Boston, or are near-sighted. They are never soul-snatchers.

Sixth Avenue—under the shadow of the overhead railroad—is lined with saloons, theaters, dance-halls, and establishments with red lamps flickering in the windows. Music from pianos, accordions, and fiddles drift on fumes of beer to the sidewalks. Drivers whip foaming horses pulling at wagons. Drunks urinate against walls. Veneered women skulk in alleys waiting for a quarter and a cock. Titanic men in derby hats swagger as if they own the street. From a tenement window a hag throws garbage to the sidewalk. A crazed cat, squealing, shoots across the street only to be crushed under the wheels of a cab. A loose pig roots in the gutter. Many souls here are in need of salvation.

"A hell-hole, Mr. Bierce." Barnum sadly shakes his head. "The Tenderloin is sometimes called Satan's Circus—a circus with no similarity to my own."

Police Inspector Williams boasts he is responsible for the Tenderloin's name.

"I made me reputation as the toughest cop in the Gas House district, but I always had me sights on the Twenty-ninth Precinct, which used to be known as the Rialto on account of it's where the theaters is. When I finally get transferred to the Rialto, I tells a reporter from the *Herald* how I had nothing but chuck steak, and now I'm gettin' me a little of the tenderloin. The name sticks, so it's the Tenderloin now. I form a Strong Arm Squad on account of there's more law at the end of a policeman's nightstick than in any ruling from the Supreme Court. That's why they call me Clubber." The clergymen huddle close to him for safety. "With due respect, reverends, there ain't no danger in the Tenderloin with me here. Mr. Bierce, hand me your timepiece. Now." Bierce reluctantly complies. It's the watch given to him by his Uncle Lucius. Clubber drapes the watch by its chain over a lamp-post. He leads the group around the block and when the men return, the watch, defiantly, is still there. "See how safe the Tenderloin is, gentlemen."

Bishop Simpson decries the Tenderloin as having as many prostitutes as there are Methodists, twenty-one thousand forty-three—and growing. Bierce asks if the prostitutes are all former Methodists or include other denominations. The Reverend Beecher advises Bierce to attend church loyally. Bierce, who never attends church, particularly when advised, suggests to Beecher that church is where the parson worships God and the women worship the parson. Beecher is not amused.

Anthony Comstock, progenitor of the Comstock Law, announces that he's a puritan and proud of it. "When it comes to vice I aim to get all I can."

Bierce says, "I've always viewed a puritan as one who believes in letting all others do as *he* likes."

Comstock nods in approval. "I've been appointed a special agent to withhold from the mails all material *I* deem inappropriate."

"I'm not sure what's inappropriate, Comstock, other than holding divine services during a dog fight in church."

"I'll have you know that six months after the Comstock Law went into effect, I seized from the mails one hundred ninety-four thousand obscene pictures and photographs, one hundred thirty-four thousand pounds of books, fourteen thousand two-hundred stereopticon slides, five thousand five-hundred sets of playing cards, thirty-one thousand one hundred fifty boxes of pills and powders—mostly aphrodisiacs—and sixty thousand three-hundred rubber articles. All having to do with conjugal activity."

"Comstock, in my opinion conjugal activity is merely the yoking together of two fools by a parson."

"See here, Mr. Bierce, I was wed by a parson."

"I rest my case."

Barnum raises his hand and calls a halt to the procession. "Gentlemen, this is the place, the fast-house of one Oliver B. McGuirk. We shall enter and save the soul of Mr. McGuirk, and hopefully the women he employs and the wretched men he exploits."

The piano player's fingers freeze the moment the group pours into the saloon. As the clergymen gather in a semicircle, the Reverend Talmage puts a pitch pipe to his lips to sound a note. The preachers sing. *Rock of Ages, cleft for me* . . . The Reverend Beecher thumps a tambourine and Bishop Simpson blows into a harmonica. McGuirk's is packed with boozers who stare fish-eyed at the invaders. The women, many smoking small cigars, wear flowing skirts and stockings that plunge into high-heeled black boots with bells attached at the ankles.

A hulk, unshaven, with a filthy apron at his waist bounds over the bar to confront the group. "What the hell's all this about? You people can't come in here and—"

"Here he is." Barnum raises palm on high. "Oliver B. McGuirk."

The little choir stops singing. The clergymen shut their eyes, clasp hands, and begin a prayer for the soul of Oliver B. McGuirk.

"Say, ain't you Barnum, the circus guy?" says McGuirk. The impresario is as famous as the freaks and monstrosities he exhibits.

"Mr. McGuirk, I'm going to save your soul. Not only for the benefit of my new acquaintance, Mr. Bierce, but for Arthur Brisbane, the young reporter from the *Sun,* and for all the sinners who patronize your establishment."

"*Save* my soul?" McGuirk snorts. "That's been tried before."

"Ah, but I know your family, and how you've hurt and disgraced them. Your emaciated mother, lying ill in her Brooklyn bed. Your father, grieving for both you and his blessed dying wife. And your three kindly brothers, two of whom are Presbyterian preachers, the third a Methodist missionary in the Philippines. I happen to know you were destined to join the ministry. That you once enrolled at the Union Theological Seminary. That you abandoned your ministerial studies after an infatuation with a duplicitous young woman. It wasn't your fault, Mr. McGuirk. You're only a man. You fell. You turned to hard liquor and soft women. 'Twas drink that did it. Take it from a reformed drinker."

McGuirk gasps. "*You* were a drinker?"

"Why, I saw so much intoxication, even among men of wealth and intellect, I asked myself what guarantee I had that I might not become a drunkard too? I forthwith pledged myself to abstain from any kind of spirituous liquors. I took my champagne bottles, knocked off their heads, and poured their contents on the ground. I signed the teetotal pledge. I launched a lecture tour at my own expense to spread the word of temperance."

"How does drink most affect us, Mr. Barnum? Externally or internally?"

"Mr. McGuirk, it affects us *e*-ternally!"

Amen! Amen!

"Mr. McGuirk, I present a drama in my Moral Lecture Room, *The Drunkard.* In the first act, we see the moderate drinker on the path to ruin. In the second, his increased appetite for strong drink, the distress of his relations, the embarrassments of himself and his family. In the third act, we witness his drunken orgies on Broadway, his barroom debauchery, his degradation and the vileness of his companions. In the fourth, despair and attempted suicide. And in the fifth and final act, we celebrate his restoration to sobriety with the help of the Bible and the Temperance Society. Mr. McGuirk, it's your story told—or can be."

Amen! Amen!

"Salvation is at hand, Mr. McGuirk. You're going to be saved tonight." He turns to Clubber. "Okay, Inspector, bring her in."

Williams opens the saloon doors wide. Into the room walks a group of police officers in blue uniforms and domed hats. They carry a cot. On it, bundled in sheets and blankets, is a wizened, frail woman, white hair streaming across her face. The police officers lower the cot at the feet of Oliver B. McGuirk.

"Do you know this woman?" Barnum says.

McGuirk looks wide-eyed at the tiny, misshapen figure before him. The woman raises her withered hand. So weak she is.

"Mama? My dear *mama?*" Tears gush from his eyes.

"True, Mr. McGuirk." Barnum lays his hand on the barkeep's shoulder. "Your saintly mother. On her deathbed. All the way from Brooklyn to see her son one last time."

"My dearest boy, my darling son."

"And Mr. McGuirk, who is this man walking into this very room? A man you once knew well. A man who bounced you on his knee. A man you haven't seen for more than twenty years."

The gaunt, stooped figure of an old man limps into Oliver B. McGuirk's arms.

"Father?" McGuirk says. *"Daddy?"*

"My son, how we've grieved for you."

The Reverend Talmage puts the pitch pipe to his lips. The clergymen sing. *Abide with me! Fast falls the even tide . . .*

"Yes, Mr. McGuirk," Barnum says as the ministers hum in the background, "God has reunited you with your virtuous mother and father."

Tears flow down McGuirk's cheeks as he embraces his aged parents. "Praise be, Lord."

"See the light, Mr. McGuirk. Ask for salvation. Do you want to be saved?"

"Glory, glory, glory. I does want to be saved."

Bierce notices the Reverend Henry Ward Beecher eyeing a beefy woman in black stockings, faint mustache above her upper lip. Even as he does, this man of God places his holy hand on the saloon owner's head. "Oh Lord," Beecher beseeches, "deliver this poor soul into your hands and protect him from evil and Godlessness now that he's seen the light. Amen." No doubt, Bierce surmises, Beecher is wondering how he might maneuver the whore into a cubicle and fork her without being discovered by his confrères.

"What will you do, Mr. McGuirk," Barnum says, "now that you've repented?"

"I'll close my saloon every Sunday like the law says."

Amen!

"Every day at the start of business I'll gather my girls, my bar-keeps, and my musicians and read to them from the Scriptures."

Amen!

"When my girls retire with their customers to the back I'll give 'em a Holy Bible to take with them."

Amen!

"On every table there'll be a hymnal."

Amen!

"Two mornings a week, an hour before the saloon opens, I'll hold a prayer service, to which you all is invited."

Amen!

"Ain't that satisfactory, Mr. Barnum?"

"And the booze, sir?"

"On Mondays, I'll serve non-alcoholic cider until five in the after-noon."

"Hmmm," hums Barnum.

"Mr. Barnum, ain't I repented enough?"

"It's a start, Mr. McGuirk. You're saved."

Amen!

The showman puts his arm around Bierce. "Sir, as you've just wit-nessed, I saved a soul and saved my circus as well. There's an after-noon performance of my circus at Madison Square Garden tomorrow. As per your agreement, you shall repent before the multitude."

"I envision public humiliation."

"Don't be so crestfallen, Mr. Bierce. The only thing you stand to lose are your evil ways."

Bierce slinks back to the Navarre Hotel and takes the elevator to his room. He is dispirited, but he also smells a rat. What was it he him-self said about sham? The profession of politicians, the science of doc-tors, the knowledge of reviewers, the religion of preachers; in a word, the world. Could he have been humbugged by the Prince of Hum-bugs? He sits on the edge of his bed. By the gaslight he watches a crawly creature climbing the wall. Finally he puts on his coat, rides the elevator to the lobby, and retraces his steps to the Tenderloin, where he stands outside of McGuirk's saloon. Light blazes from within, the accordion is abrasive, bells jangle from the boots of the hookers. As he walks through the swinging doors he feels the sawdust crunch under his shoes. McGuirk sits at a table near the bar, a woman of ample poundage on his lap. He and the woman have their mouths together separated only by her tongue. His hand navigates the veins in her breasts.

"McGuirk?"

"Who wants him?"

"I was here earlier tonight. I thought you were saved."

"Saved?"

"By P. T. Barnum."

McGuirk pushes the harlot from his lap. "Take a walk, dearie, and bring me another ale. Yeah, I remember you, mister. With all them preachers you was. Sure, I repented. Ain't no secret. I got an understanding with Mr. Barnum. When he needs a sinner to repent, he pays me to repent. Hell, I've repented forty-two times already."

"Your mother, your father . . ."

"I'm an orphan."

"But I saw . . ."

"Mr. Barnum provides 'em. From the circus. Every time I need a ma and pa, Mr. Barnum comes up with 'em."

"The clergymen with Mr. Barnum. Do they know?"

"Hey, they gotta fib in order to save souls."

"Barnum, that damned old charlatan!"

"Stick around, mister. It's almost time for the rats."

"Rats?"

"I got a rat pit in the basement. You ain't seen nothin' until you seen a rat fight. I takes bets. Anyone who places a bet gets a drink on the house."

Poor Bierce. His venture in the Black Hills ends in humiliation. His attempt to salvage his reputation fails. He is conned by P. T. Barnum. It's time to tuck his forked tail between his legs and retreat to California. The next morning, he buys railroad tickets and wires Mollie of his plans, asking about the children as an afterthought. The night before he is to ride the ferry across the Hudson to the train he dreams.

He knows it's a dream. But unlike a player piano he can't switch it off.

Banging at his door. Barnum. "Tom Thumb has been abducted for ransom, Mr. Bierce! It's the gangster Albert E. Hicksey Hicks. He's leading a coalition of gangs. The Plug Uglies, the Gophers, the Hudson Dusters, the Gas Housers, the Shirt Tails, the Five Pointers, and the Dead Rabbits. They've commandeered the William Vanderbilt mansion at Fifth Avenue and Fifty-second. That's where Tom's being held captive. You were a topographical officer in the war. We need you to draw a map. Show us the enemy's defense and our best offense. And don't forget your gun. Inspector Williams will lead the charge."

Bierce dives into his trousers, struggles into his boots, and grabs his bowler.

They pour out of the Navarre, all Barnum's circus people, living and dead. Lavinia Warren, Tom Thumb's wife; Jenny Lind; Joice Heth, nursemaid to George Washington; Madame Clofullia, bearded lady; the Siamese Twins; Commodore Nutt; Major Atom; the Aztec Children; Alexander the Conjurer; the Tallest Man in the World; the Fiji Cannibals; the Fattest Woman; Captain Georges Costentenus, the tattooed man; Yellow Bear, Chief of the Kiowas; Miss Dora Dawron, the Double-Voiced Singer; the White Negro, white and getting whiter.

"Climb on board." Barnum points at the ladder.

They scale a ladder to mount Jumbo the Elephant. Behind them come the Woolly Horse, the Fejee Mermaid, assorted lions and tigers, a hippo with two horns, a herd of buffalo, various snakes, seals, bears, and camels. In an enormous wagon enclosed by glass is the Great White Whale, water jetting from its spout.

"How do we proceed, Mr. Bierce?" Barnum says.

Bierce checks the map he's just sketched. "A frontal attack across Fifth Avenue is the only way."

"You heard him, Inspector. Lead on."

Clubber Williams, standing in an ox cart, raises his nightstick, and directs his army forward. The gangsters fire muskets from the windows of the Vanderbilt mansion as the circus people attack. Several fall, including the Tattooed Man, Major Atom, and the Fattest Woman. The Siamese Twins are mortally wounded.

"Stand your ground!" shouts Williams. Bullets fly. Smoke rises. Blood pools.

Jumbo splinters through the front door of the mansion. All the gangsters of New York are inside: Jane the Grabber, Johnny the Mick, George Leonidas Leslie, Shang Draper, Banjo Pete Emerson, Traveling Mike, Marm Mandelbaum, Black Lena, Kid Glove Rosie, Sheeny Mike Kurtz, Hoggy Walsh, Fig McGerald, Googy Corcoran, Spanish Louie, Roo-Roo, Red Rocks Farrell, Slops Connolly, Lizzie the Dove, Italian Dave, Crazy Butch, One-Lung Curran, and Baby-Face Willie. Hand-to-hand fighting. With her beard, Madam Clofullia smothers a Plug Ugly. The Tallest Man in the World propels a Hudson Duster through a window. Jenny Lind raises her voice into a high-pitched scream that cracks the ear drums of a Dead Rabbit. The Great White Whale jettisons a stream of water that drowns a Gopher on the spot. Chief Yellow Bear scalps a Shirt Tail. Clubber Williams smashes his way through a pocket of Gas Housers. The Fiji Cannibals corner a group of Five Pointers in the attic and eat them. It's Bierce who subdues Albert E. Hicksey Hicks and marches him from a basement bunker, gun to the gangster's head. The surviving gang members are shackled to each other to wait for the paddy wagon ride to the Tombs. A disheveled Tom Thumb, with his thumb up, emerges small and scared, but safe.

Barnum says, "Excellent work, Mr. Bierce. Your map got us across Fifth Avenue."

Bierce pushes his way through the crowd of joyous circus people. He's elated but dizzy. He loses his breath. His asthma flares. He stumbles, then leans against a wall. Into focus appears a man with a shotgun.

"I'm the only one you didn't get," the gunman says. "No way out this time, sissy boy. I should have finished the job on you back in Indiana."

"Harley Purvis? You're dead."

"So are you, sissy boy." Purvis pulls the trigger.

Bierce's brains splatter against the wall. He puts his hand to his face. Feels the liquid. He sits up in his bed. Barely breathes. Turns up the gas jet. The light throws empty shadows against the wall. He's alone. His hand is wet with his own sweat. He wipes his face with a monogrammed Navarre Hotel towel. Dammit, the dreams! They won't go away. At least there's no white horse this time. He takes no chances, so he forces himself to stay awake until morning.

Now, at Celaya, Bierce is a decrepit warrior with little to do. That old fake Barnum, at least, made him a topographical officer. Here, he's supposed to be a mouthpiece conning the press. Stepping outside the caboose, he observes Pancho, looking through binoculars, astride Seven Leagues. Bierce knows the commander of the *División del Norte* is seeing only what he wants to see.

Through the battle haze Pancho can just make out Obregón's gun emplacements, nearly invisible below the high ground. He don't like the visions in the fuckin' spyglass. Maybe the gringo's right. Villa knows from his spies that the man in charge of Obregón's artillery is Field Marshal Maximilian Kloss of the Imperial German Army. Pancho once encountered Kloss at the Elite Confectionary in El Paso. Back when Villa was an exile on the run. The kraut wore a crisp uniform and a mustache that twirled upward like a devil's horns, and offered money and armaments in the name of the Kaiser. They argued. The two fought with their fists. Kloss ended in the sawdust, his uniform stained with chocolate syrup and blood.

To Fierro Villa says, *"Formación de batalla."*

Pancho's troops roll their artillery into place, but most of their big guns remain with the brigades of Generals Angeles and Urbina, unavailable for the battle. Villa, his heavy bandoleers clanking, climbs to his stallion. Fierro mounts his horse as well. The Butcher looks down at Bierce and grins. He points his finger at the American and squeezes it as though firing a revolver. Bierce turns away, knowing Fierro would love to kill him, but today there are others more important to kill than some insignificant white-haired son of a bitch. Villa raises himself in the saddle and again peers into his binoculars at the battle line. "Begin firing, General," he orders Fierro, who in turn signals the artillery. The earth begins to thud. Clouds of dust and smoke start to darken the fortifications of Celaya.

"All right, you sons of whores!" Pancho shouts to his Dorados. "Let's see how good you really are!" He whips Seven Leagues forward as the bugles sound and the horsemen charge.

"¡Viva Villa!"

Bierce hears the cry, but knows it lacks heart. How do they say it in Spanish? *Corazón triste.*

Chapter Fifteen

A rowdy pack, those damned newswhores, especially the Americans. After preserving his anonymity for so long, Bierce, smarting under Pancho's orders, enters the lion's den—tent. The reporters work and bitch in a capacious canvas pavilion only yards from the hospital train. He's no stranger to the newspaper trade, from his failed effort as a printer's devil to flourishing as the star columnist for William Randolph Hearst. Yet he is mistrustful of the press and joyfully lashes out at it when it caters to the most common instincts of its readers. His relationship with Hearst sours soon after that fateful day in Oakland when Bierce, down on his luck, is rescued from oblivion by the newspaper magnate-to-be. Even en route to Mexico, Bierce dabbles on his exposé of Hearst as a dangerous demagogue—but doesn't come close to finishing it. Hell, the only thing he's going to finish now is his very being. The correspondents are being kept at gunpoint by Villa's guards from entering the battle zone, and they don't like it. They glance up briefly from their typewriters, card games, and whiskey as Bierce walks into the press tent. They've seen the old gent around, Villa's valet. A light-skinned Mex. What the hell does he want?

"Gentlemen, may I have your attention? Your attention, please. General Villa has instructed me to inform you . . . Gentlemen, please. Attention, dammit! That's better. No doubt you've all heard the guns, so it's no surprise to you that the battle for Celaya's underway."

The reporters fall over each other to swarm around the messenger, who is wearing a Stetson and eyeglasses hoping they help to disguise his face. He reads the names on their press badges. Floyd Gibbons, Frederick Palmer, Gregory Mason, George Clements, William A. Willis, Edmund S. Behr. No one here from Hearst? No, Hearst is too cheap to hire foreign correspondents. For Hearst, the wire is satisfactory enough for foreign coverage. Wait, he notices a Hearst movie team.

"As the siege is in its early stages I have no further information, other than to say General Villa is confident he will subdue General Obregón and permanently expel all federal forces from the state of

Guanajuato. It's General Villa's view that Venustiano Carranza, president of Mexico in name only and deposed from the capitol, will soon be permanently overpowered by the Division of the North."

When are we going to get to go to the front?

Why are we being kept so far behind the lines?

How many men does Villa have?

Where's General Urbina?

Why isn't General Angeles in position?

When are we going to be taken to the action?

Say, what's your name again?

"Grile. Dod Grile."

Floyd Gibbons of the Chicago *Tribune* is particularly obnoxious. "Listen, Grile, why the hell are we stuck back here when the battle's up the road? And why's some Americano like you speaking for Villa anyway?"

"Who says I'm an American?"

"Then I'm a monkey's uncle. Just who the hell are you? You look damned familiar. I always assumed you were one of Villa's lackeys, but now I'm beginning to wonder."

"I'm General Villa's auxiliary press attaché, and that's all you need to know. You're behind the lines because the general is doing battle and he doesn't want civilians in harm's way."

"We're newspaper correspondents, not civilians. Used to taking risks."

"Then I will put it another way, Mr. Gibbons. He doesn't want a lot of damned useless newspaper reporters like you under his heels. Now go back to your booze and card games and stay the hell out of his way."

The Hearst newsreel team grinds away as Bierce speaks. Later, the film will turn out to be underexposed. The reporters yell and whine.

"Gentlemen, you've heard all I have to say. I'll give you additional briefings when I have more information."

Bierce tries to flee, but Floyd Gibbons catches up with him outside the press tent.

"Grile, I question your right to keep us from the front."

"It is not I who is keeping you from the front, but the orders of General Villa. And what makes you think you have a right to go there anyway?"

"I'm a newspaperman and war is news."

"To publish news because it's news has no basis in law."

"Ever heard of the First Amendment?"

"Ever heard of Mexico?"

"Just trying to do my job, Grile. Got to make a living, you know."

"So does a burglar."

"Damn, I think I've seen you before—or someone who looks like you. Say, you couldn't be . . ."

"Put it out of your mind, Gibbons. Whatever you think, you'd be wrong."

The two men glare at each other. Gibbons backs into the shadow of the press tent and disappears. He's a busy man. No more time to waste on some old coot in a Stetson. A tight smile comes to Bierce's lips. Gibbons will go to the front all right, no matter what. Bierce knows the type. The threat of battlefield annihilation, arrest, censure, dismissal, a lost eye, even a bullet in the brain will never dissuade a man like Floyd Gibbons. In another war they might be drinking pals.

Flashes of artillery illuminate the sky like lightning. He huddles close to the scant protection of the hospital train. The cars wait to be filled. The doctors inside, he imagines, are shuffling cards, the nurses sipping coffee, joking with one another as they anticipate their moment. The crackle of far-off arms sounds almost benign, like an Indiana Fourth of July. Then it all changes. He feels the thud of shells thwacking the ground, as though the turf is being pounded by pile drivers. Obregón's cannon. A colossal wallop knocks him to the earth. A geyser of dirt erupts. On his stomach, he covered his ears with his hands as if that might protect him.

¡Madre de Dios!

Shells sail overhead. An explosion. Another. The last so loud that for a moment he loses his hearing. He's been in battle before, unafraid. But now . . . He isn't fearful of death, so he keeps telling himself, but so anonymously? To be minced into fragments like chopped meat? To vanish without a trace in this scorching desert?

¡Madre de Dios!

The hospital train's hit. Steel splinters into shreds, wood pulverizes into dust. Doctors and nurses are torn apart. Debris cascades. When he raises his head he sees an arm disconnected from its body, the fingers curled as though gesturing. A few playing cards flutter to the ground, jacks, queens, ace—God's way of providing theological solutions. He wonders if any of the correspondents are among the victims. Correspondents. The past flashes through his mind. The day Hearst transports him from the penury of satirical weeklies into the real newspaper world. Shortly after his separation from Mollie and his exile to Oakland.

His room boasts two windows overlooking Market Street. Writing desk, two chairs, single bed, chest of drawers. His uniformly black suits hang neatly in a mahogany wardrobe. Outside of a small library Bierce's possessions are meager. He likes the fact that his life is simple. He owns no house, no horse, no wagon. He vows never to possess more than his books, typewriter, and the arrowheads he collected as a child. The fewer the distractions, the more he can concentrate on what matters. Parting from the *Wasp* was difficult, and for the moment he is without a venue for his work. Still he writes. Stories. Terrible tales. About the war, his war. Confederate horseman silhouetted against the sky in the sight of a Union sharpshooter. Deaf-mute child thinking the carnage of battle is a game. Captain who trains his artillery at the house occupied by his own wife and child. Hanged from a railroad bridge, a soldier who believes he has escaped death even as he dangles from the noose. Execution of a captured soldier shocked to find he is to die without the military honor he'd expected. Soldier trapped in rubble, his own hair-trigger rifle aimed between his eyes. Some of the tales have been told to him, some he has seen with his own eyes, some he creates out of whole cloth. He writes about scoundrels and fools and murderers and his own secret terrors. He writes. Sardonic stories with twists of irony.

He steers his pen to a sheet of paper, dates it March 1887, and writes the opening words to a story. "Early one June morning I murdered my father—an act which made a deep impression on me at the time."

At the door a tentative knock. A gangly, horse-faced young man, hesitant, stands in the hall. In his hands a hat, folded newspaper, and walking stick.

"Mr. Bierce?" Voice high-pitched, demeanor nervous.

"You're not here to serve me with a summons, are you, young man?"

"Summons?"

"A joke."

"Oh. No, I, I'm from the San Francisco *Examiner.*"

"From Mr. Hearst you say."

"Sir, I *am* Mr. Hearst."

"Come in, come in. Sit down. Yes, sit. No, no, not in that chair. This is the more comfortable of the two. Let me dust it first. Sit, sit."

Hearst sits, knees together. The young man tries to gather his words but nothing comes.

"So, Mr. Hearst, what may I do for you?"

Hearst clears his throat. "I . . . I came to make you an offer."

"What sort of offer?"

"I want you to work on the *Examiner.*"

"In what capacity?"

"I've admired your column 'Prattle,' first in the *Argonaut* and later in the *Wasp.* I believe you're the most brilliant satirist in America. I want you to do the same thing for me in the *Examiner.*"

"Need I say I'm flattered?"

"My proposal is for you to write three columns a week, including one for the Sunday edition. All on the editorial page."

"Tempting, Mr. Hearst." Hearst doesn't know how tempting, how much Bierce, with no prospects, needs a break. "What are we talking about in terms of remuneration?"

"Thirty-five dollars a week. In addition, the *Examiner* will publish anything and everything else you write at better than the usual line rates."

A veritable fortune for a man with such a fuzzy future. "Hmmm. I've read your paper, Mr. Hearst, and there are no bylines."

"Except in your case. You'll be the only writer on my editorial page with his name attached."

"I'm inclined to accept your offer."

"Splendid." Hearst holds out his hand

Bierce declines it. "On condition."

"Oh?"

"Not one word of my copy is to be touched."

"Well . . ."

"Not a word."

"But you and I might have differences that would lead us in opposite directions editorially."

"In that case, Mr. Hearst, feel free to suspend the article. But I have no intention of permitting second-rate editors and sycophants to mutilate my words."

"There are no sycophants and no second-raters at the *Examiner*. I intend to make it into the leading paper in the world."

Bierce has his doubts. Already hating the fledgling *Examiner* with its sensational headlines and exploitive reporting, he is sure he will despise Hearst in the long run, but what the hell? "I accept." The two men shake hands. Bierce is startled at how soft Hearst's hand is, how weak the grip.

"May I offer you tea, Mr. Hearst?"

"With pleasure."

Bierce leaves the room for a moment to ask his landlady to bring a pot of tea and two cups. When he returns, Hearst is standing over Bierce's writing table reading the story newly begun.

"Is this how you've been occupying your time, Mr. Bierce, writing tales?"

"Mostly about soldiers. And civilians."

"As one of your biggest fans, I am not unfamiliar with the literary side of Ambrose Bierce."

"Literary, no. Fiction, yes. Literature is permanent. Fiction is born, flourishes, and dies without hope of resurrection."

"Like journalism."

"And like journalism, fiction is vigorous in its youth, decrepit in old age, and detested in its grave."

After the landlady leaves the teapot, the two men sip, eyeing each other. From outside they hear the voice of a fishmonger calling his wares. Children sing as they skip rope.

"You're a much younger man than I imagined, Mr. Hearst."

"I'm twenty-three."

"And I forty-five. Old enough to be your father."

"My father. The senator wanted me to follow in his footsteps. Mining. Ranching. But when the *Examiner* fell into his hands as the result of a debt, I begged him to give the paper to me. He was losing so much money on it he told me he planned to give it to an enemy."

"And your experience at running a newspaper?"

"Business manager of the *Lampoon* at Harvard. I was expelled for some silly prank, but soon after I became a reporter on the New York *World*, where I learned that within three years Joseph Pulitzer boosted the circulation from fifteen thousand to two hundred fifty thousand. He did it by reaching the people, not the intellectuals. There are those who think the *World* is vulgar and trashy, but I'm going to emulate Pulitzer— and do him better. My circulation is less than twenty-four thousand. Within the year, I intend to make it thirty-two thousand. Within three years I'll have more readers than the *Chronicle* and the *Call* combined."

"By becoming more vulgar than the *World?*"

Hearst gulps his tea. He is enthusiastic. "The fact is, I'm hiring the best newspaper staff in the world. Taking on causes, starting with a campaign against Collis P. Huntington's Union Pacific Railroad monopoly." He returns his empty cup to the writing table. "There's a grip man on Powell Street who takes his cable car out at three o'clock in the morning. While he's waiting for the signals he opens the *Examiner*. I want my reporters to think about him when they write their stories. I don't want them to write a single line our grip man can't understand and won't read." He shakes open the paper he has brought with him. "I've given the *Examiner* a whole new look. See, now seven wide columns instead of nine narrow ones. I've expanded it to eight pages, and I've lowered the advertising rates."

Hearst's biggest advertiser is a Dr. Prentice, who boasts of straightening one hundred thirty-eight cross-eyes in a single month. The *Examiner* sells space to other advertisers of similar dubious reputation. Peck's Cure for the Deaf, patent improved cushioned ear drums that perfectly restore the hearing. Buffalo Lithia Water, a remedy for Bright's Disease, Gout, Rheumatism, Acid Dyspepsia, Malarial Poisoning, etc. A Professor Shipley claiming to have removed one thousand two hundred tapeworms in the past five years. Rubifoam Liquid Substitute for Tooth Powder. Barry's Tricopherous for the Hair, guaranteed to force hair to grow, fasten falling hair, make the hair thick, and cure scurf and dandruff. Paine's Celery Compound, which purifies the blood, regulates the kidneys, and cures their diseases. Pfeil's Antidote for Drunkenness, costing only a dollar and guaranteed to cure alcoholism forever—in less than a week.

"Mr. Hearst, when I saw in your newspaper the ad for Pfeil's Antidote for Drunkenness I ordered a bottle, sampled it, and liked it so much I started ordering it by the case. Then I realized I'd broken the booze habit, but was now addicted to Pfeil's."

Hearst laughs. "Perfect, Mr. Bierce. Just the sort of humor I want to read in your column. As the paper grows, the advertisers will improve in quality and quantity." He gets to his feet and performs a silly little jig. "I'm going to make it the most talked-about periodical on the West Coast. Every time it jumps in circulation I'll blaze the fact on the front page." He holds the paper before Bierce's eyes. "My first revised issue."

MONARCH OF THE DAILIES

LARGEST, BRIGHTEST AND BEST NEWSPAPER ON THE PACIFIC COAST

THOUSANDS OF NEW READERS

THE MOST ELABORATE LOCAL NEWS

THE FRESHEST SOCIAL NEWS

THE LATEST AND MOST ORIGINAL SENSATIONS

"Modesty's not in your vocabulary, is it, Mr. Hearst."

"In fact, most people consider me quite modest, but not when it comes to promoting the *Examiner*. My mother still calls me Willie." Hearst flips opened the paper to the editorial page.

A GREAT PAPER

"Your column's going to be on this very page." Hearst stabs at it with his finger. "'Prattle' by Ambrose Bierce. San Francisco will applaud you."

"Agreed, sir, but for how long?"

After Hearst leaves the modest room, Bierce soars to the heavens but soon returns to the reality of Oakland. As he sips a glass of Martell, he thinks of Mollie and the kids. When had he last seen them? Poor Mollie. Damned little passion in their marriage. Truth be told, she bores him, annoys him. The whining. Pedestrian music she laboriously fingers on the piano. Popular novels she reads. Her bewilderment at his brilliant observations. Her noxious little homilies and platitudes. He imagines nefarious things about her, such as when he discovers that she has an admirer, a mutual acquaintance who has the effrontery to write her ornate and flowery letters bordering on the romantic. Bierce might have shot the bastard had not Mollie tearfully defused the crisis by insisting the relationship was purely platonic. Nevertheless, there are moments, in frustration, when Bierce wants to shout at her, thunder brains into her head. Instead, he closes her out of his mind and heart.

The air is as sharp as his bite as he finds his way to the *Examiner's* offices at 10 Montgomery Street carrying his first column for William Randolph Hearst. Bierce notes that Willie's excitement excites others. Hearst writes the glaring headlines himself until the staff gets the idea. He tinkers with the printing press and feels grease on his hands. He splits his nails setting type. He suggests ideas for features and motivates his staff with the flair of a Stonewall Jackson. He does it quietly and courteously, never raising his voice, rarely issuing a command as such. The excitement rubs off onto Bierce, who launches his attacks on the Southern Pacific as the worst, most greedy railroad in the nation. The railroad's biggest champion is a U.S. senator and former governor whose name Bierce spells £eland $tanford.

"Magnificent column, Mr. Bierce. More of the same, please."

Hearst and Bierce sit in the young publisher's office, crowded by a collection of Egyptian mummy cases.

"I see you're looking at my mummy collection. I purchased them on my last trip to Cairo. They're here temporarily until I send them to my ranch. I also bought a Pharaoh's tomb. Plan to have it reconstructed. Not only that, when I was in Verona I acquired a circular well-head made of stone. Weighs five tons."

"I see you also collect German beer steins and porcelain, Mr. Hearst." The steins, faces alternately glowing or glowering, line the room like gargoyles.

Hearst laughs. To Bierce the voice is annoyingly high-pitched, a womanish timbre for such a big man.

"My collections have no limit. Stamps, coins, rare books, paintings. Some day, I hope to build a place big enough to show them all. A castle, perhaps. Are you a collector?"

"I am, but outside of my childhood arrowheads, I don't acquire objects."

"What else is there to acquire?"

"Words, ideas. Like you, I also store them. But in the reservoir of my mind. I can take them out and display them at a moment's notice. Eminently portable. And I don't find it necessary to show them all at the same time."

In his columns, Bierce teases, taunts, twits, torments, and occasionally drops an accolade. He receives fan mail from a budding novelist named Gertrude Franklin Atherton. He is susceptible to letters applauding him, especially when signed by women, about whose faces and bodies he will fantasize. He over-praises Atherton's writing.

When an *Examiner* editor cuts Bierce's obituary of a famous actress, which read that she was "always famous for her composed manner, and she is now quite decomposed," Bierce pens a furious letter of resignation to Hearst, accusing the publisher of breaking his promise that Bierce's prose would never be touched. He storms off to Angwin's Vacation Camp on Howell Mountain in search of solitude. Somehow, Hearst, although exhausted by the climb, finds his way to the camp and comes upon Bierce sitting moodily on the cabin's front porch.

"Ah, the publisher of the San Francisco *Examiner* comes to the mountain."

"The mountain wouldn't come to me."

Through the cabin's open door, Hearst sees a fleeting movement inside.

"Is someone with you, Mr. Bierce?"

Bierce calls. "Carrie."

A young woman, slender, with hair as blond as Hearst's, steps to the doorway. She holds a broom.

"Mr. Hearst, meet Miss Carrie Christiansen."

"How do you do, Miss Christiansen?"

"Very well, sir."

"Miss Christiansen is a schoolmarm in these parts, Mr. Hearst. A family friend, in fact."

"Indeed."

"She is working as my secretary."

"Oh?"

"A much better typist than I. She is trained on the Underwood. I use a mere two fingers."

She disappears into the cabin. They hear her inside. Sweeping.

"Just why have you come, Mr. Hearst?"

"As a committee of one to persuade you to return to the *Examiner*."

"Out of the question."

"I implore you."

"Absolutely not."

"Write about anything you like if you'll only write."

"You blue-penciled my column, Mr. Hearst."

"The work of an over-enthusiastic editor, I assure you."

"No excuse."

"For God's sake, don't end 'Prattle.'"

"My mind is made up."

"It's the best thing in the *Examiner*. I don't intend to lose it. Without Ambrose Bierce on the editorial page, I'd cancel my own subscription to the damned old sheet."

"Subscribe to the *Chronicle*."

"It's time for a raise, Mr. Bierce. Another ten dollars a week?"

"You can't bribe me, sir."

"Fifteen."

"Money will not change my mind."

"Twenty."

"I'm a man who can't be bought."

"Twenty-five."

"Mr. Hearst, I've just been bought."

"Welcome back."

They shake hands.

"Sit down, Mr. Hearst. No, here, in my rocker. I'll sit on the steps. I just happen to have a jug of moonshine at hand."

"I don't drink."

"Then you won't mind if I . . ."

"Certainly not. All my reporters imbibe."

"They do indeed. Some have even taken the Keeley Cure before returning to the bottle."

Hearst hikes down the trail. Before he vanishes into the dusk he turns and waves. Bierce waves back. He knows the youthful publisher thinks his star columnist is an oddball. But a brilliant oddball—and one Hearst needs for now, although now doesn't mean forever. Carrie Christiansen steps barefoot from the cabin, places her arms around Bierce, and puts her mouth against the back of his neck, raising a hickey. God, he likes it. She's practically a kid, while he's a . . . Don't think about it, old-timer. There's a lot to be said for the young. Besides, she knows how to wield a broom and damned if she can't type. He realizes now that that clackity Underwood is good for something. And where did she ever learn to brew beer? "It's all in creating the wort and proofing the yeast, Ambrose," she tells him.

Here, within canon range of Celaya, Bierce can't see the heat of the battle, although he can damned well hear it. Pancho's cavalry melts under withering machine-gun fire. The field, layered with land mines, sends red-hot shards of steel into the riders' bodies. Mortally injured soldiers writhe in agony, groping for severed body parts. Dying horses snort and squeal, legs kicking. In the midst of the slaughter, Villa stays in the saddle waving his rifle and screaming at his troops to regroup and recharge. Again. And again. Foam pours from the mouth of his stallion. A burst of machine-gun fire blows Fierro from his mount. His arm bleeding, The Butcher manages to grab his horse and climb back on to continue the attack. Once more the *Villistas* surge against the fortifications and at one point the cavalry breaks through, trampling the enemy with heavy hooves, firing at close range. Briefly, Villa's men make it to the Zócalo and ring the church bells in a pyrrhic victory, but Obregón's auxiliary troops surge forward to drive the guerrillas back and back and back. The ground, slimy with blood, becomes littered with bodies as the survivors retreat like drunkards to their fires, dragging their rifles in the muck.

Pancho limps to his caboose, shaking in fury, dirt filthy, sweat pouring from every gland, his blood and the blood of others staining his uniform. He sinks at the table, puts the bottle of tequila to his lips, immediately feels the rush. He curses the day, curses Obregón, curses Carranza, curses Urbina, who vanished when Villa needed him the most, curses, yes, the Americano who has turned him into a drunk. The fuckers should die, all of them. The Americano. He'll do for now.

Pancho calls for the gringo, who arrives shaken and disheveled. He'll be so easy to kill. One bullet in the . . .

"You seem ruffled, Meester Señor Americano *idiota.*"

"I was nearly obliterated, General, by Obregón's artillery."

Pancho spits. "So the fuck what? Have you seen my casualty list? Do you know how many of my men have been—what is that word you use—obliterated?"

"I learned long ago that every time one is faced with death it's like the first time, so I confess I was frightened. But once again the Damned Thing passed me by."

"I thought you welcomed death."

"What I say and how I feel may not be quite identical."

"What are you holding in that trembling hand of yours?"

"A playing card. Red ace. Symbol of all that is left of your hospital train and everyone on it."

"*Estoy hasta la madre*—enough." Pancho puts his hands over his face. "My soldiers is being sliced down by the thousand. They charge head on, like warriors, while Obregón stays buried in trenches behind barbed-wire, cutting us to pieces with machine-gun fire. What am I to do?"

"General, it is a new and appalling kind of warfare."

"Cowering in a trench?"

"I've tried to explain it to you. In Europe they're even using poisoned gas."

"I poisoned wells, like throwing a dead mule's carcass inside, but what is this gas? No, don't tell me. I want to know about Urbina."

Bierce shakes his head. "General Urbina detached his private train and went away, abandoned his brigade."

"Not Tomás."

"He stole a one million peso payroll belonging to the troops."

Villa hurls the tequila bottle to the wall, where it shatters into re- flective bits. The odor of pulque, oozes to the floor, fills the caboose.

"Now I will have to kill him." Villa closes his eyes and falls back in his chair. His head nods, he snores. Bierce takes off his coat and covers the exhausted general's shoulders. A moth floats in a circle around the candle flame. Bierce snuffs out the light and the moth loses interest.

In the morning, Villa, head pounding, again charges Celaya. Once more his cavalry becomes hung up in newly strung barbed-wire entanglements as bullets tear into the flesh of men and horses. Again, Villa's buglers sound the retreat. Fierro suffers two more wounds and in terrible pain is carried from the field and put into a newly arrived hospital car. He tries to slap the gringo doctor, but this time the doctor slaps him back. After three disastrous charges, Pancho retreats for good. The general, eyes brimming, sits in the caboose across from Bierce.

"I failed, gringo. Celaya. I lost it."

"You've failed before, General, but you recovered."

"My men is deserting by the thousand. Even my officers. Too many to shoot."

"You started from El Paso with only eight men and three whores."

"One whore she got strangled by mistake, I told you. I lost maybe six thousand men at Celaya. Another five thousand surrendered. I don't know how many are wounded. More than the hospital trains can carry. When I fell back, there was bodies on the ground as far as my eye could see. I ain't afraid for myself, but for the *Revolución*. Here, they call me a cattle thief, they call me a killer, but at home in Chihuahua they call me invincible. I know every trail, every arroyo, every boulder, every cave. Even if I am the last man in my army to survive, I will be protected by my people. They are behind me." He puts his palm over the flame of the candle, and when he pulls his hand away he savors the pain because it means he's still alive. "General Francisco Pancho Villa don't surrender to filthy, thieving turncoats like Obregón or to deceitful, phony revolutionaries like Carranza. Do you know what I am? I'm a *cucaracha*."

So it goes, so it goes.

Villa and Obregón carry the fight from Silao to León.

Bierce, writing in his secret diary, notes the course of the general's escalating fall. Short of bullets, Pancho discovers that the ammunition sent to him by his incompetent brother Hipólito from Ciudad Juárez is the wrong caliber, worthless for 30-30 Winchesters and Mausers. Hipólito, supposedly in charge of Villa's arms shipments, spends his days and nights at the roulette wheel in the sporting houses, a whore on either arm and a glass of Scotch in his hand. At León, a burst of *Villista* artillery severs Obregón's arm. Obregón's second in command, a general named Hill, surges forward with his troops. In the face of

Hill's unrelenting artillery and massive cavalry charges, Pancho's men throw down their empty, useless rifles. Scatter into the hills. The survivors of the *División del Norte* load onto the waiting troop trains to retreat to Chihuahua City. Hill hesitates—a miscalculation. Pancho's army escapes liquidation, but barely. Obregón, missing an arm, occupies Encarnación, Aguascalientes, Zacatecas, and San Luis Potosí.

Bierce agonizes with Villa over the defeats, and hesitantly gives him still more bad news.

"I heard on the wireless that President Wilson has abandoned his neutrality to recognize the Carranza government. That means the United States is embargoing shipments of munitions to the Division of the North. General, you can't fight a war without arms and supplies from the U.S."

The hour is late. The smell of death hangs in the air. Bierce finds it hard to recall the names of Villa's battles. So many places have been won, lost, won, and lost again.

The general puts the bottle to his lips. "I will still fight, even if it means crossing the American border and taking whatever I need. That'll get the damned Yankees' attention."

"It would mean U.S. intervention on behalf of Carranza and Obregón."

"I ain't afraid of no Yankee—how you say—intervention. I am still the Centaur of the North."

"There's still Zapata. Perhaps he—"

Villa fists the table with a thump. "Cowardly dog. I give him guns and ammunition and he stays home. He refuses to come out and fight. Zapata don't care what happens to Mexico as long as his peons in their pajamas are safe and content in Morelos." Villa puts his head on the table and closes his eyes. "I am tired, so tired. I could fall into my bunk and sleep for twenty years. I barely know who I am fighting anymore. How long has it been since I been to a bullfight, to a cockfight? Since I heard the mariachis play? Since I last fucked?"

Bierce puts his hand on Villa's shoulder.

"General, this may sound like a ridiculous suggestion, but why don't you take a vacation?"

"You're loco, you old gringo. I'm fighting a goddamned *revolución.*"

"There's a lull. Things are on hold. Fierro can take charge."

"And where the hell do you suggest I vacation? Acapulco? Cancún? No place outside of Chihuahua is safe for me. They would hunt me down like a rabid dog."

"America."

"Huh?"

"I'll take you to the United States. We'll go by way of El Paso. The train."

"Aha! You swore you would never return. That you had a new life—and death. That you would write no more letters to nobody in the States. That no one in America would ever hear from you again."

"We'll return under assumed names to a remote part of my country where no one can possibly expect us."

"You think I don't know, *amigo,* but I see you writing in some little book that you keep hidden from me. Hand it over. Now. I need to know what you're up to."

"So keen of eye you are, General. It is a diary, a daily record of a part of my life that I can relate to myself without blushing. But it is gone now, burned, thrown into a pit of burning corpses. You're looking at a man who carries nothing but himself, a Colt forty-five, an old watch, a book or two, and—I reveal this only to you—the chiseled face of a goddess on a tiny cameo pin."

"Shit, you are loco."

Bierce holds up a magazine page. "Look at this. It is an advertisement in the *Saturday Evening Post,* which your American fliers had. "General, we'll relax with our bottle on some clean, wide porch and count the stars. We'll wait for the cool breeze of the north to dry our tears. We'll take in the pretty ladies in their long skirts. We'll smell the pines. And then . . ."

"And then what?"

"When it gets very late and I'm oh so drunk, I'll take my forty-five and we'll play The Game."

SARATOGA SPRINGS, NY

THE QUEEN OF SUMMER RESORTS
PEERLESS IN ALL THINGS THAT MAKE
FOR HEALTH AND PLEASURE

Mineral springs of the most infinite variety, alkaline, diuretic, saline and cathartic. No other place has such large and attractive hotels. One may travel the whole world over, and nowhere else find such avenues lined with stately elms and lordly maples. Within its borders is the beautiful Saratoga Lake, and it is in close proximity to Lake George, Lake Champlain and the Adirondack Mountains. One of the finest Race Tracks, under the supervision of the New York Jockey Club. The dry, pine-laden air wafted from these fir-clad mountains is a natural health-giving tonic. No malaria nor mosquitoes here to poison anyone.

INFORMATION ON APPLICATION TO
THE PUBLICITY COMMISSION
SARATOGA SPRINGS, NY

Chapter Sixteen

He is in hiding. He fans himself with Hearst's New York *American*—a newspaper he considers good enough only for displacing flatulence—and bobs in the wicker rocking chair. Long ago, his every literary and political notion was set into type and printed in that newspaper and the others in the Hearst chain, but he feels no loyalty to it, only disgust. Fashion, taste, and youth have passed him by. All along the great veranda of the Grand Union Hotel in Saratoga Springs scores of other wicker chairs tilt back and forth in unison like so many rocking horses in the afternoon heat. Female hands flutter Japanese fans, male hands wave fans provided free by the local funeral parlor. Waiters in starched whites serve drinks and tiny pastries. The men rock in stiff collars and women sway in billowing skirts, parasols at their sides should they decide to stroll in the gardens by the Saratoga elms. A string quartet plays the popular favorites. "The Glow-Worm," "The Merry Widow Waltz," "Vilia."

Next to him sits a companion, younger, swarthy, with a reddish mustache curling downward on either side of his mouth. He too rocks, uncomfortable in his new, tight-fitting suit, Arrow shirt, string tie, and shoes with spats. He'd be happier in a sombrero, boots, and a bandoleer astride a horse or crouched on the roof of a commandeered railroad car barreling down the track behind a gush of steam.

¡Viva! ¡Viva!

The older man swats at a fly with his newspaper, then opens it to the sports pages. Reading of the exploits of the athletes amuses him. He is out of touch—preoccupied too long with a faraway war—but is quick to analyze the baseball season.

"General, I think it's clear from reading the newspaper statistics that Boston will win the American League pennant this year."

"Boston?"

"The Red Sox."

"Who wears red socks?"

"On the other hand, the Phillies are, as they say, a cinch in the National League."

"The Phillies, señor? Sounds like a cigar."

"Nickname of nine unhappy men from a place called Philadelphia, desperate to win the Series."

"What you mean Series?"

"A sequence of events leading to either honor or disgrace."

He sees sports figures as men who discharge their brains into their muscles. To him, the manly arts, noble games, and national sports represent little more than emptiness and vanity. Yet he savors, reveres, the passion of combat. The long-healed bullet wound in his scalp attests to that—as does the Colt .45 that is usually wedged in his belt. The bloodshed of the past has made him hard, often unforgiving, but the crack of a rifle shot still thrills his veins. When he smells the odor of gunpowder he has visions of the dead or dying. When he climbs a rise he studies the terrain and weighs its tactical advantages. He isn't packing the Peacemaker at this moment because of the heat and the fact that it seems somehow out of place amid the potted palms on the civilized veranda of this resplendent hotel. Besides, so many years of violence in his life have passed that he can think of only one person he's inclined to kill. But he hasn't quite made up his mind. He will let The Game settle the question.

He turns to what purports to be the newspaper's arts page, overshadowed, of course, by the comic strips: "Happy Hooligan," "Alphonse and Gaston," "Bringing Up Father," "Krazy Kat." Stomach-turning. Candidly, he rather admires "Krazy Kat," but not enough to acknowledge it. He notices an item about a recent novel written by an old antagonist, Gertrude Atherton, something called *Perch of the Devil,* having to do, it appears, with copper mining in Montana. What the deuce would *she* know about mining? He, at least, does, having led a mining operation in Dakota Territory way back when. Merely because it failed ... It's just like the woman, taking on subjects she knows nothing about, no doubt starring some phony, indomitable heroine. The thought of it makes him want to puke. The damned girl ... Kissing dogs. And cats. But never him.

A little boy darts through the wicker and around the palms, nearly toppling a waiter balancing a tray on an upturned hand.

"Johnny, come back here!"

Johnny, who looks to be about five, is dressed in the popular uniform of the day, a sailor suit. His white shirt is topped by a blue-striped collar under which is a carefully knotted silk tie. The suit, along with his full and well-brushed blond hair, makes him appear childishly elegant while at the same time spoiled. When the man was a boy a sailor suit would have been an affection his father wouldn't have tolerated. Clothes were handed down from one sibling to the next.

"Johnny!" Undoubtedly the voice of boy's mother.

The boy trips as he nears the man and sprawls face forward on the floor. A box of Cracker Jacks flies out of the child's hand and the man's lap is showered by the caramelized popcorn. He brushes the sticky caramel from his suit and examines the container from which he was deluged. The slogan on the box reads, "The More You Eat the More You Want." He doubts that. The child looks up at the man who has piercing, deep-set blue eyes and a white mustache. His visage is severe. He could walk over fire and brimstone to hurl bolts of lightning. The boy begins to snivel.

"Look here, lad." The man's voice is cold. He's never made an effort to moderate his tone or manner for the benefit of children, not even his own. Especially not his own. "There's a coupon in this box of Cracker Jacks. If I read it correctly, upon redemption of the coupon you're entitled to a free gift by mail. Certainly, for a boy, that's an estimable achievement, to win a prize merely for consuming the loathsome victuals in a box of Cracker Jacks."

The boy wipes his nose with the back of his hand.

"On your feet, sir. The floor is no place for one wearing the uniform of the United States Navy."

The boy stands.

"Here's your box of Cracker Jacks, lad. May your teeth never rot and may your prize appreciate in value."

Johnny grabs the box, turns, and careens into a young woman.

"Johnny, haven't I told you to stop your running?"

The man rises, standing militarily erect, the remaining kernels of Cracker Jacks falling to the floor. His companion with the drooping mustache also climbs to his feet.

"My dear sir." The young woman clasps her hands. "Please accept my apologies and those of my son. Johnny should never have been dashing around on this crowded porch. He is, well, precocious."

"Precocious, madam? Such as a four-year-old who elopes with his sister's doll?"

"It's a wonder no one got hurt, Mr. . . . Mr. . . ."

The man bows. "Dod Grile, at your service, madam. And my companion, Señor Doroteo Arango of Mexico."

Self-consciously, the Mexican also bows. He's not used to bowing. In fact, he has never bowed to anyone before—not to anyone.

"May I inquire as to your name, madam?"

"Dumont. Mrs. Elizabeth Dumont, originally from California . . ."

"A state I know well, land of rogues, scalawags, fools, pretenders, rascals, and pirates."

She laughs. "But from my earliest childhood my family has lived in Buffalo. I've been a guest in Saratoga Springs each season since I was three. The Grand Union Hotel is virtually a home away from home."

Her dress is maroon. She wears a single strand of pearls at her neck. Her blond hair is swept high on her head. She's pretty, a word long ago defined by the man as a woman with kind eyes, smiling mouth, and cheeks painted by nature. Mrs. Dumont certainly qualifies for the term. She has imperfections, of course. He has a knack of finding imperfections in others. There are fine light hairs around her mouth. One of her nostrils is slightly larger than the other. Her ears are too large. Ears. Think of the comic quality of ears. Look at a handsome man or a woman, admire their beauty, then observe their ears, their useless ears, like the strange growths that affix themselves to potatoes. He adores the female sex, yet treats them with a certain contempt. His favorite toast is, "Here's to woman. Would that we could fall into her arms without falling into her hands." Of course, it's something Mrs. Dumont will never hear him say. He owns, secretly, a delicate cameo, which is chiseled with the face of a goddess who saved him from the honed fangs of fiendish bears. It would be nonpareil were Mrs. Dumont to wear it, but that's out of the question. Or is it?

"Won't you join us, Mrs. Dumont, for a glass of iced tea?"

"Johnny and I should . . ." Fine drops of perspiration collect above her upper lip. Her extraordinarily long tongue slithers up to tastes the salt. She opens her fan and waves it, barely stirring the heavy air around her.

"Quite warm this afternoon, madam, a veritable heat wave. Unusual for this northern clime. A glass of tea will do you good."

"A pleasure then, Mr. Grile."

He motions for her to sit and commands a waiter to bring a fresh pitcher of tea as the quartet performs "Humoresque," the older man's favorite melody, although he can never recall the title or the name of the composer.

"What the deuce is the name of that melody?" he asks her.

"I'll think of it a moment. Isn't it Dvořák?"

The child begins to hop. Grile suspects Johnny's been in constant movement since infancy. He imagines the child, even in sleep, rhythmically banging his head against the side of his crib for hours, a thumping that disrupts the entire household, and a harbinger of many sleepless nights and days.

"I've an idea," Mrs. Dumont tells her son. "Why don't you play with your Tinkertoys? You know how much you love your Tinkertoys."

Johnny darts away, still clutching the empty Cracker Jacks box. As he does he sticks his tongue out at Grile. If Johnny were an adult, he and the man would be enemies on equal terms. The boy and the man both know it.

The young woman laughs. "You know children. They have such energy. And they expect so much."

He sips his drink, iced tea exchanged for brandy. "In childhood we do, indeed, expect. However, in youth we demand. In manhood, we hope. And in old age, we beseech."

She smiles in an uncertain way. "You too must have children."

"I've a daughter, Mrs. Dumont, now forty years of age. And the memories of two sons, struck down prematurely."

"I'm so sorry."

"The mad race run, my dear."

She fans her brow and turns to the gentleman from Mexico. "And you, Señor Arango, have you children?"

She's a woman of curiosity, Grile imagines, no doubt even as a girl asking bold and direct questions to her parents' chagrin. *Why doesn't Mr. Knott have any hair?* she asks within earshot of Mr. Knott, the haberdasher. Or, to the butcher, *How did you get your thumb cut off, Mr. Baldwin?* And to her aunt, *Is what Mama says true, that you're dying, Aunt Doris?*

Arango looks at Grile helplessly.

"Forgive my companion, madam. While he and I communicate quite well in our special way, his English is not proficient. But I might answer by saying Señor Arango has had many wives; many, many mistresses; and many, many, *many* children."

Señor Arango laughs. Too loudly. Nearby guests curiously look his way. The Mexican shrugs, scrapes his finger against his teeth, then draws on his cigar and lets the smoke billow from his mouth. Mrs. Dumont giggles, hiding her mouth behind her Japanese fan. The waiter pours her tea and hands her the glass, chilled by the newly cut crystals from the icehouse. She sips, feeling the lemon coolness in her mouth. Grile also swallows from his glass.

"I see you're no longer drinking tea, Mr. Grile."

"Correct, madam. It's a cordial known as brandy, specifically Martell, a cognac. True cognacs come only from the Cognac region of France, and they're the finest of all brandies."

"My late husband drank brandy."

"My regrets about your husband."

"As you said, the mad race run."

He holds the Martell to the light. "I tell my enemies that brandy is composed of one part thunder and lightning; one part remorse; two parts bloody murder; one part death, hell, and the grave; two parts clarified Satan; and four parts Holy Moses. Even Señor Arango occasionally puts away his usual tequila and lime to sip the drink of heroes. Until he met me, the good señor never touched alcohol and rarely smoked, although he'd dance the heels from his boots. I'm afraid I have been a bad influence on him."

Arango nods and raises his glass in a kind of salute.

"What do you do, Mrs. Dumont, if I may ask?"

"I fancy myself a writer."

He knows something about writers and writing. A lot. "I must caution you, my dear, if women did the writing of the world instead of the talking, men would be regarded as the superior sex in beauty, grace, and goodness."

She waves her hand dismissively. "That's silly, as well as insulting."

"On the contrary—"

"Hear me out, sir. Certainly women can aspire to the literary craft and be as accomplished as men."

"However, history records—"

"That women were dragged by their hair into caves."

"That women occupy a special place."

"Such as in the dining room with their tea discussing sewing patterns while the men drink their brandy and stink up the parlor with their cigars and plan the destruction of the world."

He leans forward. "I'm beginning to feel as though I'm meeting my match."

"Match? As though we're two ignorant prize-fighters exchanging sweat, blood, and blows? Really, sir. I thought our discussion was on a higher level, not about the battle between the sexes."

"May I concede the point, Mrs. Dumont? Even though sweat, blood, and blows are *precisely* what the sexes exchange."

She becomes pensive. "Since you concede, Mr. Grile, in your fashion, I must also make a confession. I'm a novice. I've only written a few short stories. Some poems. All awkward, perhaps. However, I'm attempting a novel."

"The craft of the word remains a worthy art, my dear. It has always been my opinion that writing illuminates the mind, cleanses the soul, and purges evil. Regretfully, it fails to save us from doubt or fear."

"Yes, I do have doubts and fears. It's clear that for you to hold such firm convictions about writing you must be involved in literature in some way. A publisher perhaps?"

"I'd rather commit suicide."

Señor Arango snorts.

"However, madam, I'm experienced in the literary world. I've known and encouraged many young authors. Perhaps you'd favor me by allowing me to read some of your work."

Grile imagines her late at night, a bound book of blank pages before her, writing with a Parker fountain pen that inevitably stains the first joint of her index finger. Stories of her bitter relationship with a cheating husband; her ambivalence about her son—a difficult and potentially destructive child; the hate she feels toward her jealous and cunning mother; her infatuation with an aloof and distant father; her sexual initiation with a wild and inappropriate West Point cadet, Oakleigh, a man who knows how to swallow a revolver's barrel; her masturbatory guilt, which she expresses on paper only by metaphor. She admires her words but isn't totally prepared to reveal herself by allowing anyone else to read them. Perhaps after her demise her writing, like that of Emily Dickinson, will be discovered hidden in a trunk opened by smashing the lock. Scholars and critics will discover the cache and be awed by her style and her insight and her understanding of the human heart. Grile actually doesn't know all this, but he couldn't be more correct.

"I've never been published, Mr. Grile. I'm not sure what I've written is even literature."

"My dear, literature is the collective body of the writings of all mankind, except most writers who have committed *illiterature*."

"I'm afraid my work is too personal, too revealing. Still, I'd so much love to see something of mine in print. Phooey, I don't even care whether I'm paid or not."

"But you should be paid. The quaint nineteenth-century custom in which the publisher drank wine out of the skull of the writer has been rudely disturbed. Now, many authors are demanding some of the wine and are refusing to supply the skulls."

She sips her tea. "Not long ago I attended a lecture by the noted New York publisher Mr. Henry Holt, who complained about literature's commercialization. He said he hated the systematic promotion of certain books and the trend of editors who go after best-sellers for a fast dollar. He insisted that literature has fallen from its high estate, and he urged writers not to expect to earn a profit, but to have some means of support other than their writing."

"Tauri excrementum, if I may use the expression, madam. I've never heard anyone advise publishers, such as the melancholy Mr. Henry Holt, that *they* should have some means of support in addition to their publishing."

She laughs again and looked closely at his face. She sees bold, handsome features not even age can disguise.

"Grile, Grile. Such an unusual name. Is it Anglo-Saxon?"

"Anglo-Saxon through and through. My family moved from Connecticut to Ohio, where I was born on a farm near the Ohio River."

"And just when were you . . ."

"You wish to know my age, Mrs. Dumont? I was born on June twenty-fourth, eighteen forty-two, making me seventy-three years old."

"Do you think of your childhood, Mr. Grile?"

"The past is all we antediluvians have. I remember *things*. Ducks floating on a shallow pond. Tadpoles scattering like underwater ants. Larkspur, black-eyed Susan, goldenrod, May apple. Sunflowers springing up everywhere, even around the privy. The wooden table on which I ate and studied. The flickering of the oil lamp. The homemade chairs. My father's farming tools and animal traps. My mother's clay dishes, bottles, and bowls. Her linen. The Chauncey Jerome mantel clock that chimed each hour. An old flintlock musket. The trunk filled with neatly folded, hand-sewed clothing. A narrow looking-glass that stood as high as a man. The crate containing our balls, bells, baskets, and blocks. Things, Mrs. Dumont."

A wisp of the young woman's hair pulls away and flutters cunningly on her forehead.

"If I may not be too bold or impertinent for asking, Mr. Grile, what is your relationship with Señor Arango?"

"We are business associates in a way." He drains his glass and places it on the table. "He and I are playing a game. Señor Arango is trying to decide whether to kill me. If he doesn't, why, then I may have to do it myself."

"Mr. Grile!"

"Oh, don't take me seriously, Mrs. Dumont. It's a running joke between Señor Arango and me. Would you care for another glass of tea?"

She does not, excuses herself, and departs abruptly to look for her son.

"I think you scared her off, *compadre.*" Arango cackles. "I also think you like her."

"Mrs. Dumont is lovely. She reminds me of . . . a woman I used to know."

"When was this?"

"Eighteen eighty-nine. Sunol, California. I remember the date precisely. The very day, the very hour when I first saw her stepping from a train. I recall everything she wore. And her hair, like Mrs. Dumont's, was combed high on her head."

"You loved this woman?"

"I hated that woman. We argued. About everything. Anything."

"And what became of her?"

"She has become quite successful. Without me. She writes books.

People read her today, while I've been forgotten. Not that I mind, of course. You know me, General. I never relive the past."

"You are such a *mentiroso*—how you say?—liar. Order more ambrosia and tell me about her."

Gertrude Franklin Horn Atherton's letters to Bierce are as intellectually provocative as flirtatious. She tells him she hates him generally but thinks he might be interesting. She praises his handwriting as models of calligraphy and characterizes his every sentence as a treasure. Atherton's novels have had modest success and Bierce praises them a little too much in his column in the San Francisco *Examiner*. She invites him to visit at her family's home in Ross, saying he could sleep in the hammock when he becomes tired of talking to her. He replies he will never go all the way to Ross to sleep alone in some hammock. He invites her to Sunol, where he is recovering from the trauma of his older son's death, and where he is taking in the air, which is better for his health. They agree on a date and she sends him her photograph so he will recognize her at the station. The train's wheels spark as they brake, bits of smoke and fire. Atherton, carrying a parasol and a travel kit, steps to the platform. He is there to meet her.

"You're older than I thought, Mrs. Atherton, but attractive."

"It's indelicate of you, Mr. Bierce, to comment on a woman's age. I'm thirty-four. How old are you?"

"I stand chastised, Mrs. Atherton. I'm forty-nine."

"Hmmmm. Older than I thought. But attractive."

Bierce harrumphs.

They stroll arm-in-arm to Bierce's hotel. He eyes his companion as they walk. Her hair is blond, swept high on her head. One of her nostrils is slightly larger than the other. There is a single strand of pearls at her neck and she wears a blue dress and shoes with pointed toes. She sees a middle-aged man of striking good looks, with a bristling mustache, beetling brows, and beautiful hands. Bierce has a mysterious quality about him that interests her. Men with dark pasts are intriguing.

"Let me say I'm deeply sorry about the loss of your son."

"I'm touched by the sentiment, my dear."

"I, too, lost a son. When he was just six. Of diphtheria."

"So sorry."

"And I lost a husband. Poor George. For his health, he went to sea and died of a hemorrhage after receiving a dose of morphine for a kidney stone attack. In Tahiti, they embalmed him in a barrel of rum and shipped him back."

"Rum? I salivate at the thought, Mrs. Atherton. I might consider going that way myself."

"It's been bandied about that after the ship docked in San Francisco they brought the barrel of rum with George's body inside to my door. A fairy tale. George is buried with his parents in the family mausoleum. I refused to look at George's body. I'm in horror of the dead."

"Death is always difficult . . . for the living."

"Frankly, I was glad to see the bugger go. Eleven years with George Henry Bowen Atherton more than served its purpose, which was to bring two children into the world."

"I have two remaining children, Mrs. Atherton. Leigh and Helen live with their mother."

"And your wife, Mr. Bierce?"

"I don't see her anymore. Twenty years with her also served its purpose."

They approach the hotel, white framed and quaint. She stumbles on a rock. He keeps her from falling.

"Clumsy of me, Mr. Bierce. I'm prone to accidents. Once I drank from a glass of ammonia thinking it was water and almost had to have my stomach pumped."

They walk up the front steps.

"I've been in isolation too long, Mrs. Atherton. But Mr. Hearst makes it possible by sending my check to wherever I choose to be. I'm pleased to receive guests, especially one so attractive as you. Were all my visitors as comely I'd be a happy man. I've always believed that when God makes a beautiful woman, the devil opens a new register."

He sees by her expression that Atherton is irritated by his transparent flattery and annoyed by his remark about women and the devil, but, he gives thanks that she lets it go. The two rock on the porch of the Sunol Glen Hotel and muse, sipping lemonade and watching guests playing croquet on the lawn.

"Mr. Bierce, in one of my letters to you I asked you why you seem to hate dogs so much. You never answered."

"In St. Helena, once, I was walking through the woods with my daughter when a dog snapped at our legs and ankles. I saw an indo-lent-looking fellow leaning against a tree, watching the whole thing, and I shouted at him to call his dog off. When he didn't, I pulled out my gun and shot the animal dead. I asked the man why he hadn't called his dog away. The fellow shrugged and said, 'Shucks, that mutt weren't mine.'"

Atherton laughs. He tells a good story. "I hope you don't make a habit of shooting dogs."

He becomes expansive. "I think I can best summarize my antipa-thy for the beasts with a little verse I wrote. 'Snap-dogs, lap-dogs, al-ways-on-tap-dogs / Smilers, defilers / Reekers and Leakers.' Trouble with the modern dog is that he is the same old dog. Not an inch has the rascal advanced along the line of evolution."

"Perhaps dogs weren't meant to make evolutionary progress, but always intended to be the companion to our breed."

"Nonsense. Nothing in our existence is *intended* to be—dogs in-cluded."

"It is not unreasonable to believe a superior power orchestrates our life."

"I'd hate to deflate your views on religion. It would be unfair to one as young, naive, and pretty as you."

"You're condescending, sir. And we're discussing dogs, not reli-gion."

"The dog is an encampment of fleas and a reservoir of sinful smells. He has no manners. No discrimination. His loyalty is given to the per-son who feeds him, whether his master is honorable or a blackguard."

"Mr. Bierce, your criticism could apply to humans as well as dogs. Have you not known certain humans to be encampments of fleas and reservoirs of sinful smells?"

Bierce throws up his hands. "It is hopeless speaking to you on this subject. Women adore not one dog but the entire disgusting species. Then, of course, a woman will love anything."

"That, sir, is an insult."

"Tell me, Mrs. Atherton, have you ever kissed a dog?"

"Certainly I've kissed a dog. And cats as well. Fuzzy, furry, vulner-able little creatures."

"Likely you've kissed more dogs and cats than men. It is my opinion that the female who holds a dog to her heart is without other lodgers, namely those of the human male species."

Atherton's eyes burn. "Ridiculous. You seem to have as poor an opinion of women as you do of dogs, and I resent it. I didn't take a two-hour train ride all the way to Sunol to be insulted."

"If that's the way you feel about it, Mrs. Atherton, you're welcome to take the next train back."

"Perhaps I will."

"Good."

The two sit in angry silence. They hear the click of the croquet balls struck by mallets. A horsefly zooms across the porch and circles Atherton's head. She angrily brushes it away. Bierce shakes the lemonade pitcher, ice tinkling.

He makes a peace overture. "Would you care for some more refreshment, Mrs. Atherton?"

"Not at the moment."

He refills his glass.

"Mr. Bierce, I came here to discuss literature with you, not dogs."

"As I recall, it was you who raised the subject."

"Now I'm trying to raise the conversation to higher level."

"Then proceed."

"The novel."

He shakes his head. "Don't waste your time thinking about the novel."

"Waste my time? I've already written four of them. And because of discrimination against women writers I've had to use a pseudonym to get them published."

"Madam, in any one quarter-century there can't be more than half a dozen novels posterity will take the trouble to read."

"Hang posterity, Mr. Bierce. I intend to write for now."

"And I'm telling you contemporary novels are only read by reviewers and the multitude. They will read anything as long as it is long, untrue, and new."

"Ridiculous. You're asserting we must read only the classics. If we were to listen to you, there would be no novels written today at all. We'd all be stuck in the past."

Bierce sputters. "You're starting to annoy me, Mrs. Atherton."

"And you're long past annoying me, Mr. Bierce."

"Dammit." He composes himself. "Let me try to explain to you that the modern novel is the lowest form of imagination. It is a diluted story filled with trivialities and nonessentials. I have never seen one that couldn't be cut by a half or three-quarters."

"Sir, the novel affords the writer the opportunity of developing characters in the way a short story can't. It allows the telling of a story that may take place over many years, generations, with many, many participants."

"No, no, no. The novel bears the same relation to literature that a panorama bears to painting. A panorama lacks that basic quality needed in art—unity and totality of effect. As it can't be seen all at once, the panorama's parts must be viewed successively. It is the same with a story too long to be read in a single sitting."

"Just because you've never written one."

"What?"

"You heard me. I've read your stories in the *Examiner*. They may be models of craftsmanship and style, but they cry out for development, for amplification, for expansion."

"You have the temerity to tell me how *my* stories should be written?"

"Somebody should. Your stories have no humanity. They're as cold as ice. And since they don't touch our hearts, your stories will never be remembered."

"I don't write the kind of silly, trite, romantic pap you do, Mrs. Atherton. So don't ever try to tell me your work will be remembered. If, indeed, you find some intelligence other than me to read it."

"Pap? You've praised my work, given me encouragement. You've written to me of my potential. And now you call my work pap?"

"Obviously I was mistaken."

"You're jealous, Mr. Bierce. Because you can't write novels, and you know I can and will. Any clever, cultivated mind with a modicum of talent, such as you—"

"Modicum?"

"—can manage a short story. But it takes a special person with a special endowment to master the novel. You don't have it. All you can do is to criticize and to write bloodless short stories, twaddle, and mean-spirited verse."

"Twaddle? Mean-spirited? What effrontery for you come to my place of residence to criticize me!"

"I'm not the only one who is critical of you. A critic in the *Argonaut* wrote that the world laughs at Ambrose Bierce, that you plagiarize yourself, that you're the most complete literary failure of the century, that you're only a signpost marking the wreck of an utterly wasted life and the grave of a literary bully."

"How dare you show me such little respect!"

"Oh, ho, so you expected me to be a pilgrim carrying incense, wending my way to the shrine in order to sit at the feet of The Master."

"I'm outraged."

"Yes, The Master. That's what your sycophants call you. Master, indeed."

Bierce gets to his feet. His face is red. His eyes tear.

"Excuse me, Mrs. Atherton. I must take my leave."

"Mr. Bierce . . ." She reaches out her hand.

"I'm having a little trouble breathing."

He leaves the porch and walks across the lawn, stabbing his walking stick into the ground. Not only is he furious with her, he's furious with himself for losing his composure. She watches him disappear into a grove of trees, and starts to feel sorry for him. Given a few more years, he could be old enough to be her father. He's had a terrible bereavement, has parted from his wife, his health is delicate. Perhaps she hasn't been as respectful to him as she should be. He's practically a legend in letters. And she has, in effect, imposed herself on him. She finds him sitting on a log. Appropriately, a dragonfly circles his head, pauses for a second on his shoulder, then pirouettes away.

"Mr. Bierce, I'm afraid I was rude to you."

"Indeed."

"You have my sincerest apology."

"In that case, perhaps I overreacted."

"Truce, Mr. Bierce?"

"Truce, Mrs. Atherton."

They shake hands. He holds her hand slightly longer than he should. They walk back to the hotel. In the dining room they sit by a window, the sun pouring in. They dine on pickled oysters; clear leek and parsley soup; a salad of walnuts, apples, and chicory; potato yeast biscuits; rabbit simmered in red wine and thyme; mashed sweet pota-toes; succotash; yellow sponge cake, and iced coffee.

As they eat, Atherton says, "Do you feel the same way about cats as you do dogs, Mr. Bierce?"

"Absolutely not. Cats have a distinctly useful purpose. They're a soft, indestructible automaton provided by Nature to be kicked when things go wrong."

"That's not particularly funny, Mr. Bierce."

"It is not particularly intended to be funny, Mrs. Atherton."

"At times I question your humor."

"And I question humor that fails the test of wit."

"Mr. Bierce, I find you caustic and biting."

"You were aware of my reputation long before you stepped off the train that brought you here."

"Do you actually think I came in homage to you?"

"I'd never use a term quite so grandiose."

She expels a breath. "I suppose I did have some curiosity as to why you're so loved . . . and hated."

"Mrs. Atherton, did you know that each of us in his or her own way is a hypnotist? Hypnotism is a mysterious force. Why is one per-son loved better than another who may be more worthy of love? Per-sonal magnetism. Some people have the quality to draw other persons to them like a magnet."

"That's malarkey."

"Young lady, one's success in convincing another depends on the degree of one's hypnotic power, one's opportunities of exerting it, and one's susceptibility to it. Look at Congress. Each party votes predicta-bly, no matter how convincing the arguments on the other side. The members do the bidding of their more magnetic party leaders. I admit my ability to hypnotize is limited. Despite my worthiness, I'm content to be only occasionally loved . . . and hated."

"Your argument is specious. Who's to say one person is more wor-thy of love than another? Love has ramifications all its own and has nothing to do with worthiness, personal magnetism, or hypnosis. Try again, Mr. Bierce."

"You dismiss my argument cavalierly, young lady."

"Perhaps you *are* right. Your ability to hypnotize is quite limited.

And I don't appreciate being referred to as a young lady. I'm a woman in my thirties."

Bierce glares at her. Spoons rabbit into his mouth and chews furiously. Who is this girl to challenge everything he, The Master, utters?

"Obviously, you're an emancipated woman, Mrs. Atherton."

She sniffs. "Hardly. I won't become emancipated until women's suffrage comes about. When do you suppose that will be? Twenty or thirty years from now?"

"Why the rush? Men and women have survived without suffrage since time immemorial. What's a few more years?"

"Precisely what I'd expect you to say. What's the hurry? No need for you. After all, *you* have the right to vote."

"Perhaps, Mrs. Atherton, I'm old-fashioned—"

"Really?"

"—but I'd like to know how the enlargement of a woman's sphere by her entering commercial, professional, industrial, and political life benefits the sex? Whatever employment women obtain displaces men who would otherwise be supporting women. Where is the general advantage?"

"The general advantage, sir, is that it gives women the same opportunity as men to succeed—and in the same fields. It allows women to broaden their minds and horizons in the way men do. And I believe that is salutary for the general population."

"Mrs. Atherton, no woman is under the obligation to sacrifice herself for the good of her sex by foregoing employment so it may fall to a man. But it is my opinion that the enlargement of women's opportunities has not benefited the sex as a whole. And I believe it has distinctly damaged the race."

"They would never call you progressive, would they, Mr. Bierce?"

"Not without a fight, Mrs. Atherton."

"What you do is to sit back and survey the world around you, find fault with it, cynically ridicule it, and not once offer a suggestion as to how to advance society."

"I am not employed to advance society."

"No one is *employed* to advance society, but most thinking people are obliged to try."

"I view myself as an observer."

She puts a fork filled with salad into her mouth, chews rapidly, and swallows. "You support no cause, see no need for change. You deal in ridicule and sarcasm. You play the cynic's role. You stand for nothing."

"I think I've had about enough of you, Mrs. Atherton. No matter what I say—"

"No matter what you say, you talk like an old crank."

"How dare you!"

"I dare. Dare indeed."

They eat their sponge cake in silence. Bierce refuses to look at her until she removes a cigarette from a small, flat case in her purse.

"Mrs. Atherton . . ."

"May I have a light, Mr. Bierce?"

"The hotel frowns on women . . ."

"Who smoke in their bloody dining room? I'm sure I'll have no difficulty if you intervene on my behalf."

"Your language, madam."

"Oh? Did I say something amiss?"

He finds a match. She places her hand on his as he lights the cigarette. Contemplative silence as the smoke from her cigarette wafts over the table. Finally, Bierce announces he is tired but, in a gesture of reconciliation, invites her to his room to rest. She consents, neither afraid nor shy. The room is small, a single chair, a table and lamp, a chest-of-drawers, an armoire, and a narrow bed. He motions for her to take the chair while he sprawls on the bed. She, feeling awkward, wishes they had returned to the porch. He closes his eyes and breathes deeply. Uncomfortable and ignored, she squirms in her chair.

"Mr. Bierce?"

No answer.

"Mr. Bierce?"

"Yes?"

"Are you falling asleep?"

"No."

"Mr. Bierce?"

"Yes?"

"You're sure you're not going to sleep?"

"Resting my eyes."

"Perhaps I should—"

"Perhaps, Mrs. Atherton, if you'll be silent for a few moments I will regain my stamina."

She stands. "Be silent? You're rude."

"I, rude? I simply asked for a few moments of quiet while I gather my strength."

"If it's solitude you wish, I can arrange that. Expecting me to sit here and watch you snooze—"

Bierce sits up. "You're becoming hysterical, Mrs. Atherton."

"The pot calling the kettle black."

"You're a challenge to my sanity. And sanity is the state of mind that immediately precedes and follows murder."

"A threat, Mr. Bierce?"

"I'm too much of a gentleman to threaten a naive girl like you." He puts his feet on the floor.

"A gentleman doesn't fling himself on a bed in a woman's presence, close his eyes, and start to snore."

"I did not snore."

Suddenly, blood flows to his cheeks. His face and ears turn red. His breathing becomes coarse. He gasps for air. He gropes for a chloroform bottle but bumps it from the side table. The bottle smashes as it hits the floor. The room fills with sweet, sickening fumes. Atherton runs to the window and opens it to allow the vapors to dissipate. She puts her hand on his arm.

"Are you all right?"

"Asthma." He chokes.

"The broken bottle. Chloroform."

"For my breathing." He gasps.

"Lie back, Mr. Bierce." She's afraid he's having apoplexy.

Wheezing, he reclines on the bed.

"Let me get you something."

He waves his hand. "No. Just give me a minute."

Gradually he composes himself. Again, Atherton begins to feel pangs of guilt for goading him. But not too much. He's insufferable. She hates people who are so unalterably convinced of their own genius and correctness that they dismiss out of hand the views of others, especially hers. Besides, too many people consider Bierce the final arbiter on matters ranging from literature to politics. Who is he anyway but a middle-aged blowhard convinced of his own infallibility? Still, there's something vulnerable about him. A blusterer who tries desperately to hide his susceptibility with wind and steam. A melancholy man.

"I'm better now, Mrs. Atherton. I apologize. Sometimes I need to rest after a meal."

She places her hand on his. He takes it. Squeezes it. "I was angry, Mr. Bierce. Perhaps I was too hard on you."

"No, no, I was too hard on you."

"Let's forget it, Mr. Bierce."

"And you're right, Mrs. Atherton, I can't write novels."

"No, you're a great writer."

"A hack. A failure. In the employ of William Randolph Hearst. The money he spends for a single Egyptian mummy in its case would feed me for years. I've spent virtually my entire life writing and have nothing to show for it but three slim volumes of humor and a tiny book of short stories. I labor for a man I barely respect, a man who is not content to cover the news. He must create it, which he trumpets in vile and obscene headlines. He dreams of orchestrating a war for the sake of circulation. And, by God, some day he will do it. My name is associated with Hearst, and always will be."

"But your stories . . ."

"All published in newspapers. Read, then discarded. Used for wrapping fish and garbage."

"The stories in *Tales of Soldiers and Civilians* are brilliant."

"But, as you said, bloodless. Cold as ice. Twaddle."

"I regret what I said. Your fiction is as good as any I've ever read. Better. No one has written about the Civil War with such clarity and keenness. And your supernatural stories still put a chill up my spine."

"Thank you, my dear." Bierce rolls his legs to the floor again and sits on the side of the bed. "And I didn't mean it when I said your fiction is pap. You're a fine novelist and someday you'll be a great one."

"I know, Mr. Bierce."

He holds her hand as he walks her to the station to catch the evening train to San Francisco. They come upon a pigsty, and stop to watch the porkers rooting in the mud, an immense sow and several offspring. The sun is disappearing beyond the pines.

"I apologize for being so cantankerous, my dear. The stress of losing my son and the flare-up of my asthma made me disagreeable."

"I thrive on disagreement."

"I noticed."

In the distance they hear the whistle as the train approaches. Suddenly, Bierce seizes her in his arms and puts his lips on hers. She doesn't struggle but doesn't kiss him back. His mouth presses against hers, but he feels a hard resistance, like stone. He stops, back steps.

Atherton throws back her head and laughs. "The Almighty God Bierce. Master of style. The god on Olympus at whose feet pilgrims come to worship."

"You're an outrage!"

"Trying to kiss a woman by a pigsty."

"You detestable little vixen!"

"The Master."

He grabs her by the arm and half drags her to the platform. They get there just as the locomotive pulls in, its wheels gnashing and grinding like Bierce's teeth.

"I never want to see you as long as you live, madam."

Atherton laughs again. "The feeling is *not* mutual, I assure you."

He points his finger at her. "I've had a horrible day, and you're the one who has made it horrible."

"Isn't that odd, Mr. Bierce. I've had a wonderful day. I've learned something about you."

"What, pray?"

"That The Master is human." She skips aboard the train and waves. "Shall we stay in touch? I'd adore seeing you once more. My hammock has room for two."

The little bitch, he thinks. Yet with women . . . Some of whom you want you obtain, and some of whom you don't.

The weather in Saratoga Springs remains unseasonably warm. The windows are open and the overhead fan in his suite turns sluggishly as he again picks up the newspaper. A little light reading as bedtime nears.

He tells his Mexican friend, "I see in Mr. Hearst's *American* that Pancho Villa is giving American landowners in Chihuahua the hopping fits."

"That so?"

"Seems Villa's bandits looted Mr. Hearst's Babicora Ranch. Killed one of Mr. Hearst's employees and took four prisoners."

"*¡Caramba!* Such terrible bloodshed."

"What's worse, Villa's men made off with sixty thousand of Mr. Hearst's prime cattle. He's mighty vexed and expects the Mexican government, such as it is, to act on his anger."

"Pancho Villa must be shaking in his boots." Señor Arango grins and twists his mustache.

"Wilson is calling a conference of Latin American nations to do something about the revolution in Mexico. Everyone's invited but Mexico."

"What do you suppose they'll do at this conference?" He snorts

"Don't dismiss it, General. President Wilson recently dispatched Marines to Haiti. He can do the same to Mexico. America, in fact, can do anything it damn wants. The world just doesn't know it yet."

"Mexico's no damned Haiti."

"Mexico's an ally of Japan. There are those who see their alliance as a threat."

"Threat to who or what?"

"America's security."

"Too complicated for me. I'm a simple peasant, an Indian from Durango. What do I know about international affairs? But it seems to me it is an injustice for one country to meddle in another's business. Why should a big country like America threaten a little one?"

"Because it can. America has become used to getting its way, General. And if it's bad now, wait one minute."

"That so-and-so *bandito* in Mexico is also used to getting his way. What's his name? Oh, I remember, Pancho Villa."

Something in the motor of the ceiling fan begins to click.

click

click

"That sound, *amigo*. It says . . ."

"The Game."

Grile picks up the Colt .45 he has carried for years. Always clean, oiled, and loaded. It's heavy, but his hand is steady. He spins the chamber and puts the gun to his head. Then lowers the gun.

"I don't think I'm in the mood tonight, General."

"The young señora on the veranda?"

"Perhaps."

Chapter Seventeen

Mrs. Dumont and Mr. Grile stroll arm-in-arm through the gardens of geranium, arbutus, aster, violet, goldenrod, and sunflower. Dinner consumed, coffee cups cleared, Johnny in the playroom, sun starting to fade.

"A pity Señor Arango is unable to join us," she says.

"Indeed, but he has important business regarding his investments in Mexico."

"Exactly what does he do down there?"

"He is involved with armaments mostly, as well with horses, and has many thousands of men in his employ in the state of Chihuahua. One might say he is in charge of manpower and deployment. His logistics are vast and complicated."

"How did you meet him, if I may ask?"

"Following a lecture on aesthetics at the Literary and Scientific Institute of Chihuahua, which was founded in eighteen thirty-five to promote the local culture. Señor Arango was, and is, an ardent proponent of education."

"Aesthetics? Do you mean the movement championed by Oscar Wilde?"

"Spare me the thought, Mrs. Dumont. Despite his rough edges, Señor Arango is a self-made man who has an appreciation for beauty in all its manifestations. In Mexico he is famous for his floral arrangements and his skill at baking pastries."

"I hope he has managed to avoid that awful revolution."

"He is completely unfazed by it, Mrs. Dumont."

Mr. Grile sees no reason to tell Mrs. Dumont the truth about Señor Arango's absence that evening. The Mexican has taken a cab to a brothel at the edge of town, a well-established house of bliss he has learned about from an enterprising stable hand from Spain, the two speaking nearly the same language but not quite. Two dozen women ranging in age from fourteen to forty-two, locally famous for their looks, imaginations, and essence, and all like the legendary Josephine, who promised her beloved Napoleon that, for him, she would never bathe in the right places.

"I see you're carrying a diminutive book, my dear."

"Borrowed from the hotel library to read to Johnny. It's called *The Happy Prince and Other Stories*. Have you heard of it?"

He harrumphs. "I'm afraid I have."

"By the estimable Oscar Wilde."

"Estimable, Mrs. Dumont? Obviously you know not about whom you refer."

"On the contrary. You must think widows who happen to live in Buffalo are isolated from the world."

"I mean no insult, my dear. However, the lavender morocco of the book is garish, and I think much the same about the man, if I may use the term."

"Your aspersion is insulting to his memory, Mr. Grile."

"Then we should change the topic, Mrs. Dumont. Each year of my life has made me more prickly, particularly with regard to subjects for which I have a profound distaste."

Grile is aware that she considers him a man of strong opinions, not the least of which are his notions about Oscar Wilde, but he doesn't want to stretch it too far. She smiles, although in a way he'd find condescending were she not so fetching in her straw hat with its red ribbon. He also knows she's aware she's fetching, and is using it to her advantage.

She sighs. "Since you wish to change the subject, Mr. Grile, perhaps you could tell me why a year seems to go by so slowly."

"Slowly for *you,* perhaps, but for me a year is but three hundred and sixty-five disappointments."

"You're not bitter about your yesterdays, are you?"

"Yesterday is the infancy of youth and the youth of manhood. In other words, one's entire past."

She looks into his eyes as she touches a rose whose stem winds around a picket fence.

"Despite your cantankerous ways, you appear to have an extraordinary mind, Mr. Grile, if I may be so bold."

"My dear, the mind is a mysterious form of matter secreted by the brain."

"Your response is a glib way of sidestepping my observation." She shakes her head. "I know so little about you, and you're not particularly forthcoming."

"I've nothing to withhold. I grew up in humble circumstances in the Midwest, spent a single year in military school, fought and was wounded in a war I believed in—or at least wanted to fight in. And then I wrote. Poetry, fiction, criticism. With marginal success. As a young man I published three books in London, but the leading American publishers dismissed my best work, finding it not commercial. Those few who published my writing were charlatans or rogues, and cheated me. I was forced into compromises I despised, dependent upon a journalist's pay in the employ of a man I loathe. But there is at least one positive aspect to my life: now that I am in my dotage I no longer have that insatiable yearning to write."

"And yet you seem to be encouraging me."

"It's different with you. You have the passion of youth. Besides, if you didn't write what would you do? Wipe your Johnny's nose? Clean your kitchen? Sew your skirts? Sweep your parlor? Total your annuities? Certainly that mysterious gray mass within your skull is capable of more than those pursuits, meritorious as they might be."

"But you speak of publishers as charlatans and rogues."

They sit side by side on a cast-iron bench opposite a cobalt blue garden globe into which they observe their distorted reflections.

"My dear, I once wrote a satirical essay about the famous writers' rebellion, which was on a par with the railroad walkout of eighteen eighty-four."

"I don't believe I've ever heard—"

"Much before your time. We all went out, members of the Americans Authors Guild. William Dean Howells, Julia Ward Howe, Joaquin Miller, Hamlin Garland, young Henry Mencken, Richard Harding Davis, Thomas Bailey Aldrich, Mark Twain, Lew Wallace, Bret Harte. The Publishers Association—Macmillan, Arenda, Lippincott, Stone and Kimball, McClurg, Houghton Mifflin, Harper Brothers, and all the rest—used Pinkertons and government troops to put us down brutally, sometimes fatally. Victorious, the publishers announced that no author involved in our failed strike would ever see his or her name on a title page. The defeated strikers, having no alternative, sought immediate employment as waiters and bartenders. Some of them are serving us here at this great Grand Union Hotel. I shall not reveal their names."

"You've made this up. I adore it." Giggling girlishly, Mrs. Dumont opens her fan and waves a breeze onto her cheeks. The sun is beginning to retire. "Still, a discouraging picture you paint about the state of writers, Mr. Grile."

"If you're easily discouraged, then writing isn't for you."

"I'd so much like to read some of your work."

"All out of print. I've not one volume I can share with you, nor does the hotel library have a sample of my work." He's fibbing, of course. The hotel library has more than a sample, but none under the name Dod Grile. "Writing is ephemeral in any event. Acidic newsprint preys upon itself, books are destroyed by negligence and disuse. Printed or spoken, words tend to vanish over time. Paper merely takes longer to disappear."

"Minutes ago you hushed me when I spoke of Oscar Wilde, Mr. Grile. But he once voiced something profound about achievement in writing and art. Mr. Wilde said artists, like gods, must never leave their pedestals."

"My dear, I've no opinion regarding Oscar Wilde's pretentious assertion about gods, but I don't believe his name should be bandied about in polite company, especially among women."

"And just why?"

"Because he . . .he . . . Obviously, you know. Mrs. Dumont, I once met Oscar Wilde, and I assure you he was not a man that men consider a man."

"May poor Mr. Wilde rest in peace. A victim of cruel persons and, if I may be so bold, those perhaps not unlike yourself."

"I had nothing to do with his imprisonment nor his ostracism by society. And I certainly was not responsible for his death."

"Oscar Wilde died a broken man, bankrupt, banished from his homeland, forever separated from the people he loved. Nothing he did warranted that which you seemingly endorse."

"You don't understand about these things, young lady."

"Oscar Wilde was a mere human, Mr. Grile. Perhaps *you* don't understand about *those* things. And kindly don't call me a young lady. I'm a mature woman with a child."

"Mrs. Dumont, you're still youthful, impressionable."

"Compared to whom?"

"To me. There are certain despicable acts that some men—even depraved women—commit with one another. Can you imagine the physical interaction of one woman with another woman?"

"Yes, I can. Perhaps, Mr. Grile, you might describe to me such an act, and explain why you think it's despicable. Go ahead, tell me."

An august man of letters in disguise, he possesses no words, no imagination, to arrive at a gentlemanly description of coitus involving either sex in any combination or any combinations of combinations. An indecent drawing might make it easier, a filthy photo, even a ribald narrative, but he has never had the time. The world is changing, he thinks—dammit—and one of those who helped to refashion it was . . .

Songs are composed to celebrate Oscar Wilde, like "Twenty Lovesick Maidens We," by the peerless W. S. Gilbert and Arthur Sullivan. Ambrose Bierce is far from celebratory, however. Eighteen eighty-two. He attacks the flamboyant Irishman in the *Wasp* as "the sovereign of unsufferables, an ineffable dunce with nothing to say, a hateful impostor, a stupid blockhead, an offensively daft crank, an intellectual jellyfish, a man with no thoughts and no thinker, a gawky gawk, the littlest and looniest of a brotherhood of simpletons, an idiot who would argue with a cast-iron dog, a speaker with the eloquence of a caller on a hog-ranch, a dunghill he-hen who would fly with eagles." He characterizes Wilde's lectures as verbal ditchwater, meaningless, trite, incoherent. He accuses him of posing as a statue of himself, of blowing crass vapidities through the bowel of his neck, of uttering copious overflows of ghastly bosh.

Bierce has never attended a lecture by Wilde, nor has he read a syllable written by him. But Bierce reads and then digests, in his way, the newspapers, and Wilde's reputation precedes the Irish writer.

"Reginald Bunthorne," self-proclaimed genius, rage of London, master of the facetious, and champion of the Aesthetic Movement, invades San Francisco at the finale of his North American lecture tour, coinciding with the arrival of *Patience*. When Oscar Fungal O'Flaherty Wills Wilde places his card on Bierce's desk, the American is more amused than annoyed, especially by the Irishman's outlandish costume. Bierce, as is his custom, dresses in black, but Wilde is garbed in a maroon velvet suit edged with braid, pale silk shirt with a turned-down collar, flowing green tie, knee-breeches, and buckled shoes. Brown hair flows over his ears. In gloved hand he totes a felt hat with a vast brim. A carnation matching his tie springs from the lapel of his coat. His eyes are lidded heavily, his lips delicate, almost feminine.

"If I knew you better, Mr. Wilde, I'd say you were over-dressed."

"The only way to atone for being over-dressed is to be over-educated, Mr. Bierce."

"That's a colorful flower in your buttonhole."

"Assuming the one you're referring to is that in my lapel, a well-made buttonhole is the only link between art and nature."

"I observe the nature but I'm unsure about the art."

"I believe one should either *be* a work of art or *wear* a work of art."

"Which describes you?"

"Both." Bunthorne sits on the edge of Bierce's desk and crosses his legs. Bierce notices his limbs are shaped almost like a girl's.

Bierce shakes his head. "I'm afraid I don't have the time—"

"I agree, sir. Time's a terrible waste of money."

"—so I must ask you to state your business, Wilde. I'm busily working on a kind of lexicography of definitions that some might find cynical, others amusing."

"And what do you call it?"

"'The Devil's Dictionary.'"

"And you're just the devil to write it." Wilde raises the carnation in his buttonhole and inhales. "Regarding cynicism, I understand you've been saying awful things about me in the *Wasp*."

"I say awful things about everyone in the *Wasp*."

Wilde paces the room. Rather graceful, Bierce thinks, for a man who will probably turn to fat. The visitor straightens a framed photograph of Chester A. Arthur, twenty-first president of the United States. "Mr. Bierce, I've come to invite you to my lecture on the Irish poets and the Aesthetic Movement at Platt's Hall."

"I have a definition for a certain movement, but it's not in my dictionary, if you understand my meaning. Further, Mr. Wilde, a lecturer is one who has his hand in your pocket, his tongue in your ear, and his faith in your patience."

"It's obvious you aren't enchanted with certain celebrity. In particular my own."

"I avoid celebrities. For the same reason I avoid horseshit in the street."

"My infamy is only partly of my own making. You journalists must accept your share of the blame. Let me present you with a peace offering." He hands Bierce a slim volume. "My first book. *Poems*. One of only two hundred fifty copies, signed. It shall be worth a fortune some day."

Bierce leafs through the book. "You actually expect me to *read* this?"

"Indeed not, sir. Few have read it and only a few more will do so. My first idea was to print a mere three copies. One for myself, one for the British Museum, and one for heaven. Then I had doubts about the British Museum."

Disarmed, Bierce, despite himself, offers Wilde a drink. Cognac sipped from jelly jars.

"I trust you don't find it vulgar to drink good wine from a jar, Mr. Wilde."

"Mr. Bierce, although I firmly believe that while no crime is vulgar, all vulgarity is a crime. The consumption of decent cognac from any receptacle is never a crime."

Bierce advances the notion that intoxication is a spiritual condition that goes before the following morning. Wilde notes that alcohol taken in sufficient quantity produces all the effects of drunkenness.

From a silver case Wilde withdraws a cigarette, puts it to his lips, and lights it. He removes the cigarette from his lips and offers it to Bierce. "Smoke?"

Seeing the damp end of Wilde's cigarette, Bierce declines, repulsed.

Bunthorne inhales, releases the smoke. "When I stepped from the boat in New York I walked through customs declaring only my genius. I then set upon the road, seeing more of America than I cared to, finally reaching the conclusion that if one had the money to go to America, one wouldn't. I wore oilskins to stand under Niagara Falls, which looks like a lot of unnecessary water going the wrong way before falling over redundant rocks. I saw groves of orange trees, green fields, and purple hills, and decided America is almost like Italy without the art. The best scenery in your country is Yosemite Valley and Delmonico's. During four miserable days on the train from Omaha to San Francisco, I scribbled frantically in my journal because I desperately needed something sensational to read. When I arrived in San Francisco, four thousand people were waiting to get a glimpse of me, not one of them you. Mr. Bierce, you *must* come to my lecture tonight. Let me present you with this ticket for a seat in the loge. And join me backstage for a libation before the lecture."

Damn, there's something irresistible about Oscar Wilde. Against his better nature Bierce decides to attend the lecture, but that evening as he enters Platt's Hall he senses something wrong. The atmosphere is ominous. He hears a grumbling among the men, obviously dragged there by their wives. The two front rows of seats are empty, reserved. In a small dressing room backstage, Bierce finds Bunthorne smoking, drinking absinthe, and admiring himself in a mirror.

Between two fingers Wilde pinches a strand of hair. "Horrors, I just plucked this gray hair from my head, and I'm but twenty-eight. Recently I sat for my portrait. The painting was beautiful, but I thought, 'How tragic. The portrait will never grow older and I shall. If it were only the other way.'"

"To be old is to be rendered obsolete by time, Wilde, like an old book."

"Mr. Bierce, the old believe everything, the middle-aged suspect everything, and the young know everything." He pours Bierce a flute of absinthe. "I'm led to understand, sir, you don't approve of my Aesthetic Movement."

"Aesthetics are the most unpleasant *tics* affecting the human race. Art isn't necessarily truth any more than truth is necessarily art."

"I believe a truth ceases to be true when more than one person believes it."

A rap at the door.

"Ah, the time has come to face my accusers. In some ways I feel like a defendant standing in the dock at the Old Bailey, not that that fate would ever happen to me."

"You're quite sure about that, Wilde?"

"Absolutely. I'm one of Queen Victoria's most respected and admired subjects."

To a smattering of applause, Bunthorne strides onto the stage as Bierce watches from the wings. Tonight, Wilde wears a purple coat and knee-breeches, black hose, and shoes with silver buckles. His coat is open, showing a lining of lavender satin with lace at the wrists. Over one shoulder he carries a yellow velvet cloak. The applause dies. A few hisses. Down the center aisle thump perhaps thirty young men, all dressed in knee-breeches and silk stockings, coats with lace billowing from the cuffs, red neckties, green carnations sprouting from the lapels, and huge brimmed hats. Each carries a sunflower. Bierce recognizes them as students from Berkeley. They collapse into their seats at the front of the hall, then sit listlessly, eyes dull, wrists limp. The audience bursts into laughter.

Wilde smiles. "Goodness, save me from my disciples."

In unison, the young Berkeley men cross their legs and half lower their eyelids. They look at the ceiling, indescribably bored. Wilde lights a cigarette. "Perhaps it's not proper to smoke in front of the young aesthetes before me, but then it's not proper for them to disturb me when I'm smoking." Hoots from the front row. "Cigarettes, at least, have the charm of leaving one unsatisfied." A few police officers carrying billy clubs slip into the hall and stand unobtrusively in the rear.

"I come before you to talk about a trend in beauty and art known as Aesthetics. Let me cite the hatrack. Yes, a humble pole usually standing in a hallway on which to place a hat. It is not only ugly but is as hideous as the rack of the Middle Ages. Cloaks and hats should be stored, not on a hatrack, but in an oaken chest." Groans. "Our furniture is a travesty. Queen Anne appointments should serve as our model." Boos. "We heat our homes with hideous grates in preference to open fireplaces with tile hearths." Hisses. "Observe the ridiculous bonnets worn by the women of today. How would the Venus de Milo look in the ludicrous bonnet of a modern milliner?" Catcalls.

"Dear people, it sounds as though some of you would like to put me to death. Yes, you would send me to the gallows on clearly proven charges of addressing the sublime entities of art, music, and beauty, not to mention romance and sorrow." Whistles and shouts. "To those of you who are so loud, let me say you're prodigiously tolerant, which is why I love you. You forgive everything except genius."

One of the students jumps up and with a little concertina begins playing god-awful discordant notes to hee-haws from the front rows. Then rotten tomatoes, beets, figs, apples, peaches, and lemons begin to fly. The Berkeley boys, having concealed their watery weaponry under their coats, leap to their feet, to hurl the garbage at the stage. Wilde ducks behind the lectern but not before he is smacked by an overripe tomato.

"Fairy!" screams someone.

"Disgrace to the Irish!" yells another.

"Faggot!"

"Nancy!"

"Fruit!"

"Lavender boy!"

The pelted produce mushes into disgusting mounds as the cops dash forward, raising their clubs. In confusion, the stage manager of Platt's Hall turns down the gaslights when he should have turned them up. Shrieks and shouts spring up as the place darkens. Pandemonium. Several boys jump onto the stage. One of them drags Wilde from the lectern, another snatches his hat and flings it into the confusion below, still another grabs Wilde's cloak and begins to pull, ripping the fabric. Wilde is about to be soundly pummeled when Bierce strides from the wings and aims a fist at the jaw of one of the attackers, who falls backward. Bierce's boot collides with the stomach of another man. He shoves still another assailant into the orchestra pit. Then Bierce pulls his revolver and waves it in the air, firing a warning shot. Dark as the stage is, there's enough reflection for all to see the Colt Peacemaker. The attackers fall back in panic, tumbling off the stage. The cops swing their clubs, enjoying the cracking of heads and arms. The Irish author runs in confused circles before falling into Bierce's arms. Bierce drags him from the stage, through a back door, and into the alley. Wilde—panting—leans for a moment against a wall to catch his breath.

"You saved my life, Mr. Bierce. The mob might have murdered me. At the very least, I might have been beaten into irreversible paralysis, forced to die beyond my means."

Bierce harrumphs, unamused. The two men take a cab to the waterfront to escape the bedlam at Platt's Hall. They walk along the wharf, the masts of the tall ships towering like redwoods.

"You might have put up some sort of fight back there, Wilde."

"I don't even play cricket because it requires me to assume indecent postures."

"While you're obviously no aficionado of the manly arts, perhaps you've heard of John L. Sullivan. This year, Sullivan won the heavy-weight bare-knuckle boxing championship by defeating Paddy Ryan in Mississippi. Sullivan is now touring the country giving boxing exhibitions under the rules of the Marquis of Queensberry."

"The Marquis of . . ."

"Queensbury. Countryman of yours. A man devoted to the rules of physical combat. You should pay attention to him."

"He sounds dreadful. Not the sort of chap I'd ever have any business with."

Clouds chase by in a hurry. Bierce thinks he sees a shooting star but isn't sure. A breeze blows from the north. The waves lap at the timbers of the pier. In the bay, a ship is at anchor, lights screaming from every porthole. Wilde removes the wilted carnation from his lapel and throws it into the water to drown.

"In their light opera *Patience,* Gilbert and Sullivan good-naturedly mock my love for flowers—and for my favorite color, green. But flowers symbolize what's good and right in a world where there's so much bad and wrong."

"Those students tonight, Wilde. They question your sexuality, which I must say does appear to be, well, ambiguous."

"I'm courting the most beautiful woman in the world, Miss Constance Lloyd. I wish the stability of marriage. I crave children and shall have them. What is true in a man's life is not what he does but the legend that grows up around him. In any event, I'd rather have fifty unnatural vices than one unnatural virtue. Sometimes I think the artistic life is a long and lovely suicide. I'm but a dreamer, Mr. Bierce. Your Walt Whitman is also that sort of man. I met him at his humble home in Camden, New Jersey, a house so narrow I could almost stretch my arms to reach wall to wall. We drank a bottle of red wine together. I put my hand on his knee. He kissed me on the lips. May I kiss you on the lips?"

Bierce shudders. "Wilde, you're too familiar. It's unnatural."

A buoy clanks on the waves somewhere in the dark. Bierce thinks of the way buoy is pronounced, like *boy.* Wilde opens his case, withdraws a cigarette, puts it into his lips, and brings it to life with a flame. He holds out the cigarette to Bierce.

"Smoke, Mr. Bierce?"

Impulsively, Bierce takes the cigarette from Wilde's hand and puts it into his own lips. He feels the dampness where the lips of Oscar Wilde had been.

"I'd like for you to be my friend, Ambrose, and for you to call me Oscar. May I kiss you now?"

The day Bunthorne leaves San Francisco for Salt Lake City Bierce finds a wee package on his desk. A silver cigarette case, engraved "Ambrose from Oscar." He throws it along with Wilde's autographed book of poetry into the trash. Bierce is angry, no, furious with himself for succumbing to Wilde's charms. Even ashamed. There's something fragile—and eminently sad—about this very public young man. Wilde will come to a bad end. Bierce knows it. And the collapse will be spectacular, like a rocket bursting into incandescence before dying.

Exhausted, breathing heavily, Dod Grile is alone in his room following his sunset stroll with Mrs. Dumont. She has bested him in their Oscar Wilde debate, and he's pissed. Damn, some slip of a girl . . . Arango remains outré, doubtless still sampling the wares at his favorite whorehouse. Grile swallows from a glass of cognac, then another, and another. He's hot, perspiring, and strips off his coat, then his shirt, his trousers. His underwear. Hot like a fever. He thinks again about Wilde and the man's sensuous, womanish lips. He has hated Wilde ever since that night in San Francisco on the wharf when, disarmed and exploited, he let down his guard after Wilde's amorous proposition. Now he's beginning to wonder. Might Mrs. Dumont be correct? Could he be counted among the sort of cruel men who put Oscar into his purgatory and untimely death? Was he in error in attacking Wilde so viciously in print, like the boys from Berkeley, deluded and caught up in the hysteria of the mob? No, dammit, he's never wrong—rarely—and too old to change. Yet . . . His notions are easy to come by, nearly impossible to revise. In the playful Devil's lexicon he published, he dismisses the word "apologize" as a verb, meaning to lay the foundation for a future offense. He knows his mind and body are ebbing despite his fierce resistance, and perhaps he has much to apologize for: his abandonment of his wife, effectively leaving his children fatherless, friends who became enemies, enemies who remained enemies. Is there anyone, anyone, left in his life who loves him?

When Grile struts with his walking stick through the corridors of the Grand Union Hotel, he isn't unaware of his appearance. Military straight. Dressed in black. Assertive. In command. He has spent a life-time honing his image. But his parts are worn. He needs to pee every hour. Sometimes it leaks into his underwear. He expels gas more often than not, and there's no definition for that in his dictionary. He sits on the toilet for hours, waiting for something to drop.

Goddammit, hellfire, shit! I'm worn out. My mind is outliving my body.

Mind?

What's the point of having a good mind in a bad body, when all you think about is piss and chills and shit and smells? The old, young days were eminently better. Then you had the stuff of poetry on your side. Poetry is about love, grief, despair, anger, hate—not excrement. And if no one likes you as a poet, to hell with 'em. You personified your art, your convictions. Now it's all about constipation, diarrhea, flatulence, urethritis, asthma, ulcers, arthritis. Shit and sorrow.

Disappointment, loss, and loneliness are now as much a part of him as the panic of asthmatic suffocation, the ancient bullet wound in his skull, and the most recent scars on his body. It's outrageous, he thinks, that we're told we're put here for some undisclosed purpose and must wait to croak until summoned, whether by smallpox, the bludgeon of a blackguard, the kick of a mule. Put here, indeed! We were damn well positioned by our parents, who had no authority to do so and likely no intention. The claim that suicide is cowardly or lunatic is wretchedly misguided. Smug, self-righteous contentions like these inevitably emanate from priests, philistines, and women. The real cow-ard is one who lives on after endurance has ceased being a virtue. Yeah, I've outlived my purpose, whatever that might be, if I ever had a purpose. Why must I wait like a lamb to be assassinated by the Damned Thing? To hell with the wild ass of popular opinion. My ideas are fixed by time, my time, and no jurisdiction has the authority to condemn to life me or anyone else who wishes not to remain.

He reaches for the Martell but knocks it off the table with a crys-talline crash, the cognac oozing expensively on the hardwood floor.

My gun. Let's do it now. Where's my damned Colt? Where the hell did that Mexican scalawag hide it? He opens drawers and closets errat-ically, throwing out the contents.

No, do it right, dammit.

He plops on the floor.

Wait until the general returns.

He'll be back soon.

Damn, I broke the bottle.

Is it sanitary to lick the floor?

Will I get shards of glass in my mouth?

The Game.

I know the general is anxious to return to Mexico, but he won't leave this place until I'm dead. He's a cutthroat with honor. Hang on, mister, not so fast. There's Mrs. Dumont. She . . . she . . . Could it be that . . . Is it possible that . . . Might I be . . . Perhaps the deed might be put off for another . . . Maybe I should get up and . . . I have a few good years left in . . .

The door opens and Señor Arango enters, smile on his puss, which rapidly dissipates when he sees the disarray and the naked gringo, cock dangling, tongue lapping the floor.

"What the hell's going on here, you old fart? *Pinche pendeja.* Stand up. Put on some clothes or rent your own room and pay your own way. And clean up this fuckin' mess. In Mexico I'd have you shot. And maybe I will here too—and do it myself."

Chapter Eighteen

The horses go through their morning workouts at the track in preparation for the afternoon races, the trainers leading the thoroughbreds
through their paces, humans and horses strutting proud. Mrs. Dumont
and Mr. Grile amble along the picket fence. Petunia, geranium, jewel-
weed, aster, and morning-glory blaze with color in contrast to his un-
varying black suit. Mrs. Dumont, however, is turned out gaily in red,
and she carries a little parasol with tassels at the rim. She's cheerful.
Johnny's off swimming with a group of other young hotel guests,
thank god, and she savors her temporary freedom. Mr. Grile is subdued, although he tries not to reveal it to the young widow. Not only
has he a severe hangover, he is conscious of having dreamed about the
violent demise of his eldest son, Day, in a murder-suicide. Had he been
he a dutiful father, a father who actually resided with his wife and children, perhaps he could have prevented the tragedy. In the dream, he
goes to Day's room in Chico, where, horrified, he sees remnants of the
boy's brain and blood on the wall next to the bed. Just before he wakens
with a scream that jolts Señor Arango in the next room, he encounters
again the pure white horse, speaking to him again in that hideous, unde-
cipherable tongue, the mouth drooling blood. Red, so red.

"You seem rather pensive this morning, Mr. Grile," Mrs. Dumont
says. "Is something wrong?"

"Not at all, my dear. A sleepless night, that's all."

"Bad dreams?"

"Always."

"About what, if I may ask?"

"Visions of one of my late sons, and how his death was purposeless. But of no account."

"I'm so sorry."

"Let's not spoil such a lovely day with morbid thoughts. May we
change the subject?"

She's willing to do that, and she knows something about morbidity, death, purposeless or not. Oakleigh. Her husband. Why did he keep

his gun so clean, so oiled? Damn, the blood, and the cost of fresh wallpaper.

He breaks off a morning-glory and hands it to her. She puts it to her nostrils. He sees her as delicate. She sees herself as resilient.

"May I ask, Mr. Grile, how long you'll be staying in Saratoga?"

"I may never leave."

"And your friend, Señor Arango?"

"He will be here for the rest of the racing season. Then he will return to Mexico. He has a job to go to, a payroll to meet, inventory to count, horses to water. I, alas, have no responsibilities to tear me away."

"If you're planning to stay, Mr. Grile, let me warn you that winters become quite cold here. As you know, I reside in Buffalo, and just as the rest of the North enjoys autumn, often we have blizzards. Although Christmas can be lovely."

"Ah, Christmas. A day consecrated to gluttony, drunkenness, maudlin sentiment, gift-taking, public dullness, and domestic misbehavior."

Mrs. Dumont titters. He is enchanted by her sound. She knows it.

"You seem to have a definition for everything, Mr. Grile. What's your definition of a woman?"

"An animal usually living in the vicinity of man, and having a rudimentary susceptibility to domestication."

"Oh, bother! I imagine you're not in favor of women's suffrage."

"The introduction of women's suffrage into our scheme of things would be one of the most momentous and mischievous events of modern history."

"And just why?"

"I don't question the fitness of women for political activity, but the fitness of political activity for women."

"Really?"

"I believe society wants to have women who are different from men in knowledge, character, and accomplishments. That being the case, women must keep themselves in an environment unlike that of men."

"You talk like a fuddy-duddy."

"On the contrary, Mrs. Dumont. If a woman wishes to intrigue a man she must retain some scrap of novelty. A bit of mystery. She shouldn't disclose the baser side of her character, as men often do."

Mrs. Dumont's eyes flame. "I dispute your argument that a woman who has the right to cast a ballot is in some way less intriguing to a man. Is the man who votes in any way less intriguing to a woman?"

"Men will *always* be intriguing to women, Mrs. Dumont, because of their trailblazing nature."

"You're saying that men and men only are the trailblazers?"

"Women don't tend to be pioneers or innovators. Go to the tallest building of any large city and look down. Nowhere will you see the work of women. All is the product of men, built into form and substance as the result of conscious creations of men's brains. It's probable that the sum total of intellectual energy expended by women since the Garden of Eden amounts to no more than the genesis and evolution of the modern bicycle."

"Outrageous, Mr. Grile, and a slander. As if there's sex in the brain."

"Mrs. Dumont, there's sex in every organ, tissue, cell, and atom of the human body. In nothing else do women and men differ so widely, so conspicuously, as the mind. It is my conviction that if a man who has lived all his life in New York were suddenly to become a woman while walking up Broadway, she would be unable to find her way home by refusing to ask directions."

"On that issue I'll agree with you, Mr. Grile. A man will *never* ask directions."

"Touché, Mrs. Dumont."

On the track, a rambunctious stallion rears on his hind legs before being calmed by the trainer. Grile twirls his walking stick.

"Mr. Grile, you decline to take into account the repressive nature of education and custom that have conspired against women."

"Nobody is holding women from greatness in poetry, which needs no special education, or music, in which they have always been specially educated. Yet where is the great poem by a woman? Where is the great musical composition? In literature what is the feminine of Homer, Shakespeare, Goethe, Hugo? What female names are the equivalents of the names of Beethoven, Mozart, Chopin, Wagner?"

"I'll have you know many women are sublimely accomplished as musicians."

"On the contrary, they merely sing and play instruments."

"Sir, yours is a hopeless position. No matter your assertions about the mental competency of women, the tide is against you. State by state, women are earning the right to vote. I believe within five years that right will extend to all women."

He scowls—or appears to. "Oh, yes, you women will remove your little tapers and set the rivers of thought all ablaze, going from stream to stream until all are fired. It's not enough that we men have lifted you onto a pedestal and perform impossible rites to celebrate your distinction. It doesn't matter that, with never a smile, we assure you you're the superior sex. I must warn you, Mrs. Dumont, intellect is a monster that devours beauty. A woman of exceptional mind is inevitably masculine of face and figure."

"Ridiculous, sir. What you're saying is that intelligent women are ugly and attractive women are stupid."

"I speak only in the most general of terms, Mrs. Dumont. It's obvious to me your beauty is matched by your intellect."

"So patronizing. Beauty and brains as compared to the opposite."

"I'm in bondage to your charms, which is something I could never say of a man."

"So to your way of thinking a man, unlike a woman, doesn't have the capacity to be charming."

They meander to a cluster of tables covered by red-checkered cloths. Tea and biscuits are being served under the elms. Steam spouts from the teapots.

"An important thing, Mrs. Dumont." He holds her chair as she sits. "There's one service of incomparable utility and dignity for which I esteem women as eminently fit."

"Oh?"

"To be mothers of men."

She looks at him in astonishment. "A lofty sentiment, Mr. Grile, but hardly convincing and absolutely irrelevant. Giving birth is a physical characteristic having nothing to with a woman's intellectual prowess. A man is physically more capable of lifting heavy objects than a woman, but a man doesn't think with his muscles any more than a woman does with her uterus."

"Mrs. Dumont, I'm shocked at your language."

"Uterus? My language is perfectly acceptable, Mr. Grile, as well as being anatomically correct. Uterus, uterus, uterus. So *there*. And while I'm at it let me throw in vagina, clitoris, and perhaps a peehole or anus or two. Do you know the word anus, Mr. Grile? Or the word fart?"

He laughs his non-laugh. God almighty, she really stuck it to him, so to speak. In terms of vocabulary, at least, she's his equal or more. For the moment he is speechless. Watching the horses, they sit in silence sipping their tea. His headache is easing. By god, he's developing increasing regard for this feisty young woman who isn't afraid to challenge his Victorian notions. He knows how to provoke, sometimes rascally, and he relishes the role, but she's not bad at it either.

"Mr. Grile, may I change the subject?"

"Gladly, and with much relief."

"If I'm being too bold, kindly tell me. You mentioned you had three children, two of whom died prematurely. Would it distress you too much if you told me of the circumstances of their deaths?"

"Ah, it remains painful, Mrs. Dumont, although I'm not necessarily averse to discussing it with you. Sometimes it helps to recount unfathomable events. My oldest son, not quite seventeen, was the first of the two to go. I read the newspaper accounts about it, interviewed the sheriff and the coroner, and spoke to all those directly involved, the survivors, piecing together the tragedy bit by bit." He stops, puts his hand over his eyes as if to brush away tears. "However, the tale is so bitter, perhaps I should narrate it at another time."

"I understand. Maybe when we know each other better."

"*When* we do, yes."

Day is his father's son and he proudly carries the name Bierce, although he hates the name Day, his mother's maiden name. He begins calling himself Raymond. Like his father, he carries a gun. His father has trained him in the use of the weapon, how to site it with a level hand, how to squeeze the trigger without destroying the balance, how to get off a single shot that so neatly finds its way to its target. Day goes to Red Bluff, a small town in Tehama County north of San Francisco, where, thanks to his father's influence, he lands a job as a reporter on the *Sentinel*. It pays nine dollars a week, but Day knows he will some day return to the Bay area, maybe even to work on the *Examiner*. South of Red Bluff is the metropolis of Chico. The owner of the *Sentinel* sends Day to cover a lodge picnic in Chico at which many prominent local figures will be partying.

"Put down as many names as you can," the publisher tells Day. "Folks like to read about themselves in the paper."

Young Bierce arrives by horse, but instead of covering the picnic he discovers a girl. She's eating a sausage. Beside her is a tall young man.

"Name's Neil Hubbs." The young man smiles and holds out his hand.

"Raymond Bierce," Day says. The two shake hands. He can't take his eyes off of the girl.

"This here's my girl, Eva Adkins," Hubbs says. "Say, keep an eye on her, will you? I gotta play in the horseshoe competition."

Hubbs leaves. Day and Eva are alone in a crowd of picnickers. She chews her sausage, open mouth. He gets as close to her as possible.

"You're beautiful," he tells her.

"Aw, you're just sayin' that."

He follows her through the picnic grounds.

"You're fresh, you are," she says.

"How old are you, Eva Adkins?"

"Mighty personal you are, Mr. Fresh."

"Raymond. Call me Raymond."

"Well, Mr. Raymond, I'm sixteen."

"I'm nearly seventeen."

"If I should care."

"But you should care."

"How come?"

"Because I'm going to marry you."

"And what's Neil Hubbs going to say about that?"

"Hang Neil Hubbs."

"Mr. Raymond, I plan to marry Neil Hubbs."

"Over my dead body."

Day Bierce knows at that moment that he can never go back to Red Bluff. He'll have to stay in Chico to be near the girl. Her hair is dark, cheekbones high, hands and feet narrow, breasts small, hips wide. He wants to bury himself in her. He meets Eva's mother. She's divorced from Eva's father, remarried to a man named Barney, and is now separated from him.

"I love your daughter, Mrs. Barney."

"That's silly, young man."

"I'm quitting my job in Red Bluff and moving to Chico. I've got to be near Eva."

"You don't even know Eva. You just met her."

"I know what I want."

Against her better judgment, Mrs. Barney allows Day to board in one of her rooms. Eva works at the Bidwell and Sierra Canning Company. Day gets a job there too just to be near her. He doesn't mind the smell of tomatoes and beans on his hands. He and Neil Hubbs become drinking companions. They share a bottle in a graveyard because the place is quiet.

"Eva loves me, Hubbs."

"I think not, Bierce. She loves me."

"Fuck you, Hubbs."

"I'd hate to put it to a test."

"I'd hate to also on account of I like you."

"Not sure I feel the same way about you, Bierce."

"Fuck you again, Hubbs."

Mrs. Barney's estranged husband, drunk, comes calling late one night and begins slapping her around. Day hears the noise, leaves his room, orders Mr. Barney to stop hitting his wife.

Barney says, "You must think you're runnin' the ranch here, boy. Goin' from room to room in this house like you own it. I reckon I ought to take you out."

Barney grabs Day by the neck. Day kicks the older man in the testicles. Barney goes down good. For good measure, Day kicks him again, in the head. Blood rolls into Barney's eyes. When he opens them he sees Day's ivory-handled revolver pointed at his brain.

"Better leave this house now, Mr. Barney, or so help me I'll pull the trigger."

Limping, bleeding, Barney complains to the constable, who takes Day to the lockup. Next day, the judge releases him on twenty-five dollars bail put up by Mrs. Barney.

"See what I did for you and your mother?" Day tells Eva. "Now you understand how much I love you."

"But I don't love you, Raymond. You got to forget about me."

Day laughs. "Eva, no romance is complete without a tragedy."

Day goes to the courthouse and applies for a marriage license. The clerk tells him the prospective bride will have to sign too. Day promises Eva's signature will come. He finds a minister to officiate at the wedding. He tells his friends at the cannery. Invites them as guests. He tells Hubbs.

"She's not marryin' you, Bierce. I told you she's spoken for."

"Hubbs, you're going to be a disappointed man. Eva's mother approves of me."

"It's Eva who approves of me."

When Day goes on trial for assaulting Mr. Barney, Eva Adkins and her mother both testify Barney struck the first blow. The charges against Day are dismissed and the bail Mrs. Barney put up is returned to her. Two days later, Eva and Neil Hubbs elope. They go to nearby French Camp where they find a man who claims to be a minister and they take the vows. They stay in a cabin there and both Eva and Neil enjoy the loss of their virginities. The Chico *Enterprise* gets wind of the love triangle, announcing that the course of true love has run amuck, that the son of the famous satirist has been jilted by a Chico girl who elopes with a more desirable man. Day flees to Sacramento where he sits in a room at the Antelope Hotel, toying with the gun his father has shown him how to use. He puts it to his head several times. Once he pulls the trigger. There's a single shell in the chamber and it doesn't fire. He returns to Chico, back to Mrs. Barney's, and tells her he almost committed suicide.

"So sorry, Raymond," Mrs. Barney says. "You know it was you I was hopin' she'd fall for. Get some rest, Raymond. I put fresh sheets on your bed."

Day is lying in bed in his room when he hears the happy couple return. They sit in the parlor drinking tea and eating little cakes from Mrs. Barney's pantry. Day walks down the stairs and Hubbs, wary, stands up. He, too, keeps a gun under his coat.

"You're a damned fine pair," Day says.

"Is that any way to talk to newlyweds?" Hubbs says.

"Congratulations then, Neil." Day extends his hand.

Neil shakes it, still on his guard. "Thank you, Raymond."

"And my best wishes to you, Eva."

"I also thank you, Raymond."

"I hope the both of you will be very, very, very happy."

Day smiles and leaves the room. Hubbs sits down again, but he draws his revolver and holds it at his side.

"Gosh, Neil, you got your gun out."

"He's gonna try to kill us, Eva."

"That's silly, Neil. He just gave us best wishes."

"He'll kill us if he can."

Day bursts back into the room. Before Neil can lift his revolver Day shoots him just over the heart, but Hubbs doesn't fall. Day fires another shot. It hits Eva above her ear, the bullet bouncing off her skull and leaving a path of blood. Hubbs, bullet in his chest, manages to knock the gun out of Day's hand. He grabs Day by the throat and chokes him until Day falls, gasping for breath. Neil, coat and shirt bloodied, stumbles to his bride. Blood is streaming from her ear. He picks her up and carries her to the door. Day revives enough to see them leave and to hear Mrs. Barney, running from the kitchen, scream, scream, scream.

He yells after Hubbs. "My God, Neil, what have I done? Your gun's still here. Come back and put a bullet in my heart." He looks at Mrs. Barney. All he sees is her open, screaming mouth. He shouts, "Kill me! Kill me! I'm not fit to live."

"My God, Raymond, you've murdered us!"

Day says, "Telegraph my father. Please, my father."

Mrs. Barney's neighbor hears the shots, finds Neil and Eva crumpled in the front yard. He hitches his carriage and rushes the young couple to the doctor. Day, carrying his gun, gets to his feet and stumbles up the stairs to his room. He throws his gun on the bed. His neck is red with welts from where Neil nearly throttled him. He goes to the closet where Mrs. Barney keeps a bottle of chloroform. He saturates a towel with the chloroform, falls onto the bed, and places the towel over his face. He breathes deeply, inhaling the fumes. Let the fumes take his life away. Let it be done. But the more he inhales, the more acutely aware he becomes. He flings the towel against the wall, grabs his revolver, and puts it against his temple, pushing it into the flesh. When he fires, half of his brain spills onto the bed's counterpane, the rest on the wall. Somehow he is still breathing when they carry him to the doctor.

Eva Adkins's wound is superficial. Her husband is less fortunate. Neil Hubbs and Day Bierce die within minutes of each other in the same room on the morning of July 27, 1889. Day is sixteen years and eight months old. Ambrose Bierce arrives in Chico on the train the following day. At the undertaker's, Bierce handles the gun with which Day caused so much destruction. He turns the gun round and round in his hand. He looks at his son on the undertaker's slab. Much of his boy's head has been blown away. Bierce has seen worse on the battlefield, but when everything is said and done, they're all dead. His eyes mists but he doesn't cry. Day may have pulled the trigger, but he had been eaten alive by the Damned Thing.

A reporter from the Chico *Enterprise* stops the great pontificator to ask him a couple of questions, something you gotta do as a reporter.

"How do you feel about your son's death, Mr. Bierce?"

"How do I feel, young man? You ask a reporter's simplistic question for the purpose of eliciting a response from a grieving or defeated soul. Something printable, you hope. I'll give you something to print. My son did wrong. And after he committed wrong he did what he thought was right, and I have no more to say about it."

"Where are you taking the remains, sir?"

"To his mother in St. Helena."

Bierce and the casket containing his son wait for the train. The undertaker rolls another coffin onto the platform. It is Neil's body, about to be sent in the opposite direction.

Eva Adkins appears. The side of her head is heavily bandaged.

"You're his dad, ain't you. Raymond's."

"And you're Miss Adkins."

"You ain't mad at me, are you, Mr. Bierce?"

"Angry with someone like you, my dear—Why should I be?"

"Your son and all."

"Another's son died as well."

"If you think I done wrong in marryin' Hubbs, what would you do if you was a sixteen-year-old girl and placed like me?"

"I shudder at the prospect, Miss Adkins."

She puts her hand on one casket, then the other.

"Now ain't that queer? One goes one way and one goes another, but here I am."

Day's body is delivered to a cemetery plot in St. Helena's. Mollie is waiting as it arrives, as is Helen, Bibs. Mollie doesn't ask to open the coffin. She can't bear to look at her son's remains. Tears ooze from her eyes. Bierce reaches out and almost puts his hand on her shoulder but pulls it away at the last second.

"Say something to me, Ambrose," Mollie says. "You have the gift. Say anything just to prove to me you're human."

He can't, of course. He has nothing to say, nor does he trust himself to say it.

"You murdered our boy, Ambrose."

"Mollie, you're irrational. I had nothing to do with his suicide."

"Of course you did, Ambrose. You left us, him. I despise you for it."

"I can intellectualize your loathing for me, my dear, but, frankly, I no longer give a shit."

"Ambrose, you're dead to me."

"Mollie . . ."

"If you ever want to reach me, do it though Bibs."

Bierce's former employer at the *Argonaut,* Frank Pixley, now a bitter enemy, wastes no time in cashing in on the tragedy. He writes that the death of young Bierce should serve as a lesson to the elder for his bitter, heartless, and unprovoked assaults on his fellow men. "Perhaps the man with the burning pen should recall the names of those he's held up to ridicule and shame, the men and women he's tortured and abused. . . . We are too sincere an admirer of this gifted writer not to regret that when his remains shall have been gathered for entombment in the grave of literature, nothing will be found worthy of preservation."

Mrs. Dumont places her hand on Mr. Grile's arm. It shocks him into the present. He looks around, startled.

"I'm so sorry for you and your family."

"M'god, I appreciate your sentiment, my dear, but I find myself suddenly depleted of energy. I must take my leave. I have an appointment with Señor Arango."

Abruptly he leaves the table, rocking it. She almost laughs, this remarkable man ever unpredictable. His rendezvous is in the spa, where the two men recline side by side, immersed to their necks in the carbonated water of the mineral spring. Bubbles nip at their skin. The water has the odor of rotten eggs.

"So you walked round the track with the young señora. You're like a bull calf when you're near that woman."

"I admit, General, I find Mrs. Dumont singularly attractive."

"So the old gringo feels he can recapture his youth. Could you be in love?"

"Love is a disease."

"And that's why we sit up to our beards in this stinkin' water? To be cured of love?"

"The only thing that will cure love is marriage, General."

The Mexican's voice echoes across the bathhouse. "*Sí*, you've come down with the disease of love, you silly old ass."

Grile splashes the water with his hand. "Love is a malady similar to dental caries. It is prevalent only among so-called civilized nations living under artificial conditions. You won't find it among barbarous nations that breathe pure air and eat simple food."

"But isn't energetic love-making the perfect the way to meet one's end? I have fucked and fucked so much I thought I was going to die. But then I got my—how you say?—vigor back and fucked even more. Señor, take it from me, it's more pleasant to croak from love than from a bullet in the brain."

"There's always drowning, General. Here we sit in this warmed-over pool, nobody in the bathhouse but us. What is to prevent you from placing your hand on my head and pushing me under the water? I wouldn't struggle. How long does it take to drown? One minute, two? Imagine, canceling a lifetime of more than seventy years in two minutes time with the pressure of a hand."

"You would want me to drown you in *this* water?"

"It is medicinal. It has salines such as chlorides of sodium, potassium, lithium, and ammonium. It contains such alkalines as bicarbonates of sodium, calcium, magnesium, and iron. The waters are a natural compound of a super-saturation of carbon dioxide and an unknown flow of free gas. What better liquid in which to drown?"

"These springs actually restore health?"

"General, for years they have been boasting about Saratoga's one hundred sixty-three springs as the cure for disorders of the heart, the circulatory system, the nervous system, the gastro-intestinal tract, difficulties with metabolism, and arthritic conditions."

Arango stands, water dripping from his bathing suit. "No, señor. I don't think I'll drown you in the very water that cures. That would be too easy."

"You think it is easy to drown?"

"It is if I have to assist you." Señor Arango steps from the pool, feeling a slight burning sensation as the air meets the mineral residue on his skin. He picks up a white bath towel and dries himself. "You're a coward, that's what you are." He throws his towel onto the pile of other damp towels.

The American sits upright. "I have never in my life been called a coward."

"Oh, I don't question your personal heroism. You saved my balls once. You're a coward because you won't take responsibility for your own death. You don't want to wait for time to do its work. You want someone like me—or even chance—to do it for you. But only when you say so. Who says you have the right to decide when you go?"

Grile, glaring at the Mexican, lies back, sinking deep into the water. His head goes under. Bubbles from his body mix with the froth on the spring's surface. Arango crosses his arms and grins. In less than a minute, Grile's head bursts from the water. He spits, coughs, nearly gags. Coughs again.

"You weren't under very long, señor."

"Didn't like the taste." He spits again. "I never particularly favored the odor of eggs, even when fresh."

"Señor, I hear they bottle this water and sell it for American dollars. What does it taste like?"

"Like piss."

"Then I will improve its flavor."

The Mexican lowers his bathing suit. He takes his penis—much darker than the rest of his body—and aims in the direction of the spring. A curve of yellow urine cascades into the water where the American sits.

"Now the water is fit for a Chinaman to drink, señor, or a gringo like you."

Chapter Nineteen

Saratoga Springs turns unseasonably warm, almost like the summer corn days in northern Mexico when he was a boy. Señor Doroteo Arango often thinks of his youth—but not fondly. No son of an illiterate sharecropper on the *Rancho de la Loyotada* in Durango could have an idyllic childhood, forced by the age of six to labor in the sun-parched fields. How strange it is now, money swelling his pockets, meandering through the Yankee gardens of the magnificent Grand Union Hotel with his gringo *compañero*, Meester Señor Dod Grile.

The two men hear a commotion.

"A fight perhaps," Arango says. *"¡Caramba!* I love a good fight." Ah, that he does. "The only thing better than being in a fight is watching one."

"As do I, and in my younger days I managed to be in the middle of quite a few of them. Did I ever tell you about the time in Washington when I was set upon by two murderous thugs employed by the unscrupulous railroad baron Collis P. Huntington, and how I fought 'em off with my bare hands? And a little help from my Peacemaker."

"*Sí,* you old buzzard. At least five times. Now hurry up or the fight will be over before we get there."

Two little boys are on the ground grappling with each other, egged on by some of the younger guests and a few of the busboys and stable hands. One of the youths rolling in the dirt is Master Johnny Dumont.

Johnny has the upper hand over the other boy, who looks considerably younger. Johnny sits on him, first choking the boy, then bringing his fists down on the boy's face. Blood streams from the smaller boy's nose and from a cut on his mouth. One of his eyes is half closed. His clothes are torn and caked with dirt. The spectators shout more encouragement to Johnny Dumont. They like the blood.

"Hit him!"

"Smash him!"

"Kill him!"

Grile says to his *compadre,* "I'd certainly hate to intervene in a private fight."

"I'm not sure the smaller boy would mind."

"In that case . . ."

He pushes his way through the crowd and lifts Johnny by the back of his shirt from the victim, Johnny's fists still swinging in the air.

"You've had your fun, m'boy."

With his antagonist pulled away, the smaller boy sits up. Tears flow from his eyes and down his face, mingling with the blood. He crawls away on all fours. "Mama!" he screams as he runs into the hotel to find his parent. "Mama!"

Grile sets Johnny on his feet. He is barely scathed. The spectators applaud.

"It's over," Grile tells the crowd. "Go on about your business."

They ignore him and mill about.

"You heard the señor," Arango tells them. The onlookers are still slow to disperse until the Mexican yells, "Vamoose, you fuckin' bastards. *¡Ahora! ¡Tu madre es puta y pendeja!*" He reaches inside his coat as if to withdraw a weapon. They scram. Who the hell would argue with a fiery Mex with a gun?

"What was that all about, young man?" Grile asks Master Dumont. Johnny smirks.

"Your opponent was smaller and younger."

No reply.

"You were taking advantage of him."

Johnny remains sullen, tight-lipped.

"You might have seriously injured that boy, lad. You had the advantage. Why did you keep beating him?"

Johnny's eyes narrow. Proud he is of his victory.

Arango says, "I think this *caca muchacho* don't want to talk to you."

"Then he'll have to talk to his mother."

Johnny takes from his pocket a small lead figure of a Prussian general in a red uniform. He holds the soldier for the two men to see.

"I got it," Johnny says. Self-satisfied.

Grile says, "Is that what you two were fighting over? A lead soldier?"

Johnny nods.

"The other boy stole it from you?"

Johnny shakes his head no.

"Then whose is it?"

"Mine."

"So why were you fighting?"

"It was his. I wanted it. I took it." Johnny laughs. He scampers off, plunder in his hand.

Grile says, "Little Johnny is not only a bully but a thief. General, I've known lots like him. Unfortunately, most are born that way. Something in the genes. You've heard me speak of Collis P. Huntington, a felon I once described as railrogue. He too was a tyrant and a plunderer—but an ingenious one. Ultimately, however, the only difference between Huntington and Johnny Dumont is that Huntington was rich enough to hire thugs to do his dirty work."

"Maybe the *muchacho* will grow out of it." The Mexican removes a cigar, bites the stem. "The señora I feel sorry for, raising a kid like that. I was a nice quiet boy, toiling in the fields and minding my business until I had to kill the cocksman who raped my sister."

"You have a knack of putting things into perspective, General." The two men walk a winding path through the gardens. A hummingbird flutters close to Grile's ear. "A child is the happenstance of a carnal alliance. And those responsible for their creation never know what they've got until it's too late for all concerned."

The men stop to poke at the pink and yellow carnations growing from a bush. Grile snaps a flower from its stem and inserts it into the buttonhole of his coat. Arango, too, places a carnation into his buttonhole.

"Do you ever think of your children, *amigo?*"

"Never." Then . . . "Certainly I do. But children—*all* children, not only my own—weren't that important to me. I don't mean it quite that way. It's just that they were never much on my mind. I spent my life writing about politics and poetry, war and wonder, death and deceit. Children didn't enter into it. Then one day I woke up and my children were gone, and there was no one left." Talk of children and loss depress him—but then, he is depressed too much of the time these days. "There are moments I feel as though I never really got to know anyone, no one I was truly and genuinely close to. I can't think of a soul with whom I shared my deepest emotions."

"You ain't a man to share, you old jackass." Arango puffs at his cigar. "But what about us two? Think of all the days and nights you and me have talked."

"Just talk, General, prattle."

"*Pinche pendeja.* As if by talking you could hide from yourself and from me. I know you better than you do."

A horsefly buzzes around the gringo's ear. He brushes it away, not wanting to discuss himself anymore. He has revealed too much to a man-at-arms who knows him too well. His asthma is coming on, and he wields his atomizer to ward it off. They see a huge dog, part collie. A stray. Truly filthy. The dog approaches a tree, sniffs at it, then lift its leg to urinate.

"Notice that feculent dog, General. Think of that animal as a symbol of the human condition. There are those who never advance beyond the level of pissing against a tree. Morons, Mormons, Methodists, missionaries, mutts. All my life I took it as a holy crusade to expose boobs, blockheads, boneheads, and bandits, not to mention any number of Christians, for what they were. I was reviled for it."

"I have my own share of enemies, señor, some waiting to kill me back in Mexico even as we speak."

"Fortunately, as a newspaperman, I had a bully pulpit."

"Bully . . .who?"

"Something more than a soapbox. Theodore Roosevelt used it routinely to elaborate on his particular notions."

"My enemies wish to eliminate me, señor. And when I return to Mexico they may do so—if I let them."

"I've had some close calls myself, General. Did I ever tell you about the time in Washington when I was set upon by murderous thugs . . ."

"How many times do I have to hear . . ."

The reporters cluster, as if for protection, while the locomotive shrieks into Washington's Union Station. He is surrounded the moment he steps from the Pullman. As Hearst's biggest cannon against the railroad monopoly, Bierce himself is news, an invader come east from California to launch a new offensive.

He tells the reporters, "Gentlemen, my instructions from Mr. Hearst are to inform the American people about the mischief of the railrogues. It's about taking, meaning to acquire, usually by force but often by stealth. Collis P. Huntington and his late partners—Hopkins, Crocker, and Stanford—are guilty of taking. Not satisfied, Huntington wants to take even more. He's a veteran calumniator and he uses his familiar weapons: a paid press and a sorry pack of conscienceless bribe-taking rascals on Capitol Hill. I don't mean to imply that Mr. Huntington is altogether bad. He says ugly things about his enemies, but he is careful that what he says are mostly lies.

"Huntington's record of thievery speaks for itself. He is the swine of the century, deserving to hang by his dromedary head from every branch of every tree of every state and territory penetrated by his railroads. When he testifies before the House, I predict Huntington will recommend that the negative be stricken from the commandment, 'Thou shalt not steal.' Gentlemen, Huntington borrowed from the taxpayers an estimated seventy-five million dollars to finance his railroads. Now he has the gall to demand that Congress allow him to repay his debt over eighty-three years in low-interest bonds. That is tantamount to not repaying it at all. The petty politicians who support this man are eels in the fundamental mud of organized society, politicians who, as compared with statesmen, suffer the disadvantage of being alive."

That week, Bierce sits in the congressional hearing room as Huntington arrives to testify. Huntington's full beard, once black, is snow white. His head is bald, nose meandering.

"Mr. Bierce," Huntington says, "I recognize you from your pictures in the Hearst newspapers."

Hearst's cartoonists James Swinnerton and Homer Davenport are drawing caricatures of Bierce as a David taking on a Goliath. Bierce's images in the paper are striking, romanticized, while Huntington is shown as the epitome of evil, grasping, his hands picking the pockets of the American people.

Huntington holds out his hand. Bierce refuses to either stand or to touch his adversary's flesh.

"You won't shake my hand, Mr. Bierce?"

"My hand is not suitably protected, sir."

"I wanted to see how big you are, Mr. Bierce. Now I know."

Bierce waves a copy of the New York *Journal* like a fan, as if to ward off a loathsome odor.

"Mr. Bierce, it's not I that smells of an open sewer. It's the newspaper you are waving in the air."

After the head of the Southern Pacific is sworn in, he undergoes the most relentless grilling of his long life. The room seethes with antagonism, despite his claims that the railroad will go bankrupt without passage of the Funding Bill.

Huntington says, "Gentlemen, if the Southern Pacific Railroad fails, it will take with it the entire state of California, and ultimately the economy of the United States."

Boos from both sides of the aisle. Bierce and Hearst have done their job.

It is cold with a chill wind blowing across the Potomac, but Huntington is perspiring as he leaves the hearing room and walks down the Capitol steps. Ahead he sees Bierce, surrounded by admirers, speechifying. "I have to give the old bastard credit. Huntington took his hands out of his pockets long enough to be sworn." General laughter.

Huntington pauses on the steps. "Mr. Bierce, a word with you." The railrogue stands on a step just above Bierce and looks down at him. Bierce evens the position by moving up one step so the men stand nearly eye-to-eye. "Every day of the week, you and your employer Hearst accuse me of plunder."

"Pity there aren't more days in the week."

"Have you no shame, sir?"

"And you no conscience, sir?"

"Without me there would be no railroad."

"Tauri excrementum. I only regret the government didn't condemn your railroad and build one of its own."

"That is socialism."

"If so, Mr. Huntington, it is preferable to banditry."

Behind his beard a smirk appears on the old robber's lips. "Mr. Bierce, I've been around a long time, and I've encountered many a man. I've concluded that every man I've ever known has his price. So let me ask you. What is yours?"

Bierce, scowling from under his thick eyebrows, takes his time to answer and to enunciate for all within hearing distance. "My price is seventy-five million dollars in the form of a check made out by you personally to the Treasurer of the United States. I will take no less."

After living in California for so long, Washington is an adjustment for Bierce, although Carrie Christiansen is there to nurse him when his asthma acts up, to type his stories, and to warm his bed with her ample thighs. He likes things military: the way the nation's capital is laid out in precision; streets long, straight, connecting to circles like spokes on wheels. He doesn't mind the city's flatness, dominated by its tallest building, the Capitol, but he cares less for the weather. The land is low and damp, humid even in the blast of winter, which chills him to his marrow. He drinks away his evenings at the Army and Navy Club near Farragut Square, reconciled to the sterility of Washington, but not to its lack of decent dining establishments. To eat well means railing the B&O to Baltimore, home of the East Coast's finest eateries, where he engorges on steamed crabs, baked oysters, fried clams, flounder, and porterhouse.

Returning to Washington one night, and only slightly tipsy, he sees on the wicker seat next to him a worn copy of the Baltimore *American*. He reads about the travails of the Orioles, a hometown baseball club that was first in the league for the past two years before sliding into a slump. The newspaper prints an outraged ode about the team composed by a fan named Henry Louis Mencken, age sixteen. Bierce is amused by the poem, although it is far from art. He hopes young Mencken will never face the ordeal of having his eyelids sewn together for telling the truth.

After still another asthma attack, Bierce flees to higher ground, the Eagle Hotel in Gettysburg. For the most part he stays in his room, neglecting the hallowed battlefield. There are moments when he thinks he's a goner, wants to be a goner. He survives. No sooner has he recovered, back in D.C., than he takes a fall from a two-wheeler and breaks two ribs. After his bones heal he adopts a safer pastime, canoeing with Carrie in Rock Creek Park. Carrie, ah, poor Carrie. How the young woman hopes, but so little role does she play in his intellectual life, and so little does she understand it.

Collis P. Huntington has a trick up his ruffled sleeve. He engages his congressional surrogate, Grove L. Johnson, to return fire at Hearst. Johnson, fat on the Southern Pacific payroll, stands on the House floor to accuse the publisher of trying to blackmail the S.P. for cutting off its advertising in the newspaper. Hearst, Johnson bellows, is a debauchee disbarred from San Francisco society, a dude in dress, an Anglomaniac, erotic in tastes, regal in his dissipations, tattooed with sin, ungrateful to his friends, unkind to his enemies, unfaithful to his business associates, unfit to associate with pure women or decent men, low, depraved, and a seeker of relief from a loathsome disease contracted by contagion in the haunts of sin.

Bierce is infuriated, not by the ferocity of Johnson's assault, but because it has the cowardly benefit of congressional immunity. Reporters surround the Hearst columnist in a Capitol corridor. A photographer, setting off a flash, snaps Bierce's picture. The smoke from the flash hangs suspended in the air along with his fury.

"Gentlemen, Johnson's attack was scurrilous. His accusations are a pack of lies, not atypical of the man. Mr. Hearst is a wealthy man in his own right. Why would he attempt to blackmail Huntington for losing a mere eight thousand dollars in railroad advertising? Besides, most of the newspaper's dealings with the Southern Pacific occurred while Mr. Hearst was traveling in Egypt. No, I shall not reveal the names of his traveling companions, and I deny emphatically that Mr. Hearst has a loathsome disease. Further, tomorrow's editions of the Hearst newspapers will reveal that Congressman Johnson was not only indicted in Syracuse for forgery, but fled to California under an assumed name. While Johnson claims to be a member of the Odd Fellows, the Red Men, the Knights of Pithiest, and the Exempt Firemen's Association of Sacramento, I question his veracity in everything except his lodge affiliations."

That afternoon, Bierce reaches the Chief in New York by phone.

"Mr. Hearst, the reporters are asking why you didn't sue the Southern Pacific for the eight thousand dollars in advertising revenue it owes the *Examiner.* I tried to answer, but—"

"In confidence, Mr. Bierce, at the time of the advertising deal I was sailing the Nile with a young woman who was not my wife. If I sued and it went to trial, her name would be dragged into it. In addition, Huntington controls the courts in California. I'd never get a fair hearing had I sued. However, I have something more important to address. My papers are about to support the presidential bid of William Jennings Bryan of Nebraska."

Bierce fumbles with the phone's earpiece. "But Bryan supports unlimited silver coinage and you're against it."

"His cause is the people's cause. He is for the income tax. He believes in regulating railroads and corporations. Above all, the man is sincere."

"Mr. Hearst, sincerity is no road to the White House, and Bryan is the unstudied act of his own larynx. His larynx says, 'Let there be Bryan,' and there is Bryan."

"I trust, Mr. Bierce, you'll not adopt such a position in your column."

"Bryan is a buffoon and a demagogue. McKinley will surely win. If you support Bryan it will hurt your newspapers in the wallet."

"I'm already losing one hundred thousand dollars a month on my newspapers, Mr. Bierce. Why should I be afraid of losing a little more? May I count on your support?"

"With due respect, sir, on the issue of Bryan you may not."

"Then with similar respect, sir, as we don't see eye-to-eye regarding Bryan, from now please report, not to me, but to my new editor. I've hired him away from Pulitzer. His name is Arthur Brisbane."

Bierce is stunned and outraged. To be cut down like that. Could there have even been a Hearst empire without Ambrose Bierce? He has always reported to the Chief, never to some underling. Brisbane . . . Yes, Brisbane, the young reporter who long ago once tiptoed through the Tenderloin with Bierce and P. T. Barnum.

A sylph-like mist hovers as he leaves the Army and Navy club. The Capitol's dome, spotlighted, rises dimly through the fog. Bierce walks south on Connecticut Avenue, his heels clicking on the pavement, intending to take a turn around Lafayette Park before retiring. Carrie Christiansen will be waiting for him. His fluffed pillows and a glass of Martell will be at the ready. As he nears the park, two shapes rise before him. Big men dressed—like him—in black and wearing bowler hats.

"Mr. Bierce?"

He is wary. There are nearly as many thieves and robbers outside the Capitol as inside.

"Would you please come with us, sir? Mr. Huntington wishes to see you."

"Tell your Mr. Huntington I'm available for appointments only during daylight when I can see his hands."

"Mr. Huntington understands the hour is late, but he's a busy man. If you could spare him a few minutes in his carriage, he'd be most appreciative." So polite, so menacing.

Bierce considers his options. Outweighed, outnumbered. "Gentlemen, although I use the term loosely, lead on."

Two carriages are parked along the curb. He enters the first and finds Huntington alone in the dark. Huntington taps the roof with his cane. Bierce feels the motion of the carriage as it surges forward. The second carriage follows.

"Thank you for your time, Mr. Bierce. Benny and Sam have their usefulness."

"Your men are benignly named Benny and Sam?"

"Even thugs are given names by their mothers."

By the occasional flashes of moonlight, Bierce sees Huntington's crooked nose, the lines and ridges on his face above the white beard. An old man who wants vastly more than he needs or deserves.

"Where are we headed, sir?"

"A ride around the Mall, Mr. Bierce, to get better acquainted."

"I feel sufficiently acquainted to want to vomit."

"Did you know I'm a Connecticut Yankee?"

"Strange word, Yankee. In Europe, it means an American. In the North, it means a New Englander. In the South, the word is unknown."

Huntington doesn't laugh. "Are you a liberal or a conservative, Mr. Bierce?"

"Neither. A conservative is enamored of existing evils. A liberal wants to replace existing evils with new ones. Personally, I believe in the doctrine of free will so that I can reject it."

"Always the clever one, aren't you, Mr. Bierce? I was born more than twenty years before you. I had only the rudiments of an education. When I was fourteen I took to the road selling pocket watches, and got good at it. I wandered the world for ten years. Learned to survive in the worst of conditions, learned about hunger and cold and wet, learned about violent men and the nature of violence, learned how to outsmart other men. Once I was marooned for three months on the Isthmus of Panama. I taught myself how to trade, and I out-traded them all. I had one thousand dollars in my pocket. By the time my ship got to San Francisco from Panama I had four thousand dollars. I had tenacity and vision. I became part of a group that realized a great system of railroads, built by private enterprise and financed by the government, would unify America."

"Hmm. Governmentally financed private enterprise. Obviously, you were unaware of the contradiction."

"I was a storekeeper in Sacramento when I had a vision of a project vaster than the building of the pyramids—a nationwide rail network. My colleagues Crocker, Stanford, Hopkins, and I studied the land for the best rail routes. I went to Washington with a trunk filled with two hundred thousand dollars and returned to California with an empty trunk and a federal charter for a new railroad. On Capitol Hill I'd run into the hungriest men I'd ever met."

"The bastards awarded you a license to steal."

"Committees demand fixing, bureaucrats have to be convinced, senators must be switched, House members need persuasion. Sometimes it seems as though there is no end to it. But today I can travel all the way from New York to Yokohama without having to switch from my own lines."

"Sir, you have corrupted the nation's bureaucracy in such a way that it will never recover. Whenever some local constable or judge or alderman or public works official is arrested for petty bribery, you will have been his handmaiden. Anyway, Huntington, I'm tired of this jabber. Why did you drag me here?"

"Mr. Bierce, you publicly embarrassed me on the Capitol steps when I asked you to name your price. I read the headlines the next day. 'The Man Without a Price.' You performed for the crowd. But I think we can work out a private arrangement to fix that."

"And you propose just what, sir?"

"That you gradually withdraw your attacks on me. That at some point you will make it clear you've had a change of heart; over time you will let it be known that you've come to support my point of view. The topical mouthings of a journalist are discarded the next day anyway, like the remains of dead fish wrapped in a newspaper. You will go on to new campaigns, other crusades that won't involve me or the railroads."

"Why should I do that?"

"I happen to know Hearst pays you one hundred twenty-five dollars a week."

"One hundred thirty-five. I just got a raise."

"What if I were to offer you two hundred dollars a week, Mr. Bierce, *in addition* to what Hearst pays you? A lifetime guarantee. Eventually, you could quit Hearst and write your books full time. And I can make sure all your books are published. Your son Leigh is now in New York, working for a newspaper, the *Telegraph*. He is earning, let's see, twenty-five dollars a week. Leigh could have a much better job. I can ensure that."

"Huntington, you old buzzard, haven't you heard of a conscience? As long as I have both conscience and principle you will never take 'em away from me."

"I hope you will reconsider, sir."

"It will never happen, and now I wish to leave your odious presence."

Huntington decides there is no reasoning with this whoreson. He has offered the bastard a deal any other man in America would gladly take, and he still won't accept it. Huntington taps the ceiling of the carriage. The horses stop.

"You're right, Mr. Bierce, about conscience and principle. I have none. I bow to you. You may exit here, sir. My associates will take you to where you need to be."

Bierce steps from the carriage. He has been delivered to Rock Creek Park across from Georgetown. There is a little shack by the water's edge. He knows the place well: it is where he rents a canoe on warm weekends. A full moon breaches the darkness as Huntington's carriage pulls away. But the second carriage, the one containing Benny and Sam, stays behind, parked and still, like a hearse. Bierce hears the carriage door open. Things aren't right.

"Bierce?"

He walks briskly toward the boathouse.

"Halt, Bierce."

He hears an explosion. Feels a whisper past his ear. A bullet. Then another shot. Outside the boatshed two towering stacks of canoes are lashed together with rope. He crouches as another shot severs the thin wood of a canoe, spewing splinters, one of which spears him in the cheek. Damn, he thinks. He feels for the splinter, pulls it out. A trickle of blood rolls down his face.

"Bierce?"

"Where are you, son of a bitch?"

"You can't hide."

"I think he's over there. By the shack."

"Cover the path, Sam. I'll go to the canoes."

Bierce tries to open the door of the shed, but it's locked. He hears footsteps and crouches. Benny comes from around the stack of canoes and finds his prey.

"Well, well, Mr. Bierce, it looks as though I got you. Cowering in a piss-stained doorway." Benny holds a gun, a strand of white smoke drifting from the barrel. "Ain't a very dignified way for a man to die, is it? Grovelin' on the ground. You're brave when you got a big newspaper to hide behind. But you don't look so brave when it comes to standin' up like a man." He laughs. "Damn, I hate shootin' a man on his knees. Once I had to kill a man who was in a wheelchair. No sport in that."

Bierce rises to his feet, joints snapping. "So your overseer sends creatures like you to do his dirty work."

"Mr. Huntington pays us well for what we does. I worked in a slaughterhouse house once, hangin' slabs of beef on hooks. Dead men ain't no different than slabs of beef."

It never occurs to Benny that Bierce might be armed, some writer, after all, and one gettin' on in age. But as Bierce stands he pulls the Colt from under his coat and fires two rounds before Benny can get off another shot. Benny feels the impact of the bullets in his gut, but, strangely, experiences no pain, only an immense weakness that makes his gun a dead weight, too heavy to carry. He drops the gun and falls backward. He never even lets out a cry. In the instant before he dies Benny thinks about the little bitch he's been ballin' in Baltimore. Woman with red hair. Decent looker in spite of her limp and the boil on her ass. Has two kids. Shit, he'd wanted the woman again. And now . . .

"Benny?" Sam's voice from a distance. "You shoot the guy, Benny?" If Bierce reckons correctly, Sam is immediately on the other side of the stacked canoes. With his pocket knife Bierce saws the rope lashed around the canoes. "Where is ya, Benny?" Bierce slices almost to the rope's final thread. "Hey, fuckin' answer me, Benny."

"Benny can't answer you, Sam."

Sam is confused. Bierce is the one who was supposed to die. Then Sam understands. He wildly fires a shot, another. The slugs tear through the canoes and embed themselves into the door of the boat shack. Bierce cuts through the final strands of the rope. All it takes is one . . . kick. The canoes totter, then pitch forward, the canoe at the top of the stack falling first, then the others, like dominos. When the first canoe strikes him Sam thinks the sky has fallen. He has heard stories about people seein' stars when hit on the noggin. The stories was right. Sees, he does, stars, comets, meteors, Jupiter, Mars, all sorts of flashin' lights. Then he's buried under the fallin' canoes and crushed under their weight. When it's all over, Rock Creek gurgles, as if nothing has happened. The Damned Thing has come and gone, taking with it Benny and Sam.

In his room at the Olympia, Bierce wakes, his body dripping with perspiration. He has fallen to the floor. The damp covers of his bed have slipped around him. He sits up, breathing heavily. He reaches for the glass of water on the night stand. Then he drops the glass, which breaks into little pieces, spreading water on the floor. Carrie hears the crash and, barefoot, rushes into the room from across the hall.

"Are you all right, Ambrose?" She lights the lamp.

"Another bad dream, Carrie."

"You fell out of bed. There's broken glass on the floor. Everything's wet."

She helps him back into bed, tucks a dry blanket around him.

"You're bleeding, Ambrose. Your cheek."

He puts his hand to the side of his face. It is sore from where it has been pierced by a splinter of wood at the boathouse.

"Must have happened when I fell out of bed."

"Little piece of glass did it. I'll get a bandage."

"Let it alone, my dear. I want to feel the blood."

"Ambrose, dear . . ."

When the congressional vote is tallied it is to Bierce's satisfaction. He celebrates the defeat of the Funding Bill by consuming three additional cognacs in the space of twenty minutes. The Boss, however, while he takes pleasure in defeating the railrogues, can't convince America it needs Bryan as president. After the election, Hearst sends

Mrs. Bryan five thousand dollars' worth of orchids as solace for the Silver-Tongued Orator's defeat. Bierce knows, however, the publisher hasn't lost his enthusiasm for more power.

Hearst dispatches Richard Harding Davis and Frederick Remington to Cuba to stir up trouble against Spain. He also fills his readers' minds with gags, froth, murder, mayhem, sex, sleaze, nonsense, games, puzzles, and contests. Hires Rudolph Dirks to sketch a comic strip called "The Katzenjammer Kids," which Bierce finds abysmally drawn and funny as a cleft palate. Hearst's dream is to occupy the White House. Bierce, who has few dreams other than nightmares, shudders at the prospect.

Mr. Grile and Mrs. Dumont sit in lawn chairs watching the tennis matches. The players are dressed in white. The balls fly back and forth striking one racquet, then the other, over and over, the sound as hypnotic as a metronome.

"I'm sorry Señor Arango was unable to join us for the matches," she says.

"Tennis is not a sport Señor Arango is familiar with, I'm afraid. It would depress him. He is hunting in the woods for a bird called a quim, which, while not an ornithologist, I assume is something like quail."

"I want to thank you and the señor for interrupting Johnny's fight."

"It seemed to be the right thing to do."

"The other boy, Nathan, wasn't badly hurt. Some scratches. A black eye."

"I'm sure Nathan's mother was relieved to find that her son survived. Although probably not as much as Nathan."

"I told Johnny to apologize. And I made him return the lead soldier they were fighting over. Johnny must grow up sometime, Mr. Grile. He can't remain a child forever."

"Oh, he will age in chronological terms. That is to say he will become older, but not necessarily wiser. However, I've discovered there are certain advantages to aging. Study closely primordials such as myself. Invariably, you will find us distinguished by our seriousness. We are not given to frivolity. We don't play at tennis. We don't contribute jokes to the comic pages. We don't waste our time kissing the girls. We are all business. Everyone, Mrs. Dumont, can be that way as long as he or she becomes old enough. And I'm certainly right for the job."

She laughs while squeezing his arm. It's a familiar, almost intimate, gesture that startles and enchants him. The old sensation in his groin dormant for so long is awakened.

Chapter Twenty

She is adorable, he thinks, her hair swirled high with a blond wisp that curls fetchingly on her forehead. But he's had his fill of kings, queens, hearts, diamonds, clubs, aces, spades, and jackasses, thank you. Mr. Grile, barely concealing his boredom, watches half-lidded through his cigar smoke as Mrs. Dumont competes in the duplicate bridge tournament, an all-day ordeal that resumes in the evening following the players' hot and cold buffet. She and her partner, a matron from Worcester, Mass., fail to score sufficient match points to win the Ladies Pairs trophy, a grotesque silver-plated dish suitable for preserving human ashes. It would look lovely next to the preserves on someone's basement canning shelf. Afterward, Mr. Grile and Mrs. Dumont find refuge on the veranda, untenanted except for them.

"I find bridge tedious," he says. "But I'm amused by the terms. Trick, trump, rubber, dummy. Especially dummy. As far as I'm concerned, bridge is a substitute for conversation among those for whom Almighty God, who cherishes us all, has denied a single idea."

"Are you using the Lord's name in vain, Mr. Grile?"

"Never. I always wait for the appropriate occasion."

She laughs. "So I lost the tournament and that hideous gunmetal memento. Piffle. Never played cards well. Social obligation. Every Thursday in Buffalo at those afternoon bridge parties orchestrated by my mother, I serve tea and crackers and cheese and little stale cakes, and take my place at any card table lacking a player."

They sit on the steps and gaze into the sky, night so unclouded the stars seem within their grasp. Taurus for takers, he muses. Libra for lovers, Aries for the angry, Virgo for the virtuous, Capricorn for the capricious, Cancer for the cantankerous, Gemini for the gentle, Pisces for the peacemakers, Scorpio for skeptics. What pap. Astrology is the science of making the dupe see stars. Unexpectedly, the stars seem to rearrange, taking the form of a woman's body, yes, unmistakably a woman's—breasts, thighs, legs . . . Absurd. They're nothing but luminous balls of plasma. Yet . . .

She touches his sleeve, then her fingers drift onto the flesh of his wrist. "Lost in the stars, Mr. Grile?"

He is startled for a moment. "I was contemplating celestial bodies, my dear, but you've brought me down to earth, and in the nick of time. I might have gone the way of an shooting star."

"Then allow me to ask you about something unrelated to our present conversation."

Damn it to hell. At the very moment he thinks she fancies him she changes tack. He says, "You're going from astral balderdash to terrestrial reality?"

"Exactly."

"Then proceed, my dear."

"I have the impression you're a strict grammarian."

His substantial eyebrows flare. Terrestrial reality, indeed. "Admittedly, I rage at the philistines who defile the language. If we are going to communicate we should do so precisely and without deviation from the rules. In that I staunchly disagree with a young Baltimorean whose name you undoubtedly have never heard. Henry Louis Mencken."

"Ah, you are mistaken. Mr. Mencken co-edits the *Smart Set* with George Jean Nathan. He's become quite the rage. Everybody reads their magazine. All the famous writers are in it. James Branch Cabell, Sherwood Anderson, Sinclair Lewis, Theodore Dreiser, Willa Cather, and this elusive young poet named Ezra Pound."

Grile is furious with himself. "Beg your pardon for misjudging the breadth of your erudition, my dear. I've been out of the country for a long time, so I'm not up on what everybody is reading—or who is being published where." One-upped by this slip of a girl. He isn't unfamiliar with magazine publication, of course, having written a regular column for Hearst's *Cosmopolitan*, but still . . . He feels diminished in some way. Damned if he'll reveal it. "Aside from Mr. Mencken's magazine, this linguistic novitiate encourages the notion of a forever-evolving language, while I'm content to say halt, dammit, halt."

"You make no allowance for discrepancies in casual conversation?"

"Never."

"Like you, I relish words. I am an authoress, after all."

"*Authoress?* Is that like a *poetess?* Spare me another word needlessly added to our vocabulary. You're an *author*, or at least one who aspires to be."

In the dark, he doesn't see the flaming of Mrs. Dumont's cheeks. He must believe she's a simpleton, she thinks.

"I've much to learn, Mr. Grile."

"Only death ends the learning curve, my dear. But our language has gone haywire. We say a coat of paint when we mean a coating of paint. We talk about building a fire when we mean making a fire. We refer to an empty house when we mean a vacant house. When we say, 'She got married,' we might as well say, 'She got dead.' We talk about a criminal being hung when we mean hanged. We refer to dirty clothes as laundry when a laundry is a place where clothing is washed. We say one loaned another person ten dollars when we mean one lent. We refer to luncheon as lunch. When we're angry we say we're mad, as if insane. We say noise when we mean sound. It is vulgar to say pants for trousers, but we do it anyway. We say Jones promises to quit drinking, when we mean Jones promises to cease or stop. We refer to a self-confessed assassin, even though self is superfluous. We confuse sense with smell, set with sit, sick with ill. We say avocation for vocation, literally for figuratively, recollect for remember, which for that, that for which, who for whom, whom for who . . ." He stops to catch his breath.

She gets the idea. He has overstated his case. "Mr. Grile, I concede we frequently lack consistency in our language. However, since language constantly evolves, as Mr. Mencken points out, why shouldn't the rules change *because* of popular usage? If most of us—you the exception—decide pants is preferable to trousers, what's so wrong?"

"Tauri excrementum. I may be outnumbered but I will not surrender. I once published a slim volume of my idiosyncrasies about language. A mere seventy pages. It states all I have to say on the subject. A few people bought it. It went into a couple of printings. But I suspect even fewer read it. Except young Henry, of course."

"Might you tell me more about this Mr. Mencken?"

"A literary upstart who may some day become a passable writer. He has published books on Shaw and Nietzsche, but he only fancies that he knows something about the English language."

"You've encountered him?"

"Of middling height, hair slicked back, parted in the middle, addicted to cigars, often clinched but not smoked. A man of vile bigotry, which I wrote off as immaturity. We were brought together by a mutual friend, the literary critic Percival Pollard. Henry was city editor of the Baltimore *Herald* when Percy and I trained up from Washington to observe the smoldering ruins of the great Baltimore fire of nineteen aught-four." He chuckles. "Not long after the ashes cooled and the smoke dissipated, I returned for a session of young Mencken's Saturday Night Club at which he and his fellow amateur musicians performed. Respectably, I think, although I have a metallic ear."

The instrumentalists play in some violin shop on . . . where? Fayette Street, Baltimore. Brahms through nicotine clouds, the floor awash in musical scores. An all-German program, save for a composition by a Czech, a concession to their guest from the District of Columbia. Bröedel keys first piano, Mencken second piano, Hildebrandt cello, Daniel violin, Gottlieb flute. Heinrich, Buchholz, Hemberger, and Woollcott all take their turns. Woollcott is the composer of the club song, "I am a 100% American!" He is a glue manufacturer whose brother Alexander has literary aspirations. Promptly at ten, Mencken marches musicians and guest to the circular bar at the Rennert Hotel on Liberty Street to guzzle beer and wolf liverwurst sandwiches, onions, and German pretzels.

Mencken says through the haze and the odor of hops, and out of earshot of the others, "Mr. Bierce, just as there are two kinds of Jews, unsuitable and exceptional, the same relates to music. German music and bad music."

"Yet you performed that lovely melody composed by a Czech. I can't recall the name."

"Antonín Dvořák. 'Humoresque.'"

"The first time I've heard it. I'm not musically inclined, although I once attempted to play the Jew's-harp, if you'll pardon the expression. You hold it fast with the teeth while at the same time trying to brush it away with the finger."

The Baltimorean guffaws. "I fear my piano technique is godawful due to a succession of lady teachers."

"On the contrary, young man, I am quite impressed with your talent as a pianist. As you know, the piano is operated by depressing the keys as well as the spirits of the audience."

"When my father had unwelcome visitors to our home on Hollins

Street, he would demand I play something lively on the piano, louder the better. Would make 'em evacuate the place pronto."

"Mencken, about that vituperative comment you made about Jews. Seems to me most of your fellow musicians are, in fact, Jews."

"Of the preferable sort, the type who don't behave stereotypically, those who don't demand membership in, say, the better clubs. Bartender, more lager all around. Another cigar, Mr. Bierce?"

"I'm not sure whether I like you, Mencken, but I can tell you this. The aroma of smoke and spirits is the sweet smell of life, conviviality, and the urinary tract."

"You see how little it takes to make life perfect, sir? A good sauce, a little Brahms, a cocktail after a hard day, a cold beer, and a girl who kisses with her mouth open."

Like Bierce, Mencken consumes twelve or fourteen steins, yet his mind and hand remain as steady as a well-tuned piano's C note. He shares with Bierce a mutual contempt for progressives, prohibitionists, socialists, communists, utopians, vegetarians, visionaries, suffragettes, and faddists in general. Further, neither man, even when shown the error of his ways, is likely to concede it.

At the Rennert Hotel, such a nuisance is the interminable journey back to Bierce's room—eerie corridors, useless alcoves with mirrors, doors leading nowhere—that he dozes in the elevator until a brass-buttoned midget nudges him to the proper bed on the eighth floor.

"I know you," Bierce says as the midget tucks him in. "You used to work for that old fraud Barnum."

"I assure you, sir . . ."

"You and I dined together at Delmonico's in New York."

"I've never stepped foot out of Baltimore, sir."

"It was in eighteen eighty thereabouts. You sat on a stack of books."

"Sir, I hadn't yet been born."

"I saved your arse. You were kidnapped by a coalition of gangs and held for ransom in the Vanderbilt mansion. The Plug Uglies, The Five Pointers, the Dead Rabbits . . . I forget the rest. I led the charge that rescued you. I and Jenny Lind, the Fiji Cannibals, the White Negro. I met your wife, Lavinia Warren. I think your name is . . . is . . . My memory is broken."

"You certainly have slipped, Mr. Bierce. Shall I turn out the light for you? If you need anything else, just ring for Tom."

In the morning, a chipper, cold-sober Mencken escorts Bierce, head echoing jazz or worse, a hullabaloo quite afield from Dvořák, on a sightseeing excursion. By god, thinks Bierce, the recoverability of the young. Pasty-faced, hair middle-parted little SOB. Leeches should suck him dry. But Bierce rallies sufficiently to take particular pleasure in examining the five-pointed star of Fort McHenry, the fortifications sparing Baltimore from the British horde in 1814. Bastard Brits. Had he been born sixty years earlier, he might have served at this fort. Better to whip the Limeys than the rebs, but the rebs deserved it too. He and Mencken lunch at Dunlop's Oyster House on Howard Street. "Finest seafood in Maryland," Mencken insists. Oysters, shad, crab. "Crabs are prepared in fifty ways in Baltimore and all of 'em good." Baked potatoes, string beans, corn off the cob, cheesecake, cordials, coffee. Bellies full, they wander among the effigies in Mount Vernon Place, where the cast of George Washington rises with majesty from atop a marble tower. Lesser statuary are planted here and there representing Roger Brooke Taney, George Peabody, Severn Teackle Wallis, John Eager Howard. Bierce once proposed, only partly in jest, nickelplating the dead as an alternative to burial or cremation and then standing the metalloidal cadavers in the parks.

"Mencken, do you realize in another twenty years every sixth grader in Baltimore, brought to see the statues before us, will look at each other, baffled, and ask who the hell was Severn Teackle Wallis?"

Mencken hauls out a stogie and lights it. "It's strange we're both disciples of the English language yet don't see eye to eye about it."

"Precision counts in language, Mencken. That's what separates us. What's wrong with exacting English?"

"You're of the old school."

"And glad of it. Even though it was a one-room schoolhouse in Indiana."

"Mr. Bierce, some indefatigable Indiana schoolmaster, such as yours, for years has tried to teach his pupils the rules of correct English. But as soon as the school bell rings, the kids revert to their loose, natural speech habits of home and workplace. Slang. I'm not offended by it."

"I am. Slang is the grunt of the human hog with an audible memory. *Pignoramus intolerabilis,* I call it."

"But colloquialisms widen the boundaries of metaphor. They provide us with new shades of meaning."

"Confound it, Mencken, few words have more than one literal and serviceable definition. I don't give a damn how many metaphorical, derivative, related, or even unrelated meanings you and your lexicographer cronies think worth gathering. You bloat your absurd and misleading dictionaries with nonsense. In truth, you and your linguistic allies believe a dictionary is a malevolent literary device for cramping the growth of a language and making it hard and inelastic. It wasn't Webster who inspired the dictionary; it was Dr. John Q. Satan. Even with your mitts desecrating it, the dictionary is still one of man's most useful works. It will drive a screw, repair a red wagon, and apply for a divorce. It will build a barn or a privy. It is a good substitute for measles. It will make rats come out of their holes to die. It will win wars and end famine. It pays the mortgage and the iceman. It is a dead shot for worms and it cures rickets. And children cry for it. That, dear Henry, is a dictionary."

It's not Bierce's last word, nor the last he sees of Mencken and of Baltimore.

He returns for an occasion considerably more somber than Mencken's Saturday Night Club: the funeral of the literary critic Percival Pollard, one of Bierce's few champions, dead, a victim of, in his opinion, quacks. The tiny band of mourners gathers in the undertaker's chapel for the sendoff. Percy, as a critic, roasted many a writer, and is now about to experience his own roast. Unable to resist, Bierce cracks open the casket and peeps inside. In death Pollard's features reflect his final agony. Hair gone, ragged gash encircling the skull where the surgeons entered his brain in an ineffectual effort to save him from the Damned Thing. At forty-two, the corpse looks ninety-two. Bierce blames homeopathic humbugs for Percy's demise. Had he received urgent treatment for his brain tumor instead of relying on charlatans at what Mencken called an E-flat homeopathic hospital, Pollard might not have gone into convulsions and rushed to Johns Hopkins for emergency surgery. Bierce believes that despite Mencken's indisputable acumen, he is a loony hypochondriac. Deservedly, it has fallen upon the Baltimorean to make the final arrangements.

Pollard's coffin is loaded onto a horse-drawn hearse to be carted to the crematorium at Loudon Park Cemetery. Bierce and Mencken follow in a chauffeured Daimler, the widow and the few other mourners choosing to retire to the Belvedere Hotel for tea and frosted cake and those wicked eensy-weensy cherries smothered in chocolate. The tiny funeral cortège wheels west on Fayette Street past the endless formations of row houses, red brick, each with a set of polished marble steps.

"Watch the arraber!" Mencken shouts to the Daimler's driver.

"Arraber?" asks Bierce.

"Local idiom. Street arabs who sell fresh produce. Africans mostly. Some wops, a few micks. Not many like you. Or me."

The sedan maneuvers around a horse pulling a cart filled with watermelons and other fruit. A primordial black man on watery legs walks alongside shouting words that spontaneously turn into song. "Waatameloons! Peeeches! Oraanges! Froot! Froot for Sale! Waatameloons!"

Bierce becomes thoughtful, lights a cigar. "Henry, that arraber out there. Looks as if he's a hundred. But our poor Percy. Never thought I'd outlast him. Now he's worm's meat—at least until he's fried."

"My father is buried in the cemetery where Pollard is about to be relegated to ashes, Mr. Bierce. My father believed in cremation, but when his time came my mother said, no, he had to be buried."

"What is cremation, after all, but the process by which the cold meats of humanity are warmed over?" Bierce puffs his cigar. "Once, in the sacred city of Sacramento, the mourners gathered at a crematorium to bid farewell to one of their own, a particularly offensive pious type. When smoke appeared from the rafters, the mourners assumed that the proprietors of the crematorium had prematurely put the match to their late *amigo*. But as flames licked their toes they realized something was amiss. It was they who were on pyre. Such a crush at the only unlocked exit that the surging humanity plugged it tight. Hot time in the old town, indeed. Burnt to a crisp inside the crematorium." Bierce chortles. "Strangely, the dear departed whom they had come to toast was singed not a bit. Train was late so the corpse hadn't arrived."

The Daimler, close behind the hearse, turns south onto Fulton Street. Bierce passes Mencken a narrow flask of brandy.

Mencken sips. "In my opinion man doesn't die quickly and brilliantly but leaves by inches. Burn a man's mortal remains and you probably burn a good portion of him alive."

"Henry, my boy, a corpse may only appear to be detached from his environment. Once, in a crematorium in San Francisco, a late acquaintance of mine, a delightful sybarite bloated by his prodigious consumption of alcoholic beverages, objected to the whole business of incineration. His carcass, mounted on a funeral pyre and ignited by the diligent crematory workers, exploded, singeing the asses of all the Jesus-lovers within fifty yards. Terrible mess. Worth two days on the front page plus days and nights of feverish hosannas."

"Typical Christian reaction, Mr. Bierce. They have a knack of proving that God is a monstrous bore."

"The Christian mind is a small mind and the Christian hand is a brutal hand. They carry with them unbridled conceit and outrageous ignorance. I recall a matron who prayed for the demise of her husband who, like her, was a loathsome Methodist. Finally, the harridan got her wish. The corpse was mounted on the funeral pyre and set ablaze in the name of her Lord. But the widow was so frightened that her unlamented husband's soul would escape the flames that she, armed with matches and kerosene, kept the fire going day and night until she at last succumbed of dehydration. I personally examined her corpse, eyes bulging, tongue purple. The ogress was just as lovely then as she had ever been in life."

Mencken raises the flask in a salute. "When I was a boy, a porch monkey who lived in the alley behind our house ran amuck and slit his woman's throat. He was promptly hanged at the city jail. Before they planted this blackamoor, my brother and I sneaked into the Negro funeral parlor to observe the cadaver. I shudder to this day. Haunted we were for many a night by the marks of the rope on that corpse's felonious neck."

"Hell, these days a rope is an obsolescent appliance. Once it actually reminded assassins they too were mortal. Now they have no fear." Bierce swallows from the flask, returns it to his pocket.

"Mr. Bierce, if all criminals of a plainly incurable sort were hanged instantly our next generation would be free of crime."

"Perhaps. I once wrote a fable about waking after more than a century of sleep. I saw an enormous building covering a square mile surrounded by a wall patrolled by armed guards. Warden told me it was the new state penitentiary, one of dozens. I was surprised the criminal population had increased so enormously as to warrant such vast penal facilities. But the warden said the criminals had become so powerful, so bold, so fierce that no one was arrested anymore. Prisons were built to protect the honest inside."

Mencken says, "There's truth in that."

"I'm feeling the itch, young man. Need to go to a war in a distant place. Perhaps Mexico. Some sort of revolution is going on down there."

"Always a revolution in Mexico, Mr. Bierce. You can choose better."

"It is the most convenient damned war to home. When you get to be my age you can't be fussy about your wars."

"I'm no admirer of Mexico, nor of anything that comes from that squalid country. Once I saw an exhibit of Mexican arts and crafts at a gallery on Charles Street, all sorts of squat pottery, gaudy blankets, and crude jewelry. What was most shocking were two human skeletons propped up at sixty-degree angles. One skeleton was that of a peon who had been shot by a bandit. The bullet hole was clearly visible in the center of the skull. The other was the skeleton of the bandit who had shot this pitiable creature. One of the killer's cervical vertebrae was dislocated to show the effect of the noose around his neck."

"By god, Mencken, you've made up my mind for me. I *shall* go to Mexico. Perhaps look up those skeletons you saw. And send home some squat pottery, gaudy blankets, and crude jewelry. You look to me like someone who could use a gaudy blanket."

Occasionally, the procession comes to a subtle rise where Bierce beholds the anonymous homes, windows blank, stretching side by side in eternal precision. The urban landscape is monotonous, unbroken, the city's magnificent harbor obscured by sinister warehouses, rail yards, and forever unknown warrens. As the party aims west the houses shrink, two stories rather than three. On the sidewalks, kids play age-old games and new ones known only to them.

Mencken notes that behind the row houses are unpaved alleys lined with shacks where the city's blacks live and die in transient anonymity. "The jigaboos are happy in their alleys, Mr. Bierce. They're simple, good-meaning people, adept at hoodwinking us white folks. It's the Anglo-Saxon hillbillies, lintheads from West Virginia and Kentucky, I despise. They're filthier than anything I've ever smelled and a hell of a lot more ornery. And the Jews, while cleaner, aren't much better—the pushy obnoxious ones, I mean. Give me an African any day. At least he knows his place."

Bierce eyes his fellow mourner with a measure of repugnance. Bierce, himself an Anglo-Saxon descendent, neither Christian nor Jew, once fought and nearly died to free the "jigaboos."

"One thing I admire about you, Mencken, is that you spread your contempt regarding the races evenly. If you keep it up you will become as cynical as the man who unhappily shares the rear seat of this auto with you."

"Mr. Bierce, a cynic is one who, when he smells flowers, looks around for a coffin."

"Something I might have said, and perhaps did." Bierce becomes pensive, thinking of the past, which intrudes more and more often.

"Mr. Bierce?" Mencken puts his hand on Bierce's shoulder and gently shakes it, bringing him back to 1911.

"What? Oh, sorry. Sometimes I get lost in my reveries, the way of old men."

The funeral procession turns onto Wilkens Avenue for its final leg. As the hearse rounds the corner, a rear wheel—loosened by the rutty pavement—twists off the axle and rolls into the gutter. The hearse spills its cargo onto the street, casket lid flying open. Out pops the late Percival Pollard, limbs akimbo as though he is about to fly. Or to bless. His eyes, minus the nickels, are open but gaze at no one in particular. The Daimler driver hits the brake, checking the car before it clobbers the corpse, an act that otherwise would have imposed still another indignity on the deceased.

The spectacle draws a crowd slightly smaller than Buffalo Bill's Wild West Show. Housewives drop their flatirons to run to the street. Elderly widows grope for their specs. Blacks dash from their alleys. Little kids abandon their scooters. Old men on their canes hobble to the scene. Arrabers neglect their songs and squash. The postman throws down his mail, the iceman his tongs, the ashman his barrel, the milkman his cheese. Dogs follow their noses. The first police officer onto the scene knows his duty. Constrain the spectators. Officer O'Hara boots a nosy twelve-year-old in the ass and lays his baton on the head of an adrenalized African who has never seen a white man's corpse. The undertaker's factotums, chagrined, scoop up the cadaver and stuff it back into the coffin. It doesn't fit as well this time, rigor mortis perhaps, and the lid can't quite close. The hearse's driver manages to remount the wheel and upright the vehicle.

Mencken shakes his head. "Percy didn't look especially comfortable sprawled in the street."

"Hmmm. I thought he appeared rather unconcerned."

"What do you think should be done with his ashes?"

Bierce thinks for a moment. "Molded into bullets and fired at the publishers, notably Messrs. Scribner, Putnam, and Doubleday."

"Perhaps the ashes of the departed deserve some respect, Mr. Bierce."

"Sentimental about a few burnt remains are you, Henry? On my writing desk are the ashes of my late wife in a cigar box next to the skull of a former critic."

"I marvel at your humor, Mr. Bierce."

"What humor is that?"

At last, the funeral caravan passes through the gates of Loudon Park Cemetery. Bierce looks around with approval.

"Ah, the cemetery. An isolated suburban space where mourners match lies, poets write at a target, and stonecutters spell for a wager."

The graveyard is bleak on this winter day, trees bare except for an occasional evergreen. Beyond the tombs, mausoleums, and rows of crosses, a thin, whitish column of smoke spirals into the air.

"By Jove, they've stoked the fires and the ovens are in operation." He barely restrains his glee.

Mencken says, "May I speak candidly, Mr. Bierce?"

"I listen to no other form of speech."

"With all due respect, there is none of the milk of human kindness in you, captivated as you are by the spectacle of human cowardice and folly."

"I take that as a compliment."

"But some of your ideas are questionable, such as ranking Sterling and Longfellow over Whitman."

"And some of your ideas are objectionable. Ranking German culture over the English, which may lead to your downfall."

"Touché. Nevertheless, let me say you're the first American writer to lay cultural destruction with absolute gusto, no head escaping your furious thwack."

"Are you saying I'm berserk?"

"Berserk men are rare in America, and you, Mr. Bierce, are a runaway locomotive yet to run out of steam."

"Henry, my boy, more and the same might be said of you. And, sorry to say, no doubt you will be dead before you can separate your decent qualities from your crude prejudices. Perhaps you should write a book with that very title. *Prejudices.*"

"Mr. Bierce . . ."

"You have an arse, Henry. So stuff your damned racist palaver up it."

So sayeth the Almighty God Bierce.

In Saratoga, the night following the bridge tournament, Mrs. Dumont and Mr. Grile wander into the hotel gardens, secluded, but shadowed by an astonishing half-moon. A katydid sings, but the other insects are in disguise. Johnny dreams iniquitous dreams in Mrs. Dumont's suite while, as usual, Señor Arango reigns in the hotel bar, his foot on the rail, drinks all around, even though his English is so poor nobody knows what he saying.

She says, "You've not had a chance to read any of my writing?"

"Still in the process, my dear." He is putting off the ordeal. Reads so much drivel by would-be authors he's afraid she will reveal her shallowness in the writing, and he will no longer regard her in the same way. A talentless writer not only discloses her character in her writing, but her ignorance.

"What I'm most frightened of are the critics."

Blah, blah, blah. Now he's sure she's written shit. Someone who has put down virtually nothing, yet she's worried about the *New York Tribune's* reaction? Still . . . "Aren't you being premature, my dear? Perhaps it would be well of you to complete your book before concerning yourself with what others might say, especially the big city press. The judgment of the critics or the public hasn't much value in any event, other than fattening or depleting the author's bank account."

"I'm not certain living in Buffalo is conducive to my art. Perhaps I should move with Johnny to New York City. The famous authors and publishers are all there."

M'god, as if moving someplace, anyplace, makes one a better writer. Is this girl an idiot? But he can't let her go. Not yet.

"New York has a numerical advantage, Mrs. Dumont. But don't look upon it as a literary capital. Provincial writers may suffer the same disadvantages as non-writers, but hardly enough to warrant moving to New York. There is no more idle or barren pursuit than assessing writers by their birthplace or residence. My dear, remain in Buffalo, do your work, hope for the best. Trust me."

"I do."

"Do what?"

"Trust you."

They sit on a stone bench deep in the shadows. There, her Victorian antecedents, and his, ignored, she unbuckles his belt and opens the buttons on his pants—trousers.

"Am I being too forward, Mr. Grile?"

"Of course you are, for which I shall be forever in your debt."

"And I in yours."

She lowers her head, conceding to his mind but not to his body. Resolution comes almost instantly. She refuses to take her mouth away. By god, his prowess hasn't failed him. Not yet. She raises her head and her wet lips meet with his.

Chapter Twenty-one

Into the air flies a can of what was once Armour Evaporated Milk.

Bang.

The firing has frightened off the rabbits and the crows, but not a daring, presumptuous godlike robin watching from a tree limb. The two men aim at the tin cans lined on a tree stump. They have the clearing in the woods to themselves.

"You still have a good eye, *amigo*. That eye once saved my life."

"I've always been a steady shot, General."

Bang. A neat hole through a tin of Morton's Fresh Salmon.

The smoke curls from Grile's Colt, practically an antique; indeed, he acquired it not long after the war, his war. Between them is a burlap bag filled with empty cans removed from the trash bin next to the hotel kitchen so as to have plenty of targets.

Bang. There goes Lion Canned Pineapple.

Bang. Tickler Marmalade.

Señor Arango is also a steady shot. He fires a British-made Webley revolver.

"Did I ever tell you about the time I met with President Roosevelt at the White House, General?"

"At least ten times, you old *cabron*."

"TR. Now there was a crack shot. And a self-proclaimed war hero to boot."

"No *más*, dammit."

"I've always been skeptical about his charge up San Juan Hill, although he almost got me to change my mind. The operative word is almost. Roosevelt and I were co-conspirators of a sort, way back. He was a braggart, and yet . . ." He sighs. "But enough about TR and me." Grile is becoming used to living in the bygone.

"About time, *gracias*, dammit."

Bang. Van Camp Pork and Beans.

Bang. Libby, McNeil & Libby Corned Beef.

"General, you must miss the field of battle."

"It's what I was born to do. I will be going back soon on a raft of snakes. Will you return with me?"

"Highly doubtful. The Game . . ."

Arango spits. Mexicans are savvy about the nuances of expectoration. "The Game. You ain't played The Game since we left Mexico. It's the woman, this Señora Dumont. That's why you're not going to return with me."

"Remains to be seen, General."

"You're *cogiendo*—how you say, fucking—her."

"Allow me to cite a proverb from the Chippewa Indians of Ohio, land of my nativity, that goes, 'A closed mouth catches no moths, even fewer butterflies.'"

They set up more tins on the stump and shoot them off. Arango pretends the cans are *federales* dying for their executions. Grile makes believe the cans are preachers. Arango squats under a tree to rest. Grile joins him. Ominous clouds form overhead.

"Ah, war used to be so easy, *amigo*. My Dorados and I simply rode our horses into the enemy and drove 'em to the ground."

"At the cost of many lives."

"What are lives? In Mexico we got more than we need. But as I found out at Celaya it's all changing. Earthworks, barbed-wire, mines, gas, long-range cannon . . ."

"General, war has become a more healthful occupation. There is so little direct combat the soldier of the future is sure to die of consumption, apoplexy, typhoid, or even old age."

"My soldiers won't die of no old age. They want to look the enemy in the eye and die for Francisco Pancho Villa. Die for Mexico! *¡Viva revolución!*"

"How charming. Sabers clashing against others, thrusts of bayonets into bodies, revolvers firing at revolvers. Such a pity, General, that on matters of combat you refused me permission to counsel you at Celaya."

The Mexican raises an eyebrow, which he tends to do when he imagines an insult. Who is this arrogant gringo to question his tactics at Celaya or anywhere he damn pleases? Sure, he blundered at Celaya, but who the hell could have done it better? Some cocksure *hombre* with an *enorme*—how you say?—big mouth? He cocks his pistol, points it at the older man's heart.

"General, if you please . . ."

"*¡Silencioso!*" Gingerly, Arango begins to pull the trigger as he turns the gun toward Quetzalcoatl, noble feathered serpent and god of all gods. *Bang.* The bullet plunges through the breast of the brave robin perching on a limb to contemplate the two lesser beings below. The bird, wings tight against its body, falls like a squash. So short a life, but a cocky one that got it nowhere.

"Sometimes, señor, you do not amuse me so much."

"I've been known to have that effect."

"*No seas tan estúpido.* I might turn your skull into a drinking cup—if I could stomach the local water. In matters of war I need only my own counsel. And no fuckin' gringo is—"

"I love you, General, in the way of masculinity, of course, and I bow to your audacity. Your praises will be sung and your exploits celebrated in folklore long after the foredoomed ink-stained wretch before you bows to the inevitable. But as we've discussed on many an occasion, your shooting me will only be the act of one man performing a good deed for another. What I mean to say, with all respect, is that your bullets are of little significance to me." Grile removes his watch—still ticking since the day Uncle Lucius, mayor of Akron, Ohio, gave it to him on the eve of the Civil War. Is he truly unafraid of a bullet fired from the Webley that felled Quetzalcoatl? He will never say. "General, best we remove ourselves to the hotel. It's not only starting to rain, but I have an appointment with Mrs. Atherton."

"Who?"

"What?"

"You said something about a Mrs. Atherton."

"Did I say . . . ? Excuse me. Slip of the tongue. I meant to say Mrs. Dumont."

They gather the riddled cans into the burlap bag. Arango is inclined to leave them on the ground, but Grile is tidy and wants to restore the woods as he found it. It's now pouring, so indoors is the place to be.

Mr. Grile and Mrs. Dumont are most proper, both having been born in the nineteenth century, so who can blame them for their feigned acquiescence to Victorian values? They make love. In her room, Johnny absent; in his, Señor Arango off to where only God and his favorite stable hand Hector know; under the stairs leading to the east wing; in the pantry next to the kitchen; under the bar in the saloon in mid-afternoon before the evening barkeep comes on duty; behind a row of oaks within sound but not sight of Broadway; in one of the unoccupied luxury cottages on the capacious grounds; in an empty stall in one of the stables at the track. Would even the nosiest, most annoying Methodist have ever suspected?

They meet in the billiards room to play phonograph records, flat and brittle and a half-inch thick, of the popular songs. "Chinatown, My Chinatown," "Down among the Sheltering Palms," "When You Wore a Tulip," "Ballin' the Jack," "In an Air-ship Built for Two," "Let Me Call You Sweetheart." The phonograph with its great conical horn is the finest on the market, a major advance over the contraptions that spin wax cylinders. Screwed to the side of the machine is a plate etched with an artist's rendering of a perplexed white terrier, head cocked, staring into a phonograph horn.

"I'm impressed by the technological marvel of the phonograph," he says to her. "Merely watching some thingamabob, flat as a plate, turn and produce sound is astonishing. Until now, I've always thought of the phonograph as an irritating toy that restores life to dead noises. Still, I'm disappointed by its esthetics. It hasn't accomplished all I expected of it."

"In what way, Mr. Grile?"

"The tones aren't as rich and mellow as I was led to believe. I also understand a person's voice sounds like that of a stranger when he hears it reproduced on the machine. Therefore, he retreats from the apparatus with a chastened spirit and a broken pride. As a teacher of humility the phonograph ranks with the parson, the flirt, the mirror, and the banana peel on the sidewalk."

"Oh bosh, Mr. Grile. They've made a lot of improvements in the phonograph since Mr. Edison came out with those unwieldy cylinders."

"No doubt, my dear, the recorded voice will one day be enhanced so that even the most rasping nasal twang will give off rich tones and cadences. Rather like the camera. Who can go unblushing after seeing the damage done to him or her on film? But no sooner did the merciless photograph take the conceit out of us than an ingenious malefactor rushed to the rescue with a process called retouching. The honest camera can now lie like a lover. Should we expect less from a phonograph record?"

They sit on folding chairs listening to the music and watching the sharks stalk their billiard balls with cue sticks. Her foot taps to the music. "Oh You Beautiful Doll." He is annoyed by song's featherheaded sentiments, but he loves the way she taps her foot. He knows he's an unmitigated ass, but he's come to dote on her, young enough to be his daughter—no, granddaughter. Their first moonlight physical intimacy was a rekindling for him. Fornication aside, he might make something of her. Transform her into a woman with imagination, which is vastly superior to mere intelligence.

They stroll to the hotel newsstand, where she buys a package of Sen-Sen for herself and Life Savers for Johnny while he purchases a copy of the New York *American*. The paper is always a day late by the time it arrives in Saratoga Springs, but that doesn't bother him. He's in no hurry to catch up on the news. Hearst's headlines are bellowing about the sinking of the British passenger ship *Lusitania* by a German U-boat. William Randolph Hearst himself brays in a front-page editorial that the Germans had the right to sink it because it carried munitions.

Grile says, "Twelve hundred innocent people aboard the *Lusitania* drown, including sixty babies, and Hearst excuses the Kaiser. Something that young Teutonic Mencken no doubt agrees with. Tauri excrementum."

"Why do you read that odious newspaper?"

"I need to find out if Hearst is still up to his old tricks, and he is. Nobody but God loves the man. Newspapers like the *American* are conducted by rogues and dunces for dunces and rogues. Don't get me started, my dear, but Hearst's rags are sycophants to the mob and tyrants to the individual, and they stiffen the prejudices of the ignorant."

"Yet you tell me you were in Mr. Hearst's employ for more than twenty years."

"I had a living to make and a family to raise."

He is only partially right. Conveniently, he has put it out of his mind, but effectively he'd abandoned his family even before The Boss offered him a plum spot on the *Examiner*, a bylined column plus the opportunity to publish anything he wrote, including his fiction, in the Sunday features section. How could a mere family compare to a peachy deal like that, especially for a hand-to-mouth scribe like himself?

"Besides, in my own way I tried to uplift the newspaper. I take a certain satisfaction in that."

"Obviously you've soured on the press."

"Precision in language, Mrs. Dumont, precision. There's no such thing as the press. There are newspapers and there are machines made for printing called presses."

Picky, she thinks, he's so damned picky. Could she live with this galvanizing man, senior enough to be her father? My god, how striking he is, those fathomless blue eyes, hair and mustache a lustrous white, hardly a trace of fat, hands perfect, what beautiful hands. Plus his mind, his mind. And funny. Just when you think he's made a lacerating evisceration it turns out to be simply a clever joke. No, no, it *is* a lacerating evisceration, perhaps even a diabolical one. She's an ignoramus. How inappropriate their relationship. What would her mother say? Besides, Johnny hates him, and he hates Johnny. He would never cohabit with her if Johnny is in the picture. She has her own mixed feelings about her son, and terrible guilt as a result. Mr. Grile thinks she's pure, chaste. What a hoot.

During her engagement to Oakleigh, her ill-starred West Pointer, her father treats her to automobile driving lessons in Buffalo. The instructor is a young mechanic, Stefanos. He brings the Hupmobile around and shows her how to set the brake, open the fuel petcock at the tank, make sure the oil reservoir is topped up, the bearing oilers set to drip at the right rate, then to turn on the spark, prime the carburetor, and crank the engine.

"See how simple," Stefanos says. "No, ma'am, turn the crank like this."

He puts his hand on hers to show her. His fingernails are caked with grease, which gives her a rush. She wants him dirty, but there's no way to explain why. They drive out dusty Seneca Street toward Cazenovia Park. He's at the wheel. She sits next to him, plaid blanket across her knees. He parks in a secluded grove of maples and she throws the blanket on the grass. "If you say anything about this I'll have you sacked," she says. "Of course not, ma'am." "My word against yours, and who are they going to believe?" "You, ma'am, that's for sure." She opens the buttons of his trousers while at the same time raising her skirt. On the return to the city, she behind the wheel, Stefanos says, "Tomorrow again, ma'am?" "Yes, and be on time, and what's your name again?"

But Mr. Grile . . . Mr. Grile is a fuddy-duddy, always correcting her as if she's a child instead of a lover. To top it off, he's evasive. He talks a lot but reveals little. Is his name really Grile? Sounds like a made-up name to her. She wants him. Now. This instant. But he keeps droning on and on about, dammit, everything except the two of them.

"Hearst's influence on the public and Woodrow Wilson's timidity are a lethal combination, my dear. The nation needs another Roosevelt in the White House. Or, better, Teddy himself. I understand he returned not that long ago from a harrowing expedition into the jungles of Brazil, but no doubt reinvigorated and ripe for action. I had a passing acquaintance with TR, and I'm *dee*lighted, *dee*lighted to say that through me Hearst's political ambitions were quashed. Some day, perhaps, I'll tell you . . ."

"What's wrong with right now, Mr. Grile? What better thing for us to do with all that rain outside than to sit here in the lobby while you tell me all about it?"

He raises his white eyebrows lasciviously. "I can think of something preferable."

She giggles. "I'm flattered, but it's nearly lunchtime and pretty soon I must retrieve Johnny from the playroom. There *are* practicalities." She is overwhelmed by his presence, physically in his thrall, but she knows he's just making it all up, his past. As if he's actually been to the White House . . .

At first, he chooses to ignore the engraved invitation to the reception and flips it rudely into the trash, where Carrie Christiansen retrieves it. It's not every day one receives a White House invitation, and Carrie is good about saving his letters, clippings, mementos, as well as making his bed and pouring his nightcap. She also mulls a decent beer and cooks a piping Welsh rarebit. Insouciant Carrie. Never asks for much, satisfied to teach high-school English during the day and care for him the rest of the time. She's thirty-two years younger than he. He relies on her, depends on her, but he has lost interest in her, yet she doesn't complain.

"Ambrose," she says, "you're wanted on the hall telephone."

Roosevelt, succeeding the martyred McKinley, settles the issue of Bierce's intransigence with a personal call. The president, not one to take no for an answer, succeeds in bullying a man not accustomed to being bullied.

"*Dee*lighted, Mr. Bierce."

Roosevelt, McKinley. Now there's a pair, Bierce thinks, Roosevelt so progressive he's a borderline socialist, McKinley a damned antediluvian, and good riddance. A cannon on wheels, TR is brilliant, eccentric, his mental clockworks ticking sleep or awake. Admire him or hate him, he dominates everyone within range of his histrionic voice. Bierce hears it as he enters the White House through the North Portico and is escorted to the Blue Room. Not expecting so many guests, he growls as he waits his turn in the reception line. The president, under the crystal chandelier, is all smiles and teeth.

He pumps Bierce's hand. "I'll have you know I've just read your two most recent books, *Can Such Things Be?* and *Shapes of Clay.* Bully." Damn, this Roosevelt is manipulative. "But by reading your column in Mr. Hearst's *American,* I suspect you don't entirely approve of my crusade against the trusts."

"Mr. President, it seems to me we're coming to governmental ownership and control by leaps and bounds. I have doubts about regulating the trusts."

"Despite the weeping and wailing of the reactionaries, the big corporations must be subordinated to the public welfare."

"But labor forms unions, newspapers create syndicates, department stores spring up, cities swallow suburbs, authors join guilds. There is even a congress of religions. What in tarnation is the evil in trusts among corporations?"

"Trusts demand immunity from governmental regulation, which is just as wicked as granting immunity to the barons of the twelfth century. There are many of forms of tyranny, Mr. Bierce, but the most vulgar is the tyranny of wealth. Regulating commerce for the public good is not an evil."

"Mr. President, commerce is a transaction in which A plunders from B the goods of C, and for compensation B picks the pocket of D of money belonging to E."

Mockery is Bierce's best defense, and TR chortles. "Bully, Mr. Bierce. I admire your erudition."

"Merely dust shaken from a book into an empty skull."

"When I rode up San Juan Hill on a certain memorable occasion, in my mind was the vision of a lone horseman. Yes, the soldier in your story 'A Son of the Gods,' who also went forward to reconnoiter. Mr. Bierce, just as your gallant, lone horseman reached the crest of his hill, so I was determined to reach mine."

"I believe I am being unmeritoriously flattered, Mr. President."

"Come, Mr. Bierce." He leads Bierce across the Oriental carpet to the fireplace. "Observe the painting over the mantel. It depicts me leading the Rough Riders on my momentous charge. Marvelous piece of art, what?"

Bierce isn't a connoisseur, but even he recognizes the painting as grossly romanticized. Little wonder Roosevelt admires it.

The president says, "I asked you to the White House to tell you how your story helped to engineer history and to tender the thanks of a grateful nation."

Scattered applause among the onlookers.

"I'm most appreciative, Mr. President, but I feel I must be forthright."

"Do say."

"I am of the impression your actions have been exaggerated, and that you actually scrambled up San Juan Hill on foot with the rest of your men."

A collective gasp. One of TR's beefy bodyguards steps forward.

"'Tis all right, people." He puts his hand on Bierce's shoulder. "For the record, I was on horseback while the troops were in their trenches unable to see their officers. When I saw the Spanish at the top of the hill, I realized there was no officer superior in rank to me, so I gave the order to charge. As far as history is concerned I galloped up San Juan Hill on horseback and *your* story was my inspiration."

"I stand corrected, Mr. President."

"Mr. Bierce, I returned home from Cuba a hero and as strong as a bull moose. Of course the newspapers had something to do with it, particularly your own. But no matter how I was extolled, I have little admiration for certain elements of the press, if you catch my drift. To be candid, your employer has sold himself to the devil and will no doubt live up to the bargain. He's an unspeakable blackguard who combines the worst faults of a corrupt and moneyed man with the worst faults of a conscienceless demagogue, a man with a muckrake and one of the most potent forces for—and I do not exaggerate—evil."

"Obviously, you and William Randolph Hearst agree on nothing but the war against Spain."

"Which, as I understand, you decried."

"By gads, Mr. President, I opposed the war, at least at first, but never publicly disparaged my employer for all but starting it. It would have been unseemly to embarrass Mr. Hearst, who, after all, keeps my cup full and victuals on my plate."

"Our nation needed that war. It was salutary for the common good and beneficial for morale. Knowing one can win by attacking an ineffectual enemy gives a boost to all except the foe, and who gives a damn about him? I admit I took a degree of pleasure in the war, even though malaria claimed more American lives than the Spaniards." Roosevelt puts his hands on his hips. "Mr. Bierce, I intend to launch an independent re-election bid in nineteen-oh-eight, and I'm going to ride the distance on horseback. Will you ride with me?"

Bierce admires military men—once planned to be a professional man-at-arms himself—but the idea of waging war to boost a nation's morale seems repugnant. TR led a regiment, but he was more of a fervent amateur than a true warrior, so afraid of losing his spectacles that he pinned six pairs inside his Brooks Brothers hat. Bierce, himself wounded while putting down a traitorous insurrection, inherited hand-me-downs from his older brothers, so the notion of a hat or anything else from Brooks Brothers smacks of grandiose conceit.

"Mr. President, with all respect, any riding I do will be from Point A to Point B, and not as part of an exhibition."

Suddenly, Bierce starts to wheeze in pronounced distress, air tubes in his chest clogging again. Dammit all. So embarrassing.

"You appear to be having difficulty breathing, Mr. Bierce."

"Asthma, Mr. President. I'll get over it."

"Hasten, people. Our friend is ill. Assist Mr. Bierce to the master bedroom and place him on my bed to rest."

"*Your* bed, Mr. President?" Bierce pants. "Is that a rack for the torture of the wicked?"

The president bellows with laughter.

When Bierce opens his eyes Roosevelt is standing over him. TR's own eyes are huge behind the spectacles perched on his nose.

"Your breathing has improved, Mr. Bierce."

"The attacks come and go, Mr. President."

"I was an asthmatic as a child. It was also touch and go sometimes, so I know how you must suffer. What are you taking for your malady?"

Bierce sits up, groggy. "Until recently, an atomizer that contained a potent, foul-tasting, membrane-burning chemical known only to my doctor and to God, who are one and the same."

"I know that particular god."

"Needless to say, it failed to work. I began smoking Dr. Blosser's Cigarettes, consisting of the product of a plant called stramonium, which only made me gag. Then an acquaintance, a young Baltimorean named Mencken, urged me to experiment with adopting a homeopathic approach, while not endorsing it for himself, of course. So I tried Chinese ephedra, a bronchial dilator combined with a licorice root used in the Orient for over five thousand years."

"Yes, ephedra. Didn't work five thousand years ago, and won't five thousand years from now."

"My erstwhile advisor in homeopathy, a man with a sense of humor, subsequently prescribed an herb called lobelia inflate. It is alleged to be an excellent expectorant which helps to relax the bronchial muscles."

"Indian tobacco, so called?"

"It too failed. Then I was ordered to take ginkgo leaf, which they claimed increases the blood flow to the brain, but only gave me migraines. Next I took blue green algae, which contains antioxidants to increase the respiratory tract's integrity."

"No doubt the WC got plenty of use."

"I was instructed to consume honey, gobs of it, told it would build resistance to local pollens, which worked as well as the rest. Mr. President, I view the homeopathist as the humorist of the medical profession." Bierce starts to stand. "I'm better now and ready to return to your reception."

"Easy, Mr. Bierce. You were out longer than you realize, and the reception is long over. Please remain. Fact is, I had an ulterior motive in asking you here. Two motives, actually." Roosevelt grins, mouth an expanse of ivory. "When I was a boy, Mother and I vied at crossword puzzles. See the envelope I'm holding in my hand?"

"The coffin of a document?"

TR chuckles. "Inside is a crossword puzzle. The joint project of my six children. They created a crossword made up entirely of words related to me personally or professionally. There's 'Rough,' 'Rider,' 'Sagamore,' 'Republican,' 'Progressive,' 'Harvard,' 'Root,' 'Taft,' and so on. I've nearly completed it, but two words have me stumped. You're an expert on language, Mr. Bierce, so I turn to you."

"The words are . . . ?"

"The first is a five-letter word across ending with the letter E. So the clue is, 'First name of a man, homonym for the name of a submerged container.'"

"The other?"

"A four-letter word down that starts with R. The clue is, 'Last name of a man, homonym for a word meaning to predict or foretell the future.'" Roosevelt disconnects his pince-nez, blows on it to rearrange the dust, and pinches it back on his nose. "Have you the foggiest idea of the answer?"

"I do, Mr. President."

"Kindly do not keep me in suspense."

"Sir, the word down is R-E-I-D. The one across is M-A-Y-N-E."

"Reid Mayne? I'm afraid I don't . . ."

"The first clue is a homonym for a word meaning to foretell the future, such as to *read* the future. Read. Thus Reid. The other, Mayne, is a homonym for the name of a battleship, now submerged at the bottom of Havana Harbor."

"The *Maine,* of course. Clever, Mr. Bierce, but I'm still vague about . . ."

"Mr. President, when you were a boy did you not read the adventure books of Mayne Reid?"

"I'd forgotten!" The President slaps his thigh. "My brood obviously rifled through my childhood library to come up with the name."

"I became acquainted with Captain Reid slightly when I was an expatriate in London. He died in eighteen eighty-three, along with his books and, I suspect, his readers."

"Splendid piece of literary detection. Bully, indeed." Roosevelt, almost intimately, sits next to Bierce at the edge of the bed. "Now that you've solved that little mystery, let me discuss with you a small political matter for which I am in need of, shall we say, encouragement."

"Mr. President, to hear you Republicans talk you need no encouragement because your party, by its own admission, is the nation's political salvation."

"The Republicans currently are the majority, but, candidly, I'm no longer as one with the Grand Old Party."

"Sir, majorities rule, when they do rule, not because they ought, but because they can."

"Bully, bully. The Democrats hate me because I'm a Republican. The Republicans hate me for the same reason. By Godfrey, if the GOP has its way government will come to a standstill. The South will return to slavery, textile mills will again employ the labor of nine-year-olds, steel plants will gladly sacrifice life and limb for rock-bottom wages and the twelve-hour day, and the national parks will be turned into slagheaps. We might as well board up Washington and go home. Which brings me back to your Mr. Hearst."

"One of your own, a Harvard man."

"Hardly, sir. He was bounced out. Not content with spending his vast inheritance on a newspaper empire, he believes he must also take charge of the nation. He bought himself a congressional seat, as you know, although he's never present for roll call. Now he's running as a Democrat for governor of New York, and I'm told he's virtually assured of victory over Charles Evans Hughes. If Hearst wins he will be on track for the presidency, and I shudder at the thought."

"As do I."

"I know he's your employer, but it's widely rumored you believe he is not fit for public office."

"Mr. Hearst has many amiable and alluring qualities, Mr. President, but not as a politician."

"He can be stopped, sir, and you're the key."

"I'm a mere scribe. A salaried man. He no longer listens to me, if he ever did. Refuses even to take my calls. If I try to reach him, I must go through a man called Brisbane."

"There is a perception Hearst poisoned the atmosphere that led to McKinley's assassination. Hearst's newspapers published a cruel quatrain that seemed to support the idea that an assassin, after striking down the governor of Kentucky, should also murder McKinley. And I quote."

"No, please, sir—"

"'The bullet that pierced Goebel's breast / Cannot be found in all the West. / Good reason: it is speeding here / To stretch McKinley on his bier.'"

Bierce's shoulders sag.

"You know, of course, who penned that dreadful rhyme, Mr. Bierce."

"I confess I wrote it in a moment of lunacy, Mr. President. Unfortunately, it passed the editors who were long under Mr. Hearst's orders not to blue-pencil my work."

"Apologize not. Should your poem be resurrected in the midst of the gubernatorial campaign it would cause extreme damage to your Mr. Hearst. I plan to send Secretary of State Elihu Root to Utica, New York, to campaign against Hearst using your quatrain as ammunition. I simply ask for your blessing, and that in your columns you not speak out against me."

"I'm mortified, Mr. President."

"For the welfare of the nation."

"Mr. Hearst and I have come to terms with our relationship. While I no longer report directly to him, in many respects he has given me immunity. I'm a scribbler, a professional writer whose satire is sometimes antagonistic to my actual views. However, I don't seek elected office, so . . . What can anyone do to me, other than not to buy my books? Which has been the story of my life. I concur, Mr. President."

"Bully, bully! If my strategy succeeds you may not win the applause of a grateful nation, but you'll have mine."

"Applause is nothing but the echo of a platitude from the mouth of a fool."

"I beg your pardon?"

"You being the exception, of course."

Some weeks later while drinking at the Army and Navy Club, Bierce reads with satisfaction the *New York Times*'s account of Elihu Root's speech citing Bierce's callous verse. Later he takes even greater satisfaction when he reads that Hearst loses the election by 58,000 votes, ending The Boss's political future. Hearst must now despise God, but no more than God despises Hearst.

Damn the asthma.

The climate in Saratoga Springs has made it neither better nor worse.

It has always been that way, going from good to bad to good to bad again. Seeking relief from his asthma nearly all his life, he has never fully dodged it. At times he almost accepts his affliction, which has become a part of him, like a toothache that goes on so long it almost feels normal. What is disease and injury, Grile thinks, but Nature's endowment of medical schools?

"*Amigo,* is there anything I can get you?" Señor Arango asks. "You seem to be in agony."

They are in their suite, Grile in his bed, the Mexicano standing over him.

It is an effort for the Gringo to speak. "General, agony is a superior degree of bodily disgust. And I not only have the agony but the disgust."

"I will call the *medico*—how you say?—doctor."

Grile grabs Arango's wrist. "I want no doctor." Gasp. "I saw one once after breaking an elbow while bicycling in Rock Creek Park, and he removed my temporal lobe, which alleviated my aggressions but didn't heal the bone." Gasp. "At my age, I'd prefer to supply a liberal provision to maintain the undertaker, so justly underpaid."

"Don't talk like that, *pinche pendeja.*"

"Let me be straightforward, General. I'm on the verge of providing the worthy grave-worm with meat that is not yet too dry and tough."

"Stop the jokes. You are . . . how do you say it? Too cynical."

"When it comes to death, General, I'd be willing to debate the degree of cynicism that separates us."

He wheezes, gasps, coughs, reaches for the air.

"I wish I could do something about your affliction, you old *idiota.* Other than shoot you."

What passes for a smile comes to the older man's lips. "Affliction is an acclimatizing process that prepares the soul for another and bitter world." Gasp. "I'll be better in the morning, General. Always works that way, though one day it will be otherwise."

"I think I understand, *amigo.* For the moment you have something to live for. A certain señora with blond hair and blue eyes."

"I have a date on my calendar to escort Mrs. Dumont to a fashion show. And later to a concert in the park. She has even asked me to attend church services with her. Why, my health has improved already."

"Women's dresses? Music? Church? You? You *are* smitten." Arango puts his mouth close to his *compadre*'s ear. "Tell me the truth: when it comes to death you feel fear, don't you?"

"Not fear so much, General, as morbidity. Especially if my death is taken out of my own hands. Such as by an attack of asthma." He has been faced with death before; has, indeed, known fear, feels it now, not that he will ever display it, willpower and resolve permitting. "Who or what has the right to determine my extinction? It should be my choice."

"If I take my Webley and . . . Is it still your choice?"

"Absolutely. When I first met you I knew what I was getting into. Even to the extent of being lined up before one of your multifarious firing squads and shot to shreds. I demand the right to choose my own death, and a firing squad might be just the ticket."

"Demand? *Besa mi culo.* Who are you to demand anything?"

"All right then, I beseech."

"*Amigo,* sometimes I hear you refer to death like it's more than a mere circumstance, but also an *espiritu maligno*—how you say?—evil spirit. You got a name for this spirit? You got a word for everything else."

"I've already told you. The Damned Thing. It's in this very building as we speak. It crawls through the corridors, haunts the stairwells, pervades the basement, fills the closets. It sneaks up on its victims at the most inopportune moment. But it's not quite at my door. Unless I stop it, it will assassinate me."

Chapter Twenty-two

No exercise for the horses. Rain and mud. Mud and rain. The track is a slosh, so it's another day off for the thoroughbreds. Señor Arango learns from his favorite stable hand, Hector, a young Andalusian, about the weekly cockfights in the rear of Stable D and goes to investigate. *¡Caramba!* How he loves cockfights, dogfights, bullfights, and above all men fighting men. Once, in Puerto Palomas, Chihuahua, he pays two whores to fight, and one bitch puts out the eye of the other with an awl. What *alegria*—how you say?—joy.

Cockfighting is not on the list of accredited activities at the venerable Grand Union, so on this drizzle of a day the hotel stages a magic show for the young'uns in the dining room, while in the lobby a fashion show for the grown-ups. Mr. Grile is a tad cranky on his rendezvous with Mrs. Dumont. His asthma attack of the night before has passed, but not his lack of sleep and his melancholia. All night, visions of his two sons, both dead before their time, kept him awake. Day, victim of a fatal love triangle, was the first to depart, then Leigh. He'd held out some hope for the surviving sibling, a potentially gifted writer, but it was not to be. In effect, Leigh died a gutter-drunk, so it might be said Leigh was a suicide like his brother.

The fashion show's models consist of Saratoga Spring's most bonny damsels. Their frocks, the latest fashions from New York, have been supplied by the local dress shops, including the boutique in the lobby run by Mademoiselle Yvette, whose name on her birth certificate appears as Pauline Goldfarb. Mr. Grile and Mrs. Dumont sit in French chairs and scrutinize the parade of skirts, hats, bows, ribbons, buttons, lace, sashes, braids, buckles, streamers, hooks, feathers, and plumes.

"I suppose you find all this rather silly, Mr. Grile."

"I'd find it sillier watching, as your son is doing, a magician in a top hat sawing a sequined wench in half. By Jove, I fancy the rich, bright bravery you ladies wear. I don't go along with the neutral-tinted minds of those who inflict subdued pigments on our female population."

The women pose in brilliant colors. He has never relished so much plumage all at once. Satin, silk, velvet, calico, polka dots, stripes, checks, taffeta, tartans, tattersall. Although he, of course, is garbed in his customary gabardine black.

"I'm reminded of Nature by this array of color, Mrs. Dumont. Nature spreads a wealth of brilliant hues across the landscape. Hills, air, water. Colors float like banners in the sunlight and lurk in the shadows. No artist can paint them and none dares to do so. Critics might say Nature has gone mad, but it's wicked to believe the critics."

Mrs. Dumont titters girlishly. "You make it sound as if Nature has no taste."

"Nature concocts odious, even hideous, combinations of tints swearing at one another like eye-scratching shrews. She has the unparalleled stupidity to spread a blue sky above a green plain. Nature is a dowdy vulgarian with no more taste than His Majesty, Mr. Shakespeare."

"Oh look! Now there's a dress I adore. The blue gown with the lace trim."

"Ah, you're quite becoming in blue, my dear, although I'll never forget what you were wearing the moment I first saw you. You were dressed in maroon, almost a burgundy."

"I'm flattered you recall."

After the fashions, after the applause, Mr. Grile and Mrs. Dumont, both aware of their striking image as a couple, promenade arm-in-arm through the lobby.

"The blue gown you liked, my dear? Allow me to buy it for you."

"I can't possibly accept."

"Are you saying you're unwilling to make an old duffer happy on a rainy day, an admirer who wants only to please you, especially when we're standing outside the very shop that sells the gown?"

"Well . . ."

The fit is nearly perfect. Mademoiselle Yvette needs to make only the slightest alterations in the waist. The dress will be ready by late afternoon.

"It is said fashionable women are heartless for wearing the plumage of songbirds, Mrs. Dumont, but that is pure poppycock. Women are only obeying the imperious mandate of their nature."

"Which is?"

"To be comely in the eyes of the male."

"Bunkum, sir."

"It is the end and justification of a woman's being, and she knows it."

Her nostrils flare. "Such benign contempt you have for my sex."

"Not at all, my dear. In that one thing women are far wiser than men. She may be unable to formulate her wisdom, and she commonly makes a bad attempt at explaining anything, but she knows a great deal more than she knows she knows. She is aware of how stunning she looks in a skirt, but what she doesn't understand is that the skirt enslaves her."

"Twaddle."

"A skirt is devoid of utility, Mrs. Dumont. It promises a sense of restraint and takes the character captive. If you were to invent a garment that would make its wearer submissive could you create a better one than the skirt? Think of a woman riding side-saddle. There is no valid reason for a skirt of any length, shape, or material. The strongest evidence of a woman's unfitness for a larger role in the affairs of the race is in clinging to her skirt. Or rather permitting it to cling to her."

"Like a Scotsman in his kilt?"

"Ouch. Touché."

"You sound like a dotty, woman-hating, old coot, Mr. Grile. It's not the skirt that binds women, it's the mental behavior of dunderheaded males who assign to themselves the leadership of our species."

"Mrs. Dumont, wisdom comes of mental freedom. Are we to expect intellectual development from humans who voluntarily obstruct their legs? If women want emancipation from the imaginary tyranny of man-the-monster, let them show themselves worthy of it by unbinding their bodies and liberating their limbs."

"Clothes are irrelevant in the battle between the sexes. If men wore skirts, or indeed no clothes at all, they would still remain mindless brutes who, unable to apply peaceful persuasion, inevitably resort to violence to achieve their ends. See this bracelet, Mr. Grile?" She holds up an attenuated wrist to display a narrow band made up of delicate gold links. "This is the vestigial remnant of the chains and shackles used for centuries by men to hold women prisoner. Since women are the physically weaker sex, men have subdued and subordinated us by simple, brute force. Men don't view us as equals but as possessions, like owning a Clydesdale or a Pierce-Arrow. But it's nineteen-fifteen, Mr. Grile. Western women are sick of being bullied by men. Emancipation is around the corner. Women are fighting back because collectively we're as powerful as any group of men. Further, I resent your misogynistic, patronizing attitude. And as far as the gown you bought me from Mademoiselle Yvette's . . . go wear it yourself!"

Leaving him, his mouth gaping, Mrs. Dumont stalks to the dining room to collect Johnny from the magician's thrall. Mother and son will make do with a quiet dinner in their room, by god. Then she will help Johnny complete the jigsaw puzzle he's been working on, a stupid map of the forty-eights. The boy has a decided lack of interest in jigsaw puzzles, and his mother is inevitably forced to complete them herself. Johnny is in constant movement. If only there were some pharmaceutical to slow him down. The jigsaw is a diversion, however slight, on an inclement day, although it won't be much fun. Hang Mr. Dod Grile anyway! So she's a mite wrathy. She has cause to be, despite their, well, relations. And what kind of name is Dod? Think of it spelled backwards.

He catches up with her, son in tow, as they are about to climb the stairs to their wing. M'god, a lover's spat, their first quarrel after their many sexual encounters. He touches her arm, but not enough, he hopes, to rile her any more than she is. After all, she has favored him in the most intimate ways, and there is much to be said for that.

"Mrs. Dumont, allow me to apologize for my boorish remarks. Please understand that when I was a scribe for my living I thrived on controversy, which is why it sometimes carries over into my personal exchanges. Half the time I don't really believe in anything I say."

"You're not a man who will give an inch to an opponent, are you?"

"In your case, Mrs. Dumont, I totally surrender. I'm certain there is no life after life, but if so I hope that to open the Heavenly Gates I must pass a rigid examination in the art of not being a cussed ass. My disposition lately has not been all that it should. Too many thoughts about the past, about what might have been. The sorts of tomfool things we obsolete contemplate. Please, my dear, indulge me and join me for dinner tonight. I wish to make it up to you."

"In that case . . ."

As Mrs. Dumont walks up the stairs holding her son's hand, impish Johnny turns and sticks his tongue out at his white-haired foe, who is tempted to do the same; instead, he ducks into the hotel saloon for a quickie. Martell VSOP. Bartender, another. Make it a double. The cognac goes to his head as he thinks about his two lost sons. Can't get 'em out of his mind lately. He recalls that sultry day at St. Helena in the Napa Valley, his boys so innocent. Mollie is entertaining some local parson who is calling to drum up business for the Lord, as if the Lord can't do it for himself. Bierce is, for him, on near perfect behavior until Leigh dashes into the room shouting, "Daddy, Day just said 'Damn God.'" The Reverend Mr. Soul-Snatcher is appropriately appalled, as is Bierce, who says, "Leigh, tell your brother I've repeatedly told him not to say 'Damn God' when he means 'God Damn.'"

Leigh grows up in the shadow of a famous father who revels in his reputation as a curmudgeon and misanthrope. Bierce's aloofness, accompanied by long periods of absence, makes for an uncommonly distant relationship between father and son. Nevertheless, after Day's self-destruction Bierce does what he can to get close to Leigh, arranging for art lessons and, later, entry-level jobs on the San Francisco *Examiner* and the Los Angeles *Record*. Now Leigh is in New York writing for the *Morning Telegraph,* a tabloid churned out in a former car barn on Eighth Avenue. The paper survives more on Broadway gossip and sporting news than journalism.

Bat Masterson is on the editorial staff. Former gunfighter, deputy sheriff, card shark, saloon owner, and boxing promoter, he has railed east from Denver to write about sports and to make his fortune. The *Telegraph*'s editor, W. E. Lewis, assures Masterson it ain't necessary to spell in order to plow the alphabet at a Gotham daily, that scholarly editors in green eyeshades fix the words, correct the grammar, repair the punctuation, and polish the copy. Masterson can't construct a proper sentence, but the *Telegraph* is in dire need of a celebrity-staffer, semi-literate or not.

On his first day Bat is arrested for packing a concealed weapon. The *Telegraph* coughs up his fine. Mr. Lewis assigns young Bierce, cub reporter, to keep an eye on Masterson, and Leigh promptly leads the ex-gunslinger to the Metropole at Broadway and Forty-second where the two guzzle rickeys into the wee hours. Masterson appreciates the

Metropole on account of it's got three exits, givin' him a choice of get-aways in case of an emergency. His pal Billy Hickok was plugged in the back while countin' chips in a one-exit saloon in Deadwood, Dakota Territory. Leigh matches drinks with Bat, who easily becomes maudlin. He talks about his pals Wyatt Earp and Doc Holliday and Wild Bill. He talks about the men he's killed and those he wants to kill. He talks about the James boys and the Clantons. And the O.K. Corral. Now he's faced with poundin' the implacable pavements of New York to write about Connie Mack and John J. McGraw and Gentleman Jim Corbett and hoity-toity, namby-pamby stuff like the PGA, the U.S. Open, the America's Cup. He doesn't give a smidgen about golf and tennis and yachting. So he comes from Illinois, but at heart he's an Old West gunslinger, not some milksop Eastern dude.

Masterson wipes away a tear and puts his arm around Leigh. He takes from his breast pocket a Tombstone, Arizona, sheriff's badge and thrusts it into his new best friend's hand. "Take it, young Bierce," Masterson says. "This badge was part of my life and a piece of American history. It's yours now. Accept it in friendship and, hey, bartender, another round here." Bat has the sheriff badges made up at a novelty shop off Times Square. They cost a quarter each.

Leigh lives in a rooming house on West Forty-eighth. One morning, sleeping late with his usual hangover, he hears a knock. In long johns he pads to the door and opens it. Outside is a pretty young woman holding a stack of sheets. Leigh, embarrassed, tries to close the door, but the girl bars it with her foot.

"Oh, ho, it's not as though you don't have nothin' I ain't seen before, Mr. Bierce. I got a baby brother, you know. I seen his pee-pee lots of times. Anytime I want."

"Who are you, girlie? How do you know my name?"

"I'm Flora and I'm here to change your sheets. Me ma owns this place. Now, Mr. Bierce, I got lots of rooms to do, so kindly stand aside and let me fix your bed."

Flora is dark, hair black, eyes gray, hips wide, bust narrow. For two years she attends parochial school where saints trump schooling and the nuns try to beat the dreams out of her but fail. She's got stage-light aspirations, waitin' for the right opportunity. She goes to all the castin' calls and fucks the first producer who calls her back. She doesn't get the part or the producer. Disappointed she is, but she ain't discouraged. She's a girl and she knows Leigh is smitten with her. Within the week Flora clings to Leigh between his starched sheets in the bed she made up personal.

His only thought is pouring himself into her body. Hers is in capturing a handsome young man like Mr. Bierce, a gent with real possibilities. Connected he is with a newspaper. Chum of the famous Bat Masterson. Gets press passes to the Polo Grounds and Madison Square Garden and Aqueduct. Claims to have an eminent pa she ain't never heard of. Well, she ain't never heard of her old man either. Never even met him, in fact. Leigh writes to his father that he and Flora are going to get hitched. The senior Bierce promptly takes the B&O from D.C. to Jersey City, where he ferries across the Hudson to meet the girl, after which he privately hectors his son.

"Don't do it, Leigh."

Father and son sit in the lobby of the Hotel Navarre, where Bierce always stays while in New York. The rates aren't outlandish: a dollar-fifty a night.

"I love her, Dad."

"Listen, my boy, the girl has no education, no qualifications. I spoke to her at length. She can barely read, can hardly sign her name. She can't speak a simple declarative sentence without murdering the language. Son, you're off to a good start as a writer; you've written a few decent short stories. But you'll never be able to share your life with that girl. Take it from me, she will become a nuisance to you, pull you down."

"I delight in her."

"It's purely carnal."

"She's what I want."

"The girl's trash."

Leigh leaps to his feet. "How dare you say that about her?"

"I say it as your father. Now sit down. I said sit *down*."

Leigh, face flushed, sits.

"Your brother got involved with a trashy woman. I had to take him back to his mother in a box. I don't want the same thing to happen to you."

"Why should you care, Dad? You were never there for us. When Day and I were little—and Helen too—you were never around. Always off on some mountain or hiding in some room. Anywhere we weren't. Our mother brought us up. You didn't."

"Perhaps I wasn't the best of all fathers, Leigh, but I cared about you then and do now."

"Extra! Extra! Read all about it! Ambrose Bierce Wasn't the Best of All Fathers! Put that in your newspaper, Dad. Front page. And fuck your Mr. Hearst too."

"How dare you, Leigh! Your language."

"I'm twenty-six years old and need no tutelage from you about my language. And what makes you think you can tell me who or who not to love?"

"The money I send to you via Wells Fargo Bank, that's what tells me."

"That's below the belt."

"Leigh, you're immature. Like your brother, you make bad decisions. You drink way too much."

"As if you don't."

"This is not about me."

"And what *about* you, Dad? Your Colt forty-five? I heard about the time you shot at a man in San Francisco."

"In self-defense."

"You might have killed him."

"He came to thrash me over an imagined slight to his wife. Should I have allowed him to do so? Leigh, I don't want you to repeat my mistakes."

"Mistakes? Like walking out on my mother?"

"That's none of your—"

"You cut her off. You abandoned her. When you send her money it's in care of Helen. What the hell did my mother ever do to you?"

"My relationship with your mother is none of your concern."

"Anything that has to do with my mother is my concern, Dad."

"Leigh . . ."

"You got bored with her, didn't you? Intellectually and everything else. That's why you don't want me to marry Flora. Because you got tired of Mother, you think I'll get tired of—"

"Leigh, I'm warning you that if you marry that tramp I'll wash my hands of you."

"What's new about that, Dad? If someone offends you or doesn't act the way you want 'em to, you cross 'em off your list. Non-persons they become."

Bierce raises his fist as if to strike his son.

Leigh doesn't flinch. "Dad, if you hit me I'll kill you. I'll take your gun away from you and shoot you dead."

Oblivious of the street traffic, Leigh walks to the Metropole to quaff with Bat Masterson until the sun overhangs Times Square. Masterson carries him home. Flora pumps black coffee into him. The next morning, Flora and Leigh—his head throbbing—are married by a clerk at the Municipal Building on Centre Street. The windows in the clerk's office are open and as the couple exchange vows they see the boats, barges, and tugs navigating the East River under the Brooklyn Bridge. They ride the steamer to Asbury Park, where they honeymoon at the Devonport Inn for two days before returning to Manhattan. Flora moves into Leigh's room. At dinner, she gives Leigh the largest portions.

As time wears on, Leigh's father proves to be right, and Leigh knows it. His damned father is always right—even when he's wrong. Flora starts to pall. She promises to read his stories but never does and never will. For her birthday he gives her a book by Thackeray. She never cracks it. Her mind is not disciplined. She reads about sex and scandal in the common rags, but has no interest in current affairs. She vaguely recalls the names of the mayor—Van Wyck?—and the president—McKinley?—but not those of her congressman or governor. She's unaware of the Boxer Rebellion or the gold standard. She has never heard of Frank Norris or Booth Tarkington or Edwin Markham. She knows, however, all the words to the song "Just Because She Made Dem Goo-Goo Eyes." Leigh and Flora find little to say to each other outside of tidbits about dinner and curtains and illness and money. Leigh hunkers in at the *Telegraph,* stays out later, drinks harder. He usually returns home long after the dawn and sleeps most of the day.

When it comes to civic promotion, the Empire City's gazettes are hard-pressed to compete with Hearst and Pulitzer, but the *Telegraph* tries. Editor Lewis arranges a Christmas promotion, with the entire staff compelled to pitch in and distribute food and toys to the needy. Leigh is to accompany the Christmas give-away wagon and to write a story about the *Telegraph*'s fabulous humanitarian effort. It's snowing when he gets to the city room that night, Christmas Eve. He has already fortified himself with several junipers at the Knickerbocker and is feeling warm and bubbly.

"You been drinkin' again, Bierce?" Lewis asks.

"Absolutely not, sir. I never take a drink until I finish my work."

"Make sure you don't. It's frigid out there and you got duties."

"Aye-aye, sir."

The horse-drawn wagon, chockablock with provisions, pulls away from the *Telegraph's* loading dock in Hell's Kitchen and rolls down Eighth Avenue. Banners fly from the wagon's every side heralding the *Telegraph's* good deeds. When the vehicle reaches Forty-second, Leigh tells the driver to halt. "Be just a moment. Gotta warm up." He runs into Costello's and orders a double brandy, drinks it in a single gulp, and darts back into the sleet. He almost slips on the ice as he climbs into the wagon. The snow is coming down heavily by the time the wagon reaches the Broadway Tabernacle on West Fortieth. Leigh helps to unload toys but excuses himself and runs across the street to Mulligan's, where he consumes two brandies in quick succession. The wagon goes next to Marble Collegiate Church on Fifth Avenue, where he unloads more gifts, including several fresh turkeys. He disappears for a bit, ducking into Flannagan's, and has to dash to catch up with the wagon. This time Leigh has taken the precaution of buying a bottle to pocket. More gifts are distributed at St. Francis Xavier R. C. Church on West Sixteenth. By the time the wagon reaches the Bowery, Leigh is indiscriminately throwing toys and tins of food to passersby. "Merry Christmas from the sheriff of Tombstone, Arizona!" he shouts hilariously. He holds up the phony lawman's badge Bat Masterson gave him.

The driver tries to constrain him, but Leigh scurries from the wagon, leaping in the snow, at last halting in a tenement doorway to swig. Drained, he sinks to his knees, collapses against the unlatched door. A ruffian observes Leigh's prone figure and lifts his wallet and the fake sheriff's badge. The thief pulls out the few bills before throwing the empty wallet to the sidewalk, but keeps the badge, which might become useful. The snow ends by morning and dawn breaks clear. Police Officer James Patrick Niall Fagan discovers Leigh in the doorway, wallet and a liquor bottle, both empty, next to him. Poor bastard is partially covered by snow, which makes a frigid blanket. Fagan feels Leigh's pulse. A little life in him, thank the Lord.

An ambulance rushes Leigh to Bellevue, where the doctors gradually coax his hypothermic body by applying warm compresses. Once in a while Leigh awakes from his slumber, mutters his father's name, calls for his mother, asks for his sister, Helen. The doctors find in his wallet the address of the *Morning Telegraph* and call Lewis, who in turn phones Flora. Leigh drifts in and out of sleep, develops a hacking cough, hardly able to swallow the broth Flora tries to force between his lips. She actually prefers it now that he's sick, really sick. It brings him closer to her. Finally, he floats into a coma from which there is no awakening. Flora tearfully phones his father in D.C. Carrie Christiansen takes the call.

"Ambrose, it's Flora."

"Who?"

"Your son's wife."

"Tell the chippy I'm not in."

"She says Leigh's sick, Ambrose. He's in Bellevue Hospital."

"Tell her it's none of my concern."

"She says they don't think Leigh's going to make it."

"Tell her to go to . . ."

Exhausted, Bierce arrives in New York late that night, delayed by congestion at the ferries in Jersey City, something to do with ice floes on the Hudson. Leigh lies in a monstrous hospital ward. A mere curtain separating his bed from the others affords the only privacy. His breathing is so labored it's almost negligible.

Flora stands by the bed wringing a handkerchief. She tells Bierce, "The doctor says Leigh's lungs are filled with fluid on account of pneumonia."

Asthmatic, Bierce understands the terror of being unable to breathe. Flora lets out a sob heard throughout the ward.

"Get a grip on yourself, girl," he says. "There's nothing more vulgar than a public display of grief."

"But I ain't like you, Mr. Bierce."

"Of which I'm aware."

"Leigh's my husband."

"So I've been told."

"You're bein' inhumane to me."

"Young lady, I know something about inhumanity. It's one of the signal and characteristic qualities of humanity."

After Leigh takes his last breath, Bierce wires Mollie. march 31, 1901. leigh passed away 6 a.m. send helen. will arrange to return body for burial. There is much Bierce would like to have said to Leigh, but an insurmountable gulf separates sons and fathers, and time inevitably runs out for both. Helen arrives to escort her brother's corpse back to California and attempts to remonstrate against her father, but he will have none of it.

"Bibs, I loved Leigh and I loved Day."

"Oh?"

"Christ, I lost two sons. Take some pity on me."

"And Mother. Do you love her too, Daddy?"

"She's the only woman I've ever loved, Bibs. I swear it."

"But not the only one you've consorted with. That Miss Christiansen? Young enough to be your daughter."

"I can say no more."

"Why not, Daddy? Since when has the great Ambrose Bierce ever been at a loss for words?"

Bat Masterson comes to pay his respects. He gives Bierce, as a gift, a sheriff's badge from Tombstone, Arizona. After Masterson leaves, he throws the cheesy toy into the trash. A cheap fraud, Masterson, and no doubt a bad influence on impressionable young men like Leigh. Now alone, he puts his hand over his eyes and sobs. Jesus H. Christ. Get yourself together, you worthless mongrel. What if someone sees you? What if that indecorous little strumpet, what's her name, Flora, discovers you with your defenses down? Be the man you'd hoped your sons might have been. Leigh leaves nothing behind but a threadbare suit, a few unpublished stories, and three hundred dollars' worth of bills. The widow sells the suit. Bierce pays the debts. The *Morning Telegraph* is generous to the widow: the newspaper gives Flora a check amounting to two weeks of Leigh's salary.

Saratoga Springs.

They sit across from each other in the main dining room of the Grand Union Hotel, the two of them at a quiet table. She is wearing her new blue gown. They make a startlingly attractive couple, more like husband and wife than, say, uncle and niece or father and daughter. From a distance, white hair aside, he looks barely senior to her, having preserved most of the attributes of his youth, carrying himself in a bold and vigorous way. As he speaks he occasionally touches her hand. When she speaks she often touches his. They've had intimacies, regularly, in fact—in stealth and secrecy. In public, however, their decorum is beyond reproach.

"Delighted to be able to eat with you tonight, Mr. Grile."

"I believe you mean to dine with me. Precision in language, my dear."

Precision be damned. The old stuffed shirt. Under the table she rubs her foot against his ankle.

Daiquiris for starters, after which he orders a bottle of Gewurztraminer, followed by one of Petite Sirah. Then it's champagne. Another bottle. He drinks most of it. She gets tipsy. So does he, a bit. They eat tomato aspic, hearts of palm, green turtle soup, osso buco served with baby artichokes, carrots Vichy, Dauphine potatoes, cheese bread, muffins, rum chocolate mousse, and café au lait. He is still thirsty, so he orders cognac for each of them, Martell, his usual. The meal is exorbitant, but Señor Doroteo Arango is generous with the funds of revolutionary Chihuahua and is picking up the check, as he has all their expenses. From across the room a string quartet entertains the diners with that familiar air by Dvořák.

"Listen, my dear, my favorite composition." He waves his cigar in time with the music. "What the deuce is that melody called?"

"I believe it's known as 'Humoresque.'"

"Of course. His nibs Henry Mencken introduced me to it."

Mrs. Dumont has had enough to drink to embolden her to go directly to her target. "Mr. Grile, you must have finished reading my manuscript by now."

"Alas, I'm still perusing it, my dear. However, I am, as you know, not an advocate of the novel, particularly those that are cynically conceived and constructed in ways to appeal to the broadest constituency. Not that I'm referring to your own effort, of course. Do not think of the novel as art. Nevertheless, I understand your compulsion to write in the larger form."

"I hope my prose is composed as artfully as poetry."

"Some poetry isn't art at all. Tennyson's 'Charge of the Light Brigade.' Would you consider it art?"

"Certainly."

"Resonant patriotic clatter, yes. But it's not even poetry. Far be it from me to evaluate the delicate and difficult art of managing words—"

"Far be it."

"—but there are poems that blaze like a garden of brilliant flowers while others are as chaste and pallid as the white lily."

"Even bad poetry is good poetry if it touches one's heart."

"Mere sensuality, my dear. Poetry is enjoyed primarily because of its meter and rhyme, the same sort of exultation the unlearned receive from the banging of a drum or the clashing of cymbals. Most people will hear or read a poem and be unable to tell you what it's about. Of every one hundred adults who can read and write, there are ninety-nine to whom poetry is a sealed book."

"Are there any living poets you truly admire?"

"The finest practitioner of the poetic arts in America is my compeer George Sterling, an often annoying chap who totes with him at all times a personal cyanide capsule in an envelope labeled 'peace.'"

"You know this how?"

"The man adored me, confided in me. Alas, he got on my nerves. Nevertheless, if for no other work he will be remembered for his poem 'A Wine of Wizardry.' No poet in the English language has flung such a profusion of jewels into so small a casket. Let me recite a couplet. 'The blue-eyed vampire, sated at her feast, / Smiles bloodily against the leprous moon.' That picture is vivid enough to affect with a chronic chill the spine of any philistine."

"You actually *admire* those ghastly lines? Sated, bloodily, leprous?"

"Unequivocally. George Sterling is without peer. While it is true I disavowed him for purely personal reasons, when we're dead and gone our progeny will be reciting his work and singing his praises."

"It's obvious, Mr. Grile, that I'm a mere neophyte in a field in which you are so clever. But . . ."

"Yes, my dear?"

Her cheeks mutate to white. The alcoholic spirits, the abundance of odd food, and the intolerable "A Wine of Wizardry" have done their mischief. Shakily, she climbs to her feet. Grile rises with her.

"I'm afraid my digestion . . ." She pauses, unable to proceed.

He says, attempting to be droll, "By digestion I assume you mean the conversion of victuals into virtues." Oh-oh. He sees her ashen cheeks and realizes his remark has fallen flatter than Kansas.

"You'd better turn away, Mr. Grile. The world is spinning and this philistine is about to regurgitate in close proximity to your well-pressed suit."

"My dear . . ."

"No doubt caused in part by your Mr. Sterling's repellent verse. The way I feel right now would I only to possess a cyanide capsule in an envelope labeled 'peace.'"

Chapter Twenty-three

Mr. Grile wears a damp hotel towel around his head Arab-like. Immobilized with a hangover, he can't bear the thought of moving as much as a toe out of bed. Only on occasion, this being one of them, does he suffer from overindulgence, his body for years having built a resistance to the copious quantity of alcohol he imbibes. But last night he damned well outdid himself. The daiquiris, chardonnay, champagne, café au lait, and Martell—all part of the same meal—are playing within his gastro-intestinal tract like a shootout with Billy the Kid. Naturally, he blames, not the booze, but the veal.

"Never again, General, shall I order osso buco."

"Damn, I could have told you about that *merde*. And I don't even know what osso buco is."

"Then it may have been the green turtle soup. The aspic wasn't quite to my liking either. At least I didn't vomit the way Mrs. Dumont did, and in my lap. Charming. Especially the intermingling of the colors representing all she'd consumed over the day."

"You're a bad influence on that lady, señor."

"Or vice versa. My cranium throbs so much I may kill myself."

"Now you're talking like the gringo I knew in Mexico."

Señor Arango ain't feeling so super himself. North Americano food don't agree with his tummy and he finds himself more than once forced to dash to the WC. *Estomago fiojo*. Nor does he trust the H_2O. Damn, that fuckin' gringo water. They'd warned him back in Mexico not to drink it.

pat . . . pat . . . pat . . .

From outside a strange but gentle sound. He walks to the window to investigate.

"*¡Caramba!* They're doing something loco out on the grass."

"Kindly describe it to me, General. But speak in a soft, low voice if you don't mind."

"Men and women. They're on either side of a net. And they're holding rackets. Not big rackets like in your tennis but little ones.

They're hitting—not a ball—but a plaything that looks like it has feathers."

"A birdie."

"She's no birdie, *compadre*. I know a birdie when I see one."

"It's made out of cork. Also called a shuttlecock."

"Cock, cork? You make no sense."

"Deployed in a game called badminton."

"What is this badminton?"

"After the Duke of Beaufort's estate in England."

"Don't know no Duke."

"Nor do I, hailing from Indiana, General. Take it from me: it is an effete game in which the ladies have as much chance as the men to win, even more. Thus, it is played in polite company."

"I'd rather put a bullet in my brain."

"You are speaking my language."

pat . . . pat . . . pat . . .

Arango squats, almost intimately, on the side of Grile's bed.

"Then why don't you, *amigo?*"

"What?"

"Put a bullet into your loco gringo brain. You're wasting my time and yours, and I'm almost ready to return to Mexico. What the hell are you waiting for?"

The American moans. "Pain is cruel, death is merciful." He dips the towel into a bucket of ice water, squeezes the cloth, drapes it back over his forehead. "General, I've heard it said a physician's duty is to cure disease and to alleviate suffering. So why don't *you* play physician and put me out of my misery?"

"*Friendo,* I have put many men out of their misery, but not for something as simple as a headache."

Grile sits up, removes the towel from his head. "I'm not sure I appreciate the way you say *friend*, General, because it doesn't sound quite friendly. And only vaguely Spanish."

"So?"

"Then kindly hand me my gun."

"Hell no. You might use it. On me."

"Preposterous. Why would I use it on you?"

"For not killing you."

"I wish to play The Game."

"Not now."

"Why not?"

"You must wait until your hangover goes away so you can think more clearly."

"You have already encouraged me to put a bullet in my brain, so I insist that you hand me my revolver."

The Mexican shrugs. "If you insist, *amigo*." He gives him the Colt .45, oiled and primed. "Careful. It's loaded."

pat . . . pat . . . pat . . .

Grile weighs the comfortable heft of the gun in his hand, runs his fingers over the cold steel, shakes his head, then plops the Peacemaker on the nightstand.

"Still not quite ready, you old coot?"

"Something just occurred to me . . . What time is it?"

"I think maybe seven or eight in the morning."

"Holy Christ, so to speak. I have a date in church with Mrs. Dumont at nine."

"Church? Ha! An old *hombre* in love. What about The Game?"

"Possibly tonight."

"Promises, promises."

He hastily bathes, shaves, and dons his best black suit and bowler. It is apparent, as he strolls arm-in-arm to the church with Mrs. Dumont, that she too hasn't fully recovered from her own Gewurztraminer indulgences of the night before, but she's making the best of it, or so it seems. Even if she still feels the need to puke she is damned well not going to show it, and he doesn't realize her legs are so wobbly she can barely walk or that her head feels as though it's been open by a schism as wide as the Grand Canyon. At the same time, her monthlies are just ending, and she is one of those luckless women for whom the curse means bloating, cramps, throbbing breasts, the trots, and never-ending effluvia that no number of sanitary pads will stanch.

Hygienically she is appalled by her own body, and no amount of bathing compensates for what she fears is her pervasive odor. Worse, she gets downright pissed, sometimes behaves like a fuming, frothing beast, often wanting, yes, to kill. Isn't that why her late husband, Oakleigh, came to despise her? The poor boy, a West Pointer, succumbing a bullet to the brain. His bullet, his brain. Why, just last month she slapped Johnny's face twice and once more for good luck, and spent the following week plying the little bloodsucker with kisses and sweets and anything else he wanted. Anything to make it up to him. What was it they once called her condition? Oh, yes. The red river of death. If men only knew. No, they don't want to know. Men are built so simply, the lucky bastards.

She hasn't even told her doctor how wretched she feels every month, only her mother and God, and there had damned well better be a God, as she has been assured since her bassinet days by more or less intelligent people who claim to know. It's amazing how certain people, obviously divinely favored, seem to have so much savvy about God and are willing to share it. She is not as demure as she has Mr. Grile believing, and she has no intention of revealing otherwise if she can help it. She doesn't want to lose him. And why should she? At times he seems detestable, although no more than how she sees herself, and yet there is something in him she has never experienced before in a man.

"My accident on your lap, Mr. Grile—I'm mortified."

"Osso buco will do it every time. Nothing that a little hotel dry cleaning couldn't take care of. Ah, here we are at the chapel. Such a quaint spire. Have you noticed how a church's spire resembles a bayonet?"

His contempt for churches knows no bounds and rarely will he step foot inside one, but this morning he makes an exception in order to be in the company of the shaky young woman he has corrupted, or so he naively thinks. It's a Presbyterian service, not that he gives a damn. He can't tell the various silly denominations apart, nor does he wish to fritter a single brain cell attempting to do so. The preacher is a visiting minister from Buffalo, an old acquaintance of Mrs. Dumont, the Reverend Moss Herbert having presided at her wedding, the christening of her son, and the funeral of her husband.

Mr. Grile squirms in the uncomfortable pew, the polished seat curved torturously to foment sliding, preventing the parishioners from snoozing or even relaxing. He folds his program into a paper aeroplane and pretends to launch it down the aisle. Mrs. Dumont pokes him with her elbow. "Straighten up," she hisses. When the minister beckons the congregation to stand for some idiotic ritual, he wearily creaks to his feet, knee joints snapping.

The Reverend Herbert's sermon is, "Why the Masses Do Not Attend the Churches." Mr. Grile already knows why. When the collection plate extends into the pews at the end of a five-foot pole, he grudgingly throws two dimes inside. Mrs. Dumont supplements his donation with a silver dollar.

After the services, she says, "There, that wasn't so bad was it, Mr. Grile?"

"I trust you're speaking for yourself, my dear. It was torture. Both my posterior and my head are numb. And I'm in the hole twenty cents."

At the front entrance the Reverend Herbert shakes hands and makes small talk with the congregates as they file out. The preacher is obviously delighted when he sees Mrs. Dumont and her companion, the last to leave.

"Elizabeth, I knew you were in Saratoga and I was so hoping you'd find the time to come to my sermon. Any news from your mother? And how's Johnny?"

"Mother writes that she's redecorating the parlor. And Johnny's in Sunday school. We're about to claim him."

"We?"

"Let me introduce my friend, Mr. Dod Grile."

The Reverend Herbert extends his hand, which Grile accepts limply.

"I confess, Mr. Herbert, I'm not usually a churchgoer."

"Aha, then you're precisely the person I intended to address in my sermon. The churches would be filled to the rafters each Sunday if we had a law mandating attendance. It was done back in England in Shakespeare's day, you know. Go to church or face fines or the stocks."

"And not long ago in our nation, sir, one could be pilloried for blaspheming anything ecclesiastical. But what you're admitting is that those of you in the religion racket haven't the brains to make your services attractive."

Mrs. Dumont gasps. "Mr. Grile!"

Mr. Herbert touches her arm. "No, Elizabeth. It's all right. I'd like to hear what your acquaintance has to say."

"I don't believe you can expect the police to spread your gospel by rounding up people and herding them into pews. Truth is, Mr. Herbert, the masses stay out of pulpit range because they hear so much fatiguing nonsense. They'd rather do any one of a thousand things more pleasant."

The Reverend Herbert's eyes narrow, mouth tight. "Go on, Mr. Grile."

"You parsons are like a wife who scolds because her husband won't pass the evenings with her. The angrier she gets the more she scolds—and the more he stays away. Satan, the one you people invented, may not be wise, but he's a mighty good entertainer. And he has a knack of making people want to come again and again. The clergy might study Satan's methods in order to advance your own notions of religion and morality."

"Entertainment is not the object of religious services, sir."

"But entertainment is the object of the people."

Mrs. Dumont pulls at Mr. Grile's sleeve. "I think Reverend Herbert's heard quite enough."

"Elizabeth, let him speak."

"Frankly, Mr. Herbert, the masses know Sundays are more enjoyable without a religious component. There are better things to do. Face it, sir, those who go to church are, for the most part, browbeaten into it. When you go to a doctor and you don't like the medicine he gives you, he either prescribes a different medicine or he attends to another patient. The doctor never asks the police to hold the noses of his patients while he plies the spoon."

The minister clears his throat. "Mr. Grile, the masses don't know what's good for them and sometimes need to be force-fed."

"Sir, the masses rarely beg for your churches and your services. They're foisted on them. You clerics don't perceive how alien your convictions, tastes, sympathies, and mental habits are to most of your fellow men. And women. Even those who profess a belief in your notions."

"And you, Mr. Grile, how alien are *your* convictions, tastes, sympathies, and mental habits to most of *your* fellow men? And women. Even those who profess to believe in your notions."

"Match point, Reverend."

"However, I concede that your comments are enlightening."

Mrs. Dumont says, "I apologize for my friend, Mr. Herbert. He's getting on in age. They get cantankerous, you know." She vows to herself she will never again speak to this grumpy septuagenarian whose mind she esteems, and whose body she has, well, gotten to know— enjoy.

"You needn't apologize for Mr. Grile, Elizabeth. He speaks the truth."

Mrs. Dumont's mouth opens in incredulity. "You *concur*, Mr. Herbert?"

"Elizabeth, it is inharmonious for ministers to differ with one another, so we don't. We have a particular image to protect. There are certain words and themes we are expected to utter from the pulpit. But for me it's about to change. You see . . . I intend to resign the ministry."

She takes a step back. "After all these *years?*"

"I'm sick of the falsehoods, the lies, the hypocrisy. And, frankly, I'm not certain I believe—or ever did."

"I'm astonished." She touches her wide-brimmed, feathered hat, a bit more showy than it should be on a churchly Sunday. "You never hinted about anything like this before."

"I couldn't commit ministerial suicide, Elizabeth. But now I have an alternative. I'm going to work on a fishing boat in Lake Erie. I've already learned how to weigh the sails, spread the nets, and haul the anchor. I wish to become a fisher of fish rather than of men. Mr. Grile, do you find that strange?"

"Indeed not, Mr. Herbert. A substantial improvement over spreading your nets for souls. It will prove more salubrious for both your sustenance and your mind, as well as beneficial for the general population. If there are any muskellunge left in Lake Erie, which I doubt, and you happen to catch one, put it on ice for me."

She's still miffed and snappish as they leave the church grounds. "And what would your friend, your inscrutable Señor Arango, think of your disgraceful performance this morning, Mr. Grile?"

"He would disapprove."

"I thought so."

"Of my moderation. Had he his way, Señor Arango would line up all the preachers before a firing squad and have 'em shot."

The image is so outlandish she can't help herself. She giggles.

"I admit it, my dear. I'm incorrigible. Always have been. And even when it comes to your favorite cleric I couldn't resist teasing him."

"You were *teasing?*"

"You thought otherwise?"

He has redeemed himself to her, particularly in view of the Reverend Herbert's startling metamorphosis. Anger dissipating, she takes his hand as they go to pick up Johnny, who makes no secret of his antipathy for her mother's prehistoric companion, a man who understands Johnny better than Johnny understands himself. On the way back to the hotel they buy him ice cream, which he manages to spill down the front of his clean white shirt. They make an appointment to attend the band concert in the park that evening.

He finds himself alone, standing under an elm, seeing framed flashes of blue sky above the leaves. God knows where Señor Arango has gone—mostly likely to the cathouse he favors at the edge of town. The Mexican has been extolling the merits of a stout mulatto woman whose most intimate orifice boasts an amazing ability to propel small objects at high velocity. This moment of woodsy privacy gives him time to ponder the subject so familiar to him: death. He knows it to be as common as life, and yet many, in their arrogance, see it merely as a vague abstraction. Death comes in three overlapping varieties, he thinks. First, that of an impersonal nature, such as in disaster or battle, its victims nameless and often countless. Next, one's own death, almost impossible to contemplate until actually eye to eye with the Reaper. And the worst of the three, at least for him, when death claims an intimate friend or a family member, and God knows he's suffered that. He *has* loved, in his dithering way, and the Damned Thing has never given him an inch.

He remembers the telegram from Bibs ten years ago. After tearing it open he read it again and again, as if the words were in an unknown language he couldn't decipher—like the babble of the sinister white horse that speaks to him in his nightmares in some inexplicable tongue. APRIL 27, 1905. MOTHER DIED THIS MORNING OF HEART FAILURE. Only the year before, Mollie had obtained a divorce in Los Angeles on the grounds of desertion. Desertion? Harsh, the term's too harsh. But he has no defense. What should he have done? Is life so cruel as to force him to remain indefinitely with a woman with whom he had so little in common? *Yes, you should have stayed for the sake of the children.* My children never liked me. Besides, they're merely the physiological result of the sex act, nothing more. *The sex, then—you should have stayed for the sex.* What sex? One gets so used to another's body it's like having sex with oneself. *Think of the early days when you held each other, confided in each other, that counted for something, something to preserve.* You don't maintain a relationship based solely on youthful confidences. *You tired of her, deserted her.* She deserted me too, dammit, in her way. *You're rationalizing, and you know it.* Mollie was a decent woman, a good mother. The opposite of himself. That's why he's alive and she's dead, and why the worst tend to live and the best tend to go. No, that's categorically untrue. Palpable nonsense. But his eyes tear as he recalls the poem he once penned, certainly applicable on the occasion of Mollie's death.

> I lay in silence, dead. A woman came
>> And laid a rose upon my breast, and said:
> "May God be merciful." She spoke my name,
>> And added: "It is strange to think him dead."
>
> "He loved me well enough, but 'twas his way
>> To speak it lightly." Then, beneath her breath:
> "Besides"—I knew what further she would say,
>> But then a footfall broke my dream of death.
>
> To-day the words are mine. I lay the rose
>> Upon her breast, and speak her name, and deem
> It strange indeed that she is dead. God knows
>> I had more pleasure in the other dream.

They sit in Congress Park just shy of the bandstand. The folding chairs are hard but strangely comfortable—especially in comparison with those miserable churchly pews. The band plays the last of three encores, and he is thankful the concert is over. He has heard "The Washington Post March," "The Thunderer," and "The Stars and Stripes Forever" more times than he can stomach, and curse you to hell, John Philip Sousa. It's dark now, but the gas lamps—encircled by moths—are burning yellow to guide them back to the Grand Union Hotel. On younger nights, absent the saloon, he would have protected his flank with an emergency flask, easily accessible in his breast pocket.

This night, his only intoxication comes from stars and summer and Mrs. Dumont. Most of the concertgoers have carelessly abandoned their programs, but she folds hers and neatly inserts it into her purse. He wonders if she is saving the program as a memento. Hopes she is. He, a man who carries little baggage, leaves his on his chair.

"Mr. Grile, can a writer be trained?"

He is startled by the non sequitur. Somehow, he'd been counting on the night to fuel his romantic fantasies and for her to share them. But her mind is on something far afield from his naive notions of intimacy, Victorian as he is. Despite the lovemaking they've shared, why should she feel about him the way he thinks he feels about her? Their ages, my god. Return to reality, old-timer. She is barely thirty, for Christ's sake, and he is . . . But just the other night she'd said to him, whispered to him, "Eat me." "What?" he answered. "You heard me." He didn't know what she meant at first. Obviously, he knew the word eat. Then . . . He understood. Idiot, such an idiot. And so he did. But these girls, these modern girls . . . Must they misconstrue the language like that? Now, he hears the click of crickets and tries to click like them.

"Did you just make a strange noise?" she says.

"Merely my attempt at cricket-clicking."

"I think you're avoiding my question."

Once he climbs onto his academic soapbox, his sexual fantasies will be replaced by the cerebral. He has been asked the question so many times it's tiresome to respond, but he is a natural pontificator.

"My dear, anyone with natural intelligence and a fair education can be taught to write, just as he or she can be taught to draw, play billiards, or shoot a rifle. But to be great at any of those things is another matter. Since most of us can't be great, the trick is for us to do the best we can and think it's great."

"I'm not sure I understand."

"I mentored enough acolytes that I became rather proud of some of them. Did they become great? No. But they persisted in the belief that, if they were not yet great, one day they would be. It gave them the incentive to go forward."

She nods. At times his words are sharp, filled with wisdom. Other times, they seem to be nothing but hooey. "If I were your pupil, Mr. Grile, what advice would you give to me?"

"Advice is the cheapest form of gift, my dear, the smallest coin. But here goes. You must train. If I perceived the possibility of greatness in your work, and if you were my pupil, I'd need five years of your life in which to educate you. And in those five years I'd not permit you to put pen to paper for at least two years, except to make notes."

"Two years without writing?"

"Two years spent in broadening and strengthening your mind, teaching you how to think, and giving you something to think about. Sharpening your faculties of observation, dispelling your illusions, and destroying your ideals."

"How painful!"

"Oh, it would hurt, Mrs. Dumont, indeed. You would sometimes rebel. You would have to be subdued by a diet of bread and water and listening to an ode on the return of our Spanish-American War heroes, so called, or perhaps a verse directly out of Hearst's Sunday rotogravure."

"But I could read books, could I not?"

"Of course, but not a newly published novel, except by way of penance. If I found you reading the latest fiction it would go hard on you indeed. You would read the ancients. Plato, Aristotle, Marcus Aurelius, Seneca—custodians of most of what's worth knowing."

"But what of science and mathematics?"

"Of little import, assuming you've retained what you already knew of higher mathematics. Although I might permit you to learn enough science to make you prefer poetry. But to learn from Euclid the three angles of a triangle are equal to two right angles, yet not master from Epictetus the art of being a worthy guest at the table of the gods, why, that would be a breach of contract."

"And after five years I'd be a writer, Mr. Grile?"

"You'd have five years of training, Mrs. Dumont, and nothing more. It would take you a lifetime to become a writer." He opens his coat expansively. "Let me tell you what a writer is. A writer takes comprehensive views, holds large convictions, makes wide generalizations. A writer is not English, Mexican, or American. A writer is not a woman nor a man. A writer is not Christian, Jew, Buddhist, Muslim, nor snake worshipper. To local standards of right and wrong a writer is civilly indifferent. In the virtues, a writer is concerned only with general expediency. A writer doesn't waste time focusing on fixed moral principles that aren't yet before the court of conscience. Happiness discloses itself to a writer as the end and purpose of life, and art and love are the only means to a writer's happiness. A writer is free of all doctrines, theories, etiquettes, and politics. To a writer, a continent doesn't seem long, nor a century wide. And a writer has ever present consciousness that this is a world of . . . fools and rogues, blind with superstition, tormented with envy, consumed with vanity, selfish, false, cruel, cursed with illusions, and frothing *mad!*"

His face turns red. He's out of breath. Gasps.

"My god, Mr. Grile, are you all right?" Frantically, she clutches his arm.

He heaves. "I'll be fine." Wheezes. "Just need to catch my—as they say—life force."

She slaps his back.

"Don't do that. Doesn't help."

She retreats. Powerless. He takes from his pocket the atomizer he always carries with him and puffs the spray into his mouth. Gradually his color return to normal as does his breathing.

"I'm all right." One more gasp.

"You gave me a fright, Mr. Grile."

"A slight case of asthma. Occasionally it lays me low, but I invariably recover."

"I certainly hope so. I don't want to be the one to write your epitaph."

"Ah, epitaphs. My specialty as a young writer in San Francisco. However, my epitaphs were different in that my subjects were all alive, and in many unfortunate instances flourishing. Such fun I had."

As the Wickedest Man in San Francisco, he spared no one, his pen as vivid as words carved on a tombstone. "Here lies Frank Pixley—As usual." "Here the remains of Schuyler Colfax lie, / Born all the world knows when, and God knows why." "Beneath this stone sleeps Reuben Lloyd, / Of breath deprived, of sense devoid." "Here Stanford lies, who thought it odd / That he should go to meet his God."

Young he was, and he gave no ground. None. But years after his California days, long removed to the East, he takes stock of his friends and discovers he is surrounded entirely by youthful disciples. He has outlived his oldest friends, most of them literary figures. Cancer of the throat claims Bret Harte, who dies in London, his patron, Madam Van de Velde, at his side. Charles Stoddard breathes his last in Monterey surrounded by his relics: some bones of a saint, a Buddhist rosary, a piece of bark from the Fiji Islands, and an old slipper once belonging to William Dean Howells. Prentice Mulford's body is found in a small boat in Sheepshead Bay, Brooklyn, his banjo by his side, the fool preposterously in love with a little cockney tramp whose stark-naked picture on a pack of cigarettes Mulford discovers by accident. Mark Twain, of course, dead of heart disease at the age of seventy-four, thousands of mourners passing by the casket in which he lay in his starched white suit. Then there is Cincinnatus Hiner Miller, the Byron of the Rockies, the Poet of the Sierras, who refashions himself Joaquin Miller after a Mexican *bandito*.

Bierce vividly remembers this idiosyncratic apparition as, near the end, he arrives for a final visit to the place where the old fake has come to die. Joaquin has built by hand a three-room frame house ringed by patches of clarkias, red maids, shooting stars, lavender penstemons, and buttercups high up over Oakland.

The poet has surrounded himself with memorabilia. Bear claws, Western saddles, sheep horns, buffalo hooves, bows and arrows, rifles, shotguns. The walls are tacked with self-promoting photographs, drawings, sketches, and newspaper articles, while on the floor are spread mountain lion pelts and bear skins.

"I see you still have a writing desk, Miller. Guess that means you don't plan to give your readers any relief." He has contempt for Joaquin's poetic skills, but inevitably finds himself suckered by the old rascal's affability.

"Notice, Ambrose, that I still favor quill and ink."

"The quill. An implement of torture yielded by a goose and commonly wielded by an ass."

"What do you observe under the writing table, Ambrose?"

"A jug."

"And the label?"

"Radium. Which is a mineral, a constituent of luminescent plants giving off heat and stimulating the human organ that a scientist is a fool using."

"Nay, Ambrose, it's an amber fluid that affects the brain in the most enlightened way when consumed in appropriate quantities."

They share the radium, tasting suspiciously like rum, in china cups. Miller leads his on and off again friend to a pile of rocks eight feet high at the peak of the hill. Next to it a boulder onto which are chiseled the words: *To the Unknown.* They climb a ladder to the top of the pile. The sun is setting and the lights of San Francisco, Berkeley, and Oakland are beginning to bloom, one by one by one.

"We're standing on my funeral pyre, Ambrose." Joaquin suffers from diabetes, arteriosclerosis, and uremia. "When I die, I wish to fall prostrate like the Sequoia." He takes Bierce's wrist. "Remember that time in London at the Whitefriars Club when we dined with Mark Twain? You and I had a terrible falling out, and I asked, 'Why did God make Ambrose Bierce?'"

"How could I forget?"

"I now *know* why God made you."

"And just why, you old buzzard?"

"So you could write my epitaph."

Long after Miller breathes his last, Bierce reads the obituary notices more with amusement than sadness, the old charlatan being hailed as one of America's greatest bards, ranking with Longfellow, Whittier, and Whitman. Bierce knows something the obituary writers don't: the world will never remember Joaquin Miller. Let that be his epitaph.

Reduced to writing a column for *Cosmopolitan* and having lost the attention of the powers now running the Hearst empire, Bierce takes the train to New York and goes to Hearst's home to demand a private audience with The Boss, but is rebuffed by some lackey at the door. Furious, he vows to submit his resignation. That'll show 'em. Meantime, he roams the cold city streets, slapped by the west wind and punched by the north. He walks uptown, through Riverside Park thread-like and quiet along the North River, which rolls into the Hudson. New Jersey is dark and ordinary on the other side, a wretched land so close and yet so far, a place connected only by ferries and hope. The moon circles as thin and sharp as a scythe. He comes to the West Eighties, to the site of the farmhouse, long gone, in which Poe composed "The Raven." Now it's all tenements and stables and grocery shops. He thinks it ironic the name "Poe" and the word "poetry" are virtually identical. Then he feels the presence, hears the voice.

"What brings you to my street?"

"Death brings me here."

"You've come to the right place."

"I wish I could see you. I know you from your pictures. I love your looks. I cherish your twisted face, your high forehead, your mustache, your haunted eyes."

"What do you want of me, Bierce? I know only of death."

"I want to learn more about the Damned Thing. It took my sons. My wife. All my valued friends."

"Why should they be immune from the Damned Thing? You're not. I wasn't."

"I've always laughed at death."

"Out of cynicism, Bierce. You saw so much of it in war that human obliteration became impersonal. But it's not so impersonal now, is it? Besides, your cynical laughter was only a façade to disguise your fear."

"Don't tell me about fear. You died drunk and delirious in some Baltimore gutter. That's where your spirit should be, not here."

"I died drunk and delirious in a hospital room on the highest ground in Baltimore. They put my remains in the old Presbyterian Cemetery. Lot twenty-seven. My funeral lasted three minutes. Eight people bid me gone. My spirit haunts New York because it is where my love died. In a cottage in Fordham. On her deathbed, Virginia, with palsied hands, removed from under her pillow a picture of me and kissed it. Then her eyes shut. No, *I* shut her eyes with my very lips."

"You were a dysfunctional aberration of a man, clouded by drugs and alcohol."

"And you are moved by my work because I *was* a dysfunctional aberration clouded by drugs and alcohol."

"You wrote about loss, and that is why I am moved by your work."

"It was many and many a year ago . . ."

"What do I do?"

"But our love it was stronger by far . . ."

"My god, a phantom more tormented than myself."

"And the wind blew out of a cloud, chilling . . ."

"Have you no answers for me? Where are you going? I said . . ."

"And so all the night tide, I lie down by the side . . ."

Like the fading wraith, Bierce melds into the darkness, emerging two blocks east on Broadway near the IRT entrance. A blind Croat is selling papers at a corner newsstand. The bulldog edition of Hearst's *Journal* is just out. He buys a copy for two cents, reads about the formation of the nation's first billion-dollar company, United States Steel, which controls sixty percent of all the iron and steel produced in America, making Andrew Carnegie and his fellow moguls the richest men in the world. The subway ride is a nickel. It runs all night, all day, never stops. He hops the train and he doesn't care if it carries him into hell.

"Mr. Grile, Mr. Grile." She shakes his arm. "You're off somewhere again."

"What?" He puts his hand to his face, keenly embarrassed. "Ah, yes, my usual reveries. Forgive me."

"You were telling me about your asthma."

"Indeed. A lifelong malady, but one I've become used to, if one ever becomes use to an ailment. Never know when it will strike."

"I hate to see you suffer, Mr. Grile."

He loosens his tie. "I'm a believer in suffering, Mrs. Dumont. What we learn in suffering we teach in song and prose. It is the way of a writer."

She admires the cleverness of his words, but . . . "Why should a writer suffer more than anyone else?"

"Pain and remorse are educational. If a writer is lucky he will be blessed with heavy affliction. Cancer or asthma perhaps. A bereavement or two is always welcome."

"Oh, bosh. It sounds as if you favor a writerly life without joy."

"On the contrary. A writer should have a measureless exuberance of joy. Along with hate and fear and hope and despair and love. Inexhaustible love. A writer must be a sinner and a saint, a hero and a wretch. Mrs. Dumont, experiences and emotion are the necessities of literary life. To the writer they are as indispensable as sun and air to the rose, or fat, edible vapors to the toad."

They walk through Congress Park under the gaslight glow. They are just in time for a crushed ice and syrup from a vendor who is ready to retire. In the lobby of the Grand Union Hotel, she kisses him on the forehead before saying goodnight. They are both exhausted, still recovering from their overindulgences of the night before, so no lovemaking tonight, but he carries her kiss away like a gift. Thank god Señor Arango is asleep and snoring when he returns to their suite. He doesn't want to play The Game, perhaps ever again. There's something to live for. He puts his fingers to his forehead where her lips had been. Damned if he doesn't have a hard-on.

Chapter Twenty-four

The young woman wears boots, jodhpurs, and a velvet riding hat, her clothing mannish but fetching. Indeed, fetching is the precise word for her, he thinks, and he knows words. He is also familiar with horses but, at his joint-popping age, is out of shape despite his trim physique. The act of placing the foot in a stirrup and swinging the torso into the saddle is almost more than his body can tolerate. But he mounts the horse with surprising grace, refusing to reveal his aches, much as he had when he rode in Mexico with Señor Arango. They ride into the woods, Elizabeth Dumont and Dod Grile. The trails are still wet from the recent rains. Water fills the ruts and grooves where the horses trot. Occasionally they brush by a low branch or bush and horse and human are sprayed by mist. She is on a sorrel, he a roan.

He is pleased she isn't riding sidesaddle. He has contempt for such a feminine affectation, although his regard for women is a mixture of disdain, awe, and lust. At heart, he's a cognac and cigar man who still believes in a smoke-filled, Caucasian male-dominated world, and little does he contemplate, even now, well into the twentieth century, that history will pass him by, that many of his notions will become not only obsolete but flawed.

Deep in the woods, they dismount and find their way through the trees to a clearing, private. She totes a picnic basket and blankets, which she spreads on the damp ground. They each sit crossed-legged. A butterfly pauses on his shoulder before fluttering off to some secret place. She opens the basket and produces sandwiches and Saratoga chips. She pours lemonade. An envious bluejay lands in the grass to watch them.

"You're an accomplished rider, Mr. Grile. I'm impressed."

"For a man of my age you mean."

"Pshaw. Such humility, and I don't buy a word of it."

"In that case, I'm also an expert canoeist, although my colleague Señor Arango doesn't realize it, and I'm not about to tell him. He is a man of the desert and understands little about water, outside of poisoned wells." He chuckles in his strange non-chuckling way. "I observed him once on a barge at the floating gardens of Xochimilco, and he was astounded, not only by the proximity of the water, but by the riotous array of vegetation in aquatic suspension. Here, however, the sulfuric quality of the local water doesn't agree with him. It has been a delightful vacation, but he is anxious to return to his familiar haunts south of the border."

"But summer is not quite over."

"Saratoga Springs is admirable, my dear. However, he has many duties in Mexico, and with the revolution unresolved he hates to be away too long. I, on the other hand ... Let's simply say I'm still formulating my plans."

"I still don't understand what took you to Mexico in the first place, Mr. Grile."

"I went to Mexico in a premeditated act that was neither impulsive nor impetuous, but the inclination of an adventurous geriatric who had nothing to lose."

She brushes away a bee that comes too close. "The more I learn about you the less I know."

"I don't wear my heart on my sleeve, Mrs. Dumont."

"But you do have a heart, don't you?"

"A heart is merely an automatic, muscular blood pump."

"Oh, it's much more than that. It's the seat of our emotions and sentiments."

"Nonsense, Mrs. Dumont. It is well known that emotions and sentiments reside in the stomach. They evolve from food by a chemical action of the gastric fluid."

"You joke with me."

"You obviously haven't read my monograph on the subject. My treatise describes the chemical process. We are eating roast beef sandwiches, are we not?"

"Seasoned with mustard."

"The mustard alone is bound to produce an emotional response. The exact process by which a beefsteak becomes a feeling is derived from the *tenderness* of the animal from which it was cut. Think of the stage by which a caviar sandwich is changed into a quaint fancy and then reappears as a pungent epigram. Consider the marvelous functional methods of converting a hard-boiled egg into religious contrition. Ponder how a cream puff is transformed into a sign of sensibility."

She almost chokes with laughter. She reaches out to touch his hand. "Mr. Grile, have you had time to read what I've written?"

He finds her touch electrifying, her question off-putting, but he is quick to recover.

"I am in the process, my dear. Your work is, shall I say, interesting."

"I hope you're finding my words exquisitely touching and beautiful, Mr. Grile."

He laughs his non-laugh again. "I once received a note from a publisher describing a book of mine in those exact words, Mrs. Dumont—stories about soldiers and civilians. In fact, it was the best I could write. I rushed to the publisher to say how pleased I was that he was so favorably disposed to my words and would publish them. But I had jumped to the wrong conclusion. The publisher told me that its being touching and beautiful wasn't sufficient reason to publish it. He said that publishing a book, even one as superior as mine, was expensive, and the money rarely came back. I reminded this candid gentleman that he often published material any thinking person would consider rotten. He told me, indeed, he *intended* to."

"Intended?"

"He said publishers need books that sell, particularly rotten ones."

"And you said?"

"I reminded him that he often printed new editions of some of the great works in our language, and that my book, modest as it was, might have steady and perhaps increasing sales, and eventually become famous. He acknowledged he made money by republishing the classics, but he said those books enjoyed the advantage of generations of scholarly endorsements, and more important had no copyrights; therefore, no royalties to pay. This year is, what, nineteen-fifteen? Time passes so quickly I often forget. He said he would be delighted to put my book on his list—provided some other publisher kept it going for a hundred years, say in twenty-fifteen."

"Your book was rejected."

"It was rejected because it was exquisitely touching and beautiful."

For a long time she gazes at him. "Mr. Grile, I have something, nothing quite literary, to show you. Something, some might say, personal."

"Yes?"

"But you must close your eyes. No, tighter. Even tighter."

He hears rustling noises.

"Not yet."

The whoosh of leather against cloth against flesh.

"You may open your eyes now."

When he does he looks up to see her standing before him completely nude, save for her riding hat. Her fingers are interlocked behind her head to present the darkish curls in her armpits, her pelvis thrust forward to display the pelt between her legs.

"Am I beautiful, Mr. Grile? Tell me, tell me."

"Mrs. Dumont . . ."

"Elizabeth. Call me Elizabeth."

"You *are* beautiful, Elizabeth."

Crouching over him, she takes his head in her hands and pushes all her vulnerable wetness into him. They make love on the blanket, not once but three times. When they are through, packing their picnic items, he remains semi-erect.

"I'm not sure I can ride in this condition," he says, smiling, a bit embarrassed, but mostly vainglorious.

"Perhaps I can help," she says, lowering her head.

At last they mount their horses.

"Shall we gallop?" she says. "A race back to the stable?"

Sycamores hang over the trail. The sun pokes through the leaves. She digs her heels into her sorrel, which takes off. He does the same with his roan. His horse gets there first. He has no apologies for winning the race even though he is achy and limpy as they walk back to the hotel.

"You had no intention of allowing me to win," she says. "Even after what we shared on the blanket in the woods."

"Indeed not."

"You might be more gracious."

"My dear, if women wish the same privileges as men, then they must suffer the same defeats."

"Perhaps a bicycle race next time."

"I accept the challenge."

He will feel his ride tomorrow, so he plans to soak in a warm mineral bath. Perhaps the waters will soothe the aches in his joints and muscles, although he doubts Saratoga's miracle waters perform any sort of miracle at all—outside of luring gullible tourists. As they near the hotel they encounter a hearse followed by a line of automobiles on the way to the graveyard, Greenridge Cemetery no doubt.

"Do you see what I see, my dear?"

"The hearse?"

"It may be a hearse to you, but I call it Death's baby carriage."

She knows it's a joke, his sometimes failed effort at humor, but she still shivers. She feels an empathy for her afternoon lover, not that death might be nearer for him than for her, but that he thinks about it so much.

After dinner, they sit on the veranda's wicker. He leafs through her manuscript. She is nervous, afraid of what he might think of it, despite her neat penmanship. If he hates her writing he is likely to hate her.

"In some respects I felt like a voyeur as I read your material, my dear."

"Why?"

"Your writing is somewhat, well, personal."

"They're merely stories."

"I'm not sure you can hide behind a pen."

"It's fiction."

"Did you have difficulties with your late husband? Did he actually strike you?"

"If I did and he did, I have no intention of discussing those matters with you. The heroine in my novel, who is not necessarily me, has problems with her husband."

"And the child . . ."

"Johnny is difficult. My heroine coincidentally also has a difficult child."

"You have certainly employed a lot of blue ink, a villainous compound used to facilitate an infection of idiocy and the promotion of intellectual crime."

"You're ridiculing me."

"A jest, my dear."

"Another of your silly, cynical definitions. I'm not amused, Mr. Grile, and it's clear you're avoiding an assessment of my work."

"No, I'm impressed."

"Do you mean it?" She clutches his sleeve. "Do you think I can write? Do you think I have a future as an author? Will I get published? Might I have written a bestseller? Will I—"

"Tarnation, my dear. I simply said I was impressed. You say you are interested in writing a bestseller. I'm not enamored of popular fiction. From the heights on which Tolstoy sits, the popular writers today are visible only as black beetles. No, visible only as slugs in slime. However, it is clear you have a way with words and the ability to express them adequately."

"Adequately?" A curl from her hair cascades to her forehead, much like the sinking of her heart. "That's not much of an endorsement."

"You will become better with practice." He has spent more time going over her manuscript than he has ever done for his previous disciples. It is not very good, but, for her, he has tempered his comments. No doubt their intimacies have had something to do with that. "Do you have a future as a writer? Perhaps, if you actually write and not just chatter about it. Will you be published? Possibly, should you become good enough to impress some lord on the throne of thought. I've marked each page with specific comments. You'd be advised to study my observations and see what you can do with them."

So pompous, she thinks. He is so pompous. But she doesn't say it. He is too important to her. "Such a letdown. I feel myself becoming depressed."

"Don't, my dear. Depression is the state of mind produced by a poem in the newspaper, a minstrel performance, or the contemplation of another's success." Another phony chuckle. "And don't underestimate yourself. I understand all the young people are going around reading some trifle by that Burroughs fellow, *Tarzan of the Apes.*"

They hear a commotion from the street. A team of horses pulling a hay wagon. Frolicking in the straw is a group of young people, shouting and laughing and clutching one other with a familiarity unheard of in his day. There had been hayrides in Indiana when he was a boy, but he'd missed them, along with the picnics, the skating parties, the barn dances. He wonders now about all he had forfeited. So insular he was, so bookish, caught in the spell of his scholarly mentor, Mrs. Octavia Oona Rich, schoolmarmish champion of Swift and Pope and Fielding, she of the peach-toned cameo containing the chiseled face of a goddess, which he carries to this day. He remembers her Seth Thomas clock chiming away their literary togetherness as one by one she undid the portal leading to his most intimate anatomy, while from outside came the rugged shouts of the boys playing lacrosse. Why couldn't he have been like the others?

"Penny for your thoughts," Mrs. Dumont says.

He shakes his head. "The reveries of an old man."

"Stop thinking of yourself as old." She smiles coyly. "You weren't old with me on the blanket in the woods this afternoon, as I can confirm empirically."

"I'm flattered, my dear, and I'd like not to think of myself as superannuated. But that would mean to stop thinking altogether." Despite their intimacies, he, a Victorian when all is said, is embarrassed by her coquettish demeanor, her candid chatter. My god, the way young girls speak these days! Christ forbid what the nineteen-twenties will bring: no doubt short-skirted women dancing with knees exposed, swilling gin from flasks, exhaling cigarette smoke, even casting votes, say, for the likes of that madman Eugene V. Debs. "Shall we walk for a bit?" he says finally.

They amble through the garden but the ground is still a bit soggy and they are careful to stay on the stepping stones.

He says suddenly, "I had a wicked dream last night."

"Do you want to share it with me?"

"It was one I have had many times before. My dreams have recurred ever since I was a child. Some have been categorically nightmarish."

"Tell me." She puts her hand on his arm.

"I am passing through an open glade in a thinly wooded country. Through the belt of scattered trees I glimpse cultivated fields and the homes of strange intelligences. It is nearly dawn and the moon, almost full, is about to vanish in the west. The grass at my feet is heavy with dew. It is early summer. Near my path is a horse eating the herbage. It lifts its head as I am about to pass. It regards me benignly for a moment, then walks toward me. It is milk-white and seems mild and amiable. I say to myself, 'This horse is a gentle soul.' I reach out to caress its forelock. The horse keeps its eyes fixed on my own. Then . . ."

"Yes?"

"It speaks to me in a human voice with human words, yet unintel-

ligible to me. I am in horror. Then instantly I am . . . back in our world
where I awake shaking, perspiring. In the dreams the horse speaks in
what appears to be my own tongue, but I don't understand it. I desperately need to know what the horse is trying to convey. I am afraid
there will come a time when I encounter the horse that I will finally
understand it—and return no more to our world."

"Don't think about it anymore, Mr. Grile. It's just a dream.
Dreams often make no sense."

"I know you are right, Mrs. Dumont, but . . ."

"Elizabeth."

"Pardon?"

"You're supposed to call me Elizabeth."

She wants to call him by his first name, but somehow 'Dod'
doesn't sound right to her, nor has he suggested she address him in
familiar terms. Once again she thinks: could it be that Dod Grile isn't
really his name?

At the Playhouse that night, they watch a vivid, flamboyant road
show revival of George M. Cohan's *Little Johnny Jones,* expressed with
endless exuberance by a young traveling troupe from New York. Following the performance, the two walk under the elms, a horseshoe's
throw from the Grand Union Hotel. Elizabeth, more through habit
than need, fans her face with the theater program. The weather has
turned a bit cooler and is especially delightful. She takes his arm.

"A shame Señor Arango couldn't have joined us tonight."

"Señor Arango again sends his regrets. He had longstanding plans
to oil his gun, shine his boots, and count his pesos in preparation for
his return to Mexico. Besides, he says he has little appreciation for
what he calls gringo music."

"Ah, the music. Don't you just adore George M. Cohan? Those
songs of his. 'Give My Regards to Broadway.' 'The Yankee Doodle
Boy.' Doesn't he make you want to dance?" She sings in a sweetly
passable voice,

> "'I love the name, Billie
> My dad's was the same, Billie
> I love the way they laugh and say:
> How silly to call a girl Billie . . .'"

He nods, charmed, but fully aware she will never realize an audience outside of her parlor or, at the most, beyond an amateur theatrical. "It is captivating to hear your trill, my dear, although I find your Mr. Cohan's lyrics pedestrian. And, after enduring tonight's performance, I remain uncertain whether your Yankee Doodle Boy wrote music or noise."

"Noise? You call it *noise?*"

"Noise is nothing more than undomesticated music, a stench in the ear. It is the chief product and the authenticating sign of civilization."

"Oh, why can't you just enjoy the music without such sarcasm?" She doesn't know whether to be angry or sad or loving, but decides on the last. So much of his cynicism is mixed with humor that it's hard to tell them apart. She touches his cheek. He feels the softness of her palm. His own hands, too, are delicate and soft, evidence of a writer— or a haberdasher. As they walk, lightning-bugs—flashing yellows and greens—illuminate their path just for them.

"I confess, my dear, Nature has denied me an ear for music. Enjoying music is purely sensual. It tickles the ear and does nothing else. Music never touches the springs of the intellect. It fails to generate the process of reasoning and never expresses a truth, artistic or otherwise. It has no intellectual character whatever."

"I think you underestimate the intelligence and skill of those who compose music."

"Just the opposite. Musicians are not distinguished by their mental capacity. The greater their gift, the less they know."

"Preposterous. For you to say an artist is of pure sensuality and of no intellect would negate the ability of, well, writers. Such as yourself."

"I concede music started out as a kind of intellectual pursuit. Before men became wise and deft enough to make instruments, they merely sang. Just as the birds do now. And why did primitive man and woman sing? To communicate in terms of love. Abundant vestiges of this practice survive, aided and abetted by composers such as your Mr. George M. Cohan."

She says, "You make music appear to be a primitive pastime. I could tell you so much about music and what it means and how it matters to the soul, and you would never, never understand."

"I bow to your superior sense of aesthetics, my dear. Did it ever occur to you that if men and women were born happily married the entire musical edifice would fade and vanish like a palace of clouds? But since they do not, there must be siren songs and songs of adoration."

They stop under an elm where it is dark and private. Something unexpected happens. He begins to sing. Yes, he. A song of pain and rain. A song of his past.

Beautiful Dreamer, wake unto me,

His voice is untrained. Off key. But true. Who would have suspected?

Starlight and dewdrops are waiting for thee

She has been holding his arm, but now throws both of hers around his shoulders and presses her lips against his. The tickle of his mustache is erotic. She feels the wetness forming between her legs. What is right and wrong? It is of no consequence. What matters is flesh and the mind. And damn the mind! His mouth and body is not that of a man older than she but of a man. Her body is not that of a younger woman but of a woman. His breath is her breath. Her breath is his.

Neither wants their days to end. After a bicycle race, in which he again is the victor, they, clothes damp from perspiration, observe the horseshoe players, big, brawny gents mostly, the kind who favor the heft and feel of rounded pieces of molten metal, an alloy useless for any purpose other than for shoeing horses and throwing.

Clang!

"A ringer," he says.

The man throwing the horseshoes is a volunteer fireman vacationing from Elmira with his wife and two sons. He has saved up mightily to stay at a hotel he really can't afford, and the entire family is sharing the cheapest of the rooms. Mr. Grile and Mrs. Dumont recline on canvas lounge chairs in the shade. They sip lemonade as they sneer at the tournament. He has spiked his drink with gin from a flask secreted in the inside pocket of his coat.

"I'm afraid I've never appreciated the fine points of the game of horseshoes," she says.

"There are no fine points."

"A strange form of recreation."

"Not as strange as the most common recreational activity in San Francisco."

"What's that, Mr. Grile?"

"Stoning Chinamen."

It isn't funny, not really, but she laughs despite herself.

"I have thought of one additional use for a horseshoe, my dear: mounting it over the barn door for luck."

"I fail to see how that would bring luck."

"The luck comes when the horseshoe stays mounted and doesn't fall on the head of the person standing below."

"You're pulling my leg."

"Pulling your leg? Hmmm. A terrible cliché, and a disservice to the language."

"Is there any way to say it better?"

"How about 'pulleg'? It is as good a word as any." He sips his fortified lemonade. "We have certain awkward phrases we might as well condense into single words. For example, 'join in the holy bonds of wedlock' might be changed to 'jedlock.' The familiar 'much-needed rest' would become 'mest.' Instead of saying that something 'reflects credit' on someone we could use 'refledit.' Or instead of referring to a man freshly dead as he was 'much esteemed by all who knew him,' we could say 'mestewed.'"

"How clever . . ."

"By using such a simple and rational device our language would be noticeably shortened. And in that way a newspaper obituary a few lines might be saved for the death of some poor poet."

Clang!

She refills their glasses with lemonade. When she turns away to watch the horseshoe tournament, he again spikes his glass with gin.

"I am willing to reform the language even further, my dear. As you know, a number of common words have been condensed. 'Not either' into 'neither,' 'not ever' into 'never,' 'no one' into 'none.' So how about 'neven' for 'not even'? Perhaps 'nout' for 'not out.' I also advocate 'nirish' for 'No Irish.' 'No Popery' could be 'nopery.' 'No matter' might be changed to 'natter.' Or 'never-to-be forgotten' altered to 'notten.' Why, the principle is pregnant with possibilities. And Henry Mencken would certainly approve."

"Most people would think you're joking."

"Would I joke about a matter as serious as the English language?"

Publicly, the two behave with the greatest propriety. To appear to have had avaricious, but genuinely satisfying, bodily intimacies would embarrass him and disgrace a woman so freshly a widow.

They bid each other goodnight.

It is late now. Mrs. Dumont, in her room, barely hears the knock. She is only partly awake. Johnny, asleep in the other bed, dreams of red-coated Fusiliers, or so she imagines. At first she thinks the sound is the limb of a tree outside, rapping softly against the hotel window. Again the knock. Louder. Someone at her door. She swings what she thinks are her embarrassingly knobby knees out of the bed and dons her robe, the blue thing with lace trimmings that had been the last Christmas gift to her from her husband before the son of a bitch croaked. Her husband had a knack of presenting her with expensive but overly practical gifts. The year before his suicide he had given her a straight razor for her legs. It was pure sterling silver, her name engraved upon it, and Cartier pricey, but it was still a straight razor. He had treated her shabbily, she fancies, and by dying so bloodily he had compounded his abuse. Not the way she would have gone. No, she will die a dignified death. Everyone will be proud of her, and in particular Mr. Grile.

The knock. Persistent.

It is he, she supposes. Who else would knock so late? Who else would be so erotically presumptuous? She giggles in a girlish way that makes her seem younger than she is. Propriety be damned! He has never been other than a gentleman, even when he makes the most outrageous statements, both public and private, even during their physical acts, luscious and liquid. He makes her feel safe. She feels she can turn to him always and he will protect her, even though she isn't sure she can ever know him, really know him. He can be gregarious, at the same time distant. He hides behind words. Her father was that way. He managed the local railway company in Buffalo. Every night he came home with stories about the trolleys and the people who ran them and rode in them, about the tracks and the men who laid them and kept them straight. Her father was filled with words, words about everything but himself. Or her. She had wanted to know her father, to unlock his mind. To get past the words. When he died she felt as though something in her life was left undone and unknown. Could it be that by turning to Mr. Grile she is trying to replace her . . . ? Nonsense. Mr. Grile drinks, you know. She *saw* him spiking his lemonade when he thought she wasn't looking. She discovered that he usually heads for the hotel saloon after saying goodnight to her, that he stands at the rail with that barbaric Mexican man for hours, often buying brandy to take to his room after the bar's last call. She has friends employed at this hotel. They tell her things.

She opens the door a crack. It is the Mexican with the auburn mustache that droops over the sides of his mouth. She is wary. Not that she expects Señor Arango to attack her, but his appearance at her door is so unexpected. How can you trust a heathen like that? She is aware that he goes to brothels and cockfights and god knows what else, and in her mind distantly, perhaps not so distantly, is the thought of what it might be like to sleep with him.

"Señora . . ." he begins. She sees that he is trying not to look at her bare feet and she almost laughs. Modesty in a crudely handsome brute like him!

"Hush. My son's asleep. What do you want?"

"Señora . . ."

"You said that."

"Meester Grile. It's bad."

"What's bad?"

Señor Arango's English is poor. So is her Spanish. With some enterprise, they communicate.

"He has had an attack, señora. He wants you to come. He needs to see you before he, he . . ."

"Did you notify the hotel clerk? Did you call a doctor?"

"Señora, he wants no clerk, no doctor. He wants *you*. You must hurry, *por favor*."

Warily she shuts the door to a crack, then dresses hastily but quietly so as not to wake her son while Señor Arango waits outside. She barely brushes her hair. Her ribs strain with the thudding of her heart. Maybe the Mexican is right. Or is this a ploy to get her to . . . ? Nonsense, nonsense. He escorts her through the long, dim, slumbering hallways of the vast hotel.

"I hope we're not too late, señora."

"Mr. Grile and I have been on bicycles, horseback riding, rowing, and . . ." She almost reveals their secret, but doesn't. "He seems to be in excellent health."

"The asthma, señora. He is fine until the asthma. The attacks come pronto."

When they get to the suite she finds him stretched on his bed. Eyes closed. Still. At first, he appears to be dead. But then his chest shudders and his eyes open, just a bit. He is wearing his usual black suit, but his collar is open, tie pulled aside. The room is neat, but Mrs. Dumont sees on the table a flask of brandy, two empty glasses, and a Colt .45.

"We were drinking, señora, playing The Game when he got the attack. I put him to his bed."

She sits on the edge of the mattress and places her hand on his forehead. His flesh is neither warm nor cold. His eyes gradually fill with recognition. His breathing is shallow, almost non-existent. He tries to speak, but hardly has the breath with which to make words. His lips quiver. Mrs. Dumont puts her ear close to his mouth in order to hear him.

"The Game."

Only faintly does she hear the words.

"What, Mr. Grile? What's The Game?"

"I lost."

"What do you mean?"

He whispers. So softly Mrs. Dumont isn't sure she fully understands. His words come hard. He struggles to make her hear. "Kept spinning the chamber. Each time I pulled the trigger nothing happened."

"I don't know what you're saying, Mr. Grile."

"Played The Game for the last time." Breathing coarse. "Lost again. My bad luck."

"Don't talk anymore. Just rest. I'm getting the doctor."

"No." It would have been a shout if he'd had the strength to shout. "Doctors had their chance. Too late for doctors. It is just outside."

"Who is outside?"

"It."

"What is It?"

His lips move. Just barely she captures his words.

"Told you about my dream. Horse speaking to me."

"I remember."

"Dream came back. This time horse talked to me. I understood. Horse told me . . ."

"Go on, Mr. Grile."

"Horse said . . . The Damned . . . Thing . . . has come for me." He struggles to speak more, but the words no longer come.

Mrs. Dumont takes his hand. Holds it tight. She says to Señor Arango, "He's delirious."

"I think not, señora."

"Something about a Damned Thing."

"Señora, he knows what he is saying."

His eyes close. His lips stop moving. He has ended the struggle. He is calm. The Damned Thing, never known for its sensitivity, takes him away more gently than he ever expected. Mrs. Dumont puts her ear to his heart. No beat. She takes his arm and folds it across the other arm on his chest. She wants to cry but can't. He would never cry. She wants to recite something, to make a gesture in ritual. The way mystics do. Crossing themselves. Fingering beads. Mouthing drivel. Lighting candles. What the *hell* is she thinking? She is beginning to think like him, a man who would chortle at such superstitious nonsense. Still, some sort of rite is in order.

"He wants to be buried here, señora, in Saratoga. He told me. I will pay for it."

"I'll make the arrangements. Mr. Arango, what's that on the table?"

"Brandy. Gun. Timepiece."

"Pour me a brandy."

"*You,* señora?"

"Pour it into the same glass Mr. Grile was using."

He does. And pours a brandy of his own. They touch glasses. Drink. To their late *amigo.* And to all he was. The brandy is pitiless as it flows down her throat. She isn't accustomed to harsh spirits. She wonders, for a moment, how he was able to force himself to consume so much of it. It had been his glass. She hopes her lips had touched the same place as his.

"Señora, the watch, he gave it to me, but why don't you keep it? He told me he had carried it since he was a young man in your American war, that it has never stopped ticking."

"What is the gun doing on the table, Mr. Arango?"

The Mexican shrugs. "His gun. Not mine."

"I asked why it is on the table."

"He, how you say, utilized it."

"For what?"

"The Game."

"So tell me, Mr. Arango, about The Game."

"It was nothing, señora. Just some silly, senseless thing men do."

"Explain it."

He is embarrassed. Americano women aren't as subservient as the women south of the Rio Grande. He manages to communicate despite the language hurdle. "It started as a joke. In Mexico. I thought at first maybe he was a spy. For your President Wilson. Maybe an informer for the *federales*. I don't know. I could have had him shot. I had lots of men shot. So I gave him the choice. He could empty the gun except for one bullet, then spin the chamber, and, and . . ."

"Pull the trigger."

"*Si.*"

"Russian Roulette."

"Well . . ."

"You made him play Russian Roulette."

"At first, señora! Only at first. It was, as you say, a prank. Then I got to like the old devil. Hell, he saved my life in Ojinaga. He shot down two *federale* swine after my horse stumbled and threw me. He was a soldier too. Once was. A hero. I got that much out of him. And then we started to talk, and I liked his talk. We would stay up all night with only a candle between us and his gun. And talked and talked. But he was, how do you say, odd. He got used to The Game. At first he played it a lot. Over tequila, brandy. He'd spin the chamber and pull the trigger, but night after night after night the bullet stayed in the gun. After he met you he would only pretend to play. He was pretending tonight. The bullet is still in the gun. A doctor might say it was the asthma that killed him, but he would tell you the Damned Thing killed him."

Mrs. Dumont picks up the Colt. She knows something about guns.

Her late husband had one. Showed her how to fire it. The very gun he used to . . . She still owns it. Keeps it more as a memento mori than for protection. It is in her dresser in the bedroom of her home on Goodell Street in Buffalo. Mr. Grile's Colt. 45 is heavy. An old gun. But oiled. Well maintained. She points at the single bullet in the chamber without disturbing it.

"Mr. Arango, if he'd pulled the trigger one more time without spinning the chamber, the gun would have fired the bullet."

"But he didn't, Señora Dumont."

"It would have killed him."

Arango drains his brandy. "The Damned Thing took him before that could happen."

"Ah yes, The Damned Thing."

"That's what he called it."

"Death?"

"He explained it all to me. Señora, there is lots of ways to die. If he had died from The Game, then the Damned Thing wouldn't have been able to take him. The Damned Thing is an assassin that takes you only when you don't want to go. That was why he played The Game. Señor Grile didn't want to be taken. He wanted the choice to be his. In the end, he had no choice. He was, you might say, assassinated. The gringo lied a lot. He was brave, but not as brave as he made himself out to be."

"Mr. Grile's feelings about death were somewhat ambiguous, I'd say."

"Am . . . ambig . . ."

"Not important. Is Arango really your name?"

"I was born with that name, I swear."

"Just who are you?"

"An Indian. A peasant. A revolutionary. A soldier in Mexico. Some call me a bandit. I too am *muy bravo*. That is the truth, señora."

"And Mr. Grile. Exactly who was he?"

"Just some gringo."

"Was Dod Grile his real name?"

"That's all I know. He said he wrote words. That he worked for a bastard called Hearst. Wrote a few books. Saved my life. Was my *compadre*. Ah, I remember now. At first he called himself Bierce, and then he stopped. You ever hear of a man named Bierce? I ain't never hear of no one called Bierce."

"*Ambrose* Bierce?"

"You know the name?"

"Of course I do, but he never—"

"Señora, just before I left the room to fetch you he asked me to give you this."

A small book bound in brown cloth, rather heavy, made of good stock. *Tales of Soldiers and Civilians.* She opens it and reads on the front endpaper a hand-written dedication, the script small and neat. *Dearest Elizabeth, I have written many words, but now need only five. Love is man's greatest adventure. With adoration, Ambrose. August 31, 1915.* Her eyes tear. She can't help herself. She flips through the book. Opposite the copyright page are the printed words, "Denied existence by the chief publishing houses of the country, this book owes itself to Mr. E. L. G. Steele, merchant, of this city."

"Señora, he said it was his best work."

"Yet he could find no one to publish it but some merchant in San Francisco."

"Why do you suppose that was?"

"Because it was exquisitely touching and beautiful."

Afterword

General William B. Hazen, appointed Chief Signal Officer in 1880 by President Hayes, was court-martialed for criticizing the Secretary of War's botching of the rescue of a scientific expedition stranded for three years in the Arctic.

Jubal P. Pemberton, former sergeant in the Army of the Confederate States of America, died of gangrene after stepping on a sharp stalk of wood. It happened near the Coosa River, Alabama, 1878, the same river where he'd taken Ambrose Bierce prisoner. He was fifty-nine.

William Ewart Gladstone occupied the post of British prime minister four times. He neglected in his memoirs to mention his abortive odyssey with Bierce to reform London's prostitutes. He died at Hawarden Castle, England, in 1898.

The radical Denis Kearney, surviving Bierce's attempt to assassinate him, became a pariah even in his own Workingmen's Party. Fleeing to the East to organize a national party, Kearney was caught up in a scandal over the misappropriation of party funds.

Boon May died of yellow fever in Brazil.

Captain Ichabod M. West took up residence in Mexico with a woman companion. By the end of 1882 he turned up disheveled and ill— without the woman—in Silver Creek, New Mexico, where he announced plans for an enormous mining operation.

Corruption charges were brought against Alexander S. "Clubber" Williams eighteen times, but he was never convicted. He retired from the New York City police department with an annual pension of $1750. He died in 1910.

Anthony Comstock departed to the burial ground of hypocrites in 1915, but both he and the New York Suppression of Vice live on in various guises.

Major Sherburne B. Eaton and Bierce never spoke again after the dark days in the Black Hills. Eaton, president of the Edison Electric Light Company, died in 1914.

P. T. Barnum left an estate of more than four million dollars when he died in 1891 of what the doctors said was an acute congestion of the brain. Barnum's last words were, "What were the receipts?"

Ina Coolbrith, the former Josephine Donna Smith, became California's poet laureate. A park is named for her in San Francisco.

Gertrude Atherton became a prolific novelist. She wrote about her encounter with Bierce at Sunol Glen in her 1932 autobiography *Adventures of a Novelist*. She died on June 14, 1948.

William Randolph Hearst's estate was so enormous it took the courts five years to probate it after his death. Shortly before he died at the age of eighty-eight in 1951, he was asked about Ambrose Bierce but couldn't recall the name of his most famous columnist.

Rodolfo Fierro, The Butcher—heavily weighted by bandoleers, pistols, spurs, and a fat money belt—was crossing a swollen stream near Casas Grandes in 1915 when he was caught by a strong current. His men refused to go to his rescue and he drowned.

In 1916, Villa's man, Pedrito Gómez, remembering to the end his miraculous vacation with the bandit and the gringo in Saratoga Springs, was kicked in the groin by a horse in San Luis Potosí and died twelve days later of peritonitis.

Emiliano Zapata was lured into a trap and assassinated in Morelos in 1919. His assassin was rewarded with fifty thousand pesos and a promotion to general.

General Alvaro Obregón succeeded Carranza as president of Mexico. On July 17, 1928, as he was sitting in a dining hall, Obregón was assassinated by a young artist who approached him on the pretext of wanting to sketch his portrait.

Jack London, kidneys fatally diseased, was overweight, in constant pain, and agonized by rheumatism. On the night of November 21, 1916, legs swollen to twice their normal size and cursing the name of Ambrose Bierce, he swallowed a fatal overdose of morphine.

Once beloved brother Albert Grizzly Bierce died of apoplexy in March 1914. Albert's friends claimed his death had been accelerated by a hostile letter from his younger sibling.

The night Theodore Roosevelt died on January 6, 1919, in Oyster Bay, Long Island, he placed aside his copy of Bierce's *The Shadow on the Dial* and said, "Put out the light."

Bat Masterson went to his reward in 1921 and is buried in Woodlawn Cemetery in The Bronx. With him, in his grave, is a fake Tombstone, Arizona, sheriff's badge.

The poet George Sterling fell on hard times and in 1926 was living in a room at San Francisco's Bohemian Club when he opened the envelope bearing the word "peace," removed a cyanide capsule, and swallowed it.

H. L. Mencken never conceded the profound influence Ambrose Bierce had on the Baltimorean's work. In January 1956, after suffering a debilitating stroke that ended his career, Mencken listened to *Die Meistersinger* on the radio, then turned to a friend named Cheslock and mumbled something about ambrosia or Ambrose. Mencken died that night in his sleep.

Carrie Christiansen, bereft following the disappearance of her lover, committed suicide in San Francisco on December 14, 1920, after swallowing bichloride of mercury. Bierce's publisher, Walter Neale, advanced the theory that Bierce and Christiansen were secretly married in Rockville, Maryland, in 1904. Neale is unreliable.

Johnny Dumont flunked out of Amherst College and joined the United States Navy. In 1930 he was serving as a reluctant recruit aboard an American gunboat that came under enemy fire on the Yangtze River in China. The gunboat exploded. Johnny Dumont was never accounted for.

Three books published in 1929 speculated wildly on the disappearance of Ambrose Bierce, prompting Elizabeth Dumont to write indignantly to the *Buffalonian,* "Mr. Bierce died on August 31, 1915, in Saratoga Springs, New York, where he is buried in an unmarked grave—and I was his lover." She planned to support her claim by producing the book he inscribed to her, but the book was lost in a house fire, as was his timepiece and a cameo brooch on which was the face of a goddess. She was dismissed as a crank.

Mrs. Dumont's semi-autobiographical novel, *In the Face of Love,* was published by Scribner's in 1921. It garnered polite reviews and moderate sales. Considered eccentric by Buffalonians, she was forty-two when she was struck and killed by a trolley while crossing Delaware Avenue in 1933.

On July 23, 1923, as Pancho Villa drove a Dodge touring car through the streets of Parral, no fewer than eight snipers opened fire, slaughtering Villa and his bodyguards. In 1926, vandals dug into Pancho's grave and stole his head, which remained missing until 2014 when it was discovered on the mantel of a retired pharmacist in Toledo, Ohio. The head is a frequent auction item on Ebay.com.

In 1953, the Grand Union Hotel in Saratoga Springs was razed to build a supermarket.

On November 6, 2003, the state of Ohio, to honor its native son, unveiled a highway marker in the rain with six people in attendance.

Acknowledgments

Especial recognition to distinguished Bierce scholars S. T. Joshi, who edited the novel and provided the introduction, and David E. Schultz, who designed the pages.

This is a work of fiction; however, no piece of writing, real or imagined, comes without the labor of those before. I mined liberally from the efforts of Bierce's major biographers. Among the many sources were *The Collected Works of Ambrose Bierce* (Neale Publishing Co., 1909–12); *The Ambrose Bierce Satanic Reader,* edited by Ernest J. Hopkins (Doubleday, 1968); *The Unabridged Devil's Dictionary,* edited by David E. Schultz and S. T. Joshi (University of Georgia Press, 2000); *Ambrose Bierce: A Biography* by Carey McWilliams (Albert & Charles Boni, 1929); *Ambrose Bierce: The Devil's Lexicographer* by Paul Fatout (University of Oklahoma Press, 1951); *Ambrose Bierce: A Biography* by Richard O'Connor (Little, Brown, 1967); *Life of Ambrose Bierce* by Walter Neale (Walter Neale Publisher, 1929); *Memoirs of Pancho Villa* by Martin Luis Guzmán (University of Texas Press, 1966); *Insurgent Mexico* by John Reed (International Publishers, 1984); *The Mexican Revolution 1914–1915* by Robert E. Quirk (Indiana University Press, 1960); *The Life and Times of Pancho Villa* by Friedrich Katz (Stanford University Press, 1998); *Theodore Roosevelt: An Autobiography* by Theodore Roosevelt (Da Capo Press, 1985); *Jack London, American Rebel,* edited by Philip S. Foner (Citadel Press, 1947); *John Barleycorn* by Jack London (Grosset & Dunlap, 1913); *Splendid Poseur: Joaquin Miller, American Poet* by M. M. Marberry (Thomas Y. Crowell Co., 1953); *Adventures of a Novelist* by Gertrude Atherton (Liveright, 1932); *California's Daughter: Gertrude Atherton* by Emily Wortis Leider (Stanford University Press, 1991); *Prejudices: Sixth Series* by H. L. Mencken (Jonathan Cape, 1927); *A Mencken Chrestomathy* by H. L. Mencken (Knopf, 1949); *Citizen Hearst* by W. A. Swanberg (Bantam, 1963); *Greatly Exaggerated: The Wit and Wisdom of Mark Twain,* edited by Alex Ayres (Barrie & Jenkins, 1988); *Mr. Clemens and Mark Twain* by Justin Kaplan (Simon & Schuster, 1966); *The Gangs of New York* by Herbert Asbury (Paragon House, 1990); *Plains Indian Mythology* by Alice Marriott and Carol K. Rachlin (Thomas Y. Crowell Co., 1975).

About the Author

Don Swaim curates *The Ambrose Bierce Site,* the Internet's definitive Bierce resource: donswaim.com. A Kansan by birth, Ohioan by education, Manhattanite by inclination, and Pennsylvanian by preference, Swaim's long-running CBS Radio broadcast about books and writers, "Book Beat: The Podcast," continues on the Internet. He is the founder of the venerable Bucks County Writers Workshop.

www.ingramcontent.com/pod-product-compliance
Lightning Source LLC
Chambersburg PA
CBHW050917030726
47503CB00007BB/2343